SHIP OF THE LINE

SHIP OF THE LINE

Diane Carey

POCKET BOOKS
New York   London   Toronto   Sydney   Tokyo   Singapore

POCKET BOOKS, a division of Simon & Schuster Inc.
1230 Avenue of the Americas, New York, NY 10020

ISBN: 0-671-00924-9

First Pocket Books hardcover printing October 1997

10 9 8 7 6 5 4 3 2 1

POCKET and colophon are registered trademarks of Simon & Schuster Inc.

Printed in the U.S.A.

This novel is dedicated to the schooner *Alexandria,* sunk off Cape Hatteras, December 9, 1996, after sixty-seven hard-working years in amiable companionship with her crews and the living sea . . . a true Heart of Oak.

All chapter heading quotations, unless otherwise noted, are taken in appreciation from the works of Cecil Scott Forester, including the novel's title.

SHIP OF THE LINE

Part One

THE COLOR OF ENVY

It was a bad moment, up there at the foremasthead, perhaps the worst moment Hornblower had ever known.

Hornblower and the Atropos

CHAPTER 1

Year 2278
Bridge of the Klingon Ship *SoSoy ToJ*

"Today, my excellent warriors, our success will be etched on the gravestones of fifty thousand Federation dead. Today, my excellent warriors, you and I will fall upon nothing less than a fully populated and operational starbase."

Space boiled out before their supercharged warship, flickering on the giant forward viewscreen. The stars in the distance were the yellow and pink stars of civilization, orbited by planets bubbling with progress, the most populated sector of the settled galaxy. From this point on, all the space before them would be Federation territory.

And the commander's craggy face flexed with envy.

"Look," he said, moving his crippled hand. "Even their space is better than ours."

He sounded deeply moved by what he saw.

Was he? Or were his words for the sake of the crew, who had never seen Federation space before?

The navigation panel was particularly warm in this overpowered vessel. A short reach—the sensor grid controls also were throbbing.

Or perhaps I am the one who is too warm.

"Gaylon, look and appreciate what should have been ours."

"Yes, sir," Gaylon answered. Still perplexed then, he stole a moment to turn and look at Kozara, "Sir, how is their space better?"

"Look at it. A thousand luminaries displayed for the naked eye. Tails and sweeps and trunks, nebulae and storms, sparkling anomalies and ore-rich planetary clusters . . . they have everything. And look where we must live."

Gaylon peered at the distant suns, the nebulae, and tried to see what Kozara saw, but in truth the space before them looked like any other space he had ever seen in his career.

"We live where we have always lived," he pointed out, minding his tone. "The Federation took nothing from the Klingons. We live where we evolved, sir, I thought."

"Yes, but the Federation plots to keep us there, Gaylon. Never forget. Now . . . order the crew to begin scans. See if our plan is working . . . if we can move forward."

Gaylon nodded and threw a gesture to the sensor officer and the two crew members at the warship's complex helm.

No Klingon had ever piloted a ship like this one before. This was a refitted heavy cruiser, one of the old-style Klingon fighting vessels. Very old, very strong, thick, ready to fend off bolts of disruption from the earliest days of conflict with the Federation, in the days before modern shielding and advanced tracking sensors. Gaylon found himself envious of the helmsman and the navigator, the sensor officer and the tactical specialists here on the bridge. Of all here, he and the commander were the only crew who had no panel to man.

And he wished to touch this ship, to work it. There was something to be said for a lower rank.

The commander gazed at the open slate of Federation space and upon it, apparently, he saw etched his future.

"My new son will have a famous father," he murmured as Gaylon and the other bridge officers watched. "He will be Zaidan, son of Kozara, destroyer of an entire starbase, victorious disruptor of an entire sector . . . and all will bow before him."

Gaylon clamped his mouth shut. What was the point of speaking? Kozara was looking at glory and there was no turning his eye.

"This, warriors, is the culmination of months of preparation and plot," Kozara continued, not really speaking to any of them. "Starbase 12 is one of the Federation's longest established starbases. For months we have introduced operatives—spies—into the workings of the starbase. Our operatives have fulfilled their purpose now and have evacuated the station. Because of that work, Starbase 12 is experiencing a power shutdown. They are running on emergency power only, meaning . . . they have no weapons. Gaylon, inform the crew of the second stage of events."

"Yes, commander." Gaylon shook himself from his surprise—he hadn't understood that his commander had shifted from hopeful reverie to an address of the bridge crew.

In any case, he turned to the other officers and struggled to gather his thoughts and speak.

"We have allowed it to leak out that there will be a border dispute in the Federation's Benecia sector, approximately two hours at maximum warp from this point and six hours from Starbase 12. Now all Federation Starfleet vessels in the sector are on their way to the Benecia border of the Neutral Zone, assuming battle is coming with the Klingon fleet. Our fleet is there, yes, but with no plans to cross the Neutral Zone. Their purpose is only to make sure the Starfleet commanders *think* there will be trouble."

"And stay there long enough for us to cut across the Typhon Expanse and decimate a great structure," Kozara filled in with relish. His eerie green eyes sparkled. "Even the *Enterprise* will be drawn away. And the night sky over Starbase 12 will be ours to light."

Kozara was not old, yet he was deeply experienced, and still over the years of service glory had escaped him. Most of his crew were somewhat disappointed with their assignment with him. Gaylon would not go so far as pity, but there was an awareness among the crew that their commander greatly needed a victory. And such as this—monumental!

An entire starbase! In its place would be scattered bits of flotsam and shredded bodies forever in orbit, a bizarre museum of this day's conquest. And forever the Klingon Empire would be taken seriously by the Federation. The names of Kozara, Gaylon, and every member of this crew would be elevated in the imperial hierarchy.

Some of the commander's hunger infected Gaylon as he stood here only steps from Kozara. The ship was old, large, and powerful, and the bridge strictly utilitarian, most of the positions barely leaving room for elbows to move freely. Whoever designed this ship knew what ships were for, and that there was little sensible need for space *in* space.

Gaylon's thoughts were driven out as Kozara suddenly came to his feet, lifting his war-injured left hand as if it were a torch.

"Across the Neutral Zone!" he declared. "We have fifty thousand to kill, a starbase to shatter, and my son's legacy to ignite! Helm, plot a course across the Federation Neutral Zone. Enter the Typhon Expanse!"

CHAPTER 2

The year 2278
Fries-Posnikoff Sector, Klingon Neutral Zone Border
Bridge of the *U.S.S. Bozeman*

"Oh, that's wicked good. Isn't it?"

"Gabe, it is. An old-fashioned rum tot at change of watch can't be beat. Adding cinnamon and—what's that other thing?"

"Vanilla. Got it from my grandmother, sir. She liked her rum after a voyage."

"Best thing since synthesized mamba venom. You've got the strongest sense of family I've ever heard of. Me, I don't even know who my father was. It was just my mother and me, and she didn't talk much about her past. Hurt too much."

"I'm so sorry, sir."

"Well, those of us who have no anchorage . . . we just have to build our own. Now, you keep some of this stuff aside for Captain Spock and the two new men. Better initiate our new lieutenants right—with a slug'a rum."

"I have theirs here on the upper deck, sir. And we've picked up the *Enterprise* on long-range. They're almost here."

"*Entiproyse* . . . I love that accent, Gabe. Never lose that."

"Clings like lint, don't worry."

First Officer Gabriel Bush saw his captain smother a grin and grinned himself. The captain had on a properly mournful expression laced with just enough bastard nobility as he talked about having no family to trace. Now Bush was obliged, as always, to suffer along with his poor rootless commander.

"Mmm," his captain said. "We really ought to dispense this with meals too. Call down to the galley and tell them it's a direct order. Rum with all meals."

"Breakfast?" Bush commented. "What a happy crew we'd have. We'd have to cut it down to grog. We can't program food good enough to absorb the real thing."

"You cook, then."

"Oh, anytime. Corn flake stew, corn flake casserole, corn flake kabobs, corn flake pie, and rotisserie cornflakes."

"What about corn flakes with strawberries?"

"Never. Too pedestrian."

"You know I'm a peasant, Gabe."

"You are, sir."

"You ahh, suhh—damn, wish I could sound like that! Lend me a quattah so I can buy some chaddah in Glaastah."

"Then we'll have steemizz and crackizz with scraaad," Bush finished, exaggerating for his captain's amusement, and around him the bridge crew chuckled.

"What's 'scraaad'?" the communications officer asked.

The captain swung around. "That's the thing that comes up from the sewage dump with a head like a hammer and it's got just the one eye—"

"Baby cod," Bush interrupted before he lost total control. "Get it right, pikers."

"Is it anything like 'potatoes of the night'?"

Despite the drowsy moment, there was a hint of gallows in the humor. Bush baptised his grin with a sip of warm rum and shuddered down a lingering rag of dread. Oh!—that shudder was still with him, left over from the recent collision and fight with smugglers. The conflict had left him with a broken ankle and the ship with several crew members dead, including the

10

science officer and second lieutenant. The bridge still smelled of burned circuits, raw insulation, and a heavy blunder of lubricants that were never meant to be mixed. A few steps away from where he stood, the empty command chair reminded him of the fight. Still ripped near the front, the seat was a sly reminder that his captain would've been killed if he'd been sitting there when the upper bulkhead caved in. Bush would be in command.

Oh . . . *shudder.* His stomach clenched. He pressed his mind away from that.

Two weeks of round-the-clock work had cobbled the cap bulkhead back together, but the command chair's leather remained torn. Many other conveniences had gone wanting for repair as the more critical systems were pasted back to some echo of working order. The interior of the border cruiser looked like a junk sale. Her outer hull was scorched and even missing plates. She was operational, but only generally.

Yet the captain resisted returning to Starbase 12 for repairs. He wanted the crew to do the work.

The captain's methods often mystified Bush, but then Bush knew himself to be a simplistic and utilitarian fellow who often missed the unseen purposes of Captain Morgan Bateson, a decidedly unsimplistic man.

"Captain," the communications technician said, turning from his board, "the *Enterprise* is coming up on our port side."

"Open a channel, Wizz."

"Channel open, sir. Oh, and let's have port side visual, boys."

Bateson stepped in behind Bush and took the command chair, changing instantly from a casual rum-sipper to a more proper gentleman. The captain had both of those in him. His musketeer's beard and high forehead framed a pair of air-brushed gray eyes that were constantly working. At first meeting Morgan Bateson had seemed standoffish, but that had turned out to be merely one of Bateson's many operational personae, which he donned and doffed like theatre costumes.

In fact, the captain's fingernails were still dirty. He'd done his share of the hands-on repair work and only scrubbed up when he heard the *Enterprise* was passing through.

Stepping to Bateson's side, Bush was suddenly aware of how motley he must appear. Captain Bateson had stolen a moment from the repairs to freshen up when he heard the *Enterprise* would be transferring two bridge specialists, but Bush hadn't shaved in two days. He'd only managed a moment to change out of his utility suit and into his day-dress maroon uniform jacket.

Of course, unlike Bateson, who could buff himself up and shed the cragginess when he needed to, Bush could polish his skin off and still look like a shuttle mechanic. His hair was nondescript brown, a little darker than the captain's, and he had a forgettable face. Tended to say, "Who are *you?*" to the fellow in the mirror every morning.

The ship's half-patched bridge systems found their way to the forward screen and flickered up a port-side visual of a stunning silvery starship. The famous *Enterprise* was on final approach.

"Holy Jerusalem," Bush gasped. The starship had come up almost abeam already.

"What a sight!" Captain Bateson cried out, laughing with boyish cheer. "Look at her! Everybody turn and have a look at the *Enterprise.* Wizz, turn around. Eduardo, get your crew up from the trunks. Stand up and take a look at a ship of the line!"

No one turned him down on that one. All over the bridge, heads twisted, including the four ensigns who until now had been sprawled on the deck with their heads in the trunks.

Yes, there she was. Refitted and strong as an ox, the *U.S.S. Enterprise* hovered off their port quarter. The original of her kind, this massive starship had recently returned from her second five-year mission under the command of James T. Kirk, the shipmaster who had piloted her to fame.

"Isn't she a sight to behold?" Bateson murmured. "That design's never been beat. The big main saucer, round as a cake plate, that swanlike neck . . . deflector dish like the eye of a

12

god . . . and the nacelles, splayed out in back for all to see—
ah, it's like looking at providence formed! 'Bright phantom of
the night, mother of muse, diva of my heart's desire, dance
exotic across my path'!"

As Bateson's vibrant operatic voice rolled across the bridge,
the crew gazed in decided humility at the starship, now so close
that they could see her plate bolts.

Feeling his brow crinkle, Gabriel Bush looked and looked,
but could only see a large white ship with crisply defined hull
plates, the chunky engineering hull, gleaming polished windows, and the rocketlike thrusters. He saw the speed, he saw
the power and strength, and the size that allowed for labs and
recreation unheard of on others vessels. He knew he was
looking at virtually a colony in space. But he didn't see any
dancers.

"Where's that from, sir?" he asked. "A poem?"

Bateson kept looking at the starship and shook his head. His
voice took on a street-level roughness as he mocked himself.
"Beats me, Gabe. Heard it somewhere. Hail them, will you?"

Bush turned a quick nod to Wizz Dayton at communications, and upon getting a return nod from there, he said, "Go
ahead, Morgan."

The captain grinned again and shimmied deeper into his
command chair as if he were squaring away behind a podium.

"Morgan Bateson here. Welcome to the Typhon Expanse,
Captain Spock."

*"Good afternoon, Captain Bateson. This is Jim Kirk
speaking."*

The bridge crew around Bush all turned at the sound of the
famous voice. After Starfleet training, everybody recognized it.

"Well, Admiral Kirk!" Bateson leaned forward. "I had no
idea you were aboard the starship. A special welcome to you,
sir. Wizz, give me a bridge visual. Well, aren't we privileged
today?"

"Thank you for that." The image of the starship shifted to a
view of Admiral Kirk on his handsome bridge. *"I feel a little*

13

privileged myself. I haven't seen a genuine border cutter in a good six or seven years. That's a classic rig you've got there, Captain."

Bush noticed that Kirk didn't resemble very closely any of the photos of him, which must have been taken when he was on his first five-year mission. Now, instead of the familiar gold shirt of that earlier time, the famous captain—admiral—wore the same bristol-fashion maroon jacket and white collar as Captain Bateson. He seemed much more a settled master mariner than the wildwood scout of his youth.

Satisfied by that, feeling better that he was dealing not with a legend, but with a real Starfleet human being, Bush managed to unclench his knotted legs.

James Kirk stood up and strode toward the viewer, stepping around his helm and the two officers sitting there. *"We've taken the* Enterprise *out of the academy training program temporarily. Headquarters got word of a Klingon fleet mustering a few light-years from here, and we don't know why they're doing it."*

"Yes, I know. I wanted to head over there, of course, but we're still under repairs. I'm glad you'll be there, Admiral, given your experience with Klingons."

"Doesn't match yours, Captain," Kirk offered magnanimously. *"Records show you've had more hand-to-hand experience with Klingons in the last six years than any other single commander in Starfleet. They should be leaving me here as sector guard and sending you to the disputed area."*

How nice of him to say that! The whole crew beamed with pride. Bush felt his chest swell.

Bateson laughed merrily. "You'd have to lend me that starship too. The Klingon fleet wouldn't be intimidated by a border cutter."

"So you say, but I know the Bozeman*'s record. That's a tough ship. Don't give her up."*

"No, to be sure. I've got my sector and my line of scrimmage and I know how to defend it. Can't say that with your big roaming superfortress. Say, is our favorite battle-ax tinkerer still on board?"

"Yes, and he sends his most blistering criticisms. He says you'll fill in the blanks with the right expletives."

Bateson laughed with reverie. "Montgomery Scott, the galaxy's foremost hindmost. Tell that spacedog I'll be around to pick up after him once he dirties up that fancy upper-class engine room of yours."

"I'll pass that along to him. That's a refitted Reliant-*class ship, am I correct?"*

"You are. It's been redesignated as *Soyuz* class. Very compact, lots of power, no frills. Extra shielding, more weapons— not meant for science application as the *Reliant* class is. The *Bozeman* and the other four *Soyuz* ships are just knotted fists, and we pack a punch. Would you like to come on board for a visit?"

"Can't afford the time. We're already late. Spock should be beaming over with your new officers right now. I'll take you up on the visit when we're done dealing with the Klingons."

"Give 'em hell, Admiral."

"They'll get a tan, you can be sure. Kirk out."

As the screen flicked back to an outside view of the starship, Bush turned quickly to Bateson and asked, "Do you think he expects trouble?"

Bateson's slightly pouched gray eyes narrowed and his high brow puckered. He scratched his beard as if perpetuating a stereotype. "Wouldn't bet either way. He seemed cool as a cat, but he's in a hurry. Conflicting clues. He's been on the Starfleet Academy faculty for several months—could just be itchy for open space. We'll probably never know."

"Mr. Spock's coming here," Gabe Bush uttered, suddenly more self-aware than before. "It's hard to believe. Captain Spock, I mean."

"Now, relax, Gabe," Bateson said. "I know what you mean. He'll always seem like the ideal definition of a first officer, no matter how high they promote him. You can't help but compare yourself to that. Don't forget, though, he was also science officer of the *Enterprise,* and that put him in the middle of more situations than the typical first mate would see. I think you and I have a much more conventional relationship, and that gives me some comfort. I wouldn't want to be risking my first mate and my science officer all at once. So! I guess it's convenient that you're only my first mate, because I can risk you and not worry, right?"

"Whatever weathers your helm, sir."

"All right, crew." Bateson glanced around. "Put on your happy faces. We want the new men to feel at home. If you have any questions for them, feel free to ask after Captain Spock leaves."

"I got questions," Wizz Dayton piped. "Did Adam and Eve have belly buttons?"

Instantly heads turned all over the bridge, and one came up from inside a lower trunk. Voices popped up from all around.

"How do you know when to tune bagpipes?"

"What's the French word for 'bouquet'?"

"Was 'dead reckoning' ever alive?"

"This ship is sick!" Bateson rolled his eyes and shoved to his feet. "And 'dead reckoning' was never alive. It comes from 'deduced reckoning.' The abbreviation was 'ded.' Now you know."

"Should've figured he'd know that," somebody muttered as the double-door panels on the back of the bridge parted, and suddenly the chatter dropped off. They had company.

Out from the lift strode Captain Spock, supremely Vulcan and elegant, somehow looking smarter in that uniform than anyone else, including the spiffy young lieutenants who followed him. Both young men were tall and slim, one slightly more so than the other on both counts, and the second had a dark moustache and a narrow face. Spock strode immediately to the center of the bridge as if he could've found it blindfolded, and extended a hand to Bateson. "Captain, good morning."

"Welcome aboard, Captain Spock," Bateson said. "We're especially honored to have you here, gentlemen. My first mate, Gabriel Bush."

"Mr. Bush," the famous Vulcan replied. "The honor is mine.

The *Bozeman* has earned a strong reputation keeping the integrity of the Fries-Posnikoff Sector."

Well, that wasn't a cold voice at all! Bush felt his stomach uncrumple at the cracking of an old rumor.

In fact, Spock was encouragingly pliant. Not stiff at all, he was rather relaxed and pacific. His Gothic features, a series of brackets and sharp angles, came together less harshly than Bush had expected. His sharply trimmed black hair had lost the gloss of youth, yet Spock carried now an accessibility that youth could not muster. Bush watched him and wondered if the legends had exaggerated. Like anyone else, execs tended to size each other up.

That queasy feeling . . . happened every time somebody new came on board. Strange resentment of the intrusion . . . quick thoughts of how to prove he knew more than these two ever would, and how to hang onto the bond with officers who had died. The ship hadn't lost anyone in over a year. This recent violation lay and burned.

Now these two skinnies were here, eager to take the places of lost friends. As the faces of his dead shipmates rolled unbidden before Bush's eyes, Captain Spock began speaking firmly, but quietly.

"My condolences, gentlemen, on the loss of your science officer and your tactical lieutenant. I'm privileged to introduce your new second officer, Lieutenant Michael Dennis, and Science Specialist John Wolfe."

"Hello, boys." Bateson stuck out a hand, and Tall and Taller knocked knuckles trying to take it.

Bush let out a nervous huff. Bateson cast him a brief sympathetic look, then replaced it with a gentle smile.

Not understanding, the two lieutenants were too new to smile, and Spock, well . . .

"Sorry," Bush uttered. He put out a hand to the stately officer. "Captain Spock, I feel as if I've known you my whole life. Grew up clinging with all my toes to your adventures and the admiral's."

"Space adventures?" Bateson needled. "Way out on those

17

New England docks? With all those sea tales to feed on? Shame on you."

"Oh, you bet, sir. Us Downeasters are always fishing for a good story floating in the foam. Doesn't matter what kind of ship it happens on."

"Foam?" Spock asked.

"Bush is a Gloucester boy, Captain Spock." Bateson gave Bush a familar squeeze on the shoulder. "Long seafaring heritage. He can trace his family tree all the way back to the original Virginia colony. Had an ancestor in the British Navy on his father's side, a first mate, wasn't he, Gabe?"

"In the Napoleonic Wars," Bush confirmed. He turned away and gathered brass shot glasses from the upper deck where he'd tucked them behind a strut of the red bridge rail. Next, the thermal decanter—and he began pouring and handing out rum tots.

"Thank you, Mr. Bush," Spock offered graciously, then took a tot. "Captain, I do not mean to be impolite, but the *Enterprise* is overdue in Benecia Sector."

"Of course," Bateson said. "What's the latest word on that?"

"Several Klingon heavy cruisers have been seen massing just beyond the Neutral Zone, along with at least two dozen birds-of-prey. They have yet to make their intentions known or to communicate in any way."

Taking a sip of his rum so the others would feel free to do the same, Bateson shook his head. "If they'd concentrate as much on improving their own territory as they do on taking ours, we'd have two strong neighboring civilizations. They can't seem to get that through their knobby skulls."

Spock's black brows launched. "Not lately. Farewell, gentlemen."

He slugged his rum tot like a proper tar, nodded approval, and handed the empty cup back to Bush.

"Best luck, sir," Bush called, pleased for even the smallest chance to toss something into the meeting. "And the best to Admiral Kirk."

"I shall pass that along." Nodding with personable warmth

18

Bush would never have expected, Spock offered the new officers an encouraging look, then left the bridge without fanfare.

"Don't like Klingons, sir?" Lieutenant Mike Dennis asked as he turned to Bateson.

"Don't know," Bateson admitted. "Never met one."

His mustache flecked with beads of rum, Lieutenant John Wolfe tucked his chin as if he were being made the butt of a joke. "You've never met a Klingon, sir?"

"Not in person. Only in battle."

"How are they?"

"Predictable. And when they try to be unpredictable, they're even *more* predictable. Now, boys, before you square away your gear, let me give you a short course in border patrolling. Have you heard anything about this service?"

Mike Dennis glanced at John Wolfe, and neither wanted to speak, but as senior of the two apparently Dennis was pressed into service. "I've heard, uh . . . they call you 'Bulldog Bateson,' sir."

Bateson cleared his throat and uttered, "Ummm-hmm," and Bush caught some amusement at the new officers' discomfort. At least Dennis had the nerve to admit what he'd heard.

"You two know each other?" Bateson asked.

"No, sir. Just met," Wolfe said, as he glanced around the tight bridge and its two cramped decks, styled generally like any other Starfleet ship, except smaller and more utilitarian.

"Not exactly a starship, is it?" the captain stated. "'That's right. It's not. Tell 'em, Gabe."

Bush took one step forward. "This is a *Soyuz*-class border cutter authorized by the Starfleet Border Service. You may consider us, in a way, descendants of the United States Coast Guard, which in turn derived from the 1915 merging of the Revenue Cutter Service and the Lifesaving Service. In fact, the first United States naval commission went to Captain Yeaton in 1791, the master of a revenue cutter. The historic tag 'cutter' is picked up from the early days of the British Revenue Service, which actually used cutter-rigged sailing ships. If you want to know what that is, look it up. The United States Revenue Service used schooners rather like the fast Baltimore Clippers, but they were still called 'cutters,' and we still call ourselves that today. It keeps us tied to our long tradition of coastal security, and we're proud of it."

"Verily," Wizz Dayton confirmed from updeck.

With a nod, Bush added, "And this is no office building. No three eight-hour watches. Here we run standard military four-on eight-off. We dog our watches on the *Bozeman*. That provides seven watches instead of six, so crew members stand different watches instead of the same watch every day. The duties of a border cutter are smuggling patrol, towing, traffic control, buoy and lightship maintenance, import-export regulation, tariff and trade-law enforcement, and aid and rescue. Oh, one thing that always surprises new men is that we tow with heavy duty clamps."

"Clamps?" Wolfe repeated. "Why not just use tractor beams, sir? That's standard—"

"Why use energy that has to be replaced when you can use a clamp that doesn't?"

Oh, that moment of superiority felt wicked.

"That's right," Bateson said. "You'll also learn to set your whole being to short-range calibrations. Everything we do is short-range. We're not a powerpack, we're not a showboat, and we're never going to be in a history book." He made a gesture toward the main screen, where the great starship was just now pulling around a planet to clear herself for light-speed. "But we've got one thing that makes us equal to the *Enterprise* herself. You're wearing it."

Clinging to his tiny brass shot glass, Dennis gazed at him as if he liked what he was hearing, and Wolfe looked down at his uniform as if seeing it for the first time in quite a while. Bush understood how they felt—he too tended to forget sometimes.

"Ships are like people, boys," Captain Bateson continued. "They have jobs, specific jobs. This is a border cutter. That's all it's meant to be. The dream of this ship is not great exploration, not making headlines or even delivering cargo.

This ship wants a secure border and a stable Neutral Zone. As her crew, that's all we should want. We're cogs in a bigger machine. If a cog stops, the machine fumbles. We're a working ship, not a glory factory. We're not the knights. We're the castle guard. If you wanted something else . . . get over it."

Dennis and Wolfe mumbled a couple of dubious "aye, sir"s. Their faces dimmed at the unsparkled welcome.

Then Dennis suddenly yelped and threw both arms into the air. There went the rum tot. Dennis staggered, then looked down at a brownish tentacle twined three or four times around his ankle. A meter downdeck was the source, a squashy, squiddy creature with mammal eyes and nothing else mammal.

"Hi, George Hill," Captain Bateson grumbled, irritated that his show had been stolen. "Don't worry, Mike, he won't hurt you. He's just imitating the color of the carpet and wants you to appreciate it. So tell him it's nice."

Clasping the bridge rail, Dennis staggered again, but John Wolfe's chuckle shamed him into gulping, "Uh . . . it's nice. It's nice, George. Real . . . carpety."

Around them, the rest of the bridge crew laughed. On the deck, George Hill clicked and blinked those two big black eyes, and shifted on the coiled nest of his other tentacles.

"So," Wolfe commented, "we've got an octopus?"

"Look again," Bush said. "He's a decapus. Ten. We don't think he's even aquatic. Just looks like it. He doesn't have any suction cups on his things there. We think he's a constrictor."

Bateson nodded. "Considering what he did to the cheese sandwich I tossed him the other day."

Pointing at the carpet, Wizz Dayton corrected, "We call him a deck-a-pus. Get it? Deck?"

"Where'd you get this guy?" Dennis asked. "What a grip—"

"Don't know what planet he's from, or we'd put him back there," Bateson said. "Rescued him and a whole boatload of other exotics being transported illegally for sale as pets and for various voodoo medicines and aphrodisiacs. Some people will believe anything."

"Who's he named after?" Wolfe asked.

"Revenue cutter captain from way back in the scuppers of time," Bush supplied.

Bateson laughed. "'The scuppizz of toyme.' Love that accent, Gabe."

"All right, men," Bush said, "retire to Deck 4, Cabins 4-C and F, and square away your gear. Report back to the bridge in fifteen minutes. We'll give you a crash course in border ship bridge design."

"Aye, sir," the two chimed, but then Mike Dennis couldn't extricate his ankle from George Hill's coil.

"George Hill, turn loose," Bush said. "Turn loose. Turn loose of him, George!"

Clicking some kind of answer, George Hill uncoiled his tentacle from Dennis and placidly transferred it to Captain Bateson's ankle as if keeping a mooring.

Bush gave Dennis and Wolfe a nod of encouragement, and wished they could spare a couple inches of height to add to his own five-foot-nine frame. He hated skewering his neck to talk to Gullivers.

The two lieutenants headed for the lift, and Bateson leaned toward Bush. "Skinny. That's what you get with replicator food. See why I keep a galley with the real thing?"

"'Preciate that, sir. 'Specially the shrimp. Where I come from, shellfish deprivation's been known to cause severe depression."

"Excuse me—Morgan?" Wizz Dayton spoke from the communications board, but didn't turn. He was squinting at his readouts, not looking very happy.

Bateson and Bush instantly dropped their conversation. Wizz never interrupted anyone without a good reason. Now that he'd interrupted them he suddenly went silent again, staring into his readouts as if puzzled.

"What've you got, Wizard?" Bateson prodded when the communications officer fell silent after calling.

Dayton's bushy brows went down. "I was monitoring the *Enterprise's* subspace emissions, but just now . . ." He shook his head and poked at his controls with both hands. "Just now all my comm systems went silent. No malfunction, sir. Not on this side, anyway."

The captain stepped to the rail. "What could blank out your systems? Did the starship backfire?"

At mention of the *Enterprise,* Mike Dennis and John Wolfe paused inside the just-arrived lift. Dennis held the controls to keep the lift door from closing. Bush raised a hand to confirm that they should stay here for a moment, just a moment.

"The starship's long gone already. Warped out three minutes ago." Dayton plucked at his board, his chin getting lower and lower as he bent more forward, as if to stare his board into working again. "I'm almost completely shut down here. Got . . . yeah, still got intraship, but it's fluttery. I don't like the feel of it."

Bush moved to Dayton's side. Eduardo Perry rolled around from the port-side engineering station and met him there, squeezing his bulky form between Dayton and Bush.

"Plenty of those systems are jerry-rigged right now," Perry said tentatively. "But . . . hmm . . ."

"Jury-rigged," the captain corrected. "Comes from the French word *'jour'.* For the day. What do you think it is, Ed?"

"Looking for it, sir. I'll figure it out any *jour* now . . . Wiz, run power through system BZ-9 and circuit . . . six-J-Z-H."

"J-Z . . . H . . . six, powering up . . ."

As the captain waited behind them, Bush was aware of Bateson's gray eyes drilling up from the center deck. Under that surveillance the three men plucked at the boards, but weren't able to coax the right lights into coming back on.

Then Perry said, "This is blanket interference here."

"Internal?" Bush asked.

"No, sir, from space."

"Pinpoint it," Bateson said. "Could be that bilge wad Luke Oates coming back with his hold full of contraband."

"Luke doesn't have anything like this, sir," Perry pointed out as he scanned the board.

The captain turned to the forward screen and said, "Let's

have a wide scan. You—Mr. Wolfe. You come over here and be a science officer. Right over there. No, not far enough. One more step—that's it."

When John Wolfe hurried back onto the bridge and tried for an instant lesson in border design, Mike Dennis also stepped out of the turbolift, but had nothing to do yet. Technically, as second lieutenant, he was the command officer on third watch. Captain, then Bush, then Dennis.

What was happening? What could make that blue light go off? And why were the six main dynoscanners down? And that yellow indicator stripe was supposed to be all the way over. What could do this to the communications, but not disturb any other system aboard? Comet, maybe?

Bush went comet hunting for six or eight seconds, but found none, nor a thing like it. In fact, no energy surges of any kind—

"Got something," he blurted. "On the approach."

"Don't just stand there smoldering, Gabe, find out if it's natural. We might have to move out of the path."

"I already checked the—"

"Gabe!" Wizz sprung backward a few inches in his chair and pointed at one of his subscanners.

"Holy Jerusalem!" Bush twisted halfway around. "Morgan, we got emission signature. Sixty-four point nine enrichment!"

Clapping his hands together in a gesture Bush had come to realize was much less happy than it appeared, Bateson faced the main screen as it plumed bright with a new picture. The sensors had focused. They'd found it.

There it was.

Morgan Bateson drew a breath. His eyes drew tight and the pouches beneath them became pencil-sketch crisp. He looked like an opera singer about to belt the audience.

"Now, what do you think those upstanding citizens are doing all the way over here?"

CHAPTER 3

"Comm is totally blanketed. Nothing's getting out of the Expanse. We can't even call the *Enterprise* back."

"Red alert. Battlestations."

Turning to Wizz, Bush said, "Wake up the off watches and tell them to man emergency posts."

The captain reached toward him. "And make sure—oh, George Hill, let go of my ankle! This isn't the time!"

Bush twisted around. "Turn loose of him, George! Red alert, George, red alert!"

On the upper deck, the strange mascot of a ship remote enough to have a mascot uncoiled its tentacle from Captain Bateson's leg and wrapped another one around a strut of the bridge rail. He had to have hold of something.

Bateson climbed up to the command deck, but didn't sit. "Mike, find a post and man it."

Dennis bolted out of the turbolift. "Aye, sir!"

"John, maintain that position."

"Aye, sir," Wolfe said as he followed Dennis back onto the bridge.

"Wizz, keep trying to break the comm blanket."

"Will, sir."

"Engineering, bridge—Ham, you read me?"

"Hamilton here. I see 'em, sir."

"Good. Let's put everything we've got on line. I want all systems back on."

"Some are. I put the TT and TA systems at priority, but gotta tell ya two of the Prac-J nozzle heads are still clogged, DC's and one reaction chamber are inhibited, ARI's are acting up and the MIE's still iffy. DCA's under repair, but there's no juice right now, and the CC fractionators, well—"

"Ham, just flush some energy through those systems. Even if you can't get them working, I want them to *read* as if they're working."

"I get it. Ten-four."

Eduardo Perry pivoted with some effort until his wide form was generally facing the captain. "Tell him to flood the power transfer conduits."

Bateson nodded. "Ed says to FB the PTC's."

"Copy that."

"And how's the deuterium supply?"

"Oh, we got lotsa fuel."

"Copy, bridge out. Lucky thing I speak his dialect." Bateson stepped away from the command chair and stalked that Klingon ship again. "Can't hold that thing off alone . . . they're blocking communications . . . must mean they don't want anyone to know they're here. Not a good way to start the day . . . what do they want? Something . . . somehow we have to get a flash-SOS out and keep them from killing us long enough for backup to get here."

Attentive to the captain's words yet preoccupied with the approaching monster, Gabe Bush dotted the bridge with his attention, moving from position to position, but found himself a useless cog at the moment. Mike Dennis was manning the mates' console, so he couldn't even go over there and pretend. When that sunk in, he allowed himself twenty seconds to look at the approaching vessel on the forward screen.

Five times the size of the *Bozeman,* Goliath pulled out from behind a drifting cloud of space dust. The bulbous forward hull was linked to a pair of backswept wings by a long, thin, funnellike neck. The bridge bulb stuck out in front, as if to threaten whatever it pointed toward.

Mission accomplished . . .

Like most Klingon ships, this one's hull plates were drizzle-green, like icebergs reflecting the cold ocean. He'd seen it himself, off Newfoundland.

"The color of envy," Bush murmured. Quite involuntarily then, he turned to see who had spoken.

Was he so startled? They'd fought Klingons many times before, yet until now he never added up the simple fact that they'd never faced down a full-sized warship. Birds-of-prey, scoutships, recon cruisers, yes, and many daring smugglers, pirates, wild-souled individuals with a personal goal. Those were the most entertaining and challenging, because all rules were suspended, treaties ignored.

Shaken from his thoughts by the movement of Captain Bateson beside him, Bush stepped sideways with a twitch of nerves in his legs. His right hip bumped the ship's rail. For a moment he was off balance. He braced up against the rail long enough to regain composure and hoped nobody saw.

Morgan Bateson had done all but grow horns. His shoulders were hunched like a cat's, his hand clutching the arm of the command chair with fingernails turned tightly inward. His eyes were bright and sparkling with anticipation.

Despite the cold pit in the bottom of his stomach, Bush felt the same sizzle. They had to feel it, to tell themselves only their enemies were vulnerable, that they themselves were the predestined winners and God was on *their* side, nobody else's.

Bush got an involuntary flash of all the different humanoid beings in known space, and how many more there must be, and wondered which were made in the image of God. Wouldn't make the folks at home feel very secure to think Saint Peter had a skull ridge.

At moments like this Bush thought he was out of place, out

of time. He'd come from a small port town, not even big enough to be called a harbor, still a bit of old America, scarcely altered in the past three or so centuries. And here he was, remembering home, seeing Newfoundland ice in the Klingon warship, having theological discussions in the back of his mind. The warship was getting closer.

"Forward impulse," Bateson said, not sitting down. He rarely sat down.

The order seemed ludicrous, advancing on a ship like that.

"Helm, comply," Bush reinforced, just in case anybody doubted the captain's intent.

"Complying."

Who was even at the helm? They'd been in the middle of repairs. Oh—Ensign Welch. Not the best. Wanted to do it, tried hard to learn, basic maneuvers okay, but not very creative. A light touch, not much experience.

Bush contemplated a change of postings, but he wasn't in command anymore. Ten minutes ago he had turned the bridge over to the captain.

The tiny brass cup, still half-filled with golden spiced rum, was still warm in Bush's hand. He looked down at it. A flake of cinnamon floated on top. He placed the cup on the deck beside the helm trunk, intending to return to it later.

"Confirm shields up." Bateson's voice startled Bush, though it shouldn't have.

Instantly the anchor of protocol took a bite on Bush's nerves. The initial fear melted away, replaced by step-by-step processes forged over two thousand years ago in the military tradition. One thing at a time, each thing in order. Process, process.

He stepped forward to look at what Andy Welch was doing at the helm. So far, so good. *Bozeman* was pulling forward, angling "up" and port, into the path of the oncoming Klingon.

"Hailing frequency," Bateson said.

Dayton turned. "Sir, it's not working."

"Do it anyway. We might be able to break through on short-range. Send every signal you know how to send."

"All right," Dayton sighed with a shrug of one shoulder. "Beating a drum in a vacuum . . ."

Bateson didn't look back. "Beat proudly. Let's go by the book, Gabe."

"Good choice, sir," Bush said, raising his voice for the crew. "After all, you wrote it. Mr. Dennis, hoist the yellow jack."

Looking spic-and-span in his crisp new uniform, Dennis blinked briefly, startled, then dredged up the bit of knowledge he'd probably never used in any other duty.

"Uh—oh, yellow jack, aye," he said then, and found his way to the mates' console, a place on the bridge between engineering and sensors that presented overrides on all sections and a series of special authorization grids for use by senior officers only. Security ships were the only vessels still rigged this way, the only ship so single-minded, so basic, so clean of purpose that the mates could actually run such confrontations. The link at times like these between captain and mates was drumhead tight.

Klingons or not, they'd understand the universal sign of flashing yellow and red hull strobes. Since the first flashing lights on police cruisers, keepers of the law had carried submission lights.

Two yellow lights and two red ones on the sides of the main viewscreen came on, to confirm that the yellow jack had been lit, corresponding yellows and reds were flashing on the cutter's outer hull, and any vessel in the area was expected to heave to.

"Mr. Wolfe," Bush went on, "give us a profile of that big hammerhead, will you, when you can?"

So far, John Wolfe seemed more at home with his science board than Mike Dennis did with his mates' console. The science console was like any in Starfleet. If the rest of the ship fell apart with obsolescence, the science station would still be made state-of-the-art. It was the only station on every ship that was constantly upgraded. They might be using slingshots, but their aim would be pinpoint perfect.

The science board made no sounds except for two soft bleeps and one click. Wolfe looked up. "Klingon ship is standard full-bore design, except I'm reading thirty-two percent more raw tonnage and roughly fifty percent fewer crew on board than usual." He turned. "She's fully armed, and I'm reading some strange configurations in the cargo bay that read empty, but if they were really empty I'd only pick up the container and the air inside. Instead, I'm getting some kind of coloration on my screen."

"What do you think they are?" Bush asked.

"If this were a simulation, I'd say they were jettison salvos. On the other hand, I've never scanned real ones."

"Thanks for admitting that, John," Captain Bateson broke in. "Do you think that's what they are?"

Wolfe looked briefly at Bush for moral support, found little, then glanced at Dennis and got more. A second later than was proper, he finally looked at the captain and took a risk. "Yes, sir."

"Salvos . . ."

The captain's murmur swelled on the bridge. No one else spoke.

Jettison incendiaries. Bush got a shiver as his internal barometer dropped. Not often used, so brutal were those weapons, so entirely savage that they tended to spark revenge and rage even brighter than the thing they were set upon to burn. Many stellar wars and the occasional interstellar one or two had been ignited by a single use of such things, and few people ever spoke of them. Everyone wanted to forget those sticky, sizzling destructives. Not surgical at all. Not nice. Not fair play.

"Packed and inbound," the captain uttered. He was speaking to himself, fingering his beard, thinking. Then he shifted in his seat and tilted his head. "Go, Gabe."

Bush flinched to life and the words were out before he thought them. "Helm, block their flight path."

"Aye, sir," Andy Welch responded. He'd been ready. Course plotted. Now the ship instantly powered up around them, its inner hum bolstering them as if the deck were rising under their feet.

30

At the mates' board, Mike Dennis's face drained to the color of an old eggshell.

Bush was pretty sure his own feet were the same color. Luckily, his face had been trained long ago.

All but that one twitch at the side of his nose. Blast it.

"Steady, men." The captain leaned ever so slightly forward and placed one hand on a knee. Before them, the thick-hulled Klingon ship seemed to drift downward toward the middle of the screen, but in fact the *Bozeman* was moving up. The Klingon ship, however, was doing its own enlarging process—drawing closer, so close that no one could claim an error in navigation brought them here.

"Sir," Wolfe spoke up, "I've got the I.D. code off their hull."

"How'd you do that?" Bush asked. "They're not close enough for visual confirmation."

"New interpretation methods," Wolfe explained. "They're training us to pick up on segments of numerals and symbols. Like archeology, building a whole creature from an ankle bone and a tooth. I figure out what to look for, then the computer finds the pattern."

"Okay, who is it?"

"Ship's name is *SuSoy Duj* . . . or *mutoy muj.*"

"Mighty damn!" As if fired from a blunderbuss, Morgan Bateson stood up from the captain's chair and flexed his jaw at the oncoming ship. His eyes flared with something like brutal joy. He circled his own chair, but never took his eyes off the other ship. *"SoSoy tuj!"*

Mike Dennis asked, "Who is it, sir?"

"An old bloodblister. He's always dogging the Neutral Zone without really coming over the line. We've had to rescue a couple dozen border ships from him. Get out the handcuffs, boys. It's the universal constant . . . Kozara."

"I don't know, sir," Bush interrupted. "In that? He doesn't have one of those. He flies a bird-of-prey."

"Not today."

"How can you be sure?"

"Because *SoSoy tuj* is his mother's name. Mmm . . .

interesting . . . she must've died. I get it now—the gathering of their fleet way over there is a red herring. Starfleet's been set up. The Klingons are creating a distraction. Giving Kozara his chance to slip by."

"Slip by and what?" Bush asked.

"Isn't it obvious? The prize of the Typhon Expanse."

Bush tried to think. This sector had no particular prizes. Just outposts and storage links and—

"Don't you get it?" The captain slid him a sidelong glare, then nodded at the Klingon. "Why would a Klingon warship, a Klingon captain who's had no particular glory to claim in his whole career, want to sneak over an unguarded border, in a sector about as far from Federation central as possible, but definitely populated and growing?"

Ed Perry shifted his considerable bulk, trying to apply engineer logic to the problem. "You don't think . . ."

"Yes, I do," Bateson said with a nod. "They're here to obliterate Starbase 12."

After the horror of the statement thudded to the deck at everyone's feet, Mike Dennis was the only one to speak. "Captain, how do you know that?"

Bateson's eyebrows bobbled. "It's what I'd want."

Trying to add up that leap in logic about Starbase 12, Bush eyed his captain critically. How did he know to think like that? Captain Bateson always had these long-range suppositions handy. Bush never could do that. He never could tell more than the breed of the bird in his hand.

The chilling words drove in a moment of silence. If true, this meant the *Bozeman* stood alone between jettison incendiaries and fifty-odd thousand innocent people on a starbase whose power was flickering. Starbase 12 wouldn't be able to defend itself against anything like that ship.

Morgan Bateson kept his eyes on the Klingon ship, but moved slowly to Bush's side.

"Gabe . . . I'm very sorry."

"For what, sir?"

"I'm going to miss your wedding."

Surprised, Bush frowned at him. "What? Why would you?"

The captain raised a hand and dropped it on Bush's shoulder. His words were entirely dark.

"So are you. This just became a suicide mission."

"Bulldog Bateson!"

Kozara stood up so quickly that Gaylon had to move out of the commander's way.

They had expected a clear path. The Klingon main fleet had notified them that all known Starfleet ships were accounted for.

"Mistakes!" Kozara roared. "Always a mistake stands between me and glory! How can this happen? A simple passage becomes an incident! There was supposed to be no ship here at all! Now I have to kill him!"

"What is he doing here?" Gaylon asked. "Why is he here instead of with his fleet?"

"He must have damage. One ship, one ship . . ." Pacing like an animal, Kozara thrashed back and forth before his command center, then went behind it and thrashed across the deck again. "We blank his communication, but only if we stay here . . . if we go on, he sends a message and we are compromised. How long to reach Starbase 12 . . .?"

"Three full hours at warp factor five," Gaylon reminded, though Kozara knew very well the distance and time.

". . . and only moments to communicate with Starfleet . . ."

Kozara muttered and spat his words, some clear, others garbled, and Gaylon was careful not to interrupt his commander's efforts to think clearly through the obvious anger boiling beneath. Blocked! By one small ship! The mission of the decade, and one border patroler had stumbled into their way.

Truly Kozara's fortunes were shortfallen. Gaylon glanced around at the bridge crew and saw roaring disappointment in their faces. If Kozara never saw glory, they never would either.

Gaylon held out a hand to calm them, and hoped Kozara didn't see.

"He *must* be damaged," Kozara said, glaring at the border

patrol ship. Instantly dropping his rage for something more functional, Kozara reached past the tactical officer and clicked the sensor board for himself, scanning the bulldog's ship. "Otherwise, why would he stay here when his fleet goes somewhere else?"

The science officer shook his head. "But I read full power to all his systems, Commander."

"A lie," Kozara said. "He would never linger here with such a threat in the next sector. His main drive must be crippled."

"Sir," the tactical officer began, "he is moving to block our way."

"Is he using full impulse power?"

"Yes, but his plasma flow is . . . reserved."

"Can we destroy him? Are our systems functioning?"

"We are charging them now, Commander. Everything was inhibited for silent running, as you ordered. We did not expect a fight yet—"

"I will get you the time to rig out of silence. Hurry."

All watched as the smaller ship swung slowly around to face them and climbed toward the *SoSoy tuj's* flight path. Rusker nearly laughed, but some inner warning checked him.

Because Kozara was not laughing.

"Keep the communications blanket on," the commander said, "but give me short-range subspace. I wish to speak to the dog."

"Morgan Bateson the dog. We stand again before each other."

"Kozara the butterfly . . . yes, we do. Sorry about your mother."

"It was her time to die."

"You're wearing different clothing."

"Much larger clothing. I see that your little lights are flashing at me in the night."

Bateson's eyes glittered and he nodded, even though there was no visual connection. "Well, we all have to do what we do best, Kozara."

Audio was barely working. The words crackled and snapped

between the ships, just enough to hear each other. The Klingons were letting them talk, but just so far.

"What are you doing here, if you don't mind my asking?"

"We have catastrophic failure in our environmental control and an explosion in our lower deck flushed much of our plasma. We need assistance from a full starbase facility and request your merciful cooperation."

Bateson laughed out loud. "What a bag of bilge!"

"You insult me."

"I don't know who you talked into giving you that ship, but it must've been a scene to behold. You don't really think I'm going to let you get anywhere near Starbase 12 with that bulldozer, do you?"

As the captain spoke, Gabe Bush wedged his arms tight to his body and gripped his elbows and tried to keep them from shuddering. What a sorry display! He wasn't as afraid as he was certain he must appear, yet the appearance bothered him more than his own mortality.

"We have no unconventional weapons aboard," Kozara's voice crackled. *"Only the usual disruptors, and I shall shut those down."*

"Really?" Bateson said. "Kinda takes the starch out of an assault, doesn't it?"

There was silence, given a few snaps and fizzes, for many seconds. Then the comm cracked so loudly that half the bridge crew flinched.

"Dog."

"Butterfly," Bateson responded instantly, and glanced at Bush. "Enough shillyshallying."

Bush returned the glance, but had no idea what he was communicating to his commander. Support, probably. What else could there be? Doubts and fears were already spoken for.

"It's my intention to impound your ship," Bateson announced.

This lofty and ludicrous statement caused Bush to chuckle suddenly, and some of his nervousness broke down as he waited for Kozara's reaction.

A dull rippling sound sniggered across the impeded comm link, and surely they were hearing the amusement of the Klingon crew.

Then Kozara spoke again. *"You . . . in that . . . will detain me . . . in this?"*

"What choice do I have?" Bateson said. "It's not like I'm towing a dungeon."

"Am I looking at a single cruiser a quarter the power of this warship?"

"No," Bateson said. "You are looking at a Starfleet Border Service *Soyuz*-class cutter, with the full authority of the Federation Division of Law Enforcement and the nerve to use it. Unless you turn around right now and head back through the Neutral Zone, I'll have to hold you, your ship, and your crew in preventive custody. If you turn around, I'll log the incident as a navigational error. That's the deal."

While waiting again for the response, Bush slipped forward a step and tapped Andy Welch on the shoulder. When the helmsman looked at him, Bush whispered, "Plot evasive."

Had he whispered too loudly?

Welch nodded and worked at his board, fumbled, rubbed the blood back into his fingers, then worked again. On the starboard side, Perry tiptoed—as much as a man of his girth could go on his toes—behind the captain and Bush, back to the main engineering console on the port side. Just to be ready.

John Wolfe came to life suddenly. "Sir, I'm reading a firing solution!"

Bateson snapped his fingers. "Evasive maneuvers, right now!"

The deck dropped out from under them. Perry grabbed for balance, Dayton hunched his shoulders, and Welch leaned into the controls. Captain Bateson drew a breath and held it. Engines surged—and Gabe Bush sensed a slight buckling of the maneuver that should've been smooth. The *Bozeman* was struggling, but finding the power someplace. Unlike the men, the ship didn't get nervous and would just swim like the reef shark she was.

"No deal."

As the deck vibrated under their boots, Kozara's voice gave its final snap over the inhibited comm, and the system went dead silent. Frustrated, Wizz Dayton rammed the palm of his hand into his console, then turned a scared-puppy look at Bush.

No distress call. There was nothing to be done for that.

"Work on intraship," Bush snapped. "Keep it clear."

That would at least give Dayton something to do, and they did need to be able to speak—

A sudden queasiness seized Bush by the stomach and shoved him to one side. He slammed into the bridge rail, then caught himself and cranked around to see smoke boiling down from the port-side upper monitor trunks.

"Taking disruptor fire!" Eduardo Perry shouted. "Glancing hit, shield four! System's stressed but holding."

It was the weakened side, where the ceiling had imploded before.

At Bush's left, Bateson was gripping the command chair with both hands as the ship whined and tilted up on a nacelle to veer around a planet. "Lock it down. All right, boys, it's time to dodge, spin, parry, and thrust. Brace yourselves and, Welch, make for the inside of the solar system, a good spanking pace!"

"Aye aye, sir!"

"Why should they follow us?" Lieutenant Dennis asked. "They've got to be reading the damage. All they have to do is keep going to Starbase 12. They must know we can't stop them by—"

"They don't dare move on without killing us," Bush supplied. "If they leave, the comm blanket lifts and we contact Starfleet, and their mission is compromised."

Wolfe didn't look up from his board. "How do we avoid getting killed, then?"

"Oh, we don't," Bateson admitted. "He's going to kill us. But call me irresponsible—there are fifty thousand people whose lives are in our hands. Not to mention the crowing the Klingon Empire can do if Kozara succeeds. They have the edge on the next twenty-five years if we let him by. So keep dodging, Andy, till I think of something."

Looking troubled, Mike Dennis kept one hand on the mates' console, but turned to the captain. "Sir, there's got to be some way to negotiate with them or break the noise blackout. I didn't come on board to get killed right away."

Bateson leaned on his chair and scratched his head as if nothing at all were happening, then stretched out that patronizing grin. "Really? What *did* you come on board for, Mike?"

The captain's musical voice worked on all who heard it. If anyone else thought to protest this action, the inclination dissolved.

Bush thought of his fiancée at that moment as he watched this.

Dennis stared at the captain for a few seconds, but neither flinched nor blushed. "I guess that's what I came on board for, sir," he said amiably. "If you'll excuse me, I'll just go right back over here."

The captain straightened up as the ship's course rounded its curve and the compensators worked better. "John, quick, let's see a schematic of this solar system."

Wolfe complied without a word, and above his science station three monitors flickered to life, but one of them immediately failed. The remaining two managed to show multidimensional representations of the lovely large solar system and its twenty planets, and their positions at this time of year. Several, six . . . seven, Bush could see, were clustered on the same side of the sun, within a few degrees of each other on the orbital plane.

"There!" Bateson crossed to the rail. "That can work for us. Andy, I want you to look at that. Memorize it right now. As long as we keep Kozara from leaving the pie wedge right down the middle of those bodies, he'll be planetlocked. He won't be able to maneuver more than eighteen or twenty degrees either way with that waterlogged hog. Lead him right down the middle there, then veer on the Z-minus under that blue planet on the left."

Welch nodded and croaked, "Aye, sir," just as another disruptor javelin made the whole ship choke and grate, laying a percussive thrum onto the bridge. John Wolfe pitched forward out of his seat. Bush also had to hang on, but Batcson kneed his command chair without really sitting and managed to hold position and keep his eyes on all the monitors. Deafened by a jangle from the starboard side and blinded by a flush of gouty smoke, Bush found himself momentarily confused. When he righted himself, he realized he was looking at a different monitor than when he went down. Where was the other one?

And his head was spinning—had he knocked it on something?

"Keep the pot boiling, boys," Bateson called over the ship's gulping of power. "They're coming after us!"

CHAPTER 4

The forward screen kept a forward view, virtually a big window, giving Helmsman Welch a good look at where he was steering. So all they saw in front were planets swinging around nauseously. It was a port-side monitor, over the engineering station, that gave them the harrowing view from behind.

The massive Klingon ship dipped its forward bridge bulb and came charging at them shooting streaks of energy that blistered the *Bozeman* and caused the cutter to stumble even without a direct hit. Shields were made of energy too and reacted to the proximity of the disruptor beams as if the Klingons' shots creased the very space they were flying through.

Gabe Bush felt every sizzle on his arm hairs as the cutter turned hot inside. Environmental control was breaking down with the strain of trying to outpace such a powerful pursuer. Systems stretched their limits, infighting until something shut down and something else got the surge of power, creating their own turbulence inside the *Bozeman*'s hull.

In a turn that almost pulled the crew's heads off, the cutter dodged under an asteroid belt and angled around a small dustball with a rocky core. The Klingon ship fell far behind, too heavylegged to effect so tight a turn. An instant's victory, but there was no getting away from them without warp speed.

Over the whine of straining impulse engines, Bateson called, "We're getting gnawed. I'll take suggestions, boys, while that ponderosity comes around! Klingons aren't very imaginative. Any ideas for making use of that? After all, we're the 'best of the best,' right?"

"Might try a subspace burst in a sensor blind, sir!" Perry shouted.

"What blind?" Bush asked. "We can't stop long enough to establish—"

Dennis cut him off. "We could go around the largest planet, then maybe change course to stay there long enough to use the planet as a block."

Bateson paused. "How long is long enough?"

Suddenly on the hot seat, Dennis had to check his calculations before he spoke again; and before he could answer, the cutter was heaved on her nose by another disruptor hit somewhere on the saucer section.

"Whoa, good shot!" Bateson looked at Bush and shook his head. "Don't just stew, Gabe. Say 'Holy Jerusalem' and shoot back. You know you want to."

"Thank *you!*" Bush dived for the weapons control podium. His shout filled him with a hunger to return fire, and a shell came up and over his sense of humanity, one trait which did not serve well in a situation like this. Some things had to be jettisoned, and giving a damn about the enemy's life was the first.

Of course, that wasn't so hard lately. Quickly he got off two bursts of phasers before Welch recovered control and plunged the ship downward on their flight plane.

The ship squawked as the metal in her hull strained and her lesser systems suffocated. Flush-mounted hull plates grated like teeth as the whole ship stretched on one side and compressed on the other, and the braces all made groaning sounds.

"Sir," Dayton called over the noise, "we need nineteen seconds to broadcast a subspace message!"

"Too long," Bateson called back. "Keep the suggestions coming."

"Bridge, engineering! Joiner bulkheads in the storage areas are buckling, compromising the DP's."

Clinging like a really big barnacle to the port side, Perry punched the nearest comm link. "Take a club to those joiners, Ham. Don't let the plates break."

"My kinda answer. Mitch, where's the sledgehammer! Ham out."

A blowtorch streaked across their main screen, so close that the bright light blinded the bridge crew for a moment. Andy Welch shielded his eyes and somehow kept piloting.

"They're on top of us!" Dennis shouted. "Nine-three degrees by seven-one. Make it seven-three. Closing—"

The captain responded, "Veer off, starboard!"

Skneereeeech—

Howling, the cutter scrolled off to the right, leaving the bulb keel of the Klingon to slug around stumpily after them, and open space to spew out between.

Something about that open area of space . . . the Klingon ship grew momentarily smaller as it briefly fell behind and *Bozeman* was given the chance to hell-drive for the middle of the solar system's wedge of planets.

"We're fishtailing," Bush murmured. Had he really felt that? Were they losing control? Asking too much of the already battered border patroler? Velocity seemed to peak even though there was open space before them for a good twenty seconds. They didn't get twenty seconds more pitch-speed out of that maneuver. He felt the ship sag as if she were breathing hard.

Open space—

"Too straight, Andy!" Bush gulped then. "Take a nose-dive!

Evasive, not a flat course! Don't make us a target for a straight shot!"

"Oh—right, right." Welch shook himself out of his hypnotic trance from the planets racing past, and remembered to steer in and out between those planets instead of just past them.

At this speed, chances of being caught in the gravity of one of those bodies was very real, Bush knew, and he worried about that. The planets were all sizes, and Welch could easily forget to give the larger ones more distance.

Disruptor fire streaked past them every few seconds as the Klingon ship chased them, but the enemy couldn't get a straight shot. Even the glancing blows, though, were rattling *Bozeman*'s shields, throwing the ship into paroxysmal stumbling. The plunges, dashes, braking, and climbs of this pointless course barely gave the gravitons a chance to adjust, and Bush felt his stomach being pulled in six directions.

"Compensate like crazy, boys," Captain Bateson uttered, not bothering to be specific.

"Captain," Bush spoke up, "what if we send a hardshell?"

Bateson looked at him, probably thinking of the ten things wrong with that idea, but didn't immediately dismiss the suggestion.

"It'd never get out far enough or fast enough," John Wolfe pointed out. "A comm hardshell's only sublight speed—"

"Maybe not to help us," Bush said, "but maybe soon enough to help Starbase—"

The ship slammed downward a good two feet and gave everyone that elevator-drop disorientation. Cymbal-crash ringing blasted from the bulkheads and ventilators. Caustic smoke belched from several positions at several levels around the bridge, and Bush knew the same thing was happening all over the ship.

"Direct hit, sir!" Dennis called over the noise. "Deflector nine's down, eight and seven are weakened by fifty-five percent each."

"Not so bad," Bateson grumbled. "See what you can do to shore them up. We'll need our aft shields for those jawkickers.

Keep talking about that hardshell. Everybody pitch in. Eduardo, take a breath and suck out some of this smoke, will you?"

"Vents on double, sir."

"They'd see a hard comm marker in a second," John Wolfe said.

At the comm station, Dayton waved the smoke from his watering eyes. "They'd hear it too."

Dennis shook a burned hand and winced through the pain. "Is there some way we can launch one without having them see it?"

Letting fly another two phaser shots to the exposed underside of the Klingon's bridge bulb, Bush tossed in, "We'd need at least sixty seconds to get it out of the solar system."

"Or a terrific distraction," Dennis added.

Welch mopped sweat from his face. "Even at impulse, they're still faster than we are. They just can't *turn* as fast."

"Maybe we could blow up one of the smaller asteroids," Perry choked out.

"Take ten minutes," Bush dismissed. "Don't—" A hard surge upward drove him to one knee on the deck. From there he finished, "—have it."

From his stable seat, Bateson reached over and pulled Bush to his feet. "Can we rig a wide-range hardshell with thirty-minute broadcast delay?"

"Can do," Perry answered before Bush could speak up.

Just as well—Bush would've been guessing.

"Do it, please."

"Aye, sir," Perry said.

The captain paused as the cutter swaggered under another assault, then said, "Gabe, precautions."

"Right away, sir."

Good! Bush had been waiting for that. But he was manning the weapons console—a moment of bitter choice racked him before the captain himself stepped in and took over the weapons board.

Without acknowledging that, Bush clawed his way to a

starboard side comm to the lower decks and hoped Dayton had managed to hold back the Klingons' comm blanket enough to be able to speak to the crew.

"Attention, all hands," Bush rasped through his smoke-raw throat. "Prepare to abandon ship. Now, boys, that's not a command *to* abandon ship, but just prepare for it. Off watch, get the lifepods warmed up and running, check fuel and survival stocks. All hands, know which pod you're assigned to. Stick close to your posts until further notice. Bridge out." Swinging around to a technical ensign who was hurriedly closing the electrical trunk he'd been patching together, Bush snapped, "Ensign Nolan, take George Hill to a pod."

"Aye, sir!" The ensign scrambled along the deck without really getting to his feet and scooped George Hill's squashy "head" and tentacles into his arms. The eighty-pound decapus obligingly climbed onto the ensign's shoulder, coiled around his arm, his neck, his elbow, and one thigh, and turned dusty gray to match the utility suit, even getting a white ring around its "head" to match the suit's collar. Thus encumbered, the ensign stumbled for the turbolift.

"Gabe!"

"Sir?"

"I've got it!" Bateson slid out of his chair and prowled the helm. "I've got it. Andy, keep dodging. Gabe, listen to this. Mike, John, Eduardo, you too. I want to launch a hardshell probe into a sensor blind of some kind. A recorder marker at its highest sublight, but with a delayed broadcast timer of, say, half an hour. Once it's a half hour away, it'll send a distress beacon. We'll have to send it without Kozara's knowing, or he'll chase it down and kill it. It has to be silent for thirty minutes. That means we have to stay alive that long and distract him from scanning the area."

"And once it's gone," Bush picked up, "even if we're destroyed, Starfleet'll be warned and be able to protect Starbase 12."

Snapping his fingers, Bateson crowed. "I *like* the way you

think! Pack it with subspace broadcast on a delay. I want it to stay silent for half an hour, then scream its little ass off. Gabe, Andy, you keep us moving and distract Kozara for thirty minutes. That's all I want, boys. If we live thirty minutes, I'll die happy."

Bush drew a breath, nodded, and mourned, "And I'll die unmarried."

CHAPTER 5

"Hardshell launched! God help us he doesn't see it go."

Gabriel Bush crossed his fingers, toes, most of his chest hair, and the tail of every fish he'd ever netted as he watched the tiny dot of the comm probe gloss off into space. Was the sensor blind wide enough? Had the cutter stayed on opposite sides of this big planet long enough, yet not so long that the Klingon could get here too soon? Would the probe be fast enough to get out of the solar system, and yet silent enough to remain undetected?

Hang on, Ruby, we'll have that wedding day yet . . .

"Let's veer out of the sensor blind and try to look innocent," Captain Bateson said.

The sensor blind was small indeed, simply a funnel-shaped piece of space starting small and widening into the far reaches. Into that little wedge they'd launched their hardshell comm probe.

Now Andy Welch leaned into his controls and the cutter veered off, hoping the feint in another direction would distract the Klingon. Also, Bush was hoping that Kozara's crew weren't efficient enough to pay attention to outlying space while they had prey at their fingertips. Bateson had always said Klingons were like that, and now the cutter's crew was betting on that assessment.

How far away was another Starfleet ship? The comm hardshell would go like mad for half an hour, then start screaming for help from anyone who could hear it.

"All we have to do now," Captain Bateson said, "is distract Kozara for twenty-three more minutes. As long as we're alive, he can't move on even if he knows the probe went. After twenty-three minutes, if he kills us he still won't have time to make it to the starbase before the *Enterprise* or somebody heads him off. You know how the merchant fleet is in these outskirts—they'll move in and stand Kozara down themselves if they know to do it. Twenty-three minutes, boys. That's the deal."

"He's gaining, sir," Dennis announced.

Bush fitted together what was happening and decided to leave things as they were. Dennis was keeping tabs on the Klingon, Wolfe was monitoring the science station, Perry was keeping the engineering patched together, Welch steered for all he was worth, down in the lower decks Ham Hamilton and Mitch Trumbull were being Perry's hands, and Bush himself was firing back at the Klingon.

Firing. What a wish. Popping, more like. Spitting. Teasing. Against the shields of a full-sized warship, geared entirely for battle and absolutely nothing else, the cutter was only marking time, perhaps obscuring the Klingon's view now and then with a shot, but not much else. And the cutter was taking hits despite Welch's efforts to waggle around planets and between asteroids. This large solar system no longer seemed so large— not at these speeds.

Another spasm pierced the shields and came down through the innards of the ship like a rupturing blister. The crew was hit with waves of energy looking for a place to dissipate. For a handful of seconds Bush was riveted to his seat, frozen, unable to speak or do more than move one hand as the other hand sizzled against the weapons controls. Too far—too far from the starboard quarter weapons array firing button—he saw the red button blinking *ready ready ready.*

Just beyond his finger . . . just past his reach, and the jolt of the strike was still holding him down as if he were caught in a thunderbolt.

Ready ready ready ready ready—

The cutter veered hard under him. He felt the movement, and another second or two of the terrible seizure still kept him down. Then, abruptly, the ship tipped up on a wing so sharply that the artificial gravity slipped and Bush was thrown to the deck. On aching legs he scrambled up far enough to throw an arm over the weapons console and cram the heel of his hand into the red button.

The whine of phasers broke again from the aft hull, and judging from Mike Dennis's whoop of victory, scored a hit on the Klingon.

Not a destructive hit, but enough to gain a critical second or two, perhaps to get out of the line of fire again.

"He's pretty mad," the captain grunted, coughing on a stream of smoke from the port side. "He didn't expect us to be here. We wrecked his shining—"

The cutter jolted suddenly, and the captain and Bush both stumbled. Welch came an inch out of his seat. "Guidance is slipping!"

"What?" Bateson bolted toward him and was met at the helm by Bush.

"Why would it slip?" Bush asked—what a question!

The helmsman shook his sweaty head. "I don't know, I don't know! It's internal, though, that's for sure."

On the upper deck, Ed Perry rotated like a planet. "That can't be an accident!"

Bateson skewered him with a glare. "Can it be damage?"

"Maybe. But I wouldn't bet on that."

Straightening against the protests of his aching back and

legs, Bush looked at the captain meaningfully. "End of the chase. He'll chew us to scrap."

"Look for a hiding place, Andy," Bateson ordered. "We can't keep this up. What's around?"

Before them, the forward screen shuddered and swung as if it were hanging free, but that was only the movement of the ship around them, and all who remained on their feet were only doing so by hanging on hard to the consoles.

Andy Welch's jaw was actually dripping sweat now. "All these planets, three asteroid belts, all too thin, and over there is some kind of . . . cloud. Doesn't look like anything that would hide us."

"Cloud? Let's see it. Mag it."

"Full mag," Dennis called from beneath a terrible crackle as something burned over his head.

On the screen, through waves of acrid smoke and dust, a planet's edge dissolved and was replaced by a hazy globular mass that didn't look like anything but heat distortion. In fact, they could see another planet right through it. The smoke and dust inside the bridge here were far thicker.

"Is it energy?" Bateson asked. "Is that a nebula?"

"I don't think it's a nebula," Dennis responded. "Some kind of energy. I'm getting some funny readings."

"How we doing on time?"

"Nineteen minutes left, sir," John Wolfe declared.

With an internal groan, Bush leaned forward a little on Welch's chair back—nineteen endless minutes.

His stomach twisted. With guidance malfunctioning . . . what could make that happen? It had been working fine just before this encounter, so what could have gone wrong? Had something been shaken loose by one of the hits?

No, there was nothing in that system to shake loose. He was grasping at answers for his own comfort, and failing.

He looked over Welch's head at Bateson. "Let's go in."

"I think so too," Bateson said. "Tell me why you do."

Shrugging one shoulder, Bush said, "If it disrupts us, maybe it'll disrupt him too."

Bateson gave a quick nod. "Let's go in. Time for some naviguessing. Gabe, give it a try."

"Alter course, one-one-four-zero, Andy." Bush put his hand on Welch's shuddering arm and was gratified when the shudder faded some and the helmsman leaned into his recalibrations. "You'll have to do it manually and eyeball your course."

"I . . . know." Poor Welch.

"Full impulse," Bush decided.

Was that right? Did the captain want to reserve any power? No—that wouldn't work. Bush glanced at Bateson, but the captain was looking at the screen. Right, full speed. On any straight course, the Klingon ship could come up out of an arch and shoot right down its nose at them. Speed and a tighter arch would be all that could help the cutter now. The speed they had.

Without guidance working well, the arch was another matter.

"Hold on, everybody," the captain said. "Mike, John, help the helm. Ed, crack on all the speed you can. Andy, pilot with the thrusters if you have to. Everybody else just hang on. Hang on."

On the side screens, the Klingon ship with its greasy-green hull shone in the light of this system's star, cast slightly yellowish as it passed out of the haze of the planet just left behind by the *Bozeman*. The warship dragged a tail of the haze along behind as it veered in an upward arch that couldn't quite match the tightness of the cutter's arch. The Klingon kept its disruptors griping angrily now that there was nothing between the two ships. Bush's teeth were set on edge with every scratch and glance, but the enemy didn't land a direct hit. Good thing, at this proximity, because one hit—

Bush gripped the helm chair harder. On the forward screen, those disruptor javelins shot by, leaving a cymbal-ring to jar the cutter's shields and vibrate through the ship.

The "cloud" was hardly that at all. It barely registered on the eye, and only the enhancement on the helm screen allowed

51

Bush to really understand they were heading toward more than a mirage. Something was there, all right—if only it held some kind of energy that might choke the Klingon's weapons for a few more minutes, long enough for the hardshell to get far enough away. As for the *Bozeman* . . .

Suicide mission. Bateson had called it right.

Ruby's funny face and chipmunk cheeks popped up in Bush's mind. How teasing and quirkish she'd look in the bridal veil—poor girl, she'd wanted so much to be radiant. He had intended to tell her she was, and that someday they would have children just as radiant as she, cheeks and all.

Even if the cloud helped, there would only be a few more minutes. He damned himself for not coming up with ideas. He was dependable, but not creative, competent but uninspired. At moments like this, he wanted to go get a Vulcan for his captain.

"Entering the cloud," John Wolfe reported, and tapped at his sparking console. "It's some kind of localized distortion."

There was no sensation of entering anything, no bump or swish, no jolt, not even much of a change on the main screen. Perhaps there was nothing here at all, and it was just a mirage or some kind of sensor wash. It wasn't as if they could open a window and stick a hand out.

" We're in," Wolfe said. "It's in flux . . . we're losing power."

Welch gulped, "Captain, I'm losing thrust! Speed's reducing!"

On the upper deck, Perry shook his head. "Damn it! Pulse flow's impeded. Must've been one of those aft hits. Main systems are losing power."

"We're slowing down," Welch whimpered.

The bridge noises and the hum of the ship grew slower and weaker, like batteries running down to their last bit of charge.

"He'll be on us in two seconds," Bateson mourned, and swung around to the port monitors to see the approach of Kozara's warship.

But those monitors were empty. Only stars.

Mike Dennis had been leaning one hip against his mate's board, but now pushed himself squarely around and bent forward over something on his panel. He didn't look up. "Captain . . ."

Bateson turned. "Yes, Mike?"

Bush looked up there too, but Dennis shook his head, changed his controls, tried something else, and shook his head again. "John, you seeing this?" he asked.

Wolfe frowned and double-checked what his co-new-guy was looking at.

During that moment, Bush discovered one of the things about Captain Bateson that perplexed him so much— Bateson didn't prod or demand answers, even though he had been summoned. He didn't snap his fingers or climb to the upper deck to hustle the crew there into explanations they weren't ready to give. He just waited. In the middle of all this, he found a few seconds to just wait and let his crew do their jobs.

"Can't be," Wolfe uttered. "You got eighty-nine percent too?"

"On almost everything," Dennis answered.

"Can't be."

Bursting to ask, Bush clamped his teeth down on his lower lip and clamped his hand on the helm chair. The captain still didn't press, but only turned fully toward the port deck and continued to wait.

Dennis shook his head again, clicked at his board, and shoved aside a piece of conduit support that had flaked down onto his controls,

"Tell him," Wolfe said, looking at Dennis as if he couldn't believe what he was about to confirm.

Dennis stared at him a moment, then turned to the captain and wiped a hand across his moist cheek. "Sir, the Klingon's gone."

As if he'd been ready for the absurd statement, Bateson said, "No, he's not. Find him."

Ignoring a shooting pain down the side of his right leg, Bush limped to the weapons console. When they found the Klingon, he should be ready to keep up defense, joke that it may be. Maybe a few lucky shots . . . maybe a torpedo . . . maybe an act of desperation . . . Kozara's ship outgunned the cutter fifteen to one. Maybe an act of God . . .

At the science monitors, Wolfe turned to the captain with his conclusion. "No readings at all, sir."

"Gabe, Mike, Ed, all of you look for Kozara."

The bridge fell to a bizarre silence. Only the blips and shivers of damaged systems and the hum of ventilators made any noise at all. All faces bent to their boards, except Welch, who stared into the main screen, trying to steer without computer guidance.

"No residue," Dennis reported. "He didn't explode."

"No warp trail either," Wolfe said. "He didn't leave—"

Bush glanced up there. "Is he shut down?"

"Million-dollar question," Bateson responded. "To tease us out, maybe . . . nah, he's not that scared of us to play a game like that. Keep looking."

"Captain, I've got some kind of malfunction here," Dennis complained. "The planets are reading way off position from a minute ago."

"It's your instruments," Perry told him. "Planets don't move like that."

"Maybe, but this distortion we're in," Dennis went on, "I think it's temporal."

"Time distortion?"

"That's what I'm reading. Could be a malfunction. I'll check, sir."

"Wait—got him!" Dennis yelped suddenly. "Coming up on us fast from high forward—but the readings aren't the same. These are . . ."

"Coming in fast and high," Wolfe warned. "Collision course!"

"Great God!" Bush choked out as he looked straight forward.

On the forward screen, the fractured sensor systems coughed up a view of the oncoming vessel—and it was no Klingon ship. It was a moving mountain! The thing in front of them was triple or more the size of Kozara's ship and made the *Bozeman* rumble just from the proximity of its energy wash. God, it was big!

Bateson plunged for Welch's controls. "Emergency propulsion!"

"Haven't got it," Perry said, gawking with an engineer's eye at the monstrosity on the screen.

Stunned, Andy Welch slumped back in his chair. "I got nothin' . . ."

Bush glanced at the captain; then they both looked at the forward screen and watched the massive creamy shape freight-training down upon them.

"Brace for impact!" Bush shouted. "Everybody, brace for impact!"

He held his breath and wanted to go to his knees. Agonizing. Impending collision and no way to move, no guidance, no thrust—lie here and take death like officers.

The enormous oblong ship with something like low-lying nacelles and a sheen of dove-gray hull boomed at them, filling up the entire forward screen until he thought he was going mad with the size of it, close enough to touch. In this moment of final terror he actually reached out a hand, perhaps in defense, perhaps in relinquishment—he would never know.

He would be able to contemplate that, for at the last moment the big ship suddenly tipped upward on a wing and surged hard off, angling directly over the cutter's topknot and scratching by on the grace of what must have been raw inches. Inches!

"Ahh—ouch!" Ed Perry gasped, apparently amazed that the cutter's skin hadn't been shorn off.

"Holy J!" Bush shouted, actually bending his knees as if to duck. "They got my back teeth clean with that pass!"

Mopping a cold sweat, Bateson wallowed back into his

command chair, kneading the chair's arm. "I can't believe they missed us!"

"They decompressed their loading bay," Mike Dennis reported breathlessly. "At the last second, they blew their whole bay, including several cargo containers."

"Hope nobody was back there when they did," Bush uttered, shivering visibly. "Look at the size of it! Gotta be seven hundred meters!"

"Even bigger than the *Excelsior* design." Morgan Bateson remained seated, apparently gathering his wits, for several seconds. He stared and stared upward at the shadowy underside of the unknown giant.

"Mike, check out his emissions ratios," Bush suggested. "John, analyze the structural materials."

"Aye, sir," Dennis and Wolfe said at the same time.

The captain was already into analysis mode. "Is that Starfleet design? At least in rudiments . . . but looks like its been puffed up and stretched out. Primary hull, conduit neck, lower hull, nacelles . . . can anybody read the I.D.?"

"Not from this angle," Dennis said. "Sensors aren't working well enough. But the emissions ratios check out as Starfleet standard matter/antimatter enrichment, with some modifications I don't recognize."

"I'm detecting some new materials," Wolfe countered. "Reading some composites the computer doesn't recognize."

Bush leaned toward the forward screen, as if that would help. "Can it be a top-secret development?"

"It would have to be," the captain said. "How did they know we were in trouble? The probe isn't broadcasting yet."

"Six more minutes," Perry supplied.

Pivoting in his chair on the upper deck, Wizz Dayton said, "Captain, that ship's hailing us."

Arranging himself a little in his chair, Bateson made a facial shrug and said, "Answer it."

Wizz worked his board, and through the clearing haze on the bridge the main screen shifted from a view of that big ship to a view of a huge, wide, bright room of some kind with lots of lounge chairs and people sitting in most of the chairs. In the middle of the room were three chairs and three people, one a woman.

Humans, at least.

The captain drew a slow breath, then did his thing. "This is Captain Morgan Bateson of the *U.S.S. Bozeman.* Can we render assistance?"

As he watched, Bush experienced a wash of relief when it in fact wasn't Klingons who appeared on the screen with a ship more than twice as big. Kozara hadn't somehow switched ships.

The screen now centered on a rather stately bald gentleman of medium build, wearing a black suit, standing at the center of the auditoriumlike room's gold carpet. That gentleman was obviously the oldest of anyone there, and judging by his posture and position, he was also the most senior of rank.

"Captain Jean-Luc Picard of the Federation Starship Enterprise. *We were just going to ask you the same thing."*

Enterprise? Bush almost blurted an accusation. *Liar!*

But Bateson chose for some reason to play along. "Captain Picard . . . your ship is unfamiliar to us."

After a pause of underlying challenge, the other man asked, *"Have you any idea what just happened?"*

"Our sensors detected a temporal distortion. Then your ship appeared. We nearly hit you."

Picard seemed very reserved, even stiff. *"The* Enterprise *has been caught in a temporal causality loop. And I suspect something similar happened to you."*

"You must be mistaken," Bateson told him. "We only left Starbase 12 three weeks ago."

Another pause. Bush didn't like the pauses. Not a bit.

"Captain Bateson," the bald officer began again, *"do you know what year it is?"*

Feeling his innards coil, Bush knew what that particular question meant.

Bateson was remaining cool. "Of course I do. It's 2278."

The men on the screen glanced at each other; then the one called Picard took a couple of steps forward. *"Captain, perhaps you should beam on board our ship. There's something we need to discuss."*

For several seconds Bateson said nothing, then finally managed a by-the-book response. "Very well, Captain. I'll be there shortly."

"We'll be waiting. Picard out."

The screen flickered back to a view of the overwhelmingly large ship.

Wincing, Bush stepped forward on his bleeding leg. "Morgan, you're going over there alone?"

Bateson took his arm and helped him down from the command platform. "I think I'd better. I want to have a look inside that ship. You're bleeding, Gabe. You all right?"

"Oh, it'll fix," Bush said with a pat on his thigh. "Feels better already."

"How'd you get cut like that?"

"Guess I fell against that open panel over there."

"Are you fit to take the bridge?"

"Wouldn't leave now except feet first."

"Have a medic come up and tend that leg, at least. Even in this century we can still bleed to death."

"Aye, sir. I really don't like this, you going alone over there and all. Could be a trick. We don't really know what we're looking at. Take some men with you."

Bateson held a hand toward the forward screen. "If that's a Starfleet ship, it would be the height of indiscretion for me to beam on board with a security detail, even if we've never seen the design before."

"Or those black suits before either," Bush pointed out. "We'd know if headquarters changed uniforms, wouldn't we?"

"Maybe. We're pretty far out, you know. It wouldn't be the first time they didn't bother to tell us something."

"But uniforms?"

"If it's not a Starfleet ship . . . well, look at it. There's not much we could do, is there? I'll put on a sensor chip. You can monitor my whereabouts and physical condition. If I get hurt, zero in and beam me on out."

"Then what?"

The captain hopped up the steps to the upper deck near the turbolift. "Who knows?"

CHAPTER 6

Year 2368
The *U.S.S. Enterprise* 1701-D.

"This way, Captain Bateson. Right through here, sir."

A good looking man. Well-groomed, even elegant, and quick-witted, but with a raucous glimmer in his eye, something like a South American macaw until it started talking. Already he'd made several comments and even a joke. Something about how Daniel Boone would've liked all this "elbow room on a ship this big."

And those old-style uniforms certainly were striking—black trousers under the angular maroon jacket, the black belt, the white command-division collar, and that fold-over chest placket . . . less comfortable, maybe, but certainly more stylish than today's leisure-fitted two-piece uniforms, no belt, no collar, no placket.

"Captain." Commander William Riker kept his opinions to himself and motioned to the ready-room door, behind which his own captain waited to speak to Bateson.

Morgan Bateson hesitated where he stood on the port side of the starship's bridge, gazing at the huge vision of his own ship on the gigantic forward screen. This bridge must look very strange to him, with its beige carpeting and its wide ramps, the high ceiling and bright shadowless lights. Certainly that ship on the screen, the humble *Bozeman* possessed nothing like the place its captain now stood.

And Riker couldn't help a few seconds of awe as he gazed at the *Bozeman* too. Something about old ships . . .

There was visible damage on the cutter's hull, and that caught both men's eyes for a few lingering seconds. Then Bateson turned and came through the ready-room door at Riker's side.

The ready room was decidedly cooler than the bridge. Captain Picard liked it that way. He said he could think better.

Jean-Luc Picard was pacing in front of his desk, and now came forward with a hand extended to Morgan Bateson. Picard wasn't a large man, but he commanded a certain attention and had done so for as long as Riker had known him. He was less swashbuckler than magistrate, an old-line sovereign of a synthetic kingdom. Carrying with him little of the bravura of command, Picard instead seemed to treat captaincy as a pastorship, a trust rather than an adventure. Perhaps that was because command hadn't been Jean-Luc Picard's driven goal in life. Instead, he had simply risen to it as it came.

As Captain Picard approached them, Will Riker wondered if he himself could ever be so regal, and to take moments like this with such marksmanlike calm.

"Welcome aboard, Captain Bateson," Picard offered amiably, and indeed Riker thought the tone and posture reminded him of someone greeting the next of kin at a funeral.

"Captain Picard," Bateson responded, taking Picard's hand. "This *is* a Starfleet ship . . . isn't it?"

"Yes, yes, it is, most certainly." Picard motioned to the office. "Won't you sit down?"

"I'd rather not just yet."

Picard glanced at Riker. "Yes . . . of course."

Looking out the wide viewports that graced the ready room for just another moment, Bateson turned and bluntly asked, "Will you please identify yourselves and your vessel now?"

"I am, as I told you, Captain Jean-Luc Picard. This vessel is the United Federation of Planets flagship *U.S.S. Enterprise.*"

As if he'd already been bracing for some kind of joke, Bateson looked at Picard, then at Riker, then back to the captain. "The *Enterprise, Constitution*-class NCC 1701, length two-hundred ninety meters, is under command of Captain Spock, currently flagged for Admiral James Kirk, and is at this moment on its way to a bogus border despute in the next sector. We just rendezvoused with the *Enterprise* less than one hour ago, and this ship . . . is not that ship."

"Ah, no," Picard allowed, "this isn't that ship. But this *is* in fact the *Enterprise* . . . *Galaxy*-class, L.O.A. six hundred forty-one meters, crew of one thousand four. Our number is NCC 1701-D."

Riker held his breath. The captain had been careful to put an inflection on the "D." Bateson was no idiot. Starfleet captains weren't. Well, *most* weren't.

A, B, C . . . D. That had to represent a lot of innovation and effort—and a lot of years. It also implied that the starship Bateson knew as the Federation flagship no longer existed, that something had happened, probably something bad.

Bateson didn't ask the obvious question. He just waited, looking at Picard with those slightly narrowed gray eyes.

Rubbing his knuckles, Picard confirmed, "Yes . . . all right, I'll try to explain at least what we know. It's only been a few minutes since we stabilized our systems. We nearly struck you."

"I know," Bateson said. "You blew your loading bay at the last second. Good thing you did, because we were completely stalled."

"It's our shuttlebay. Mr. Riker's idea," Picard gallantly transferred. "We'd have all been destroyed otherwise. We're pretty sure of that. You've been caught in a temporal causality loop, as near as we can figure it, Captain. We were caught in it also and kept repeating the collision between our two ships. Finally we figured out the survival alternative and put an end to the loop."

"I'm glad you did. We couldn't move at all. For some reason our propulsion and guidance both went off line."

"There's no reason for that to happen," Riker interrupted. "They're not tied in with each other."

"I know that," Bateson answered.

"Of course . . . sorry, sir."

Bateson ignored him and turned to Picard. "Get to the bottom line, Captain. What do you think is going on?"

"Just what I told you," Picard said. "Our ships are roughly ninety years apart in development. The causality loop has put us together." He gestured at himself and Riker, then at the area around them. "We are from the year 2368."

Riker noticed that their guest instantly rejected the idea, then almost as quickly absorbed it, typical of commanders who had learned to distill situations in an instant. Bateson doubted what he heard, of course, but he also trusted the evidence of his own eyes. And he was gazing fiercely at Picard, as though the stare could make the liar break.

Letting the surroundings speak for himself, Picard blue-bloodedly remained untextured and took the glare.

"You're sure about this?" Bateson asked.

"We're double-checking everything now."

"I'll have to have confirmation, of course."

"Of course."

As Riker and his captain watched, Morgan Bateson crossed some line or other, and at least made a strong effort to participate in what he saw happening around him.

He fanned his hands casually. "Well, Captain Picard, Mr. Riker . . . if all this checks out, I'll do everything possible, as I'm sure Starfleet will, to make you and your crew comfortable in our time."

Riker actually winced. He was glad Bateson wasn't looking at him right then.

"This must be terrible for you," Bateson went on to the captain. "Perhaps there's some way to use this causality to return you to your own time."

"There isn't," Picard established. "We've been checking that more than anything else. The causality has a particular temporal flow that can't be reversed by artificial means. In fact, it's gone now. We think it's subject to its own forces and it's gone off to another era. Possibly another epoch. We can't find it anymore."

While he talked, Picard threw a glance at Riker—a deeply troubled glance, even a desperate one. The moment of terrible truth was getting closer and harder at the same pace, and the captain's silent eyes asked the ugliest question: *Are we sure it's not us?*

A chill ran up Riker's arms. Trying not to draw attention, he slipped into a swivel chair before the captain's desk and reached for the non-audio computer access tie-in. He fingered the controls, shutting off the vocal response mode. All he needed was for the computer to stupidly blurt out what it discovered.

Local celestial bodies . . . position . . . status . . . stellar correlations . . . home in on the beacon at the Linden Navigational Outpost, established only fourteen years ago . . . *please be there . . .*

Yes. Loud and clear.

He tilted his head, caught Picard's eye beyond Bateson's shoulder. Picard didn't change expression, but maintained a perfect stage distance. Riker nodded with sad reassurance, then pointed quickly at Bateson. *It's him.*

"Mmm," Picard uttered. "Captain Bateson, I'm deeply sorry, but we've confirmed this . . . the causality was apparently a *forward* time current."

Such a melodic voice when he wanted it to be. In the midst of the regret he was feeling now, Riker found himself admiring both that deep Shakespearean eloquence and how Picard could ease off on it when he needed to.

Judging from the sudden pallor in Morgan Bateson's face, Picard was playing the part of both doctor and paster—to inform of bad news and also comfort the quaking aftermath.

Bateson slowly drifted down to sit on the couch—luckily he was standing right in front of it or he'd have gone down to the deck. Once down, he somehow continued sinking. His elbows rested on his knees and his hands fell limp. His head and shoulders slumped until he was staring at his own feet. His voice scattered out on the rag of a sigh.

"Oh, no . . ."

The ready room grew so quiet that the soft sounds from the bridge beyond the doorway, tiny beeps and breathy whirrs, actually came through the insulated door panel. It had to be pretty quiet for that. Usually there was classical music playing in here, or someone was talking to someone else. Riker never noticed before how quiet this office could be, or that the bridge activity could be heard at all.

The tragedy for Bateson's crew—going forward in time—was far worse than to go backward. Anyone finding himself in the past could at least contrive to send a message forward, let relatives know what had happened. There was separation, but no tragedy. For a whole crew, the chance of success was pretty good. One message might fail, but a hundred or more, each requesting that the whole crew's families be notified, would surely succeed. Riker found himself mentally plotting out the process, just how he would do it, where to leave messages.

People who went backward in time had a chance to fit in. They would be living in a time to which they were technologically superior, and that was at least a comfort. Very little would be beyond them.

But to go forward in time was something else. No way to tell families what happened. The sense of tragic loss would endure and endure. Men from the past, in a ship that was already old ninety years ago, were instantly out of date, their hard-won skills obsolete. They were oddities. The process of fitting in would be the struggle of their lives. They'd be pathetic curiosities, and if they didn't want to deal with that, their only choice would be self-imposed isolation. They'd have to just about turn shepherd.

Riker watched sadly as all this ran through Morgan Bateson's mind. The click of thoughts was almost audible, until finally they started to come out.

"My first mate's about to be married," Bateson faltered. His face was like plaster, his eyes shallow and pained. "Our second engineer just became a father. I still have the cigar . . ."

Empathy crushed Riker to his chair. A terrible moment, worse than breaking news of a death. Should he go over there? Sit by Bateson and offer support with his presence? Just as he braced his legs to stand up, he changed his mind and decided he wouldn't like that from a stranger. Not yet, anyway. Captain Picard wasn't moving yet either, but just watching Bateson in a patriarchal way, not interfering.

This was a loss entirely catastrophic to poor Bateson and his crew. They wouldn't be able to tell their families what happened to them. That moment was gone. The mate's fiancée would never know why he didn't come home. The engineer's child would grow up without his father and never know why. That awful note in the file would read, *"Missing in deep space, lost in the line of duty. Outcome inconclusive."*

Ninety years. Even the baby was old now.

All this sat on Bateson. Riker could see the other man's mind spinning. Oddly, Riker felt just as bad for his own captain. That sorrow-filled gaze, the struggle to remain clinical for his own sake—Riker saw through it. Picard was sharing what could not possibly be shared, and Riker was too. *What if it had turned out to be us and not Bateson? I feel relieved and rotten at the same time.*

Riker flexed his arms, then fought to relax them. He'd never forgive himself if he added to Captain Bateson's irreversible tragedy by showing how lucky he felt that it wasn't William Riker going through that. He didn't dare appear smug, or hurry Bateson through this moment by being casual either. There really wasn't any posture that said the right thing, was there?

He beat down a shudder. Just like that, misplaced in time. No family, no friends, homes ground to dust, and ninety years obsolete.

Just like that.

How many times had they tampered with time? How often

would luck bail them out as flippantly as it had failed Bateson? For this captain and his crew, once was too much. *Snap*—and everything's changed. Their lives were fouled on a spur of bad luck, and that was as complicated as it would ever get.

"What can I possibly tell my crew?" Bateson uttered, almost a whisper.

The truth.

Ouch—Riker had almost said it out loud.

Steeling himself visibly, Bateson swallowed a couple of times, then croaked, "This isn't me. This is my stunt double. I'm still sleeping in my bunk. Go wake me up."

Outside the solar system, just at its edge, a comet streaked by like some kind of harbinger. Riker found himself watching it for a few moments, just to avoid staring at the lump of pathetic matter on the couch.

In his peripheral vision, Morgan Bateson's hands were ice white, and the shocked man was undoubtedly gathering up the courage he'd need to tell his crew about this.

"Well, all right, tell me," Bateson said harshly. "Did we at least . . . matter?"

"Did you!" Riker heard himself blurt the silly question and immediately gulped the words back—of course it didn't work that way.

Bateson looked up at him. His eyes were red with effort as he waited for an explanation.

"Go ahead, Number One," Picard said softly. "Tell him."

Riker stood up and tried not to be so damned tall. "On Rhodes Colony," he began, speaking slowly, "where Starbase 12 is still intact and operating, the main spaceway is called Bateson Boulevard."

Bateson's head dropped into one hand. "Oh, please, gentlemen," he sighed, "this isn't necessary."

"It's true. Everyone knows what you did. By standing down Kozara, you saved over fifty thousand people, a full-sized starbase, several colonies, and the security of two sectors.

"The incident was investigated for months. The search and

rescue alone went on for weeks. They looked everywhere for you. Starfleet teams, civil volunteers, starbase residents, and Rhodes colonists. Two sectors turned out for the search."

Bateson nodded bitterly. "They couldn't find a trace, of course."

"Of course," Riker said. "Kozara was chased out of Federation space by Admiral Kirk and Captain Spock on the *Enterprise,* who responded to your comm buoy. The Klingon plot was exposed and condemned as cowardly espionage rather than noble challenge, which embarrassed the entire Klingon Empire and shook the High Council to its bones. They went through several turnovers of power. Several families fell out of influence, including Kozara's. He was saved from execution by his one nominal victory . . ."

"Destruction of me and my ship," Bateson finished, his voice heavy with irony.

Riker nodded. "That was his one credit, sir. He never recovered from an incident you stopped from happening. His career went no farther. He's spent his life clinging to the one shred of respect—destruction of the Cutter *Bozeman* and the best border captain the Federation ever had."

"Best enough to get good and lost," Bateson derided. "Is there . . . are there any ways we could go back in time?"

"There are ways," Picard complied. "None very dependable or accurate. We know we can go back to general periods, with great strain and risk, but to go back to a particular month or even year . . . no. You may overshoot your own time by decades in the other direction."

His voice rough, Bateson said, "You don't mind if I look into it *myself?*"

Tolerantly quieter, Picard said, "Of course you should."

Sitting in front of the desk, Riker wished he weren't here, for Bateson's sake. Surely this was embarrassing enough. Bateson had a notable reputation which had naturally bloomed with time and the fullness of appreciation for his one-ship standoff with a fullly armed Klingon warship. The pertinacity of Morgan Bateson was so entrenched in society at Starbase 12 and Rhodes Colony that the official Federation mascot was a bulldog.

"Please be assured," Picard gently went on, "we'll all do whatever we can to help you, and anyone in your crew."

The offer sank in slowly, a gracious but empty gesture Bateson had extended to Picard only minutes ago. Somehow it seemed hollow the second time around.

After a few moments, Picard urged, "What would you like, Captain?"

Perhaps that seemed like rushing things, but these were not ordinary men, Riker knew. These were captains. Riker himself had enjoyed the prestige of a captain without having to continually shoulder the responsibilities of one, and he knew that would change a person. Captains had to think faster, grasp concepts faster, everything faster, bigger, more.

"I'd like—" Bateson began, then paused and gestured weakly at Riker. "I'd like your first officer to brief my crew and show them the records once I inform them of what's happened."

"Done," Riker said, then pressed his lips together. He shouldn't have spoken up.

But Picard didn't contradict him.

Bateson was gazing at the carpet now, thinking and obviously trying to be practical at an impractical moment. "I'd appreciate your help with any of my crew who want to contact their relations or . . . find out what happened to their families."

"Certainly," Picard agreed.

"Despite the time difference, and the . . ." Bateson waved both hands limply and glanced around the ready room. ". . . obvious technological gap, I'd very much like my ship to remain commissioned as long as possible. She's our only anchor now."

Picard nodded. "I'll make that recommendation and throw my influence behind it."

"I'd like to remain their captain indefinitely."

"I would like that as well. I doubt there'll be any resistance to it. Also, I'll make the ship's counselor available to assist your crew through the emotional transitions. She—"

Bateson's head snapped up. "I'm sorry—your ship's what?"

Pausing, Captain Picard seemed momentarily disarmed. "Deanna Troi, ship's counselor. She's ostensibly under the authority of the—"

"A babysitter, you mean." Bateson huffed and his eyes flared. "My crew won't need any 'counselor,' Captain. No offense, but we've got each other."

Riker frowned and embarked on a tailspin to try remembering when the counseling program had been made regular duty, but Jean-Luc Picard smiled. "None taken. Smaller vessels run on a different dynamic than a full-sized cruiser."

Without a beat, Bateson shot back, "Perhaps in *this* century they do."

Bristling at the tone, Riker clamped his lips shut and realized that Bateson wasn't trying to insult them. He'd just run headlong into a glaring difference between his time and this. His voice was harsh with bitterness at the cruel twist, and he was trying to tread water in a very big sea. Bateson wasn't alone—the concept of a ship's counselor had bothered a lot of people when it was first proposed. Even now it had its hardcore detractors, even captains who gave their counselors every conceivable duty to keep them from counseling.

"Well, there's one little quirk in your favor," Picard mentioned, moving forward.

Trying to conjure up a bright side, Bateson looked up and asked, "Which is?"

Picard held out one hand. "Your seniority."

"That's right!" Riker put in. "There's no provision in Starfleet's active duty articles that takes time travel into consideration!"

"Actually, there is," Picard corrected. "Before James Kirk traveled back in time on a mission to examine the 1960's, a provision was incorporated allowing any Starfleet personnel to retain seniority as accrued from the date of commission despite passage backward in time. However," he added, "in your case, Mr. Riker is quite right. There's nothing about moving forward in time. Your commission date still stands, making you in fact the most senior captain currently on duty. You may be able to parlay that into great influence, Captain. And on behalf of all you have sacrificed in the line of duty, I will defend that seniority."

"So will I," Riker chimed in.

Bateson shook his head and wiped a film of sweat from his cheek. "It gives me seniority of a captain four and a half times my age or experience," he sadly mused, and there was a glint of possibility in his voice this time. "I've . . . *no* idea how to use that . . ."

Briefly seeing the future through the murk, Morgan Bateson pushed off the soft simulated leather of the couch, stood up, wavered understandably, then shuffled to the huge viewports that made up one full curving wall of the captain's ready room. He drew a breath, let it shudder out, drew another, and had a little more control this time. He gazed out at open space.

"We have no mission . . . our ship is outdated . . . my crew doesn't need counseling, gentlemen. They need a purpose. They need a reason to focus their minds forward. It's my new mission in life to provide them with one."

Picard looked at Riker—they'd found a thread of hope—and back at Bateson.

"Something tells me you'll find your way, Captain. And we will unceasingly defend you."

Riker smiled. "Yes, we will. That's a promise."

CHAPTER 7

Morgan Bateson dreaded every step back to the starship's transporter room, every step from his ship's transporter room to the bridge. A thousand lies raced through his mind. Could he control his expression? A million words available—which would he choose? Were there good ones? Better ones? Neutral ones?

No, there was no neutral. No good, no better.

A chill throttled up his spine as he clumped onto his bridge. There it was, the same as it had been ninety years ago. There they all were . . . Gabe, Wizz, Ed, the new guys who certainly would be lost now, for they hadn't even had the chance to be at home here. Now they would be at home nowhere. How could their captain help them? Did anyone ever expect a captain to be at some time entirely powerless?

All their eyes were on him. They had questions. They thought he had answers.

He did.

"Boys . . ." His voice was scarcely a croak.

His cold hands motioned them to gather around. For a few

rough seconds he said nothing, but coiled an arm around Gabe Bush and lay the other hand on the next man's shoulder, who happened to be Mike Dennis.

Then he looked at Bush, and felt his own cheeks grow ruddy and his eyes crimp. His throat tightened—better speak before it closed right up.

"Gabe," he began, "gonna miss the wedding."

Part Two

THE NEAR UNKNOWN

Service in a flagship might be a way to quicker promotion, but there were many crumpled petals in the bed of roses.

Hornblower and the Atropos

CHAPTER 8

Three years later, the year 2371

Between commands. That queasy insecurity. No ship. No home port, no mission.

Commander Will Riker found the feeling unbanishable. Shoreleave was good when a docked ship lay waiting to go out again, but where there was no ship . . .

There is no ship.

As he hurried along the Promenade at Starbase 12, Riker was anxious to meet Captain Picard. Lately the captain seemed calm and unflappable as always, but for some reason, fearing some impending decision, Riker didn't like to leave Picard alone for too long at a time, alone to think. A captain with a ship had preoccupations. A captain without one . . .

The *Enterprise*-D had been Jean-Luc Picard's crowning accolade. Now the ship was wrecked beyond all but salvage, destroyed in the line of duty, crashed to a planet's surface to save the lives of her crew.

At first, the crew had felt victorious at simply having survived. Then relieved, and now deeply disturbed, living in the uneasy vacuum between assignments and trying to deal with the sad weight of having failed to bring their ship home. Unlike the grieving process of losing a loved one, which generally got better with time, losing the ship seemed to be getting worse with time.

Many of the crew had slipped away, been offered new assignments on other ships or at outposts. Some had taken chances for research assignments, others for exploratory posts. Some had decided to make those life choices that came at times like these, and left Starfleet, gone off to start families or pursue other interests. Some were still waiting, stalling.

As he nodded to someone he knew, Riker hoped that officer wouldn't come over or try to converse. Couldn't remember the guy's name anyway, didn't feel like being social. He wanted to get to the captain. This was going to be one of those days.

No—this was going to be its own kind of day, and he'd probably never forget this one. Damn, his hands were so cold—

His boots thudded softly on the deck carpet as he angled into the officer's corridor and forced himself to keep from breaking into a jog. This corridor didn't look all that different from the corridors on the ship, and his chest tightened, for in only minutes he hoped to be walking the captain back down this hall. Of course, the captain came and went regularly from here, but somehow doing that alone and doing it with someone who was having the same thoughts—

The captain had to walk down here from his quarters to get to the command officers' lounge. Riker told himself that over and over, but somehow it didn't help.

Ah—the door. He'd almost raced right past it. And almost sprained a muscle doubling back.

Hope he's alone in there. Should be, this time of day—

"Good morning, Captain." Did he sound cheerful enough? Too cheerful?

Jean-Luc Picard only nodded, and squinted at some activity outside the wide windows of the viewing portico, out to the movements of ships and workers in the protected work cavity of Starbase 12.

"How are you today?" Riker asked, vectoring toward the woodpaneled inner wall and the food replicator station. Oh, boy, that sounded like something a nurse says to a sick patient.

The captain was sitting on one of the half-dozen office couches in the comfortable old room, watching some workers on free-float tethers mount a new sensor disk on a scruffy merchant cargo ship. Pausing at the replicator while he waited to see if Picard would answer the silly question, Riker found himself fixated on the cargo ship's numbers—586490.

"Well enough," the captain said. "Same as yesterday, and the day before."

"I'll get you some tea. Just the way you like it." Riker snapped out of his relationship with the numbers and turned to the replicator. "Tea, Earl Grey, hot."

"Sounds funny with you saying it," Picard remarked as Riker accepted the steaming cup of tea from the receiver port.

"Well, I've heard you say it often enough," Riker said.

"Yes . . . I never order anything else, do I? Every time it's 'tea, Earl Grey, hot.' Perhaps next time I'll be wild and ask for 'hot Grey tea Earl.' The poor computer'll have a stroke."

Feeling as if he were about to step on a mine, Riker dodged. "We've all got our favorites, sir."

"I suppose. Or I could just be stuck in my ways."

Uh-oh. Quickly taking a seat, Riker tried to figure out some way to get off this train, but he couldn't think fast enough.

The captain leaned back and blew across the top of his cup. "One of these days I should just walk right up to that replicator and order Kahlua and cream. Or . . . oh, I don't know . . . perhaps a good stiff . . . iced tea. Wouldn't that be radical?"

"Captain," Riker grieved, and gave up trying to angle off what they were both thinking about. "Sir, it's been five months now. You've signed every reassignment request from the general crew, but haven't you noticed something?"

"For instance?"

"For instance that none of those requests have come from your command staff. Most of us are holding off on reassignment. We're assuming—"

"Don't say it." Picard held up one finger. "I know what you're all assuming. I don't know if it's the thing for me any longer."

"I hate when you talk like that," Riker said, deliberately leaving out the "sir."

"Yes, but those are becoming my clearest thoughts, I'm afraid," Picard told him right away. "I'm starting to listen to them."

"Attention all Starbase personnel, residents, and visitors. There will be a special encore showing of A Night to Remember *and Tony Feretti and Fred Lewis' award-winning documentary* The Loss and Recovery of the R.M.S. Titanic *in the ballroom at eighteen hundred hours tonight. The touring exhibit of artifacts from the* Titanic, *the* Lusitania, *and King Henry the Eighth's warship* Mary Rose *are currently on display on Decks 4, 5, and 9 of the* U.S.S. Bozeman. *Remember, the exhibit will only be here two more weeks. Thank you, and welcome aboard."*

Slumping back into the couch cushions, Riker shook his head and moaned aloud. "For pity's sake . . . I feel like I'm stroking upwind against a blast furnace!"

Picard cast him a wry and sympathetic grin. "No matter how you try to cheer me up, eh? Leave it to us to have temporary billet at a Starbase hosting artifacts from ships in various conditions of wreck."

"Of all the times in all the years, did that damned presentation have to be just *here,* just *now?"* Riker slapped his knee and shook a fist at the speaker system. "Maybe they should just put *us* on display!"

"Oh, now, Will," Picard soothed. "You're taking this far too personally. You've got to let these things subside, so you can have a chance to think clearly."

"Captain," Riker complained, "I came down here to cheer *you* up!"

"I don't need cheering up." Picard's gaunt face and dark

eyes actually showed up in the reflective surface of his tea as he held the cup to his chin, yet did not drink. He continued gazing out the big window. "This is my second loss of a command. In those years I've had hundreds of adventures, chances to save lives and advance changes far beyond my most wild anticipations. I've been absorbed by the Borg collective and survived. That's a chance denied millions of innocent victims. The Borg still have a little grip on me . . . now and then I can feel it. I never know how that will manifest itself. Is it just a memory? I really don't know. But if it does come forward again, it's not only myself at risk. It's any crew I'm commanding. Over a thousand people who have faith in me to have a good grip on whatever the situation is. Am I being fair to them?"

The captain paused then, somehow knowing that Riker certainly didn't have the answer to that and wasn't very skilled at over-the-counter comforts.

Picard blinked a couple of times and then looked at Riker. "And is any of this fair to you at all? Will you ever move on if I don't?"

Bridling his response, Riker determined not to get caught in that one.

After a moment, Picard looked away again and sipped his tea, then flinched. Too hot.

"I've managed to survive through a great deal," he went on, "though I've had to watch members of my crew suffer and die . . . even had to order some of them to their deaths. That wears on you after a bit. I've lost two ships now . . . anyone with a lick of sense becomes circumspect after that. Seven years ago I was the *Enterprise*-D's first mission commander, and now I'm her last. That should be enough for anyone."

The lounge fell silent again, and Riker found himself wishing that cursed announcer would come back on and start talking about disasters at sea again. At least that would be noise.

"You think I'm being negative, don't you?" Picard asked abruptly then, eyeing his first officer narrowly.

Fidgeting, Riker wished he'd gotten himself a drink too, so he could have something to hide behind.

"As a matter of fact," Picard went on, "I'm rather looking forward to life without that weight on my shoulders. There are other frontiers, you know, Will. I've always felt drawn to archaeology. A quiet sunlit dig somewhere, a cool drink, a big hat, a shovel and a brush—"

Riker tucked his chin. "Sand in your teeth, sunburn on your nose, callouses on your knees . . ."

Picard grinned. "And the wind in my hair?"

They laughed a little, and Riker felt better. The captain had a rare smile, but a pleasant one.

Tensions lingered between them, though. That unanswered question—*Will you ever move on if I don't?*

The captain gazed at him, still grinning.

Shaking his head, Riker uneasily chuckled, "I wish you'd stop looking at me like that."

"Like what?"

"Like Geppetto looking at the puppet and being proud of what he built."

"Well, I *am* proud of you. I'm tempted to agree with a few of those admirals."

"And turn the next command over to me," Riker huffed. "I wish they'd stop pressuring you to do that."

"Oh, it's not all that bad. We've been cleared in the loss of the ship, and that's something. They've ruled her crash a viable option in that chain of events and subject to commander's discretion. We're all free to accept new assignments . . . if we want them."

Picard stood up and strode to the large viewing windows. Outside this room was the inner spaceport of Starbase 12. The base itself was a huge hollowed-out spool hanging in space over the planet Rhodes, where the colony established a century and a quarter ago was now covering over half the planet. And at their fingertips, separated only by this window, was the protected inner docking area, where ships could be cuddled up close to repair bays and stocking complexes.

And there, permanently moored, was the reason the colony was still here and the reason this starbase was still here.

Beneath Picard, and Riker as he came to stand beside his captain, was the permanently moored border cutter *Bozeman*, docked here as a spacefaring museum. The old ship was compact and built for business, with its out-mounted sensor pods and its strong tractor mounts. Fixed up and put back in good hull condition, with its engines stripped out, the cutter was a dependable tourist attraction, coveted by the people on this starbase and the planet below. Its galley had been converted to a popular café, and even in retirement the ship continued to serve. Not so bad.

In its belly right now were precious museum collections of artifacts from famous lost ships, crews, and passengers, rescued from slow but inevitable destruction at the bottom of Earth's salty seas, brought here to be appreciated by successive generations who otherwise would forget.

And that old ship, the cutter—Riker remembered from three years ago how sad Captain Bateson had looked at his great loss, and wondered if he were seeing the same resignation in his own captain now. Morgan Bateson was here on Starbase 12 right now, Riker knew, working on the new starship that had just been commissioned when he and his crew had been transferred so unceremoniously to this century. Bateson was regarded as a hero, and he deserved to be. He'd managed to keep most of his crew together and working. That was a feat in itself.

Beside Riker, the captain's dignified voice startled him suddenly.

"I made," Picard declared, "a big mistake."

Then he said nothing else for the moment, and went on sipping his tea.

Riker paused, held his breath. He couldn't remember hearing those particular words out of Picard in all the years they'd been together.

Well, all right, might as well play this out. Maybe they could get to a goal line somewhere.

"I can't think of any mistake you made," he baited. "I was in command of the starship at the time. You weren't even there."

"I should have been. A captain commands not just a ship, but a situation."

"Sir," Riker pointed out, "don't forget . . . we won."

Picard shifted his feet and kept looking out. His expression didn't change much. There was a perplexed tightening of his brow. "Then why do I feel as if we lost?" Looking down there at the old-style primary hull and the nostalgic nacelles, Picard quietly mused, "I wonder how James Kirk handled losing his *Enterprise.*"

Riker skewered Picard with a look. "Why him, all of a sudden?"

"Not all of a sudden. I met him only briefly, through a quirk of fate, yet he made an impression on me. He wasn't the man legend declares him to be. He wasn't all-encompassing and bigger than life . . . I don't believe he saw himself as a faultless monolith at all. I presided over his death, yet I felt entirely inadequate to that charge. For a man who took things so personally, what was it like to lose that marvelous, strong, first *Enterprise?* He ordered the destruct sequence, did you know that?"

"No," Riker said. "I didn't know that."

"Yes. His ship had come to the end of her tether, but he still summoned up one last chance for his crew to live. They did live, by the way, all of them who were on that ship that day."

"And so did all of us."

"Yes, but somehow, even though it's happened to me again, I still can't imagine what it must've been like for him." Picard gazed out into the center of the Starbase spool at the moored *Bozeman.* "That was a different time, those years of early expansion. Captains were more autonomous. Their ships were really *their* ships. They were out of touch most of the time. Whatever happened, they simply had to handle it. They had to break regulations sometimes, even make up regulations. No Federation council looking over their shoulder, no civilians or desk officers second-guessing their every move, scouring their decision with hindsight . . . there's a certain loss in the civilizing of Federation space. I wonder how James Kirk managed to never lose his edge."

Unable to bring himself to ask the perfect next question— *Are you afraid you've lost yours?*—Riker came up with a completely different question and forced it out.

"Why don't you go ask him?"

The captain had begun turning away from the window, and now paused, perplexed. "I beg your pardon?"

Leaning against the vaulted window brace, Riker cast the captain a saucy look. "The holodeck computer bank has all of his adventures programmed in as holoprograms."

"It does?"

"Yes. While he was on the faculty at Starfleet Academy, he cooperated in making all of his mission logs into programs, and extrapolated on them for guest participation. Kirk told them what he was thinking, why he was thinking it, and what he thought he could've done better. Then they incorporated some of the perceptions and memories of other participants, just to make sure all the details were right. They used the building plans of the original starship and the technical schematics. The computer'll give you the real James Kirk, too. After all, it's not impressed by legends."

The captain drew his brows together, trying to imagine just how such records could be step-by-step, breath-by-breath fed into a computer and turned into a three-dimensional interactive program. Riker had wondered the same things.

Picard tipped his head contemplatively. "I hadn't given it a thought . . ."

Riker smiled. "Well, you should."

Pressing his lips tight, the captain bobbed his brows and seemed intrigued, if not entertained, and put his teacup down on one of the lounge's obsidian tables.

"Well, sir," Riker bridged awkwardly, "are you ready to visit the new starship? After all, everyone's *assuming.*"

Picard sighed. "Suppose it's my duty to stoke the rumors, isn't it?"

"Not rumors, sir. Hopes. Just the pitiful wishes of a group of ragtag misfits, alone in the universe but for each other, clinging to the forlorn museful glimmerings of—"

"I'm walking out the door, Number One. You're not still talking, are you?"

"No, sir, not me. Let's go to the right, sir, it's shorter."

CHAPTER 9

Long, long years, and many grinding sorrows. Was this the shining return of knights? No, this was the melancholy reappearance of coachmen in a not-very-impressive coach. No great warship hummed beneath, but only an exploratory tank, now crammed full of samples and specimens. Not even an unusual specimen.

Feeling as if his burdened chest were turning inside out, Gaylon rumbled out a sigh. The moment they had so long waited for was at hand. Return.

This tank ship rattled around him as he arranged the last docking maneuvers at the Zgoda Ring. With no more to do, Gaylon turned and watched the last few umbilicals screw out from the station's housings and latch onto the tank ship. He wished he were a machine too.

In the center seat on this stuffy and unenlightened bridge, Commander Kozara sat in silence. A sharp-eyed patrol ship on the outer expanse had forced them to identify themselves, so even their approach to Fortress Zgoda had not been peaceful and without identity. By now, everyone on that station and half the people in the Klingon Command structure knew Kozara and his gloryless crew were finally coming home.

Gaylon and his crewmates had hoped for a grace period, a few days to contact their families and feel out the reception, to see if public and private mockery had possibly cooled after so long. After all, Kozara's crew had paid, had they not? They had taken ignoble duty, gone out to "explore," to absent themselves from the empire they had mortified, and they had contacted Klingon Command only twice. Each time they had been told to stay out there, remain exploring the Great Waste even longer. And they had obligingly stayed. That had to mean something, entail some credit, some bank of favor, yes?

Shh-CHUNK—the final tether drew into its mount and locked there. The expedition was over. They would never have to come back to this forsaken pot of a vessel anymore. It had served, and could be cut to scrap for all Gaylon cared.

He caught a thin reflection of himself in the scratched frame of the sensor mount at the helm as he went to stand in the same general area as Kozara, without moving too close. They were both ragged now, aged by years and even more by this humiliating voyage to collect useless bits, a voyage really meant to keep them away from here. Kozara was absolutely gray. Most of the warrior had been bored out of him. The past seven years had been a constant struggle to pretend they had a mission, and to keep doing it. They had come upon a few civilizations, but none of any use. Only one proved dangerous, and Kozara had no fighting ship. The Klingons had been forced to run away.

They had run, and not bothered to be more humiliated. A man could only be so bruised. After so many blows, there was no feeling left in the nerves of the soul.

Seven grim years they had been wandering. The mission was supposed to last only five years, but those contacts with Command had extended their assignment each time. Now the ship was full to its braces with bits of trash in stasis. There simply was no room left with which to keep exploring.

Kozara looked old. He had looked old for decades now. Gaylon glanced at his commander—Kozara was tight with his small hopes.

"He may be here, Commander," Gaylon said. "Since our approach was not secret, he may have been notified."

For years Gaylon has trained himself not to care what was in Kozara's mind. Today, though, he wanted to know.

"He will be here." Kozara's voice, scratching from the old throat, made Gaylon flinch. "My son Zaidan will be in that station to greet us," the commander muttered on. "Forgiveness will be on his lips. We have done our jobs without question. We went where we were told without protest. We did a job no one wanted. Charted space no one wants to go to. We have paid our penance and earned back our place among warriors. Zaidan's open arms will welcome us back to honor."

Hope fired through Gaylon's chest. He saw each of the bridge crew swell a bit with the new chance, the flicker of logic in Kozara's voice. They *had* done all that had been asked of them, done it without protest. Yes, yes—they *could* return!

Sitting like a stone carving, Kozara stared at the forward screen, which now showed a view of the other side of the station ring from their docking place. The tank ship was plugged in afterend first, so her cargo hold could be unloaded. Gaylon could tell by the clanking of clamps and buzz of adjusting gussets that these docking ports had been updated. The ship, of course, had not. Out of range. Out of date.

They could see from here all the other ships being worked on or loading. They could see the three warships, so different from the one they had piloted . . . how long was it now?

Those new ships were much more like the blunt-winged birds-of-prey that soared Klingon skies, but more massive and stronger, and to look at them was a pain in the heart. They were painted with feathers and had only the slightest echo of the long-necked warships of Kang and Kor. In fact, they reminded Gaylon of Romulan wing-attackers.

But to look was hurting his eyes. He saw too clearly all they had been missing.

Obviously they had missed a considerable rearmament of the Klingon fleet. Why was there a rearmament? What was happening in the galaxy today?

Seven years . . .

Sharply a hunger for advancement gushed through Gaylon, a sensation he thought he had long ago banished. What a strange unbidden thought! His chances for promotion had been smothered long ago on that day with the dog captain. Many months had dragged by before he understood fully what he had lost and how much all the men of Kozara had lost their reputations that day. Gaylon had only been able to cling to his rank by staying with Kozara. Whatever his second thoughts had been, they had occurred in the middle of the Great Waste, and what did it matter out there? He had to stay with Kozara. At times even speaking to his commander was the most mocking effort of his life, worse than battle, worse than wounds, yet he had made himself do it, keep the ship going, one more system, one more planet. Keep going. Keep going.

Today there would finally be another choice. Finally, finally, he could leave, and melt into the faceless masses.

Were they still young enough to build their lives again? Gaylon hardly knew anymore. How much had things changed? Were there nothing but young men in charge now? Or were elders more respected? Who was in power now? Which families? Which sect? Which province now dominated?

Gaylon looked at Kozara. The commander sat as if he had been sculpted into his seat. Would Kozara's son be here?

The boy's life had been bedeviled by ridicule, Gaylon remembered, so difficult that Kozara had willingly taken the chance to go off into the big nowhere and relieve Zaidan's plague of nominality. When, seven years ago, Kozara and his unimportant crew had left Klingon space, Zaidan had been plodding along in a construction career, making buildings, bridges, and spaceports like this one. Only two things had saved him from the crushing weight of his father's failure. One was his natural skill with architecture. The second was his father's only success—destruction of the Starfleet border ship that had ruined the assault on Starbase 12. At least there had been that single accomplishment. Kozara had retained his rank, and Zaidan had been spared the stain of complete dishonor.

Now the humiliation had been scrubbed clean and Kozara could have a son again. Gaylon and the other members of the crew could begin again, rebuild their lives, negotiate for wives. If they were not too old, perhaps they could have sons. The stain upon them had been made to fade.

And they were old . . . all of them. All were grayed and crusty, their skull ridges pronounced and spiny. Their best days were past.

Moments passed as the ship was secured by the technicians outside, and Gaylon caught the eyes of the other crew around him. Veg, whose wife had left him after the Bateson incident. Zulish, who had been anticipating transfer to service with a favorite former captain and had been rejected. Kuru and Losh, who both had expected to be accepted to the finest warriors' advanced-training facility on the main continent.

Ninety years.

Gaylon knew what they were thinking now. Those might as well be their hands out there, doing the menial work. Warriors and skilled experts in advanced fields like Zaidan's were not as common as the enemies of the empire believed, for the imperial government could not economically support the training of more than a special few, and the private structure had been deliberately held down, so there were many positions of useful unimportance to be filled—that was understandable. But once trained as a warrior, one would find only agony in taking a manual position.

Gaylon knew what his crew members here on the bridge were thinking. Was Kozara right? Was the slate clean? Could they come back now?

Or were those manual jobs outside the ship waiting indeed for them?

If Zaidan were here, that would be a clue. There might be hope.

Gaylon held his breath when the bridge-direct access vault opened and they were once again connected with others of the empire. This would be the first time in all these years that they laid eyes upon a Klingon other than themselves.

The crew had their body armor on today. Many years ago they had ceased to wear it for daily duties. First the senior engineer had put his away, and then gradually the entire crew followed. Kozara had been last, probably because he thought he should be. Out in the Waste, what was armor for? To pick up plants, carcasses, and minerals, and to survey primitive planets, who needed protection? Who needed to look like a warrior?

Today, they wanted to wear it. They were glad they had it on as the vault port on the side of the bridge clanked and rolled open, revealing a conduit into the Fortress Zgoda Ring.

And there—there stood a young Klingon! Gaylon's heart began pounding against the shell of his body. His blood began to course. Hope!

Kozara's son was big, even for a Klingon, and had to duck as he stepped under the vault port and entered the bridge. Zaidan had the massive arms of a man who had done considerable lifting and daily physical work. His hands were strong too— from the tips of his fingers to the muscles of his neck, from the boulderlike thighs to his neatly braided hair, he was powerful and developed, though even he was no longer young. He was nearly a century old now, at an age when most Klingons should be just reaching their highest goals. He wore the black-and-red clothing of a construction specialist in the employ of the imperial government, but not the jacket of a supervisor, as Gaylon expected to see by now.

Kozara moved on once-powerful legs toward Zaidan. The two stood looking at each other, and Gaylon realized that Kozara had once been nearly that tall and brawny, but had lost bulk with the years of low activity, no battles.

The commander straightened and squared his shoulders within the armor he no longer completely filled.

"My son," he greeted.

Zaidan's head had been tilted to one side, and he now slowly tilted it to the other side.

"My *pain.*"

A shock—that was Kozara's voice from years ago!

But the words . . . the contempt . . .

Kozara, Gaylon, the entire bridge crew visibly sank. The son shriveled the father with his glare. All became clear in that instant. All became derision.

Stunned in the truest sense of the word, Kozara stared and stared until his eyes began to water and he had to look down at the deck. With his head bowed there and one hand steadying him with a grip on the command chair, he seemed to have been punched in the heart.

Pestilent disappointment shot through the crew. Standing nearby, Gaylon closed his hands and took the same kind of grip on the hem of his tunic. There he stood, holding onto his own clothing and hoping to keep control. A gush of breath, a flinch, a tightening of his eyes—unacceptable. Zaidan would see out of the corner of his peripheral vision.

In that moment a strange and unexpected shift took place— Zaidan, the son, the skilled laborer, the lower, suddenly and quite decisively became superior to imperial trained warriors. On one finger Gaylon could count how many times in Klingon history that had happened.

Now it was happening here. Gaylon felt as if he were shriveling into the deck.

Slowly, slowly Kozara's eyes rose again to meet his angry son's, but they were crimped and wrinkle-fanned. He parted his lips. No sound came for several moments, through which Zaidan harshly waited without saying anything to his father. Self-control—an effective method of torture.

"Why do you say this to your father?" Kozara croaked from the depth of his misery.

"Do you know what happened while you were gone?" the son shot back. "Your one victory was snuffed out, *that* is what happened. *That.*"

Kozara blinked in confusion. His face shifted and twisted.

"What is it you speak about? My victory was the destruction of the Bulldog and his crew. He is gone. *They* are gone. My victory stands."

"Your victory has evaporated," Zaidan charged. "Bateson is back!"

Back?

Gaylon heard what Zaidan said, but could make no sense of it. The Federation ship had disappeared in a place where nothing could disappear. Kozara and his crew had searched for them, to make sure there was no trick, and for certain the Bulldog and his *Bozeman* had disintegrated. The Federation used no cloaking device. That ship could not have disappeared. Even with a cloaking device, there were methods of detection. But there had been no trail, no residue, no distortion. Nothing.

"Back?" Kozara belched. "We drove him into a planet! He is dead!"

"He is *back.*" Zaidan poked his nose forward and glowered. "He did *not* die. He did *not* plow into a planet. He went *not* into a planet, but into a time anomaly! And he emerged three years ago, to be escorted in trumpeting victory to Starbase 12 by none less than that petrified block Jean-Luc Picard and the becursed *Enterprise!*"

The shock was almost too much to absorb. Gaylon's mind rushed with protests, but he dared not say anything. This was not his time to speak, yet he wanted to blurt out arguments, insist that this could not happen, that there was some trick. But this was Kozara's moment and Gaylon could not interfere.

And Kozara had nothing to say. The commander shuddered and sizzled in his place, but said nothing.

"Not only is Morgan Bateson back," Zaidan continued, "but Morgan Bateson is famous. At forty-two years old, Morgan Bateson is a hero. His ship which you 'destroyed' is polished and tended and fitted to a special dock. Bateson came forward in time with his ship bearing the signs of battle and his crew intact."

Zaidan's voice was controlled, his words prepared, but each sentence burned across the deck. The rehearsed explanation had obviously been cooking for three years, waiting to be spoken. Three years of Zaidan's shame.

"Since then," the son continued, "the empire has been the laughingstock of the galaxy. We have been pilloried by the lowest of the low, the weakest of the weak. Bateson brought his entire crew safely through to a whole new time. Bateson went through *time* to save his ship from Kozara. The empire has been blistered by ridicule with every celebration for Bateson and his men. A warship, an entire invasion, was turned back by a single border ship and its forty-man crew. In Starfleet, to stumble on a pebble is now called 'a Kozara maneuver'!"

Dashed to blindness, Gaylon sank back against the helm console. Good thing it was there. If only he could speak—if only it were his place to say something—

"Your one little victory against Morgan Bateson saved me from scraping animal dung from imperial streets," Zaidan snarled. "I was Kozara's son, humiliated but not stripped of my rightful place. Kozara was still a warrior and I could work. I could command teams of laborers. I could design complexes and show my designs to respectable Klingons. I could do all these things . . . until Morgan Bateson came alive again."

Zaidan took one—and only one—step toward his father, and tipped one brawny shoulder in that direction.

"Since he came back, do you know what life has been for me? Son of the warrior who won not a single encounter? I have borne the wretchedness that should have been yours. My career has spiraled down until I am scarcely able to build a shelter for a dog. No one wants a bridge, an outpost, a box, a sewage station built by Zaidan, son of Kozara. Perhaps they have a job for me in Starfleet!

Gaylon glanced around the bridge at the terrible faces of Veg, Zulish, and the other bridge officers. He knew that the communication lines were open throughout the ship and the entire crew was hearing this. That was simple docking procedure, so all systems could be coordinated and no one could subvert the process of entering a port or province. Now the whole crew heard all this, and indignity scrubbed their faces.

"Now, this week," Zaidan charged, "comes the biggest embarrassment of all. The Federation is about to launch a new starship. It is the sixth *Starship Enterprise*. And the great Morgan Bateson is master of ceremonies. Morgan Bateson has used his rank privilege to employ his crew in the commission and building of the new starship. That mollusk Picard is to be guest of honor. For two years Starfleet has been building this starship, and when the fifth *Enterprise* was destroyed four months ago, the decision was made to declare this new ship the next *Enterprise*. Recall, o warrior, that it was the *Enterprise* of James Kirk who flew in after the disappearance of Bateson and finally drove you back into the Neutral Zone. Is there no relief for me? Must everything you do haunt me this way? Bateson and the *Enterprise* through my entire pathetic life? I should rename myself 'Bateson, son of *Enterprise.*' It would be less disgraceful than 'Zaidan, son of Kozara'!"

Their lives were over. Gaylon's eyes were boiling. The faces of the other crew members were dusky with hopelessness. Surely one of them would surge forward and slaughter Kozara where he stood. He even saw Veg's hand slip back to grip his hungry dagger. Gripping his own tunic's hem harder, Gaylon vowed not to stop the murder.

Then Zaidan stepped back a pace, straightened his stance.

"I am no longer the son of Kozara," he proclaimed. "I will go away. I will change my name. I will be a pirate or a hired weapon. If I could scrape this degraded face off my skull, I would do it. There is no more Zaidan, son of Kozara. There is only Kozara, who could not make a single victory, who never had a good day to die, and who could not keep a son."

The bridge fell to scornful silence. The disgraced young Klingon pressed his mouth shut on those words and seemed to be finished saying the things he had waited three long years to say.

He turned as sharply as that, and strode toward the exit.

As Zaidan's boots clunked on the conduit deck and he dipped his head to keep from bumping it, a pitiful voice sputtered across the deck.

"I want one chance . . ."

Zaidan stopped and turned. "What?"

"One chance," Kozara begged. "Be my son for one more chance."

"What chance?"

"I will hunt Bateson down and kill him."

Waving both hands, Zaidan spat his contempt. "Who cares about that? So he would be dead! So what?"

Crushing his knuckles across his mouth and rubbing saliva into his beard, Kozara tried so hard to think that the old scar on his skull turned darker. There was every stress in his face short of blood coming from his eyes.

"I will . . . I will destroy . . . I will . . . his entire crew came through time with him, you said?"

"Yes!" Zaidan snapped. "So what?"

"There is a chance!" Kozara bolted, suddenly coming to life. "If his entire crew came through, then I am vindicated!"

"Why?" his son demanded.

"Because there is a Klingon operative on his staff."

Kozara lowered his voice and made the wild statement as calmly as if he were once again giving the order to dock. His satisfaction ran deep and cold through his crew.

But Gaylon threw it off. "We had no way of knowing Bateson would be waiting for us that day! How would you have known to put a spy on him?"

"Bateson and I had clashed before, and Bateson and others," Kozara said, enjoying the sudden upper hand. "The spy was assigned to the Typhon Expanse. I and others knew that even if Bateson were drawn away, he would be there when we tried to return."

"Why did this operative fail to help us that day?"

"How could I know that?" the old captain barked. "But if that person is still alive, then he has been working on that new starship all this time. Think of it!"

"You are fantasizing," Zaidan insisted. "There is no such person."

"Doubt me, then. I may not be Kang or Koloth, but I am a commander in the Klingon fleet and there are things I know. If my information is right, there was on that day a Klingon operative on Bateson's ship. Not a Klingon, but a human doing Klingon business. For that man, only three years have gone by. His loyalties may yet be in place. We shall see when we come up against Bateson and his new ship . . . what advantages he can give us."

Kozara circled his command chair with a flicker in his eye such as Gaylon had never thought to see again. Gaylon dared say nothing to this wild new turn of possibilities. Could it be? Was there a wink of hope in the murk?

"I will kill Bateson," Kozara promised, "and I will smash the Federation's new starship at the same time. No . . . not enough. Even more, I will make the entire Federation hate what they have built! For all time, I will vilify the name of *Enterprise!*"

Zaidan shifted his considerable weight and tilted his head to one side. "How will you and one miserable old ship destroy the new starship?"

"I do not mean to destroy it," his father said. "I mean to possess it."

Something about those words made Zaidan pause, Gaylon noticed. The son had spent his life scheming to overcome his father's shortcomings, and as such he was no stranger to clever schemes. His restraint now showed that. A chance was a chance.

Or something about the idea—to do such an outlandish thing, to even conceive of it, took some courage, some cleverness. Zaidan apparently saw a glimmer in his father which he had ceased to believe existed, perhaps believed had never existed at all. But there it was. Kozara had somehow spoken magical words.

And Kozara saw the change. His senses were not so stultified that he missed his advantage.

He swung around, then around again, until he caught the attention of his entire bridge crew.

"Yes!" he sang out with his ages-ago voice. "Listen, all of you! Gaylon! Zulish! Veg! Kuru! All of you—you will help me! We will stay together and escape failure's maw with a victory such as none has ever seen! Our enemy has returned! No Klingon will deny us a chance to defeat him! We will get a ship, a good ship! We will give the ship a name that will ring in history! The empire will not stop us from this chance to reclaim our honor! This is the continuation of the battle that was cut short so long ago by a quirk of space! I will go before the High Council and they will give me a ship. Bateson is still young, but I have ninety more years' experience to use against him. We will snatch our names back from the gullet of shame! Say it now, so my son can hear the loyalty of this crew of the forgotten! Say you will all come with me!"

A spontaneous cry of willingness rose from the crew, blasting forth like the shot of some great old weapon. In a moment, in an instant their enemy was back and they were warriors again! Their shame could become their monument!

Like a flash Gaylon remembered the long-subdued one characteristic that had made Kozara worthy of the rank of command—stunning flexibility.

On the crest of this unexpected turn, Kozara squared his shoulders, raised his chin, lifted both his hands and fanned them, and turned to Zaidan.

"This I promise, I vow, I swear to my son," he blazed. "On the blood of our fathers, there will never be another *Enterprise!*"

The ship was a thing of exquisite beauty in an exquisite setting. . . . She was a magnificent fighting machine, the mistress of the waves over which she was sailing in solitary grandeur.

Lieutenant Hornblower

CHAPTER 10

"Well, I must say . . . *that* is a thing of beauty."

A study in motion. A swan in starshine.

Riker had heard that description of a starship before, but he couldn't remember where. Probably one of those moments of wonder that trundled down from person to person, father to son.

The *Enterprise*-E. There she was.

Olympian and stunning as it rested in the welcoming arms of open space, the new starship looked as if it were going warp five standing still. This new *Sovereign*-class ship was a creature of motion, as if her designers had been leaning forward when they made the design. There was still the traditional Saucer Module, inspired by the most original H. G. Wells science fiction and found to be ironically servicable, but unlike that on the *Enterprise*-D, this ovoid saucer was turned so that its longest diameter ran with the fore-and-aft line of the ship instead of against it.

As he looked at this ship now, Riker had a hard time imagining any other design, even though he had flown another design for the better part of his career. The main body of this new ship was mounted directly to the aft underside of the saucer—there was no birdlike neck as previous designs had possessed, but the familiar V-shaped design had been cherished. The two snake-headed warp nacelles still rose like wings above and behind the main section. The hull plating was not white, as early ships were, but instead was a pattern of flannel blues and dove grays, making the ship look as if it were made of buffed pewter.

Hundreds of lit rectangular cabin windows on the saucer section were mounted up and down like wheel spokes, each pointing inward toward the bridge. The windows on the main section, however, were turned on their sides to follow the hull lines. Backlit by the Christmas-tree glitter of the boxdock, the starship looked as organic as the narrowed eye of a god.

Riker felt supremely privileged. He hadn't been in on the launch of the *Enterprise*-D, or any other starship for that matter. He'd participated in the launch of a hospital ship once, and accidentally happened upon the launch of a matched set of recon sweepers, but that was all. Until this moment, looking out at the new ship, he hadn't realized what he'd missed. Judging by the spectator pods and media coaches that hovered at the ordered distance around the boxdock, the whole Federation understood the significance of this new starship.

He felt a little guilty as the pod he and Picard were using to approach the ship was cleared by the harbormaster. Unlike all those spectators, he and Picard could go right through the restricted postings and pilot up to the starship itself. Only officers, crew assigned to the ship, and the construction and maintenance personnel were allowed in.

He glanced to his left. "Captain?" he prodded. "Here she is."

"Yes. Very pretty."

An inward groan rattled through Riker's chest. The captain simply stood there and eyed the ship sidelong as if unwilling to commit. Minutes ago Picard had questioned his relationship with the old ship. Now he was being belatedly loyal to the *Enterprise*-D.

Luckily, they couldn't see the whole starship anymore, but only the glossy hull plates rolling by as the pod came up close to the rim of the saucer section and angled its way automatically toward the airlock. Now the rivets, bolts, carvel plating, and construction stencils were up close and intimate, no longer looking like a ship at all, luckily.

Riker turned away from the captain and punched the clearance to dock. The pod would nuzzle itself in. He found himself wishing the thing were manual so he had something to do besides the two of them standing here being aware of each other.

The pod's docking cuff hissed, the security clamps chunked into place, and the airlock pressurized with a nearly living breath. Automatically the airlock port slid open, and before either Riker or Picard could escape, a smiling wraith flew toward them.

"Welcome aboard, Captain!" Deanna Troi said.

Riker grinned. Troi looked glad to see the captain here, finally. Her Grecian features were etched along narrow jaw and cheekbones, her large black eyes were prominent than in years past, her dark hair shining.

The captain seemed unmoved by her enthusiasm. Even irritated by it.

"Good morning, Counselor," he drawled. "Thank you for your eagerness, but I'd rather—"

"Jean-Luc . . ." a sultry voice interrupted, clearly to keep him from finishing his sentence.

Riker stepped out of Doctor Beverly Crusher's way as she moved across the deck and slipped her arm into Picard's.

"Beverly," the captain greeted her.

"Welcome aboard," the doctor said. "How are you feeling?"

The captain sighed. "You're being custodial."

"That's my job."

"Captain! Captain, good morning!"

What was this—a mass mugging?

Riker stepped more out of the way. Engineer Geordi La Forge, his dark features and his cybernetic eyes shining with emotion that shouldn't have been showing there, plowed between the two women and grabbed the captain's business hand and started pumping. La Forge was the same age as Riker, yet there was a perpetual boyish cheer in him that always made Riker feel like the big brother.

"And Engineer La Forge as well," the captain grumbled. "How totally unexpected. All right, where's—"

"He's right behind me, sir!" La Forge turned and craned down the corridor, where along came a familiar face. "Data! What took you so long?"

"I was distracted by the wonderful music coming from the rec area," Lieutenant Data said. His metallic-gold face was animated with delight. "Someone is in there playing Smoky Mountain music. I love Smoky Mountain music! It is so down-home and toe-tapping. Do not you all love it too?"

"You all . . ." Riker echoed, and glanced at Troi.

For years Data had been an ideal android, completely cool, a little curious, but seldom ruffled. Recently, though, he had been given a strange invention for a walking computer to possess—emotion. A chip in his positronic brain gave Data something that Riker had thought unprogrammable. How were feelings, reactions, sensations, needs, programmed into a machine?

Well, apparently it had been done. How well, nobody knew yet. The chip could be turned on and off at Data's will, but he pretty much left it on and indulged in a mosaic of appreciations denied him until lately. Fear, humor, disgust, cheer—all these things had eluded the unflappable android, even more steely than a Vulcan, because Vulcans possessed underlying emotions. Data hadn't had any . . . or at least, not many.

Riker never quite believed Data was exactly the mechanical box he was reputed to be, or in fact that the medical computers said he was. There had always been something in there which was more than just a circuit trunk with legs. The rest of the crew liked him. Riker liked him. While certainly it was possible to gain affection for objects or vehicles, homes or mementos, somehow Riker knew Data wasn't any of those.

Now Data was as human as any of them, as emotional, and about three times more naive. He'd been through a longer working lifespan than any of them. A decorated full commander in Starfleet, second officer on one of very few cruiser-class starships, Data was seeing the universe for the first time, through the eyes and with the emotional balance of a child.

"The irrepressible Commander Data," Captain Picard drawled out, nodding wearily. "I suppose there's something to be said for banjos, fiddles, and—what would be appropriate? Harmonicas?"

The two women nodded, and Riker threw in, "Yee-haw, sir."

Picard groaned at him. "Now, what is this? What are all of you doing aboard this ship? Don't tell me you've signed on already."

"Just hedging our bets," Beverly Crusher said, pulling him a few steps forward, away from the transporter room doorway. She gave him a little shake, the kind only very old friends can get away with. "Don't gripe."

"We've been waiting to show you the ship," La Forge added. "It's a very streamlined design, sir. Some atmospheric capabilities, too. When the *Enterprise*-D crashed, Starfleet decided to step up the completion of this ship, and they let us all sign in on the work."

"How gracious of them."

"The ship's got advanced long-range sensors, almost thirty percent longer-range than any ship before, and extended warp capabilities at about a forty-two percent upgrade."

Data nodded, his mouth opening every few seconds as he tried to get his two cents in. "Yes, sir, she also has an upgraded galactic-condition database, isolinear matrix chips with a memory capacity of three-point eight kiloquads with tripolymer sealant over the refractive surfaces as standard protection, improved warp-field control which allows for a greater Z-axis compression, improved hardware efficiencies, and quantum torpedoes. We're very proud of the bonny lass. If you'll come this way, please . . ."

As Data led the way down the corridor, Picard looked at Riker and mouthed *Bonny lass?*

Offering only a shrug, Riker motioned the captain before him. Troi and Crusher each took an arm and angled the captain into the open corridor of the big ship. Riker and La Forge followed.

The corridor was glossy and smelled new, but wasn't particularly bright. Easier on the eye than previous Starfleet intraship corridors, it was perhaps too subdued. The braces and doorframes had a certain streamlined liquidity, sculpted beyond function into an art form.

Riker followed Picard as they and the others strode directly through the lower body of the ship to the main engine room. Here, nostalgic red double-door panels parted for them, and their welcoming committee of one was right inside the entrance. Riker smiled when he saw who met them here. Ah . . . "bonny lass." Of course.

A rotund silver-haired gentleman with a black mustache and ruddy cheeks, looking as if he were an out-of-place organ-grinder in a street festival, came sauntering toward them with a smile bright as piano keys.

"Captain Picard, welcome aboard, sir."

"Captain Scott!"

"Sir, welcome aboard the new lass!" The famous engineer's highland roll added a melody to his voice. "Hope you're as well as I look."

"Well, thank you, I think I can come up to that."

"Been avoiding us, sir? We expected you a month back. Poor Data's been just twitchin'."

Riker poked in between Data and La Forge. "How did you get assigned here, Captain Scott?"

Montgomery Scott's sparkling dark eyes flickered at him. "Pulled a string or two, lad."

"I'll bet you had to turn down ten other assignments," La Forge offered.

Scott glanced at him. "Twenty-three."

"I'm not surprised," Picard said. "We thought you'd given up warp engineering and—"

"Retired? Oh, I did, I did."

"But . . ."

"Gave it up for Lent, sir, right along with a diet of greens. I did some lecturing here and there, then took a few engineering courses to familiarize m'self with this century's technology, got recertified and, poof, here I am."

Picard leered at him ever so briefly, then looked at Scott again. "You're a lousy liar, Captain. You couldn't stand to see an *Enterprise* built without your fingerprints on it. It's not many men who get to leave their influence on six generations of ships and actually work on three of them."

"May be the case, sir," Scott said, "but the fact is we didn't know this ship was going to be an *Enterprise* until after . . . eh . . ."

"That's all right, Mr. Scott, I know my ship crashed."

Scott's eyes went from sparkling to sympathetic, and he got that organ-grinder look again. "Sorry, sir."

"So, just which strings did you have to pull to get this plum of an assignment?" Picard asked. "As if I didn't know."

"Oh, well, Captain Bateson and I are long-time friends, and I mean *long*-time friends, after all, sir."

"You don't have to call me 'sir,' Scotty. You're a captain too, and your commission date—"

Scott waved a hand. "Ah, don't remind me how old I am. And I wouldn't know how to call a ship's captain anything other than 'sir,' give or take a few choice adjectives now and then."

The famous engineer, a man brought forward through time by a quirk of science instead of nature—the transporter— seemed supremely at home here. Riker was glad about that. Montgomery Scott had been confused and out of place when he had first been rescued from transporter stasis, but apparently his talents hadn't been buried by misfortune. He'd found his way. Riker admired him for his resilience, but found Scott's ability to fit into this starship somehow annoying at a time when Riker and his captain were having trouble finding their own places.

He glanced at Picard. The captain wasn't looking forward to the tour. His face was grim behind the forced smile, his eyes lightless, his posture stiff.

The engine-room panels parted again, and for an instant Riker thought they'd be offered a little distraction, but no such luck. The person who came in at the center of a clutch of ensigns was hardly to be any relief.

Morgan Bateson.

He hadn't changed that much in these past three years. Hardly at all, in fact, Riker noticed. Still had the neat musketeer's beard, not so different from Riker's. Bateson's sandy hair might've receded a finger's width. The uniform was updated, which was a bit startling—somehow Riker had expected to see Bateson still wearing the black trousers and maroon jacket of Starfleet past.

Bateson had his eyes down at a padd he was just taking from a junior officer as he strode in and paused in the middle of the wide deck.

"—and make sure those tests are run under full radiation bombardment. Doesn't do a bit of good to test under ideal conditions, since you'll never fight in ideal conditions."

"Aye, sir," one of the ensigns said, and all the younger officers veered off in various directions, leaving Captain Bateson standing alone, checking off details on a PADD's screen.

"Hm," Bateson grunted, shook his head, then wrote something more.

The moment was surreal—no one said anything. Bateson didn't notice them as he stood there in the middle of the engineering deck, writing. No one moved. Everyone expected someone else to move or speak. Montgomery Scott shifted once, and La Forge peered over his shoulder briefly at Picard, but that was all.

Just before bones started cracking, Bateson finished writing and stepped off toward the starboard side, then instantly noticed the crew off to port.

"Well—what's this? Captain Picard! What a nice surprise!" Bateson plowed toward them with his hand extended and pumped Picard's enthusiastically. "Beautiful, isn't she? Quite a ship Starfleet's got here. How long have you been aboard?"

"Less than five minutes, Captain," Picard said. "She's lovely."

Bateson's animated bearded face shifted instantly from joy to sympathy—how did he do that?

"I'm so very sorry about your starship," he said. "A great adventure with a great ending, though. Your crew made a safe planetfall, at least."

" 'Fall' is one way to put it," Picard said.

"Oh—sorry." Bateson shook his head at his social goof and said, "If you don't mind waiting a few minutes for your tour, I have to pass along these schematics to the engineers aboard the *Roderick*. She's being built in the other dock. They're just installing her warp core and phaser banks now and they need some numbers. Got to have some fighting ships ready, you know, with the Klingons making so many angry noises these days." Bateson angled an eyebrow mischievously and added, "We don't ignore Klingons where I come from. Come on. I'll show you the specs."

They walked off—two captains talking about a ship, their favorite subject.

Riker and the two women stood there in the middle of the engineering deck, and a sudden sense of ill ease crept between them. Riker felt it, and tried to play it down. Have either of you had lunch?"

But neither the doctor nor the counselor bought his effort. Neither answered. Both continued gazing after the captains, who had paused downdeck, on the other side of the wide engine room.

Folding her long arms, Crusher said, "It's eerie the way those two get along. Every time they get together, it's like they haven't even been apart. Worries me."

"Why does it worry you?" Riker asked.

She raised one shoulder. "Bateson's a little obsessive."

"About what?"

"Anything he's thinking about at the moment. He's been all over this ship. He's micromanaging everything, and he's got the ship littered with his own crew from the *Bozeman*."

"Mmm . . ." Riker uttered. "He said he would make it his cause in life to give them a future so they wouldn't fixate on the past. He was involved in this ship's commission, right?"

"Right. He found out a new ship was being built, and figured that was one way to get in on the ground floor of something."

"Doesn't surprise me. He's trying to jump start a whole new life for himself and his crew."

"That's the problem," Troi suggested. "It's as if he's still running a crew of forty. This ship crews over a thousand. He's the one who arranged for the ship to be built way out here, at Starbase 12. It gives him a psychological advantage. Everybody in the sector lives in the light of Morgan Bateson's success against the Klingons. It's given him quite an edge."

"Ah." Riker looked from one to the other. "Alright, ladies, let's hear the other half. What do you think is going on?"

Crusher glanced at Troi. Then Troi admitted, "We think he's jockeying for command."

"What do *you* think about this?" Crusher asked, pulling on Riker's arm. "Is Bateson qualified to command a ship like this? He can't be."

"I don't see how," Riker offered. "He was ninety years out of date three years ago. Three years isn't enough to catch up. At least, I don't think so."

"Command of this ship is going to Captain Picard," Troi said. "Everyone says so. And you saw how Bateson treated him. Even Bateson knows the captain deserves this command."

Crusher eyed Riker then and suggested heavily, "Maybe Bateson's jockeying for first officer."

Riker winced and clapped a hand to his chest. "Oooh . . . that hurts."

"There's another option," Crusher suggested. "There's talk of 'Captain Riker.'"

"She's right, Will," Troi said. "If Captain Picard wants to retire, you might not be able to dodge command now that this ship's ready for launch."

"Who says I'm dodging?"

"I do. And I think you're going to get command if the captain doesn't want it."

"He wants it," Riker declared.

Troi stepped in front of him. "Did he say that?"

Crusher reached for his arm as he sidled away. "When did he say it? Tell us his exact words!"

"Can't." Riker swiveled to one side. "Sorry. I've gotta go analyze a system. Now, look, ladies . . ."

"Shh! Here comes the captain!" Troi batted Crusher's hand away from Riker's arm and they all turned together, looking like a vaudeville show as Captain Picard approached, scolding them with his glare.

"You're a sight, all of you," the captain derided. "Captain Bateson's waiting for you on the other side of engineering. He's going to conduct your tour. I've been called away."

"Away, sir?" Riker prodded.

Picard struck him with that glower. "Yes, I've been summoned to Admiral Farrow's office."

"That's got to be it," Riker accidentally blurted, and it took all his self-control to keep from clapping the captain on the shoulder.

"I don't want to have this conversation," Picard sighed. "No choice, I suppose . . ."

"Jean-Luc, it's wonderful!" Crusher exclaimed.

And Deanna Troi smiled. "The ship is ours!"

CHAPTER 11

"Captain Picard, hello."

"Good morning, Admiral Farrow. I'm sorry I wasn't on hand to greet you when you arrived on the starbase."

"That's all right. Captain Bateson and Captain Scott were there. And I knew you needed some time to yourself after— what happened."

Admiral Farrow's sympathy fell hard between them as Picard entered the office. Was it particularly chilly in here? Or was his discomfort simply turning up the air conditioning? He wished he could avoid what was to come, for he had no idea what answer he would give the options posed.

Farrow was a big man, very blond and pink-faced, with a gap between his front teeth. He looked like something out of a Norwegian legend, and Picard knew the admiral's record read a little like that. He had a slight accent, but Picard had never been able to place it and had never bothered to ask.

Right at the moment he certainly didn't care.

"Have you seen the new starship?" the admiral asked as Picard sat on the plush antique-velvet couch.

"Just came from there," Picard said, trying to sound pleased. "She's quite a work of art. I haven't had the chance to examine the technology quite yet, but . . ."

"But you'll get to it, I know." Admiral Farrow sat in the unmatched antique chair nearby, rather than in his desk chair, which would've been, apparently, more formal than he wanted to be at the moment.

"Would you like some coffee?" Farrow asked. "Oh—forgive me, Jean-Luc. With you, it's tea, isn't it?"

"Yes, but no, thank you. I've had some this morning. Even I can only take so much. Admiral . . . please put me out of my misery, will you?"

"Yes, so sorry. Jean-Luc, on behalf of the admiralty, with all our congratulations and appreciation, I'm pleased to offer you the rank of rear admiral. Now, don't say anything just yet. You don't need to accept right away; in fact we prefer you didn't. We have a thing or two bubbling in Cardassian space. You might like to take charge of those."

As his hands tingled as if frozen in time, Picard repeated, "Cardassian space? I'm hardly an expert on Cardassia—"

"But you have unique experiences that will play into the mission we have for you." Farrow leaned forward, his pink face beaming.

"What kind of mission?"

"Leading a small team to Cardassia Prime."

"I'm not a commando, Admiral. Why choose me for this?"

"We've been contacted by a Cardassian with whom we've developed a—relationship. She confirmed some things that have only been suspected until now. She asked for you by name."

"This is entirely a mystery to me."

"It'll all make sense once you've read this." He handed Picard a padd. The top line of text read "Picard—Cardassia."

"Should I give you some time to absorb this?"

"No . . . no, sir." Picard shook himself, careful not to accept or deny the promotion. "May I only say I'm sure Will Riker will make a superb captain for the new starship."

Farrow sat back and crossed his ankles. "Yes, I know he would. But he's not being given command of the new *Enterprise.*"

Visibly stiffening, Picard frowned. "Then who is?"

"Command will be going to Captain Bateson for the ship's launch cruise."

Well, *there* it was. Despite the records of Picard, Riker, and the *Enterprise*-D, forces in another favor had won out. How much had Morgan Bateson himself fueled those fires? He'd been here all these three years, able to influence forces involved with the design and future of the newest starship. Proximity could certainly have been a factor, while Picard and Riker were represented only by reputation. Not to mention a touch of notoriety.

Angry now, Picard put forth no effort to make his physical demeanor hide how he felt. "Sir . . . I *genuinely* believe Mr. Riker deserves command."

"He well may." Farrow accepted Picard's point. "To be honest, I agree with you. But some others don't."

Picard leaned rather fiercely forward. "Who?"

The admiral was unimpressed. "It doesn't matter right now. Bateson has massive amounts of seniority."

"That's because of a quirk of time travel!"

"It was you yourself who recommended Starfleet give him full seniority consideration, to give him a boost in this century. Besides that, his record is not only spotless, but exemplary. He took risks above and beyond the call of duty several times, he effected some valiant rescues and some monumental arrests on border duty, and on top of all that he's a hero in this sector. Starfleet can do worse, don't you agree, than to recognize its own heroes, Captain? Or shall I say, 'Admiral'?"

"Don't say it yet," Picard snapped, and held up a restraining hand.

The heady thrill of a promotion was completely lost on him, totally smeared by the idea that Bateson and not Riker would have command of the *Enterprise*-E. And very likely Picard would be the one to tell Riker. More delight.

"Does Bateson know yet?"

"I thought there was some discretion in telling you first."

"Mmm." Good—then Bateson wouldn't accidentally let anything slip as he toured Riker around the ship.

"Now," the admiral said, "let us discuss the mission Starfleet has for you."

"A mission," Picard muttered. "For a captain without a ship."

CHAPTER **12**

"Thank you all for being here," Picard said. "These quarters are not exactly a ship's briefing room, but that would be strangely inappropriate today, I think."

The officers' guest quarters were more like a hotel lobby, with cookie-cutter furniture that could've been in any room, anywhere. Only a painting on the wall—looked like Georgia O'Keeffe—offered any personality. On the opposite wall, near the glass dining table where Riker, Troi, and Crusher huddled, a starbase monitor ran constant silent viewings of the exhibit of *Titanic* and *Mary Rose* artifacts. Longbows, a steam whistle, a figurine, a set of 1900's bagpipes, so on. An unlikely mixture of times and troubles.

"Before you all pop from curiosity," Picard went on, "and anticipation, I shall cut to the bottom line. I have not been offered command of the new *Enterprise.*"

Riker digested the captain's words with a heavy heart. To his right, both Troi and Crusher gaped in astounded disappointment.

"What?" the counselor huffed.

And Crusher declared, "Oh, I can't believe it!"

"You heard me," Captain Picard said as he stood at the other end of the small table, "and you shall believe it."

The captain didn't sit down.

"Please, Captain," Crusher began, *"please* tell us congratulations are in order for Mr. Riker."

Will Riker tried not to react, and thought he did pretty well. He didn't want command unless Captain Picard wanted, really wanted, to move on.

He didn't get that from the captain's demeanor.

Picard's expression hardened. Clearly he was angry, but keeping it under control. He looked at Riker for a few seconds, then bitterly turned back to Crusher. "Command for the ship's shakedown cruise has been given to Morgan Bateson."

"What?" Crusher exclaimed.

Deanna Troi shook her head. "I don't believe it! Morgan Bateson is ninety years out of date! He'd have to go through college all over again just to catch up with the ship's basic systems! How can he command the newest ship of the line? He can't possibly be qualified."

"You're mistaken about that," Picard said icily. "If we brought Benjamin Franklin forward in time, I guarantee he would be a formidable presence in government. Innate talents are worth something. Men of the past are not necessarily simple men. Galileo would flourish in these times. He would rise above the crowd even now."

"Bateson's no Galileo," Crusher grumbled, "or Franklin either."

"How do we know that?" The captain turned to her and held out a hand. "His career was just beginning to roll when he was lost in the Typhon Causality. In any case, captains of the past had to think fast, and that's what Bateson has done. Bateson may not be technically up to snuff, but I'd be more circumspect about his command instincts."

Knowing from experience that Picard was fuming behind those words, Riker didn't push the point. "We'll try, sir."

Picard sighed as if it had taken all his personal resolve to choke that out. "Thank you."

"The shakedown cruise," Troi clarified. "That's what you said. *Just* the shakedown cruise, that's all. Then Bateson's in *temporary* command, right?"

"It is in fact temporary," Picard confirmed unwillingly, "but temporary status is usually only a formality. I wouldn't hold my breath for any surprises. I've already given him my congratulations, and I expect no less from all of you. When I spoke to him, he asked me to carry a request . . . to you, Will."

Startled out of his misery, Riker looked up. "What kind of request?"

"He'd like you to come along with him as first officer on his shakedown cruise."

Aridly Riker frowned and shifted on the plush seat. "Bateson already has a first officer. He doesn't need two."

"No, but he does need someone familiar with current technology, star territory, and spacefaring until he familiarizes himself with those aspects of command. He's no fool. He knows what he doesn't know."

"Somebody else can teach him."

The words dropped like rocks.

Riker knew he was being childish, if loyal to Captain Picard. If Starfleet concurred with Bateson's logic, Riker would have no choice but to go along. It wouldn't look good on his record to demand a transfer off the new starship, but right now he felt like burning his record. Only experience and circumspection kept him from saying so out loud, or imagining he might someday feel differently.

Picard eased up a bit in his demeanor and paced around his end of the dining set. "When I went into Admiral Farrow's office, I experienced the most curious splitting of hopes. Never in my life had I been so utterly of two minds about anything. I wanted command, yet I didn't. My spacefaring career is winding down, or it's about to launch again at full warp. I tossed a mental coin, and the damned thing hit an antigravity pocket and it's still spinning about. When the admiral informed me that Captain Bateson would be taking command for now, I went strangely numb. No feeling at all, except perhaps anger on Mr. Riker's behalf. Then, the admiral started talking about something else, and I forgot all about the starship. He's given me an assignment. I've accepted."

"Assignment?" Troi repeated. "Without a ship?"

"Yes."

"The Admiralty!" Crusher blurted.

The next instant Riker asked, "Commandant of Starfleet Academy?"

"No, I'm still a captain for now, and without a desk job. This isn't just an assignment. It's a mission. Now that the Klingons are making trouble with Cardassia and the peace in this quadrant is broken, the Cardassians are motivated to cooperate with the Federation. Or at least they need to keep the lines of communication somewhat open. We have an opportunity we haven't had before. My mission is to go into Cardassian space and reclaim our MIA's."

"What MIA's?" Beverly Crusher put both hands on the table and leaned forward. "Missing in action? Federation nationals? Are you serious?"

"I haven't heard anything about this," Troi said.

Leaning forward and feeling suddenly fierce, Riker raised his voice and demanded, "You mean the Cardassians are holding Federation citizens as prisoners? Captain, is that what you're saying?"

"Not just Federation citizens. Starfleet personnel. Over the past three years, the U.S.S. Durant and several Starfleet personnel have been classified as missing in or near Cardassian space. Also there've been some merchant vessels and one satellite tender gone missing under suspicious circumstances. The Cardassians insist there are no prisoners, but I know otherwise. They also claimed I wasn't there, being held, being tortured, and I certainly was there. I intend to take a private vessel, a non-Starfleet ship, go into Cardassian territory, and confront Gul Madred personally."

"Madred!" Beverly Crusher nearly choked. She gripped the

edge of the table and shook it. "Jean-Luc, please—don't do that!"

Deanna Troi shriveled where she sat. Her hands turned white in her lap, her fingers tangled, and she pressed them hard against her thighs. "Sir . . . after what he did to you . . ."

"I know what he did to me," Picard snapped. "That's how I know what he's doing to our missing people. I'm going. Your orders are not to attempt talking me out of it. I don't even want to hear the points of argument. Stop thinking them."

Silence fell again. No one knew what to say, though all of them listened in anguish to the arguments in their own minds. Riker could almost hear Troi's mind clicking and Crusher's nearly screaming.

Feeling as if his veins were about to burst, Riker weighed a hundred versions of his request before making it. Finally, there was no other way but to ask outright. "Sir . . . permission to go with you into Cardassian space."

"That's appreciated, Number One," the captain said sternly, "but this isn't the Federation volunteer corps. This is Starfleet, and you have your assignment. I expect you to go with Bateson cheerfully. Go on the shakedown cruise, and the next time you're offered command, take it."

Startled, Riker clamped his mouth shut on anything else he might've said.

Beside him, the two women stared at Picard.

"Captain . . ." Troi began a sentence, then let her tone do the speaking.

Picard snapped her a glare. "Counselor?"

She hesitated now. "We've always been a family as well as an assignment . . ."

Embarrassed that she was defending him from the captain's rebuke, Riker bristled but didn't say anything.

The captain riveted Troi to her seat with a long stare. "We're not a family, Counselor. Starfleet isn't a social club. Our command staff is a close-knit unit of service who have been lucky enough to remain in each other's sphere for many years. That doesn't abrogate our responsibility as officers, or make our relationship to each other superior to our duty. Our ship is gone and we must expect changes. Mr. Riker has been given an assignment where his talents are needed. You, Mr. Data, and Mr. La Forge are also assigned to the *Enterprise*-E, and I expect you to serve Captain Bateson with every bit the loyalty and energy I have enjoyed from you. Now, am I going to have to repeat that anytime soon?"

A stunned silence fell briefly, a silence they knew would have to be broken. The captain would not let those words hang without a response.

Riker knew Crusher and Troi were waiting for his cue. He slumped back in his chair. "No, sir."

Crusher folded her arms and Troi sank back also. "No, sir," they half-heartedly echoed.

"Thank you," Picard responded. "Captain Bateson has assigned sixty-nine members of his *Bozeman* crew to the starship, short of two who found other pursuits and retired from Starfleet. His first officer, Gabriel Bush, second officer Mike Dennis, and science officer John Wolfe have all been working feverishly to upgrade their abilities to modern standards. The starship will also be manned by over three hundred additional starship crew members from . . . well, our time."

"Three hundred?" Riker interrupted. "That ship takes over a thousand."

"Not for a shakedown cruise. The scientists, medical personnel, analysts, and general maintenance crew won't be going on board until she receives her first duty assignment. Only department heads and technical specialists will be aboard for now. Captain Scott will remain on board as chief engineer, and Mr. La Forge will be assistant chief. Counselor, Captain Bateson doesn't want a ship's counselor on duty, so you'll be part of the medical staff. Mr. Data—well, he can do the work of almost the entire science staff, so they'll be fine. We don't know yet whether these assignments will be permanent, but I expect all of you to treat them as if they are. Dr. Crusher, on the other hand, you'll be going with me into Cardassian space."

Letting out a long sigh, Crusher muttered, "Thank God . . ."

Ignoring the knots in his arms, Riker tried to control his voice, his tone, the pacing of his request.

"Captain," he began, "at least take Data with you."

Picard put his hands on the back of the nearest chair. "Mr. Data is physically far stronger than any Cardassian or human and he's quite obviously an android. He'd present the wrong kind of intimidation. However, I do intend to take some intimidation along with me. I've already contacted Captain Sisko at Deep Space 9. I'm going to stop off there and borrow Commander Worf."

"You're trying to appear 'neutral,'" Crusher challenged, "and you're taking a Klingon into Cardassian space?"

"I want a neutral *ship,*" Picard explained. "But this is not a neutral mission. I want it made perfectly clear that I don't care how the Klingons and Cardassians feel about each other at the moment. They can't tell Starfleet who to have in it."

"As long as you're borrowing," Riker asked, "why don't you 'borrow' the *Defiant* too?"

"No. No armed ships. No Starfleet presentations. I'm taking a privately owned vessel. I want no mistakes made about my intentions. The Cardassians will know exactly how to behave if they see a warship coming at them. If I bring a neutral vessel with a hired captain, someone other than myself, they'll hesitate. And they'll be paying attention to *me* instead of a phaser bank."

As he spoke, the captain went to a closet and removed an already packed and strapped suitcase and a Starfleet duffel bag. Obviously he was vacating these quarters and not intending to return.

Riker found himself disturbed by the luggage, and he stared at it for a long time, even missing the captain's first few words when Picard turned to them again.

"Now, listen to me," Picard said. "Morgan Bateson is a man with different priorities than you and I have ever known. No matter how much we may disapprove, he believes in himself more than in the structure of Starfleet. Captains of his time had to. You can learn something from a man like that. The

124

Klingons have been quiet for nearly eighty years, but they've been a smoldering volcano. Now the top is blowing off. They've always been resource-poor, angry at having been contained by the Federation, and now they've found reasons to be our enemies again. Whether we like it or not, Morgan Bateson's attitude about Klingons is back in fashion. He is the captain of the *Enterprise* now. I expect you to treat him accordingly. Mr. Riker, Counselor, you both report to Captain Bateson at eleven hundred. Doctor, get your things and report to Captain Reynolds aboard the merchant explorer *Half Moon*. Take whatever you may need for a rescue mission. We leave in an hour."

There was a storm brewing, without a doubt, and moreover a storm which had so long been foretold would be all the more violent when it did come.

Ship of the Line

CHAPTER 13

**Cardassia Prime
"Madred Village"**

"Steve! Over here!"

"Dan—there you are. I couldn't find you."

"Are you hurt?"

"Nah, fell into a crater. Took me a while to get out. Are the others protected?"

"Under cover. Atherton's got his crew over in the gym, and David and Jack got everybody else in here before the bombardment. They're down in the basement. Y'know, m'friend, I think they're really trying to kill us today."

"Same as yesterday. Why don't you turn on that bartender charm of yours and talk them out of it."

"They're trying harder today. You really made them quite mad when you blew up their amphibious unit."

"Couldn't let them work the beach."

"Sure couldn't. Do you think the Cardies are enjoying this?"

"Hell, no, I think they're dead serious. I don't think they're having any more fun than—"

"Hey! Look! Somebody's beaming in!"

"Where?"

"Right in the middle of the compound! Right dead center of the bombardment! Those bastards!"

"Dan—stay here! Don't go out there. Can you see who it is? Is it anybody we know?"

"I can't see very well . . . it's a man . . . human . . . it's Mark! Steve, it's your brother! It's Mark!"

At the sound of his brother's name, Lieutenant Steve Mc-Clellan dropped his commanding manner and plunged past Dan Leith, right out of the protective doorway of the building they were hiding in. The last thing he saw was a flash of Dan's dusty blond hair and shocked face, too shocked even to shout a restraint.

McClellan was twenty-six and had been doing the work of a fifty-year-old senior officer for months now, but suddenly he felt like a little boy again. Now he forgot all his training and plunged past Dan's clutching hands and right out into the open, ignoring the plumes of explosive hitting the ground every few yards, every few seconds. Over the whine of salvos he shouted, "Mark! Mark! Mark!"

In the middle of the shattered spaceport mall, his brother looked completely confused. As the transport process finished and the sparkles faded away, Mark McClellan was left vulnerable and disoriented.

Damn, he looks exhausted—

Salvos deployed from the distant hills drove into the pavement every few seconds, each preceded by a telltale whine. The whines were twisting together into one vibrating sound as the salvos came more and more quickly. Each hit blew up a cone of ejecta, sharp and lethal shrapnel, too fast to be dodged. Realizing that he must appear like some kind of wraith bursting through the gouts of smoke, Steve McClellan dodged toward his stunned brother.

Mark looked like the wreck of their ship, exhausted and caved in, cheeks hollow, eyes weary and dazed, his wheat-brown hair dull and dirty. He was a ghost of the young officer he'd been when their ship had been wrecked, twelve . . . was it thirteen months now? Thirteen months, two weeks . . . what day was it? The eighth?

The eighth of May. Mark's birthday. Mark McClellan was barely twenty-four as Steve reached out for him through the sulfurous snarl of the nearest salvo. Relief and regret crashed through Steve's chest at the same time. His brother was alive, able to see this birthday, but he was also here.

"Steve?" Mark squinted in disbelief. Then, driven down by the impact of another salvo, he stumbled to one knee. A hundred yards away a water reservoir crashed to the dirt, spilling the rancid liquid inside. As the contaminated water spread, Mark turned and stared at it.

Accustomed to running on the shuddering ground, Steve McClellan wrenched his brother to his feet and pulled him into a run, wondering if he himself looked as haggard as Mark did. Everybody always said they could've been twins. The McClellans had been quite a set on the *Durant*'s bridge, one lieutenant, one helmsman, both Starfleet, nice and snappy, looking so much alike—if Mark had made lieutenant before they got caught, nobody'd be able to tell them apart.

But that hadn't happened. Something else had.

"In here, Steve!"

That was Dan calling! But from a different location than the office doorway—Steve looked toward the sound, didn't see anything, but angled his brother in that direction anyway. All around the running pair, the ground opened up every few feet under the deafening salvos. The bombardment had just started. They couldn't count on its ending anytime soon.

Steve pulled his brother into the flimsy protection of a billboard just in time to get a slap of debris across both their backs. Through a wince, Steve shouted, "Call out again! I lost you!"

"Here! This way! Straight on! Come on, come on!"

"Is that Dan?" Mark choked.

"Get up! Run."

Gritty with chunks of cracked sidewalk and broken glass, the pavement damned their every stride. With their boots skidding, the brothers scratched around a corner. Steve reached to his side and kept Mark on his feet. They plunged toward Dan Leith's call.

There was Dan, looking like an illustration for one of those adventure South Sea holonovels that women liked. Even after all these months of stress and physical taxation, he still looked good, still blond, somehow still tanned. Just one of those lucky guys who were put together like some kind of statue.

A flash of movement caught his eye. Dan—waving frantically to them from inside a partially caved-in garage. How in hell had he gotten in there from the office building that shielded the rest of their crew?

But it was a good move. The angle of the bombardment had changed. Dan had anticipated that, and found better cover.

Steve tilted toward the garage, pushing Mark in front of him. Overhead a salvo screamed in from the hills, torturing their eardrums. Ten feet from the garage, Steve shoved Mark in one fierce final dive forward as the salvo blew a hole in the street behind them.

The McClellans sprawled into the shadows together, and both fell headlong into the dimness, propelled the last few feet by the salvo's hit outside the door. The impact blew down what was left of the front ceiling. Razor-edged steel panels, window glass, and shafts of reinforcement bar speared the entranceway and would've happily sliced the men in half if they'd been standing there.

Instinctively shielding his brother from the blast and the hungry shrapnel, Steve twisted at the last moment. The move was a clumsy one. It did his brother no good, but Steve plowed full tilt into a steel tool chest with his right shoulder low. His head cleared the top of the chest, but his shoulder and hip collided with the thick metal crate. Pain bolted through his neck, his shoulder, and the right half of his body. A gray cloud swam before his eyes. Stunned and suddenly lightheaded, he rolled against the tool chest in a haze, then slipped to his side on the oily floor. Felt himself rolling. *Had to keep his senses . . . had to stay conscious . . .*

Was his shoulder dislocated? If something happened to him—

Pain was . . . stay conscious . . .

"Steve!"

Mark's voice. And somebody was pulling him over.

"Steve, you all right?"

Shuddering through the daze that gripped him, Steve blinked into the gray cloud and saw dust . . . found the outline of Mark against the dimness. Two pairs of hands pulled him to an awkward sitting position.

That was Mark right in front of him . . . right here, for real. Steve pulled his brother into a crushing embrace and rasped, "Thought you were dead!"

Only half the words cracked out past the knots in his throat.

"Thought you were too," Mark responded against his ear. "Aw, Steve . . . what's going on? Is this a Federation post or not? Who's bombing us?"

The embrace almost made Steve pass out from pain and relief. His brother had him around the bad shoulder and the gray cloud was pounding at the insides of his skull. Not that he much cared.

"The Cardassians, who else?" A cloud of dust took form beside them out of the crumbling rubble. It was Dan. That tightened British-empire accent put a stylish mockery on his words. "You men are making me cry. I'll get tears all over my tidy uniform."

Mark McClellan looked around as Dan crouched next to him. "Leith . . . you could be run through a curtain press and you still wouldn't be tidy."

Dan Leith cracked his photogenic smile through the layer of soot on his cheeks. "This from one of the recruiting-poster brothers. Come here, young man. Are you real?"

In spite of Dan's wry complaint, there were joyous tears in his eyes as he coiled both arms around Mark McClellan and hugged him shamelessly. The three Starfleet officers, trained by the academy, officers of the fleet escort *U.S.S. Durant,* hardened by thirteen months' captivity and torture, paused here in this smoldering metal-sided structure, clinging to each other like lost kids, and pretended for a moment that they were safe.

Just for a moment. These moments were all they had to sustain them, brief flashes of hope when they found each other again, or survived a trauma they shouldn't have. Rubbing his arm, Steve McClellan winced through the sharp bolts of pain and the unexpected emotions as his brother and their friend absorbed the fact that they were together again, all still alive.

Dan Leith pulled Mark back and put his hands on both of Mark's shoulders, the way a parent does to a child who's just fallen down. "Are you hurt? Did the plasterfaced bastards hurt you any?"

"They hurt me a lot," Mark admitted. "It's what they do. Where are we? I thought they'd dropped me in a Federation spaceport. Then the ground blew up around me. Is it a spaceport?"

"It's a fake spaceport," Dan explained. "The Cardies built it. They're making us live here and defend it."

"Fake? But there's what's left of a runabout right here in this garage!"

"It's got no engine, Mark. It's fake."

"No engine . . ."

"It's a shell. Trust me, eh? I'm an engineer. If it could fly, I'd fly it. Steve? You all right, Steve?"

Slowly coming out of his pain-inflicted fog and the shock of reunion with the brother he thought certainly was dead, Steve McClellan shifted his battered body. He leaned heavily on the bottom step of a stairway that led upward from where they crouched. Upward to nothing but a collapsed attic.

He rubbed his face and let his eyes clear on the blessed vision of his brother crouched only inches away.

"You all right?" Mark asked. Leaning away from a crawl of hot smoke from outside, he pulled Steve to a better position.

With only an unconvincing nod, Steve fixed his eyes on his

brother, afraid he might pass out and this would be another dream. Pressing a hand to the center of pain in the hollow of his shoulder, he bottled up his anger at the lost months, the lost crewmates.

"They're using us to train their spies and soldiers, Mark," he sputtered. "They built a whole Federation spaceport to see what works and what doesn't, so they can figure out how Federation people live and fight."

Dan Leith kneaded Steve's injured arm and shoulder to keep the muscles from stiffening up. "What scares me is that this means enough to them that they do this."

"This whole complex is a prison of some kind?" Mark glanced around, then looked at the weapon attached into Steve's belt. "But you've got a phaser!"

"They gave us phasers and some other weapons," Dan explained. His South African accent somehow made his explanation sound efficient. "They want to be able to fight us for real. But we're on a moon. Everybody comes and leaves by transporter, as did you. Even the Cardie teams who come to fight us. No vessel ever lands here, thus there's nothing to hijack. We can't leave."

Mark peered out a crack in the crumpled sheeting that had once been the solid side of the garage. "But there's a merchant-fleet recruiting office right over there! I can see houses . . . an apartment complex . . . a fueling station . . . stores, industrial supply, bicycle repair—"

"There's everything," Dan cut off. "There's even a dog-clipping shop. The plumbing works, thank God, so we can remain civilized, and the lights, sometimes. It's a textbook example of a functioning Madred Village."

Mark bolted around. "Madred? You mean, that dirty arrogant spawn of a reptile had something to do with this place?"

"These villages are his specialty," Steve said through a cough. "This place is a tapestry of little details he got from people like us who he tortured over the years. There are rumors that he's got Madred Villages for Romulans and Klingons too. The Cardassians are preparing to go to war with everybody."

"Who's shelling us, then?"

"A Cardie assault team up in those hills," Dan said. "Been here about . . . isn't it six weeks now, Steve?"

Grasping his brother's arm, Steve crushed down a wave of nausea and asked, "Where've they had you all these months?"

Mark patted his brother's hand to reassure him. "A work camp. Sometimes in a cell, if the weather was bad. Once in a while they'd pull one of us out and treat us to the zapper."

"Damn them all . . ." Steve felt his face crumple at the idea. They all knew about the insidious subcutaneous torture devices that could make the pain in his shoulder and hip right now seem like a brush with a feather duster. He'd promised his parents that he'd take care of Mark. Now this.

Forcing himself to think about something else, he asked, "How many other prisoners did you see?"

"Most of our crew disappeared eventually, like you did," Mark said. "Ensigns Seneca, Webb, Yeoman Kelly, Ensign Rankin . . . Lieutenant Barth, Lieutenant Garland, Annie Cole . . . about nineteen of us were together in the same cell block, but never in the same cells. When they had us in a work camp, we weren't allowed to talk much, but at least we could see each other. There were others there too. A couple of Maquis, some merchant spacefarers and their captain, and even a couple of Romulans. Then they started disappearing."

"We know." Dan comforted Mark. "Some of them ended up here. We'll have to compare notes and see who's still alive. The merchant captain's name is Brent Atherton, I'll bet?"

"Right, Atherton! You mean he's here?"

"Yes, along with some of his crew still alive," Dan said. "A dandy resourceful one, kept us going many times."

"Sure has," Steve agreed. "Out of our crew, we've still got Jack Seneca, David Rankin, Sarah Stockdale, Wattanakul—a handful of others who showed up, one every couple of weeks. Not everybody has survived, though, Mark. Cole and Webb, Kelly . . . Barth, Garland—"

"They're dead?" Mark murmured.

"We've killed Cardies too," Jack established. "They've

killed some of ours, but we've done in a fair few of them as well. It's not a game. Sometimes we're the defenders. Sometimes we have to be the aggressors. Every few weeks, a new scenario, some new thing they want to learn from us."

"All this," Mark gulped, "so they can figure out how humans think?"

"How we think," Steve said, "how we fight, what makes us flinch, what doesn't, how much we'll protect each other, do we protect friends more than strangers—" Dry heat from the shelling outside baked the moisture out of his body as he spoke. He felt strangely cold. "But . . . at least . . . at least we get the illusion of fighting for our lives."

Dan put a hand on Steve's knee—a gesture of solace for that tone of voice. "Now and then the Cardies throw somebody fresh into the pot to see if anything changes."

Disheartened, Mark sagged back against the tool chest. "And I'm it?"

"You're it for now."

Even in the smoky dimness, Mark's eyes were still gingham blue, but had lost the youthful glitter Steve had clung to in his memory all this time. Probably would never return.

Mark was looking back at him the same way. The exact same way. God, it hurt.

"What . . ." Mark seemed to be formulating questions, trying to distill all this. He struggled, and the others let him go through it. "They . . . provide food and water? They keep some of you alive?"

"Alive enough," Steve told him. "They make us fight for it. If we get it, we have to fight to protect it. They want us alive, if we can stay that way, but . . . for one thing, they don't see to our medical needs. They want us to take care of each other so they can see how we do it."

"We're being watched?"

"Most of the time," Dan said. "We've neutralized most of their on-site recorders, but they've still got pinpoint satellite visuals and infrareds. We can sit and talk, but if we move five feet or so, they can figure out what we're doing. Every now and then, they get an audio device in here, but we eventually find those. I'm making m'self a necklace."

"I don't understand," Mark moaned. "What does this get them?"

"They're trying to get their guys to think like humans," Steve said. "We're being used to train their operatives. We've got to fight, try to outthink them, so they can see us do it. They set up situations, and we have to try to win."

"'Win'? What do you get if you win?"

"Few days' rest. Maybe extra food. Some medical supplies if we can demonstrate a need, if we catch them in a good mood."

"Chance to tidy up," Dan said, scratching at the day's growth of blond beard. "Shave, haircut, bit of a toenail manicure, you know—"

"What if you lose?"

"Then we get treated to the subcue. The 'zapper,' you called it."

"What if it's a draw?"

Dan shrugged. "Then we fight till it isn't a draw anymore. We've got to keep up some level of success. If we stop being useful to them, we're dead."

Anger flared in Mark's eyes. "I won't do it! I won't help train their soldiers. Forget it!"

Dan nodded, weary of that old song. "If you don't, they'll walk right out here and kill you. We've seen them do it. Remember Lieutenant Garland?"

"Hell, yes, I remember him!"

"Wouldn't participate. Absolutely refused and stuck to it. Now, peer out through the crack in this flashing. See that thing hanging up on that light post?"

"That burned rag, you mean? Is that his uniform?"

"Not just his uniform, my friend."

"Oh . . . God . . ."

Mark coiled up with nausea and bowed his head. Dan offered no comfort, nor did Steve. There wasn't any.

Silence swarmed in on the small garage. Only as an afterthought did they realize the bombardment outside had stopped. That would mean a recon pass by the Cardassians pretty soon. The teams here would have to stay undercover and as still as possible. Underground, if possible. The mall was a shattered mess, the water tower was down, not that the water was much good to anyone.

"First we've got to help ourselves," Steve said, ultimately. He lowered his voice. "Besides, there's another reason to stay alive. This is backfiring on them. We're learning to think like Cardassians. We're getting an idea of what they'd do in this or that situation. We're staying alive so we can take that information back to Starfleet."

"Like what?"

"Like they underestimate humans."

"So what? Everybody does."

Steve shrugged his good shoulder. "Well, that's not the only thing."

"Is the captain here?" Mark asked. The courage to ask that question drove a visible shudder through him. "What about Mr. Court? Who's in charge?"

Dan looked at Steve as if there were some way to get out of this, but the terrible conversation was a replay of a dozen others, strung out over these months. Just when the sorrow started to blunt, they'd have to say it all over again to somebody new.

Steve parted his lips, but Dan quickly placed a hand on his injured shoulder, rescuing Steve from having to tell his own brother the ugly news.

"Captain's gone," Dan said. "The Cardies got him the first week, before we figured out what we were supposed to be doing here. Mr. Court took command for another three months. Then they got him too."

Swallowing the news with a shiver and a brave smothering of reaction, Mark asked, "Who's in command now?"

A shuffle of movement and noise broke through the terrible moment—movement on the other side of the pretend runabout in the middle of the garage. Steve came out of his mournful daze and pulled the phaser from his belt, swinging the weapon in the direction of the noise, just as Dan did the same with the phaser that had been tucked in his jacket. Their weapons were leveled exactly the same, aimed at the same spot, and for a silly instant the beauty of coordination made Steve proud of how they'd learned to move together.

"It's me—Atherton!" a voice called. "Steve, did you hear a transporter?"

"Over here, Brent," Steve responded. He lowered his phaser. Only then did Dan also lower his.

By now pretty spooked, Mark McClellan froze and watched. A form in a civilian's jacket with leather belts, the typical calf-high boots preferred by merchant spacefarers, shaggy black hair and a happy amalgam of Asian and European Earth-features vaulted right over the wreckage of the fake runabout and came toward them.

"This is my brother," Steve said as the new man crouched between him and Dan. "Ensign Mark McClellan . . . Captain Brent Atherton. I guess you've seen each other before."

"Mark," Atherton said. "I remember. Cell Block Four. Glad you're still alive."

Mark accepted Atherton's hand. "I wondered what happened to you. Is your crew here too?"

"Some." Atherton's right cheekbone was bruised, and the shoulder of his dark blue jacket had an oily rip. He surveyed Dan and Steve, noticing Steve's pain-tightened posture.

"You hurt?" he asked.

Steve nodded. "I had a close encounter with this cabinet. My shoulder's numb. Can't move my hand . . ."

Atherton took Steve's hand and pressed his thumb in the middle of the palm until the fingers curled. "Feel that?"

"Yes, I sure as hell feel that."

"Then it's not a total wreck. Put a sling on it. The Cardies blew away our no-go wall between Cafe Bilge and the paint factory. What do you want to do about it?"

Steve winced. "Damn! It'll take us another week to build that up again."

"Longer. The metal's shredded. We have to find new panels. Maybe cannibalize this garage."

"I don't want to give up this garage. It's our mid-way cover."

"Well, I hope you can think of something portable, then. Might have to start using wood for the barricades."

"What's 'Cafe Bilge'?" Mark asked.

"Our produce warehouse," Steve said. "We can use some of the plating off that runabout shell."

"Only about twelve feet," Atherton said. "We need thirty-five feet or so. Twenty feet on either end are still intact. The middle's blown out."

"Gotta protect our food. We'll have to find something sturdy enough."

"We'll wait till dark," Atherton offered. "Then Saul, Peggy, and I can gut the grain elevator and use the accordion-sheets inside."

"Not until at least midnight," Steve ordered, "when the satellites are past us. Take Rankin and Seneca with you. Peggy's not strong enough to carry those metal sheets."

Atherton smiled. "No, but she's a witch with a crowbar."

Steve shifted against the pain again, rubbed his throbbing arm, and complained, "I was holding those sheets back for something better than a no-go wall . . ."

"If you got another idea, I'm listening."

"I don't have any other ideas right now. Go ahead with yours, Brent."

"Aye aye, guy." Atherton gave Steve a squeeze on the good shoulder, tossed to Mark, "Glad to see you—sorry it's here," and ducked through a rupture in the garage's back wall.

They heard his footsteps crunch through the glass and rubble, then gradually fade away toward the gymnasium, where he had his crew holed up.

"Rebuild that stupid wall," Steve sighed. "We've got to find a better way to safeguard the food supplies. Maybe move them."

He looked up, his thoughts clearing his head somewhat.

Mark was gazing at him in new realization. "You're in command?"

Well, that tidbit was out now. Steve managed a nod. "Mmm-hmm."

"But Atherton's a captain! You're a lieutenant! You shouldn't have to do this!"

"Atherton's a merchant captain," Dan corrected. "He runs his own crew, but he knows somebody has to be in charge of the combined operation. Since the Cardies are training to fight Starfleet, he agreed to let Starfleet run the show as long as there was still an officer alive ranking at least lieutenant. If something happens to Steve, then Atherton takes over."

Suddenly angry, Mark demanded, "Do the Cardassians know that?"

Dan shrugged. "Probably."

Mark looked at his brother. "That makes you a target!"

"Oh, I know it," Steve said calmly.

"Well, you two argue about it real loud, now, eh?" Dan stood up, picked a shard of broken glass out of his trouser leg, and said, "I'll go check on the crew and make sure the way's clear for you, Steve. Don't hurry on that bruised hip, my man, or you'll hurt yourself, eh?"

"Thanks, Dan. Keep low. Can't have that pretty head blown off."

"I'm not 'pretty.' I'm 'dashing.'"

"Yeah, well, dash then."

A moment later, the brothers were alone in the smoky garage. The only sounds now were the chitter of ceiling materials and roofing as they broke and fell in bits and pieces.

The brothers sat together in that heavy silence, their heads throbbing from the fresh memory of those kettledrum salvos.

"Aw, Steve," Mark groaned spontaneously, then stopped.

Wisely for both of them, Mark cut off his own groan and didn't try to express in words the sadness that showed in his eyes. Steve McClellan was the *Durant*'s fifth ranking officer, and that meant the deaths of four senior officers before command had fallen on him. He hadn't expected command, hadn't wanted it, at least not so early in his career. He had presided over the suffering, the loss of all those carrying the burden before him. The captain and three senior lieutenants, all gone.

He'd managed to keep from most of the other crew how he felt about this. Dan had figured it out gradually, but now Mark understood right away. His brother knew him too well. Mark had already distilled the misery Steve had endured in the past few months, saddled with unwanted responsibility. Starfleet officers trained for this, but usually it came with the right number of years. Not so for Steve McClellan.

Bitterly Steve found himself saying, "I wish we hadn't pushed so hard to get assigned to the same ship. We pulled every damned string we could find, and now this."

"What 'now'?" Mark asked. "You mean, that I'm here too?"

"You're here too. Ever since the five Sullivan brothers were all lost in the demolition of one ship, the service has avoided putting brothers on the same vessel. I always thought it was kind of silly in this day and age. So you and I had to push for the tradition to slip. We just *had* to serve on the same ship. The two McClellans, together on the same bridge. We were so charming, weren't we?"

"Steve . . . cut it out."

"How long do you figure headquarters waited until they wrote to Dad and Mom and Uncle Ray and told them we were both missing in space? How long you figure Starfleet looked for us before they gave up? You think there's been a memorial yet?"

"Cut it out and that's an order," Mark insisted.

"You can't give me orders. I outrank you."

"Too bad. We've been tight as a carrick bend all our lives. Nobody could see light between us. I don't think it's so bad that we're both here. Maybe it's a good sign. We'll get out of here. Starfleet'll come for us."

"Starfleet's not coming, Mark. They think we're dead. They don't—" He was cut short by a stab of pain up the right side of his back and struggled to finish. "They don't know to come."

"Don't try to get up. What are you doing? Sit down!"

"No time. I've got to deploy an armed detail north of here. We've got to block the Cardassians off before they work around behind the produce warehouse, or we'll starve for a month."

"Let me help you. And promise you'll quit talking about Mom and Dad and Uncle Let's-Go-Fishing."

"Okay, deal. Oh, hey!"

"What?"

Steve maneuvered his good arm around his brother's shoulders and leaned on him. "Happy birthday, baby boy."

Together they crawled toward the crack in the back wall. Elbowing aside a piece of collapsed roof material, Mark McClellan blinked through the settling dust.

"Is it my birthday?" he asked.

Eighty-five years ago, the tragic loss of 1500 people aboard the R.M.S. *Titanic* forever changed the perceptions and practices of sailors. Caution was no longer a thing in the wind. "Master of the sea" was handed back to the birds and fish. Thousands more lives have been saved because hundreds were lost.

Because of our loss of Danielle, this schooner is forever safer, the crew more watchful of each other. Through the fog of senselessness comes clear appreciation that Danielle's loss has saved or will save the life of a child, a cadet, or a crewmate.

Certainly tragedy need not be devastation, for here we are back again. Rather than being fearful, we are merely smarter and more humble, for many more sailors lie there than stand here. For our lives, and the lives of the children and young adults who sail this ship, we pause in appreciation for Danielle Faucher and all those with her.

> D. Carey, Schooner *Californian.*
> read at memorial wreath service on board,
> May 4, 1997, near the appropriate latitude
> and longitude.

CHAPTER 14

"Mr. Riker, I'm Mike Dennis. This is Wizz Dayton."

"Wizz?"

"Short for Wizard. Communications Specialist. Welcome to the *Enterprise*-E. We didn't see you at the ceremony, sir. We were afraid you'd miss our launch time."

"Oh, I was there." William Riker nodded and offered the two men no explanation of why he was late.

He was late because it had taken this long to convince himself to actually board this vessel without Captain Picard as his captain. The commitment was a little hard to swallow, but here he was. Somehow the oath he'd made to Starfleet overcame his irritation at admiralty whim.

"Report ship's status, Mr. Dennis," he requested.

"Sir, we're under way at impulse speed. Course is Port Innerspace Standard on Lane Delta India Tango away from Starbase 12, trying to shake all the confetti off the hull from the launch celebrations. We're cleared for any primary spacelane. All local traffic has been detained, and we're putting on a nice show for everybody who's pulled over so we can pass. We're receiving hails of congratulations and fair weather from dozens of spectator vessels, and even one from a grizzly tanker captain who swears he took a shot at the *Enterprise*-C once upon a time. Department heads are preparing to report light-speed readiness. The captain is on the bridge."

"Very well."

"We'll show you to your quarters, sir," Lieutenant Dennis went on. "Then the captain has requested that you join him on the bridge. It's a big ship. I still get lost, and I've been working aboard for about—"

"Yes, I know," Riker cut off. "My gear was brought on board by a couple of yeomen who met me at the starbase."

"Yes, sir, we sent those two men over. Your gear is in your quarters. If you'll come this way—"

Riker followed the young officers, knowing these were two of Bateson's original crew, and that made him uneasy. Knowing they were actually the better part of a century older than he was didn't help either, but he kept a lid on that. They'd probably heard every quip, pun, and joke about that in the past three years.

"Hey, hi, bud!"

The voice sounded from inside the open door of a tool locker, and then something utterly extraordinary occurred. A drunken man, reeling slightly and clutching what looked like an antique silver whiskey flask, piled out of an open doorway and threw an arm around Wizz Dayton. "Here he is! The Wizard!"

Dayton shrugged unhappily. "Hi, Gabe. Take it easy, okay?"

This was Gabriel Bush? This hollow-eyed shadow of a human being was Bateson's upright first officer from the *Bozeman?* Riker stepped back a couple of paces just to get a better look.

"Sure, I'm easy," the man assured, nodding. Then he saw Riker, apparently for the first serious time, and said, "Oh, I know who you are."

Drunk. Incredible! Riker backed off a step in disapproval. "I'm First Officer Riker, yes . . ."

"Oh, great to have you around!"

Uneasy, Lieutenant Dennis said, "Mr. Riker, this is Commander Gabriel Bush."

Riker scarcely recognized him. They'd met briefly three years ago, but this was hardly a shadow of that man. Now he was gaunt and undernourished, barely filling out the gray work suit he wore.

Riker tipped his head. "Mr. Bush . . . are you all right?"

"Oh, I'm good," the inebriated man said. "Look at you! First mate! Oh—sorry . . . first *officer*. Big difference, right? That's a good job, you know. It's a wicked great job. It used to be *my* job, did you know that?"

Self-conscious, Riker nodded and glanced at Dennis.

"I was good at it," Bush said, his New England accent making his words more garbled. He took a sad moment to palm his rumpled hair as if he knew what he looked like. "Not so good anymore . . . but that's okay, because . . . well, now he's got you. Anything you need, you just let me know. It's a big ship, so just take one thing at a time. You'll be just wicked in no time. I'll . . . I'll see yez later."

With that Bush wandered off down the corridor, tossed back a weak "Don't worry," and disappeared into a lab.

The three watched him go, and nobody spoke until the lab door slid shut. And even a few seconds after that. Riker felt as if his chest were caving in. Now what?

"Don't feel bad, sir," Mike Dennis said finally. "It isn't you. He's been like that since we got to this century, give or take six months."

"What happened? What could possibly do that to him?"

"He was about to get married when we ended up lost."

"Oh . . . still . . ."

Wizz Dayton waved a hand as if to explain with a gesture. "We all just loved Ruby. That's the girl he was going to marry. She was about to come all the way from the East Coast to Fries-Posnikoff. Captain was going to officiate at the ceremony. Gabe was—aw, he was the happiest man in the whole sector, we figure. I never saw anybody so idiot-happy to be getting married."

"He's distraught like that, even after three whole years? I understand, but—"

He stopped when Dennis and Dayton looked at each other uncomfortably. Evidently there was more.

"Not just that, sir," Dennis confirmed. "Mr. Bush looked into what happened to Ruby. It wasn't very nice."

"What did happen?"

They seemed to be afraid he was going to ask, but there was no turning back. Even if they didn't offer the information, Riker stood there and insisted with his posture that they tell him. As first officer, he had to know.

They seemed to accept that. Dayton took the burden. "Ruby spent years looking for us. Hiring ships, scratching resources together, lobbying admirals, buying search services, getting fleeced, getting older . . . she hired some of the most disreputable characters around."

"Yes," Riker said. "I've heard that no one of any self-restraint would go into the Typhon Expanse for a good twenty years after that incident. And I don't blame them—I was there."

"You sure were," Dennis commented.

Riker glanced at him, then said, "Go on, Mr. Dayton."

"She finally used up all her resources except a single ship that she took out by herself. She had word that Gabe was a prisoner of the Klingons, from someone who was willing to trade lies for money, and she was determined to get him back. She headed straight for the Klingon border."

"The Klingons got her?" Riker guessed.

"Yes. Captured, tried as a spy, convicted and sentenced to Rura Penthe Prison Planet. The Federation tried to get her back, but she *had* trespassed on restricted territory. The charge was legitimate. The Klingons were about to let her go on a technicality, but then they found out who she was . . . the fiancée of the *Bozeman*'s first officer."

"The *Bozeman*," Riker echoed, "the ship that wrecked their invasion and sent the High Council into a tailspin."

"That's right," Wizz Dayton said. "After that, they sent Ruby back all right . . . in ten small boxes. The same number of dignitaries who were purged from the High Council."

With a wince Riker murmured, "Oh, no—"

"All because she was the fiancée of Gabriel Bush," Dennis added. "And when Gabe checked on what happened to her, there was a nice clear set of pictures in the files. He just sat there for days and stared at the monitor, eaten up by guilt."

Will Riker winced and canted forward as if he'd been punched. "Oh, my God . . . poor Gabe . . ."

With new sorrow and empathy, he looked down the corridor, empty now, wishing he could catch Gabriel Bush and—do something, anything, for him. Anything.

"I guess you can see, sir, why we protect Mr. Bush," Wizz Dayton said. "We'd appreciate it if you'd just forget what you saw. We've been pretty much keeping him away from officers for a long time now, and Captain Bateson's been running interference for him, making sure nobody finds out. He's not really causing any harm, sir. And he does do his jobs, usually. Please don't say anything, sir."

"That's highly inappropriate, Mr. Dayton," Riker began, but they already knew that. "Don't let me catch him on duty like that."

As boarding first officer, what should he do? What would he do in their place? Wouldn't he protect Troi or La Forge just the same way? Hadn't he and Picard and everyone else protected Worf during all his struggles between his Klingon heritage and his Starfleet loyalties? Those hadn't exactly been sane times. And the glasswork feelings of Data during his halting search for humanness?

Thinking of those, he couldn't muster up the second half of his sentence.

"But you can see," Dennis said, "why he just couldn't be the first officer for this voyage. We don't know when he ever will be again. He's taken the course and upgraded his technical skills to some extent, enough to pass muster—"

"Whenever we could sober him up," Dayton offered.

"And he passed reaccreditation," Mike Dennis went on.

"Has the ship's surgeon seen him?" Riker asked.

"Oh, sure," Dayton said. "Cured him eight times, enough for him to take exams and get recertified. But there's just no curing his broken heart."

Riker drew a breath and sighed. "Well, I've heard of conspiracies before, but this—"

If only there were some way to bring this up casually, talk to Bush, help him . . . but if his own crewmates hadn't been able to help, and a Starfleet surgeon hadn't been able to help, then no one could help. Real help, Riker knew, lay untouchable, ninety years in the past, with a soulsick girl and a sorrowful destiny. Some things just can never be fixed.

As the two men led him in silence to his new quarters, he combed his mind for just how to handle this. As first officer, it fell upon him to handle problems of the crew—usually not quite this personal, but certainly if those problems affected the ship. And this would.

On the other hand, his responsibility was much more to the crew than other senior officers. Bush was still a senior officer, and thus was more the captain's concern than that of another senior officer, other than the ship's surgeon, who evidently had already weighed in on the subject and decided that being custodial was enough. It might be technically appropriate for Riker to take some action, but not in the realm of polite consideration that officers gave each other.

Bateson should've handled Bush's desperate mental agony years ago. He hadn't. Apparently he had communicated to his crew that it was all right to shield Bush and deceive Starfleet about the functionality of a commissioned, stationed officer aboard a ship of the line.

By the time Riker was introduced to his quarters, and then was escorted to the bridge of the starship, he was solidly grumpy about the way Morgan Bateson ran his command.

Good way to start off, right?

The turbolift doors parted before him, and Lieutenant Dennis led him onto the sweeping, beautiful bridge of the new *Enterprise.* It was a more intimate place than the previous *Enterprise,* each brace, chair, and support designed to mimic the streamlined, forward-leaning outer configuration of the ship's hull, making each station look as if it were about to leap off a cliff and fly. The lines were all recognizable, the ceiling lower than the other ship. The lower ceiling provided more of that intimacy he suddenly felt.

The colors were muted, rather like being inside a giant computer chip. Brushed-satin structural members of military gray supported hundreds of diagnostic readouts and sensor displays. Six support pylons arched in a semicircle like the ribs of a melon, and each had a lighting panel running along its inboard side. Floor lights glowed upon a carpet of astral blue.

No station was more than four steps from the next station, which meant no one would feel alone or separated here, and they could all see one another's panels with a glance.

Otherwise, most things were basic Starfleet design, captain's chair at the center, helm before that, and the main screen directly forward of everything. The functional design had been mimicked in most spacefaring cultures. Klingon bridges, Romulans, Orions, merchants—almost everybody had the same basic design. It just worked.

Dennis immediately went to a station, leaving Riker to stand in the turbolift vestibule and look about in privacy. There were some people here, a few officers, Captain Bateson standing just over there on the port side, going over something on a padd with an engineer, and Deanna Troi was on the forward starboard upper deck, picking off some detail or other on a console. Nobody noticed him.

Nobody except a science officer who now tried to get past him and decided better of that.

"Sir, Lieutenant John Wolfe, Stellar Sciences," the young man introduced himself. "You must be Mr. Riker. Welcome aboard, sir. Permission to show you around the bridge."

"Granted," Riker said. "Just do it from here."

"Yes, sir." Wolfe turned and started pointing to stations. "Tactical, Mission Ops, Defense, Science One, Science Two, Ops Manager, Guidance and Navigation, Environmental, Main Engineering Primary Status Display, Warp Propulsion, Impulse Propulsion, Flight Control, FTB Receiving, Systems Diagnostics, Battle Bridge Co-Station, Main Computer Core Memory, Docking Control—"

"Thank you, good enough. Pretty much standard, give or take a few."

"Yes, sir."

"Thank you, Mr. Wolfe. Carry on."

"Aye, sir."

Riker paused for a few moments to appreciate the sheer newness of the bridge, the fresh smell of factory-new carpet, the glossy control panel tripolymers, the efficient and yet aesthetic arrangement of terminals and monitor screens with their pretty displays, and the brushed-metal struts gracefully holding everything in place.

And the sounds . . . he'd forgotten how comforting the soft bleeps and hums and whirrs could be. They were the voice of the ship, its great heart surging, its ventilation system softly breathing like a sleeping woman.

On the wide forward screen was a lovely view of open space, the brilliantly cluttered Fries-Posnikoff Sector, a field of space full of nebulas, elephant trunks, remnants of cosmic activity, comets, clusters, sparkling clouds, binaries—the place had become popular as a college course because so many celestial characteristics could be experienced here, in a relatively compact stellar field.

Taking a few breaths himself, to calm down, Riker stepped downdeck and strode on the plush carpet to where Deanna Troi picked at the environmental control panel.

"Deanna," he uttered quietly.

"Oh!" She spun to him and said, "I'm *so* glad you're here! I didn't think you made it before we got under way!"

Halfway through the sentence she pulled her voice down to a whisper. Her large eyes widened and she peeked over Riker's shoulder—which took tiptoes and a little hop—at Bateson.

"Wouldn't miss it for all the saxophones in New Orleans," he said. "What're you doing on the bridge? I thought you were assigned to medical."

"I am. I'm adjusting temp control in some of the lower decks. It's been a little haywire. We can't find the problem."

"New ship," Riker said. "Have you seen Mr. Bush?"

"This morning? No, I haven't. He might be down in—"

"No . . . I mean, have you *seen* him?" He rolled his eyes and shrugged in a meaningful way.

"Oh," she uttered and nodded heavily. "Yes, I've seen him. I think he saw two or three of me as well."

"What do you make of all that?"

She kept working on the panel, so no one would notice their lowered voices. "I think he's sunken into severe depression, that's what, as if it's not obvious. He's completely inconsolable. Diagnosis doesn't take a professional."

"But he certainly needs professional help."

"He does, but the captain won't let me practice as a counselor." She worked to keep her voice down through her anger. Her eyes flared in frustration. "And to tell you the truth, Will, I don't think there's much I could do for Mr. Bush. His despondency needs more intense treatment than I can administer on board ship while he's trying to do other work. Besides, I'm not sure I'd prescribe much more than he's getting right now—simple hard work."

"But it's not helping," Riker complained.

"No, it's not. And he's been cured of the alcoholism several times. We can do that in ten minutes. He's not simply *physically* dependent. He's just . . . grief-stricken."

She raised one shoulder in a hopeless gesture, and glanced across the bridge to where Captain Bateson still had his back to them.

"It's his fault," she whispered emphatically. "He keeps protecting Bush. He thinks that only shipmates can help a shipmate. When I disagree, he just brings up our loyalty to Captain Picard and to each other, and what can I say? What do you really expect me to say?"

"Nothing, I guess."

"As first officer, can't you do something?"

"That'd be patently inappropriate," Riker told her, cutting that one off before it got started. "The senior officers are the concern of the captain. I can't possibly circumvent Captain Bateson's preferred method of handling his staff."

"Well, I don't prefer his method."

"Neither do I."

"It's not the way Captain Picard would behave."

"No, it's not." Riker glared a few needles at the middle of Bateson's back, then changed mode and gripped Troi's arm warmly. "At least we can be together, you and me, Data, Geordi . . ."

Troi glanced around. "We all tried so hard to get assigned here, Will . . . we assumed Captain Picard would—"

"That's enough," he said, cutting her off.

Her eyes crinkled sadly. "You're right."

Reluctantly, Riker gazed again at the captain. "Guess I'd better report in."

"I suppose."

"I'll talk to you later."

"Alright."

She seemed sorry to let him go over there, but Riker broke away from her and crossed the fresh carpet to where the captain was picking at the controls and comparing them to a padd. Riker lagged back until the junior engineer finished his report and Bateson nodded and handed the padd back to the nearly teenaged young man.

Even then, Riker did not announce himself, knowing there was a point of no return. He'd passed it already, but still . . .

"Oh—Will!" Bateson turned and his animated face beamed. "Welcome aboard. I appreciate your deciding to accept my request. It's not an official long-term stationing. I'm sure you haven't had time to make up your mind about anything permanent yet. You don't mind if I call you 'Will'—"

"No, sir."

"Good. Excuse me." Bateson tapped his combadge, one of the little innovations that had come along during those ninety years he skipped. "Bridge to Main Engineering. Captain Scott, Engineer La Forge, Commander Data, join us up here, please. Bridge to IM Pulse Engineering. Engineer Perry, Engineer Hamilton, please join us on the bridge. And tell Gabe to get his carcass topside pronto. Captain out."

Without waiting for acknowledgments, the captain took Riker's arm and strolled with him around the upper deck, talking as they walked. "I know what you're thinking. How could Morgan Bateson, a man ninety years behind the technical times, possibly be effective as master of the most up-to-date ship in the fleet? Right?"

"Uh . . . well, sir, to be honest—"

"I always want you to be honest. I'm counting on that. I won't learn anything from polite deceptions."

"All right, sir, if you say so."

"I do. And you know as well as I do that I don't need to be technically expert at every detail of this ship. Nobody really can be, you know that. A captain is much more than that. That's why we have ship's department heads. The captain decides what needs to happen, the department heads make it happen. Finding myself ninety years behind the tech times, I need extra help on the bridge. I have officers who take command when I'm off watch, of course, but they're in the same boat I am. Oh—that would be a good joke if I'd timed it right, but I didn't."

"No, sir."

"My original crew and I know the lay of space like the backs of our hands. Spatial bodies don't alter that much in ninety years. On the cosmic timescale, we hardly missed anything. What I need is an on-call spacemaster. Essentially a pilot. You've been recommended for your own command and turned it down. Now, I know you were holding out for command of the *Enterprise*, and I suppose you rather hate my guts right now. In spite of that, I'm going to gamble on your decent sense of duty and ask you to serve for a few months, to usher me and my men through the shakedown period. What do you say, Will? Are you too bitter to do what's good for Starfleet?"

Riker paused, managed to disengage his elbow from Bateson's grip, and turned to the captain.

Annoyed, he said, "I believe I've already answered that question with my presence here, sir."

Bateson nodded his conciliation. "All right, noted, of course. You've got me there. I just had that speech all worked out and I didn't want to waste it."

"Understood, sir," Riker dismissed. "And it was a first-rate speech too."

"Thank you, I thought so . . . did you know where that phrase comes from?"

"Sorry?"

" 'First-rate.' It's from the Royal Navy. They used to rate their ships, first, second, third . . . ironically, third-rate didn't refer to lesser quality. It referred to the construction, arming, and duty of a type of vessel."

"I didn't know that, sir."

"Oh, yes. Lots of our modern slang comes from the sea. 'Down the hatch,' 'lower the boom,' 'keel over,' 'devil to pay,' 'toe the line,' 'taken aback,' 'show your true colors' . . . what else? 'Son of a gun,' 'the con,' 'lay off,' 'cut and run,' 'above board,' 'sickbay'—"

"The brig," Wizz Dayton contributed. "It's from Trafalgar. A kind of ship Nelson used to stuff his prisoners into. I know that from when I got thrown into one after shoreleave."

"And you deserved it too," Bateson reminded Dayton. Then his eyes narrowed and got mischievous. He pointed at Riker's face, at the neatly trimmed beard. "You know, we have a problem. One of us is going to have to shave this D'Artagnan imitation. Either that, or everybody aboard is going to have to grow one."

"Don't look at *me*," Deanna Troi warned from Environmental, and leaned her hip against the console's spongy edge. She obviously didn't quite buy into what she was hearing.

Riker hoped the captain didn't pick up on her coolness, but Morgan Bateson didn't seem to miss much.

Smiling, Bateson tapped his combadge again. "Attention all hands. Propulsion and science stations, confirm ready for warp speed."

The words rang. He had a resonant broadcast voice with natural stage presence, and he knew how to use it. A shiver of excitement went up Riker's spine in spite of his trying not to like all this.

He *did* like it, damn it! The launch of a new starship!

The main turbolift doors parted. Captain Scott rolled out, beaming happily, followed by Geordi La Forge and Data. Riker was instantly stung by the absence of Captain Picard, Beverly Crusher, and Worf. Would they ever be together again?

A few seconds later, hardly any difference at all, the secondary turbolift beside the main screen opened and two engineers piled out, each rushing to take the first step out onto the bridge. They almost tripped each other, and Riker smelled a bet. Behind them, out sloshed Gabe Bush, with Wizz Dayton guiding him along custodially.

Riker suddenly realized what was going on. Bateson had his whole bridge crew from the *Bozeman* here now, as well as all onboard officers from the *Enterprise*-D.

"Ah—good!" Bateson looked around. "I wanted you all here for this marvelous moment. Wizz, hold that lift door. George Hill's coming out."

Dayton stuck a hand at the lift panel, keeping it open as a big, gaudy, tentacled creature tumbled goofily out. The thing wrapped one tentacle around Wizz Dayton's ankle and promptly turned color to imitate the carpet. It blinked its two—only two?—soggy black eyes at Riker as if knowing he was new here.

"What is *that?*" Riker blurted.

"That's George Hill," Bateson said. "He's a member of my original crew and he's entitled to be here."

"What is it?"

"It's a decapus. We don't know where he's from."

"Captain . . . is this some kind of a—"

"No, he's a member of the crew. He's our official worrier. Department staff, I'll take your reports now."

Grinning like a pumpkin, and in a holiday way resembling one, Captain Montgomery Scott proudly announced, "Main core engineering, matter/antimatter reaction assemblies, dilithium integrity, plasma injection terminals, SIF and IDF conduits, and catastrophic auxiliary operations are ready for warp speed, Captain."

"Thank you, Scotty. Mr. La Forge?"

Geordi La Forge stepped forward one pace. "All tactical, mission operations, subspace relays, navigational, guidance and sensory stations, emissions receiving, and conning stations show ready for warp speed, Captain."

"Very well. Commander Data?"

Still overwhelmed by his emotion chip, which forced him to deal with feelings most people had dispatched by kindergarten, Data actually clapped his hands once. In this state, he was essentially a long-lived child. His moonstone eyes glittered as brightly as his onionlike skin.

"All mission-specific sensor systems, shipboard security, defense functions, and communications report go for warp speed, Captain. Isn't it just wonderful?"

"Yes, it is, Data. Commander Troi?"

Rather drably in comparison, Troi reported, "All medical and environmental stations, graviton control, internal damage control, and internal sensors report ship is tolerable for warp speed, Captain."

"Very well. Science Officer?"

John Wolfe stood up from his seat at the primary library computer system. "LARCS is on line, sir. All systems operational."

"Thank you. Chief Hamilton?"

Ham Hamilton, Bateson's smarmy original engineer from the *Bozeman,* drawled, "NDT's are completed, sir. MIE, DCA's, MCPC, RCS diagnostics, ODN's, and MJL's are go for warp, sir."

Bateson bottled a laugh. "A-OK. Thank you, all of you." With genuine warmth he said, "And thank you sincerely for having more faith in me than I deserve. Mr. La Forge, how about a little nostalgia? Would you like to take your original post as navigator for the first watch?"

Geordi La Forge seemed startled, then smiled. "Yes, sir! I'd like that very much!"

He quickly came down into the command arena and took the nav chair.

"Mr. Riker, your place is right here—" Bateson gestured to the seat on the right of the command chair, then motioned to the chair on the left and said, "Gabe, I want you right here beside me too."

Not nearly as jolly as the last time Riker had seen him, Gabe Bush had obviously been sobered up a little by his shipmates. Twitching with self-consciousness, he wallowed in obvious embarrassment as all eyes came to him. His eyes went only one place—to Riker's. Bush flushed in humiliation, and he couldn't look up for long.

He glanced at the captain. "Thank you, sir," he scratched out. "I 'preciate that."

Not belaboring the discomfort, Bateson took his place in the captain's chair.

"Let's see what she can do. Mr. La Forge, your course is two six zero one point six."

"Twenty-six-oh-one, aye, sir!" Helmsman Andy Welch's voice had a quake of thrill running through.

Bateson tapped the control on the command chair's arm. "Captain's log. Captain Morgan Bateson recording. Log first engagement of matter/antimatter propulsion system, *U. S. S. Enterprise,* NCC 1701-E. Mr. Welch . . . give us warp factor one."

"Warp factor one, sir!"

The engines hummed. Space on the screen blew into gorgeous distortion. The Fries-Posnikoff Sector blurred into some kind of painting, and *snap*—they were going faster than Einstein thought anybody ever could.

As she pressed her armored shoulders forward into lightspeed, the *U.S.S. Enterprise*-E was indeed a beauty, inside and out. She was a forward-leaning thing, a huge bird leaping off that cliff, but she was leaping for the first time. She was a grand ship. Only time and trial would tell if indeed she was also a great ship.

"Ahead standard."

"Standard cruising speed, Captain, warp factor four. All systems responding."

Now that they'd settled down and most people's eyes had dried up some, Will Riker turned to Captain Bateson. "What's our destination, sir? Circling the Emerson-Northern Nebula?"

"The Forest Hill Asteroid Belt?" La Forge guessed from the starboard side.

"The Civic Park Cluster at Echo-Five?" Data added hopefully. He still looked like an android, but he wasn't acting much like one right now.

"Nope, nothing so pedestrian." The captain pointed at the big main screen and made a sweeping gesture with both hands. "We're going right out to the far edge of the Typhon Expanse. Our old hunting grounds."

As Bateson glanced around in satisfaction and met eyes with his original crew members, Riker noticed that everybody else—he himself, and the engineers and techs who hadn't come through time with Bateson—were all staring in a completely different manner.

Then Riker noticed that most of them were looking at *him*. They expected him to say something. He expected it too.

"Captain," he began, stepping into the command arena, "that's directly adjacent to the Klingon Neutral Zone."

"Yes, I know."

"Sir . . . it's considered hostile space. The Federation recommends that all shipping remain clear of the Expanse. That area is scrupulously avoided by all but assigned Starfleet border patrol vessels."

"Yes, I know that too."

"Vessels, I might add, which are thoroughly shaken down, fully armed, and manned by active-duty battle-trained field officers, *sir*—"

"Yes, Will, I know, I heard you." Bateson tilted his head and surveyed the officers of the *Enterprise*-D. "What's the matter with all of you? You look like a raft of seals. Stop staring. Are you getting upset for some *good* reason?"

Riker worked to unclench his fists. "No, sir."

"Good. I had a feeling you might be a little reluctant. How long was it—seven years under Picard?"

"Yes, sir." Uneasily, Riker met the glances of Geordi and Troi, who were now standing together with Data on the upper starboard deck.

Bateson shrugged. "Well, all good things . . . no, I'm not trying to be heartless." He strolled toward Riker, much closer than Riker wanted to be right now, and the captain looked at him with embarrassing sympathy. "I was going to save this for later, but I really want you on my side and I don't want you to resent me."

"Sir . . . we don't resent you."

Damn, what a lousy liar I am. Even worse, to be watched doing it by a whole pack of other lousy liars—Data's poker face looks more like a go-fish face.

"Yes, you do," Bateson parried easily. "Don't blame you a bit, either. But look. Come over here." He crossed the bridge to the science console and put his hand on the lower trunk. "See this?"

"You mean the panel?"

"Yes, the panel itself."

"Yes, sir, I see it."

"See these little scratches that have been painted over?"

"Yes, sir . . ."

"This panel is from the *Enterprise.*"

Riker looked at the panel, brushed-satin gray like the others. "I beg your pardon?"

Tapping the panel with one finger, Bateson said, "It's made from salvaged terminium from the *Enterprise*-D's structural trusses."

Suddenly stepping back, a little spooked, Riker murmured, "Oh, sir . . ."

"That's right. Now, come over there."

Bateson "walked" across to the port side, to the most forward support pylon. He ran his hand up the after side of the pylon. "This too. Polyduranide from the secondary framework rods off your Saucer Module. And the corresponding pylon on the starboard side over there is the same. And all through the ship we incorporated little bits and pieces of the wreckage of the *Enterprise*-D. We know where they all are, too. Some of them have engraved brass plates."

Now beyond spooked, Riker slid both hands across the part of the strut Bateson had touched. It was identical to the rest of the strut except for two little pocks and a thumbnail gouge that wouldn't have been tolerated in a brand new piece. Wreckage . . .

"In the officer's lounge," Bateson said, "the table was salvaged, and it has a plaque on it dedicated to the *Enterprise*-D."

Overwhelmed, Riker looked at the rail again, then looked up at Troi. Her eyes welled with tears, her face gaunt and ashamed.

Data sniffed. Geordi clasped his hands humbly.

Bateson rubbed the bit of salvage on the ship's rail. "You know why I did this?"

Feeling obliged to fill up the pause, Riker murmured, "No, sir . . ."

Bateson gripped Riker's elbow again. "Because ships are important. Salvage is important. To *people*. I'm the one who invited the *Titanic* and *Mary Rose* exhibits out to Starbase 12. I wanted everyone out here to see the sacrifice of those who had come before them. It's special to stand a couple of feet from something that actually went down with the *Titanic*. It shows us that those people were real people, living and breathing just like we are. They really lived and they really died. These artifacts tie us to them in a concrete, physical way that we'll never forget. Everybody who's ever held his great grandfather's watch or touched his mother's wedding ring understands what I'm talking about. *Things* really are important. They take us directly back to that moment. Not to a legend or a story, but to an actual moment on a given day in the past. Because of these bits of your ship, all of us on this ship, for her whole future, will never forget you and your ship and what you did that day. It's important."

Could the human chest stand this kind of pressure? Steeped in shame, Riker gripped the pocked strut and couldn't manage to speak.

Giving him and the others a few seconds to absorb what he had just said, Bateson added, "I never really had any roots. Only my ship and my crew. When we came through time, I found I wanted some roots. So I sort of adopted Starbase 12 as my hometown. I guess that sounds pretty provincial . . ."

Riker raised his lowered eyes. His hard demeanor cracked. He smiled. "No, sir, it doesn't sound provincial at all."

Well . . . why did it feel so good to smile?

He stood back a little and offered a hand. "Thank you, Captain. Thank you very sincerely, from all of us."

Taking the hand, Bateson smiled and clapped Riker on the shoulder with the other hand, *damn him. Why did he have to be such a decent guy?*

"All right, enough partying," Bateson said. "Work, work, work, slave, slave, slave. This is Starfleet, not a sideshow. First things first. We have a mission to undertake."

"A mission, sir?" Riker asked. "On a shakedown cruise?"

"That's right. War games, Mr. Riker. In preparation for that, I've ordered shields reduced to fifty percent and phasers powered down to ten percent."

"Captain!" Riker crossed to the chair he had been invited to take, but did not sit. "Reducing phaser power while we maneuver just minutes away from the Klingon Empire?"

"That's right."

"Captain, we have to talk!"

"I thought we handled this. This isn't command by committee. We don't have to talk."

"Well, we're going to."

"Is that so? . . . All right, Will. Go ahead. Talk."

CHAPTER 15

"Captain Picard? I'm Chip Reynolds. Welcome aboard the *Half Moon*. Did you get squared away into a bunk?"

"Yes, thank you, Captain. Your watch leader showed me down to the—what was it? The Orlop Deck?"

"That's what we call it. Down there you have a chance of sleeping with your legs unbent."

"I hope the watch leader wasn't too put out by the sudden change of events. She was muttering about having totally lost control."

"Oh, no, she's always like that. I'm a little mystified about this—I mean, I'm willing to go into Cardassian space, but you *do* understand the difference in speed and armaments between this ship and just about any Starfleet ship . . ."

"Yes, I understand. In fact, it's preferable. I don't want a fighting vessel for this mission. My message is entirely different. Rather stronger, I think. As long as you keep to your top speed, we'll get to Cardassia Prime in adequate time."

Hoping to dispense with amenities before any got started, Jean-Luc Picard tried to retreat to his excuse for quarters

163

aboard this strange old rattletrap of a private ship, but the ship's lanky captain stopped him again.

"By the way, for passing the time, I've got something for you," Captain Reynolds said. He reached into a black captain's case and pulled out several computer cartridges. "They were delivered to me just before we left Starbase 12."

"What are they?"

"They're holoprograms."

"Oh, Riker . . ." Picard shook his head at his first officer's persistence, then thought of something else and looked up from the cartridges. "This ship has a holodeck?"

"Well, we didn't before, but Mr. Riker had holoequipment installed in our cargo hold about forty minutes before we left. I never saw a team work so fast. He had a guy he said was an android going like some kind of rocket on the installation. Riker told me not to tell you until we were under way." Reynolds grinned sheepishly and seemed to enjoy the conspiracy, then added, "Hope that's all right."

"Mmm, it wouldn't be the first time he did something behind my back," Picard said. He turned the top cartridge to read the label. " 'Starship Logs, Enhanced, *U.S.S. Enterprise* NCC 1701, Captain James T. Kirk. Stardate 1709.2: Romulan Incursion at the Neutral Zone'."

"Sounds like a great show," Reynolds said. "Are they completely interactive?"

"I believe so . . . these are the ship's actual logs and recordings, enhanced with the cooperation of Captain Kirk. Or was he an admiral when he made these? Of course, then he regained his captaincy—well, I've lost track. Thank you, Captain. I'll try to stay out of your way."

Reynolds shrugged. "If we can do anything for you, just say so. Not that there's much more than you can actually see—"

"Are you completely provisioned?" Picard asked. "Your fuel and everything taken care of?"

"Starfleet took care of everything. I think my crew's in

shock. We never had it so good. Starfleet even stocked up our cleaning supplies and recharged our replicators. They even made repairs on our hull. We'll get spoiled if we don't end up dead."

The statement was a casual one, and Captain Reynolds was a good sport—and pretty gutsy to take this ship out in space, never mind Cardassian space, for indeed a real danger existed from Cardassian border patrols. The Cardassians didn't like surprises. Or demands, for that matter.

"As soon as you encounter one of the Cardassian navigational beacons, notify me," Picard said. "I'll leave it up to you which course to take into their area. Do what you need to do for the safety of your ship." He flipped through the cartridges and read some of the mission titles. "If it takes a few more hours . . . so be it."

Year 2266—Bridge of the *U.S.S. Enterprise* (Holographic Simulation)

"Out—Outpost 4 . . . do you read me, Enterprise. *This is Commander Hansen . . ."*

"Kirk here. We're minutes away, Hansen. What's your status?"

"Outposts 2, 3, and 8 are gone . . . unknown weapon . . . completely destroyed . . . even though we were alerted . . . had our deflector shield on maximum . . . hit by enormous power. First attack blew our deflector shield . . . if they hit us again with our deflector shield gone . . . do you read me, Enterprise?"

"Confirm what hit you, Hansen. What vessel? Identity?"

"Space vessel . . . only glimpse of . . ."

"Can you locate the intruder for us?"

"Negative . . . it seems to have . . . disappeared somehow . . . I have you on my screen now . . . switching to visual . . ."

The poor man's voice was a rag. His back was to the screen, and all around his wavering figure was the wreckage of a bombed-out room. Bodies of green and gray smoke boiled from several spots, and from other spots open flame tangled the hot air. The color was faded, probably from burned connections in the visual broadcast system.

"Enterprise, *can you see it? My command post here . . . we're a mile deep on an asteroid . . . almost solid iron . . . and even through our deflectors it did this. Can you see!"*

"Affirmative, you're visual, Hansen. What do you have on the intruder?"

"No identification. No answer to our challenge . . . only a glimpse of . . . then it fired something at us, some form of high-energy plasma—fantastic power! And then the whole vessel disappeared. But it's out there somewhere . . . our sensors show that much . . . Enterprise—*something coming at our view-screen . . . coming at us fast!"*

"Lock us onto your screen."

"Switching . . ."

Standing beside Captain James T. Kirk on the bridge of his ship, Jean-Luc Picard was awash in nostalgia and until now had been watching the drama as if it were only that. He only half noted what was going on, at least until the screen came on and Commander Hansen's burned face gripped him. Hansen was injured, gasping, probably suffocating from the acrid smoke and the flames eating up his oxygen.

Unlike a holonovel, this incident was real. It had happened. And it was being replayed here before him, as identical to reality as modern technology—and the participation of its primary player in later life—allowed. And that was considerable.

On the forward screen, now that Commander Hansen had switched views, was a matte of star-studded space. Then, at the top center, a chalky form appeared, like wings without a body, two pods of some sort on the ends of the wings. That was about it. Just a gash in space.

It came gradually into being, out of nowhere.

"A cloaking device," Picard muttered. He snapped his mental fingers. "Oh, of course—*that* incident!"

James Kirk ignored him. Everyone did. He hadn't asked a direct question.

There was a film of sweat now glazing James Kirk's strong cheekbones. Standing on his other side from Picard was the now-youthful Captain Spock. *Mister* Spock, the first Vulcan in Starfleet, officer of the starship under its first captain, Christopher Pike, and first officer to James T. Kirk. Spock's face was younger now, his features crisply framed by his charcoal helmet of hair and his Yule-blue tunic. Spock was quite different in almost every way from his boiling-under-the-surface captain, Picard noticed. Even Kirk's topaz tunic seemed to fit him in a way that Spock's would never quite fit him, and Picard could never in a century imagine Jim Kirk in blue.

Especially not looking at him now, he thought, but didn't speak. He was more fascinated by the silent conversation occuring right next to him. There was tremendous communication going on between Kirk and Spock right now. They watched the screen together, and once in a while, very specifically, they would meet each other's eyes as if to confirm that they were thinking the same things.

Kirk's brow slightly tucked, a clear worry behind the flame in his eyes. Those famous hazel eyes—Picard recognized them as if he'd known James Kirk in these younger days. Everyone in Starfleet knew that face, those eyes. And that empathy, that pain at having had to watch Hansen die, how much of that had been ignored by history? Picard had smirked sometimes at the somewhat burlesque hindsight turned toward James Kirk's activities. This young captain was often the subject of academy jokes and spoofs.

No one would spoof him if they were here watching today. No one with any circumspection of soul could possibly take lightly the young captain's misery, the weight of responsibility he obviously felt right now. He was clearly out of range, yet he still felt responsible.

Desperation voiced itself again over the crackling comm.

"Can you see it, Enterprise? *Can you see it? Becoming visible in the center of my screen!"*

"Do you have phaser capacity?" Kirk demanded edgily. "We're still out of range."

"Negative," Hansen mourned, *"phasers gone, weapons crew dead."*

Kirk turned his head to speak over his right shoulder to his communications officer, but Picard noticed the young captain never took his eyes off that ship. "Make challenge! Warn that ship off!"

"Trying to, sir," his communications officer said. "They don't acknowledge."

The ship on the screen fired, but not a weapon Picard recognized. A plasma cloud boiled toward them, a gluey see-through salmon mass, almost pretty if one didn't know what it could do. Like the business end of an avalanche the plasma cloud rolled toward the screen. And it was *fast*—

A loud thrum blew from the forward screen's audio system. The screen switched back to a view of the command center as the systems began to break down under fire. Now they could see the pathetic, brave Hansen as he suddenly arched back in a supercharged convulsion. His hands clawed in agony, his mouth gaped toward the ceiling. He was quite aware of his own last moments, and Picard grimaced to see it.

BOOM—BOOM—BOOM—BOOM—successive surges of energy blew through Hansen's body, through the whole command center, through the whole asteroid. The noise was like a kettledrum without a damper.

The whole bridge crew, and Picard too, winced at the pain suddenly in their eyes, as the bright destruction bloomed across the entire screen, a hurtful white light of plasma reaction. James Kirk shielded his face with his right hand, and his sedate first officer was driven to flinch and blink at his side.

Picard actually looked away briefly. No point going blind, was there?

As he turned away, his gaze fell upon James Kirk, on James Kirk's sorrowful eyes, and Picard noticed the depth of sadness, of worry. In just those short seconds of conversation, Kirk had invested in a relationship with Commander Hansen. Interesting—the young captain's intense empathy with other people was palpable right now, apparently even with people he didn't know.

Commendable. I didn't know that about him.

And in that moment, Picard took a chance to appreciate where he was standing—a scrupulously detailed representation of the bridge aboard the first starship named *Enterprise*. A charmed place, rather like the secure milk-and-honey childhood dream everyone had in common, a cloud-woven place everyone recognized. This was the quixotic beginning of Starfleet's reach out into deep space, the Federation's first great manifestation of farsight, and this ship its first deep-space anticipator.

And it was a pleasant looking place as well, tidy and rather simple, slate-blue and black work areas racing-striped with bright Starfleet-red.

Now Mr. Spock moved away from the captain and quickly took his seat at the science console to confirm the terrible facts they all knew already.

"Outpost 4," he began, then turned to look at Kirk meaningfully, "disintegrated, Captain."

Spock seemed deeply affected—and Picard had been long ago conditioned not to expect that from a Vulcan. But Spock was not your garden-variety Vulcan. He was less laconic, less stiff than one might've expected, and moved and spoke with straightforward fluidity and intimacy that was a surprise.

And these were those old days, the earliest days of the *Enterprise*'s missions under James Kirk. The ship would be ten or eleven years old, if Picard recalled correctly, relatively young in the tenure of a vessel.

Shadows lay dry-brushed across James Kirk's smooth face. He was a stylish young man, Picard noticed, with a powerful presence that drew all eyes when he was in the vicinity. Now Kirk moved toward Spock and placed both hands upon the red rail between them.

"Position of the intruder, Mr. Spock?" he asked.

Such a quiet voice! One always expected a hero to project like somebody on a stage. Kirk wasn't doing that.

"Disappeared," Spock said. "Interesting how they became visible for just a moment."

Excellent diction.

"When they opened fire," Kirk murmured. "Perhaps necessary when they use their weapons."

The captain had shifted roles that instantly—no, not shifted. He was still mourning. But he had also embraced the needs of the new moment.

"Have a blip on the motion sensor, Captain," Spock said then. "Could be the intruder."

Kirk turned forward. "Go to full magnification."

The helmsman said, "Screen is on full mag, sir."

That voice—

"Captain Sulu!" Picard looked at the helmsman. "Of course . . . I'd completely forgotten—"

"I don't see anything," Kirk said, evil-eyeing the main screen. He climbed up the short steps to the upper deck, leaned back on the rail, and put a foot up on the stand of Spock's chair. "Can't understand it."

Evidently Spock took that as a question. "Invisibility is theoretically possible, Captain. Selective bending of light, but the power cost is enormous. They may have solved that problem."

"Continuing to challenge, sir," the communications officer said. "Still no response."

"Discontinue. Contact remaining outposts, have them signal us, any sightings or sensor readings in their area."

"Yes, sir."

"Blip has changed its heading, Captain . . . and in a very leisurely maneuver. He may be unaware of us."

"Their invisibility screen may work both ways. With that kind of power consumption, they may not be *able* to see us."

"His heading is now one-eleven . . . mark fourteen." Spock dropped off the reading, then turned once again to communi-

cate with Jim Kirk in that personal way they had. "The exact
heading a Romulan vessel would take, Jim . . . toward the
Neutral Zone. And home."

Home. So much meaning in a single word, and Spock had
put all that substance into his tone, into his eyes as he
connected with his captain's, and the two continued to communicate after the words were done.

Picard paused in brief appreciation. Such a charming moment, a pivotal point in Starfleet history. He took an instant to
glance around and enjoy the streamlined console desks in
glossy black, with brightly colored knob-lights and buttons for
easy identification, the rugged swivel seats, gleaming monitors
at eye-level on the upper deck, the forward screen that seemed
small compared to what he was used to, yet somehow still
dominated the bridge . . . nostalgia was a universal comfort,
and Picard found himself grinning in spite of the tense action
around him. What a nice place to be, right in the middle of a
myth. If he could only stay—

But he couldn't. He had only as long as it took to get to
Cardassian space. Then this rescue mission would require his
personal vigilance.

Riker was smart, though. These holotapes not only would
sweep Picard into confronting some of his own thoughts about
command, but would keep a senior captain out of the hair of
Reynolds and his crew, which could only be to the good.
Having a Starfleet officer aboard and looking over their shoulders could be slightly terrifying to a private crew, who knew
their jobs perfectly well otherwise. Picard was better serving
himself and them too by doing Riker's evil bidding.

On the starboard side, Kirk had given a helm order and
come down to the command deck, and Picard wasn't really
paying attention. His mind was still in other places.

"Don't you mean interception course, sir?"

"Negative." Kirk moved to the forward side of the helm,
faced the two men stationed there, and spoke to the navigator.
"You and Mr. Sulu will match course and speed with the object
on our sensors move for move. If he has sensors, I want him to

think that we're a reflection . . . an echo. Under no circumstances are you to cross into the Neutral Zone without my direct orders."

"Acknowledged, sir," Sulu said.

"Cancel battlestations, all decks standby alert."

Picard followed the captain around the helm. "If I recall, this is when the hunt begins, doesn't it?"

"Yes," Kirk said as he settled into his command chair. "The game from now on is dangerous. Every move we make will be a critical one."

"An act of war, actually," Picard corrected.

"The act of war has already happened." Kirk gripped the arms of his command chair and eyed the screen, though there was nothing to see yet but stars. He pointed at the great emptiness which held a lurking enemy. "He made it. That moment's past."

The holodeck program completely accepted Picard's presence, without admitting him in as a "character" in the drama of a situation where he did not belong. He was an observer here. This was an instructional historical program, not a game or toy, not meant at all for recreation.

In fact, the navigator had turned to address the captain, but now the program circumvented that. Picard had asked a question. Now, all the active members of the show would find something to do until Kirk's part of the program was ready to push on.

Strange. If Kirk "liked" talking to Picard, the computer would just let him keep doing it. Yet somehow the programming would sense when it was time to move to the next step. Ingenious. Nothing short of brilliant. Not the machine—the people who had invented it.

"Are you saying you're at war?" Picard asked him. "That's your attitude?"

"Not yet," Kirk said, raising his brows. "But we're not at peace either. Commander Hansen and his people wouldn't want us to pretend nothing happened. And I'm not going to."

"You're running a parallel heading with the blip?"

"That's right."

"What if they go into the Neutral Zone?"

"I haven't decided."

"You mean you may actually consider following them in?"

"I'm already considering it."

"Really . . ."

For the first time Kirk turned his head very slightly and eyed Picard with that forceful leer. "You'd do something else?"

"Once they cross back into the Neutral Zone," Picard said, "in my time we would let diplomats handle such things. They're headed back into their own territory. Why don't you let the Federation handle this? Perhaps it's a rogue. You don't know whether this action is sanctioned by the Romulan government."

"Sanctioned or not, they're responsible." Kirk pointed at the screen. "No 'rogue' developed that plasma weapon on his own. That takes infrastructure."

"Perhaps it's not even a Romulan. You're assuming."

Kirk seemed unmoved, even nettled by the suggestion. There was only the slightest tensing of his shoulder muscles beneath the gold tunic. "It's a Romulan ship, near Romulan space, slaughtering Federation outposts in an area where the Romulans once staged a protracted war against us. If you don't like assumptions, get another job."

"How do you know what their real intents are?"

Eyeing him fiercely, as if Picard were really annoying him, Kirk leaned toward him and drawled, "Am I supposed to wait for *another* declaration of intent?"

It was a good point. Picard offered an eyebrow shrug and accepted that. Four outposts violently demolished. Couldn't be ignored.

As if tiring of that line of talk, Jim Kirk got up and prowled the command area, rarely looking at anything but the screen. The soft sorrow of those moments with Hansen was completely sweated out of him now. He was hardened, or more properly he was hardening, preparing himself for what he thought might be coming.

"The Romulan government has been the silent body," he said. "They're the ones who haven't made their philosophies clear. They're the ones who haven't stated their goals outright. If they let a rogue get through, they have to bear the responsibility for their silence. If there's a war, they've brought it on themselves."

"I understand."

"But you don't agree?"

"I'm not sure yet. I don't think you are either."

"That's for me to know," Kirk said, "and *them* to find out."

He sighted-down the screen, and in some way seemed able to see that invisible enemy out there. Picard noticed Kirk trying to project his whole mind out there into that ship, that bridge, to hear what was being said and thought. The hunger to be out there was interesting—Kirk was quite a provocateur. He was anxious to get on with activities he would rather not have happen.

Well, Picard recognized that kind of paradox, but for himself he'd never been quite as forward-leaning about it as Kirk appeared right now.

"Phaser overload! Control-circuit burnout."

Helmsman Sulu's voice cut through the brief pause between Picard and Kirk, but Kirk already had his hands on the helm controls between Sulu and the navigator and Spock was also working the controls.

Picard scanned his memory about ships' systems in these days. The phaser guidance and aiming systems were here on the bridge, but actual power-up and firing controls were somewhere below, though he couldn't recall just where. A team of phaser specialists were required to operate the complex engineering that controled the gathering and release of such fantastic destructive power. These were the days shortly before such things could be automated and controled directly from the bridge. Reaction time, firing time, therefore, was slower and required a series of relayed orders. Those seconds were critical.

Now they'd had an overload. Phasers were down. Did they

have photon torpedoes at this time? Picard wasn't sure—no, no, they didn't. Those came a little later than the beginning of James Kirk's captaincy. Yes, that was right.

Spock rolled to the deck and opened a smoking access trunk, waving the smoke, batting out the tiny flame in there. He surveyed the damage. "It'll take time to correct, sir," he called over the crackle.

"Captain, are they surrendering?" Sulu blurted suddenly.

Everyone turned to the forward screen. The mystery ship was appearing out of the night, heading directly at them in exactly the same manner as it has come toward Outpost 4 during those last horrid moments.

Abruptly tense, Kirk angled back and leaned one thigh on his command chair and pressed the shipwide comm with his wrist. "Full astern!" he ordered. "Emergency warp speed!"

The ship hummed with response, trying to go to warp speed faster than was comfortable. A flower of energy bloomed from the enemy ship; then the ship disappeared and there was only the widening floret of destructive energy. Sick-pink and rolling, the discharge raced toward them, just as the same sight had come at Outpost 4, seconds before unthinkable devastation wiped the outpost from the face of space.

"Do we have emergency warp?" Kirk demanded.

"Full power, sir," Sulu confirmed. "It's still overtaking us."

They worked for more speed, but warp engines could only do so much, so suddenly.

"If we can get one phaser working, sir," Sulu wished. "One shot would detonate it."

Kirk stood between them. "Navigation?"

"Estimate it'll overtake us in two minutes, sir," the navigator responded.

"Phasers, Mr. Spock."

From the deck, Spock's sharp answer left no doubts. *"Impossible,* Captain."

"How did he know you were here?" Picard asked.

"See that comet?" Kirk said, pointing at a hazy streak in the night. "When he went through its tail, we thought we'd pick up a residual trail and be able to pinpoint his location. But he guessed my move and countered it. I had to give up my hiding place and lay down a blind firing pattern and hope to knock him down."

"There's your act of war," Picard said, holding out a hand. "You took the first shot. Now he can claim he's defending himself."

"I don't care what he claims. The Romulans have never offered so much as a finger of friendship. No hope for the future. No remorse for the past. Until they offer that, or at least start making noises about it, they don't deserve the benefits of ours."

"Ten seconds to impact," Sulu said.

On the screen, the pink rolling nosegay began to thin in the middle, becoming like a ring of smoke puffed from the lips of a cigar aficionado. Picard noticed it instantly and muttered, "It's losing integrity. Sacrificing for its own speed."

"Captain," Sulu called then, "dissipating, sir!"

The navigator hopefully agreed, "It must have a range limit!"

Sulu divided his attention between the screen and his readouts. "Five . . . four . . . three . . . two . . . one . . . impact!"

The deadly pink blob filled the screen, and suddenly the ship was rocked hard. Luckily, they were already full astern and the impact drove them farther along their own path, so that helped absorb some of the force. Had they been heading forward, into the cloud—

Kirk and the female yeoman standing with him were pitched starboard into the rail, but already Kirk was assessing what had just happened.

A tenor of victory rang in his voice. "Limited range . . ."

Glossy light from the dissipating energy lay harshly upon his face. Now he knew something concrete about his enemy. Picard smiled at Kirk's quiet appreciation. Kirk had begun the process of gathering bits of information about his enemy for which he would later become so famous.

"How are you going to use that knowledge?" Picard asked.

"I don't know yet." Kirk pushed off the rail and moved back to his command chair. After a glance around at his crew to make sure everyone was all right, he settled into the seat. "But it's a lesson. If the phasers hadn't overloaded, we'd have detonated it before it hit us, but also before we could see that it had limited range. Even out of our bad luck I learned something."

"Phasers operational, Captain." Spock shut the access trunk, got to his feet, and clicked into his sensor readouts. He bent forward and gazed into a small desktop monitor hood. "Intruder bearing . . . one-eleven mark fourteen."

As Kirk sat in his command chair, the soft red lights from the ceiling casting a deceptively warm glow upon his shoulders and his sandy hair. "Back to his old course."

"He may think we're destroyed, Captain."

"I wouldn't make that assumption. I don't think their captain will either."

"So something's changed," Picard noted. "You're thinking differently about him than you were before."

"I underestimated him. Then he outmaneuvered me by doing something I'd have done. I won't make that mistake again."

Picard leaned back on the ship's rail and smiled warmly. "You know, I can't get over how soft your voice is at times. That's simply not the image of you that we generally have. Legend has given you rather a Lord Nelsonish bearing, as if you were that way at every moment. You're rather a quiet fellow in reality, aren't you?"

Kirk shrugged. "If you're always speaking up, you can't hear yourself think."

Picard stepped aside as another science-division officer of command rank appeared from the turbolift and came down to the captain's side.

"Medical report, Captain," the man said. "Damage caused a radiation leak on two decks, both under control. Casualties are minimal, but there are some serious burns."

"Thank you, Doctor." Kirk was obviously distracted and didn't seem to give that another thought. The matter was being taken care of.

Doctor McCoy, of course. Leonard McCoy. Picard nodded at himself. He'd even met Doctor McCoy once, many years later than this particular moment. How charming it was to see him and Kirk together like this!

Yet—there was some kind of tension between them, Picard realized. The way they looked at each other. Or rather, the way McCoy looked at Kirk and the way Kirk *wouldn't* look back. Kirk's eyes were fixed again on the forward screen. It seemed he was determined not to be surprised again, as if he could see something faster than the ship's long-range sensors could.

The Romulan ship was once again cloaked, and now the enemy knew there was definitely another ship out here.

"We'll enter the Neutral Zone in one minute, sir," the navigator spoke up.

"Do we violate the treaty, Captain?" McCoy instantly asked.

"They did, Doctor," Spock declared as he came up behind Kirk and McCoy. He seemed unashamedly hostile.

And nobody seemed surprised, either. Did this instant electricity go on all the time?

Picard was suddenly aware of a power play of physical positioning. The captain in his chair, looking forward, thinking about a dozen things at once, the doctor at his side, both hands on the command chair's arm, and Spock behind them like a haunting conscience.

How poignant, the crackling energy among these three men. The captain let his officers do the arguing, yet he was still the center of attention.

"Once inside, they can claim we did," McCoy said. "A setup. They want war, we furnish the provocation."

"We're still on our side, Captain," Spock stated.

Kirk didn't like what he was about to say, but there was no hesitation when he said it.

"Let's get them while we are. Before we enter the Neutral Zone. Full ahead, Mr. Stiles, maximum warp."

McCoy now left the captain's side, and Spock stepped down to replace him. The body language was clear—Spock had prevailed in his relentless belief that aggression was today's way. Clearly that hadn't been what McCoy wanted. Spock had prevailed, and now took the coveted place at the captain's side.

Somehow they all silently just did that, and Picard got the feeling the conversation was still going on in McCoy's and Spock's minds. There was lots of dialogue happening on this bridge, most of it without words.

"Phasers stand by," Kirk said as the warp engines thrummed through the ship.

"Sir, at this distance?" the navigator asked without turning.

"We know their Achilles's heel, Mr. Stiles. Their weapon takes all their energy. They must become visible in order to launch it."

"A phaser hit at this distance would be the wildest stroke of luck!"

"I'm aware of that, Mr. Stiles. Are phasers ready?"

"Phasers show ready, sir."

"Fire."

Picard stepped forward. "You're shooting at them? Wouldn't it be better to attempt heading them off? Notify Starfleet to send assistance?"

"A starship has to assume it won't have assistance," Kirk said. "We *are* the assistance. Besides, contact with the nearest command base requires three hours of communication time. We don't have it."

"Oh, yes," Picard chided himself. "You don't have warp communications yet, do you?"

"Not until twelve years from now," Kirk tossed off, just for an instant showing that the holodeck computer wasn't entirely perfect in its representation of the past.

The little bit of computer intrusion made Picard grin briefly. "There might be more advantage to restraint at this point, don't you think?"

Stabbing him with a glare, Kirk seemed to take that as a challenge—which, actually, it was. "Rather than risking a definitive action, you want me to show ourselves to be weak? Risking millions of lives instead of hundreds?"

"I'm asking a much more simple question, Captain," Picard persisted. "Who are you to start a war with the Romulans?"

Blistered by that, Kirk squinted at him without the slightest bit of shame. His lips purposefully tightened. "I'm the captain of the flagship of Starfleet. The line must be drawn *here*. This ship is here not only as an instrument of defense, but as a symbol of strength. And determination, and integrity. It's a symbol that we'll stand that line."

Picard was at once impressed and amused by Captain Kirk's unshakable sense of identity. For Picard himself, in life there had been many uncertainties about his own destiny, about how best to spend the small click of years allotted to each human being. Should he be a scientist? Should he go into archaeology? Might he pursue music . . . the plague of a man with a bit of talent in each of many areas. Everyone who had known him in his life, he recalled, had expected him to do something different than had the others who knew him. Command had been the ironic culmination of a bunch of little accidents and unexpected turns.

Kirk's next question jolted him out of his self-involvement. "What do you think are the chances the Federation might launch an unprovoked attack on the Romulan Star Empire?"

Picard shook his head. "None."

"Zero," Kirk confirmed. "Never happen. Can the same be said for the Romulans?"

Looking at the forward screen, Picard sighed. "Obviously not."

Satisfied, Kirk kept his eyes on the screen. He seemed always to be prowling his enemy, always thinking, always anticipating, always trying to figure out what maneuver that other captain might make.

"Twenty seconds to Neutral Zone, sir," Stiles reported.

"It's not that I disagree," Picard offered, forgetting for an instant that this was something other than real. "I'd like to know your thought processes . . . why and when you made up your mind to do what you did. Are you like me? Did you ever wonder whether you were risking your ship for nothing? Should you turn tail and warn the Federation? As alone as you were in deep space in those days, how did you know when to take risks?"

"There is no risk-free maneuver," Kirk said, as if that were some kind of answer. "I don't get to choose between a right and a wrong. I have to choose between a wrong and a wrong. That's my job."

"Yes," Picard agreed, "but your approach has a certain ruggedness. How are you going to do it?"

"I'll show you." Sad resolve spirited the captain's eyes as he said, "Lieutenant Uhura, inform command base, in my opinion no option . . . on my responsibility, we are proceeding into the Neutral Zone."

CHAPTER 16

Well, there it was.

Picard held back any comment and simply watched. He hadn't remembered that part of the tale—that Kirk had actually broached the Neutral Zone without authority, without sixteen different possible plans, without mapping out every other option. He'd chosen, he'd acted on that choice.

"Steady as we go, Mr. Sulu," Kirk quietly said. "Continue firing."

On the screen, phaser bolts flashed through space on a blanketing pattern. Were they slashing the invisible enemy? Was he being rocked by those bolts? Was he faltering, or was he slightly beyond range? There was no way to tell.

Picard watched James Kirk, empathizing with those questions, those doubts.

"You seem so young to shoulder such burdens," Picard granted, and was slightly put back by the regret in his voice. In fact, he hadn't meant to speak aloud at all.

"Motion sensor signal's stopped," Spock reported, bent over his sensor hood.

"Cease fire."

"Debris scattering ahead, sir!" Sulu called. "We've hit him!"

"Mr. Spock?"

Spock squinted into the hood. "Vessel wreckage . . . metal molds, conduit, plastiform . . . and a body, Captain . . . however—"

"One body?" Picard spoke up. "Then it's a trick."

Kirk stood up abruptly at this sudden humanization of their acts. "However?"

"Insufficient mass, sir," Spock said.

"What?"

"Simple debris. Not a vessel. A trick."

"Go to sensor probes."

"Nothing, sir. No motion out there at all." Spock twisted to gaze at Kirk in that way they had. "We've lost them, Captain."

The terrible fact sunk in. They knew the enemy wasn't destroyed, wasn't even gone, but was hiding.

"All stop, quickly," Kirk snapped. "Shut down all systems. Rig for silence, all stations. Tell everyone on the lower decks to shut down and sit down. Avoid movement. Don't touch anything. Nothing's as important as silence. Go ahead."

"Aye, sir," Lieutenant Uhura acknowledged, and turned to relay the odd order.

"Everyone take a deep breath," Kirk said. "This could take hours."

"Captain's log, stardate 1709.6. We are at the Neutral Zone. Have lost contact with the intruder. No reaction on our motion sensors, but believe the Romulan vessel to be somewhere close by, with all engines and systems shut down. The *Enterprise* is also playing the silent waiting game in hope of regaining contact. Now motionless for nine hours, forty-seven minutes . . ."

James Kirk sat in his quarters, alone, recording his log entry. His voice was heavy, murmuring, overburdened.

Jean-Luc Picard sat on the opposite side of the compact area, much smaller than his own captain's quarters had ever been, and watched the young Kirk shift on the edge of his dilemma.

"You doubt your own actions, don't you?" Picard asked when the captain paused in his log entry. "Here we sit, on the edge of the Neutral Zone, as if you can *bend* a treaty without breaking it. What were you thinking?"

Before Kirk could answer, if he was even going to, the door slid open and Leonard McCoy strode boldly in, without beeping for permission. Kirk didn't seem to mind.

"I thought you'd be down here, Captain," McCoy said. "When they told me you'd left the bridge under these conditions, I didn't believe it."

"It's better for the crew," Kirk told him. "They already feel as if they're wearing anchors. Nine hours . . . why doesn't he move?"

"Maybe he's not out there at all," the doctor offered, leaning back against the doorframe. "Maybe you've destroyed him without even knowing it. Or he might've gotten away. In which case, Captain, we're sitting here in violation of the treaty."

James T. Kirk, the legendary rakehell of Starfleet, the man most revered and also most mocked by cadets, the shipmaster's shipmaster, now sat here in a puddle of sorrow, looking about as spirited as a wet rug. Anyone who thought James Kirk could not be wearied, would never be parried by turbulence, had never seen him like this. For Picard this was a kind of revelation. The man was simply completely different than he had been on the bridge.

Kirk's airbrushed brows were flat now, drawn. His eyes were rounded with hurt, not at all like the slim weapons they had been on the bridge. As Picard watched, he saw before him a man who was his own tragic flaw.

"Why me . . ." the young captain murmured. He looked up beseechingly at Doctor McCoy. "I look around that bridge . . . and I see the men are waiting for me to make the next move . . . and, Bones . . . what if I'm wrong?"

Silence dropped instantly over those words like a muffler, for there was no good answer, certainly no right one.

Boxed in, McCoy licked his lips and began, "Captain, I—"

Kirk stood up abruptly. "No—I don't really expect an answer."

But the doctor caught him by the shoulder as Kirk tried to slip past. "Well, I've got one. Something I rarely say to a 'customer,' Jim. In this galaxy, there's a mathematical probability of three million Earth-type planets. In all the universe, three million million galaxies like this. And in all of that, and perhaps more, only one of each of us."

Now the doctor turned his head but didn't quite look directly at his captain.

"Don't destroy the one named 'Kirk,'" he added solemnly.

In silent appreciation, Kirk did not answer. He gave a small grin of thanks, slipped out from under the doctor's hand, and disappeared into the corridor.

Even though Kirk had gone, Picard remained here in the captain's quarters, and found himself gazing thoughtfully at McCoy. The ship's surgeon didn't leave right away, but instead leaned on the doorframe another few moments, seeming to wish there'd been a better thing to say. His expression was still troubled, though he'd done all he could be expected to do under the circumstances. There really wasn't an answer.

"I wonder what you meant by that," Picard said, stepping to the doctor's side, in almost the same spot Kirk had stood. "Did you mean 'destroy' as in not letting himself be killed? No, there must be more to it. You must mean destroying his inner resolve with those doubts. That's what I would've meant if I'd said that to him at this moment . . ."

Leonard McCoy made no response, no acknowledgement that Picard was here. He merely gazed at nothing, his eyes full of regret that he had no bandages for the soul. Of course, Leonard McCoy hadn't participated in the creation of these holodeck programs, so no one knew his particular thoughts. That was just as well—something had to be left to the imagination, didn't it?

McCoy sighed, almost as though agreeing, blinked sadly,

looked at the deck carpet, then pushed off the wall and turned out of the quarters.

Picard almost sat down, almost stayed here, as if he instead of Kirk were the captain today. Strange how at home he felt here. Very strange. Was there another universe somewhere? Were there Cardassians and MIA's and Rikers and Datas? Somewhere, but not just here, not just now.

"Computer," he said, "take me to the bridge."

"Power on. Reverse course. He'll try to slip under us."

"Lateral power, sir."

"Coming around, sir."

"Phasers . . . fire!"

Silent standby was over. Systems were back on, once again cooking. The bridge was electric with tension. The whine of phasers surging through the starship's shaken body made a wincing kind of noise. Were they hitting anything?

Kirk was betting they were. Picard was making the same bet. Blanketed phasers like that were much the same as dropping depth charges. The very fabric of space would communicate a jolt, even if the hits were not direct ones.

"Debris on our scanners." Spock's voice cut through the phaser backwhine.

"Analysis, quickly."

"Same type as before, sir . . . except . . . one metal-cased object!"

"Helm, hard over! Phasers, fire pointblank!"

A phaser whined, and at almost the same instant there was a ghastly eruption dead ahead, point-blank range. The reaction was so instant, so gut-level that Picard was momentarily surprised. Kirk obviously knew something about sneakiness, or at least he was making good on his collection of data about his enemy's methods.

The ship lurched hard over, throwing Picard hip-first against the starboard rail. Holodeck or not, that hurt. The whole ship rocked and shuddered, then hung at an angle against her own artificial gravity. Kirk was thrown back from the forward rail onto the helm console, and both helm officers were pitched from their seats. Spock disappeared entirely into a shadow, and two engineers ended up on the command deck.

Picard found himself suddenly trying to push off the rail onto a tilted deck. He felt the tug of pressure as the graviton chambers struggled to compensate against the damage. Nausea boiled up in his stomach—well, it'd been a while since he'd felt *that*—

"They dropped a concussion device into the debris," he observed, watching Kirk and his crew try to collect themselves. "How utterly primitive! Obviously effective, though . . . " He looked at Kirk, who was pulling the navigator to his feet. "I'm surprised you didn't think of it."

"I did," Kirk muttered. "Right after it happened."

Half the lights were out on the bridge, leaving large areas in shadow. Mr. Spock came slowly to his feet, favoring one knee, and his face was bracketed with pain he probably would've denied. "Main junction shutdown, Captain. Compensators coming on line."

In fact, the whole crew was crawling back to their posts and instantly rushing to put everything back in some order, but that would take a while. Picard could actually smell what was wrong—detect little burnouts here and there, with distinct scents of different grades of lubricant and circuitry. He did an automatic scent-diagnostic in his own mind and suddenly it was no surprise that the bridge was half in darkness.

In deference to his bad knee, Spock sat down and touched his controls.

"Captain to sickbay."

"McCoy here."

"Casualties?"

"Twenty-two so far. Mainly radiation burns, mostly from the ship's outer areas. Could've been much, much worse, Captain."

"Thank you, Doctor."

Click—and most of the bridge lights came back on. Not all

of them, and some that came on were red emergency maintenance lights instead of the regular lights of day work. But they
certainly helped.

Other systems hummed to life too, evidence of an unseen
but hardworking crew below decks.

Glancing around, Picard sympathized with the shaken crew
and their young overburdened captain. And he was glad that
McCoy had offered that little gift of telling Kirk things could
be worse, after needling him that he should turn back and not
face the Romulans down.

Sitting there in a leftover panel of shadow, Kirk tensely
looked up at the starboard science console. "Report, Mr.
Spock?"

Spock turned. "Nuclear device of some kind, sir. Our
phasers detonated it fewer than one hundred meters away."

"Ship damage?"

"Mainly overloads and circuit burnouts."

Kirk tapped the controls on his chair arm. "Weapons
status?"

"We've only the forward phaser room, Captain."

"Fully operative, Scotty?"

"Yes, sir. But specialist Tomlinson is manning it alone."

"Scotty," Picard murmured, smiling. "Captain Scott . . ."

Stiles swiveled around. "Sir, my first assignment was in
weapons control."

"Go," Kirk said. "Lieutenant Uhura, take over navigation."

Spock left his controls and came down from the upper decks,
then gripped the command chair as Kirk leaned toward him to
hear what he had to say. "We have engine power now, Captain,
if you'd like to move off and make repairs."

"No, no." Kirk looked weary. "Maybe we can pull him back
to our side of the Neutral Zone. Hold our position . . . play
dead."

As Spock moved off without response, in fact leaving the
bridge entirely to go belowdecks, Kirk took the moment to
wipe a hand across his sweat-glazed face. He was probably
exhausted, Picard realized. They all were. They hadn't had a

change of watch, evidently, in those nine hours. Not unusual, under emergency conditions. It was usually preferable to leave officers at the controls they were handling when trouble popped up, but this seemed a bit of an extreme.

Kirk sat at his command, a shadow lying passively across his right shoulder, his eyes in a band of light.

"Enemy vessel becoming visible, sir!" Sulu said then.

As quickly as that, everyone came back to life.

Kirk gripped his chair, ticking off seconds as the Romulan ship faded into clarity on the screen. "Forward phasers . . . stand by . . . fire."

But there was no response, no shots fired. Nothing—

"Fire!"

"What happened?" Picard asked. "Why don't your weapons fire?"

"Coolant-seal malfunction." Kirk shoved out of his seat. "Stiles, can you hear me? Fire! Fire! Stiles, can you hear me? Fire!"

"Phaser controls not on the bridge," Picard said "—I'd no idea it had been such damnable trouble! Haven't you got men in there?"

"Yes!" Kirk snapped. "Stiles and Tomlinson."

"They'll be poisoned."

"They were. One died. Spock's on his way there—Stiles! Do you hear me? Fire!"

Fweeee—the whine of phasers finally broke out. A flash in the darkness blew toward the enemy ship, and this time the *Enterprise* was first to score a hit. The other ship never had the chance to fire its plasma weapon.

Even at this distance they could see the Romulan ship quaking bodily as if someone had struck it with a big hammer.

The forward screen flickered, blurred, then sharpened. Picard found himself looking into the bridge of the mysterious enemy ship. It was a gray and pared-down place, spare and simple, with a control kiosk in the center of a completely shattered compartment. There, bent in agony over the kiosk, was a man in an old-style Romulan uniform. Huddled in obvious pain, he gradually pushed himself up, now allowing Picard to notice the rank insignia. A full commander.

The Romulan commander was clearly injured and struggling just to breathe in the smoke-clouded bridge. His dead crew lay around him or hung over their sparking, snapping controls, dying in the poisoned smoke. One of the bodies twitched, and the sight was disturbing.

Only the commander moved now. Picard felt his own chest tighten in empathy for the destroyed man over there who was trying to breathe in that poisoned compartment.

For a moment Picard watched Kirk, expecting him to say something, but Kirk didn't. He simply sat in his chair, his legs crossed, still cowled by a stripe of shadow, and gave his enemy the time he needed to see what was going on.

Gasping, the Romulan struggled across his demolished bridge, hardly a step or two, grasped a support beam just above the viewing mechanism, then paused—he could see them now. He knew they could see him.

For the first time, the two commanders gazed into each other's eyes, each seeing the other. Kirk must've been something to gaze at for the first time.

Picard took a moment to appreciate that. Like George Washington's face, James Kirk's was known to everyone. Not so for this Romulan who had been so tightly engaged with Kirk for the past many hours, and had watched his important mission crushed by this unseen captain. Probably years upon years of preparation had been snuffed today.

And among those here, only Picard knew how very long it had taken the Romulan Star Empire to recover from this hard slap.

"Captain," Kirk said politely now. There wasn't a hint of gloating in his manner. If anything, he seemed nearly apologetic.

But he did not apologize, and that was important. Did not even voice his regret that this had to happen.

Whether he actually regretted it—Picard couldn't really tell.

"Standing by to beam your survivors on board our ship," Kirk said. "Prepare to abandon your vessel."

"He won't," Picard grumbled.

"No, it's not our way." Squeezed by the grip of pain, the Romulan's body flinched, but his eyes did not. He surveyed Kirk with disclosed warmth. "I regret that we meet in this way. You and I are of a kind . . . In a different reality, I could've called you friend."

With clear sorrow Kirk attempted to persuade the Romulan. "What purpose will it serve to die?"

"We are creatures of duty, Captain . . . I have lived my life by it. Just one more . . . duty to perform."

The Romulan took one more look at the man he wished he could call friend, then pushed away from the viewer and stumbled across the smashed deck.

Jim Kirk took a breath to argue, perhaps order a tractor beam or an emergency beam-out, perhaps to talk his enemy out of a useless end.

Then he held back. He closed his lips. Precious seconds drained away as the injured Romulan on the screen staggered to a control panel, made a small adjustment, and twisted a partially jammed handle.

A flash of energy wash, a grimace of pain, the crackle of overload—and the screen faded back to the mindless void of open space. Stars twinkled in the distance, as if nothing had happened here at all.

At first Picard almost spoke up—transporters could snatch those survivors off that ship . . . useless sacrifice . . .

And then, in an instant, he knew better. As if he'd been delivered a message by intravenous injection, he completely absorbed the depth of James Kirk's understanding of being a soldier. Anything Kirk might've said would have taken away that Romulan's last shred of pride.

Despite what Kirk had just done, he gave his enemy that little bit of advantage, a chance to control his last moments. Kirk had let him lose his life, but keep his pride. This

Romulan, who had murdered hundreds of Federation citizens, was being offered a civilized hand as a final gesture.

Strange—that hadn't been the image of James Kirk which had filtered forward in time. The tender side had never been given much due in history.

But Kirk remained silent, choosing not to diminish his enemy's last act.

"That was elegant of you," Picard mentioned, thinking aloud. "We hear about the valor, nobility, fighting talent, your ability to map a space battle in your head and always know where your ship and the other ships are . . . we know about your deeds of strength and your tricks, but until I stood here and watched you, I never knew about your mercy. You could have saved his life—"

"And wrecked his dignity." Kirk's tone was clear sadness, as if indeed he had lost something, someone. He wasn't proud of himself. He was genuinely sorrowful at what he had been forced to do.

Amazing, really. Had Kirk and that Romulan actually come to be some kind of friends in these tense hours while hunting each other through the empty tracts of space?

Could that happen?

Picard searched through his past to see if he'd ever had such an encounter, but couldn't think of one.

"Thank you, Captain," he said. "Thank you very much for this. I've seen things I never imagined. You don't have all the answers at all, and somehow, I suppose like many others, I had let myself become convinced that you did. While I was a little confused before, I can say that, now, I'm *completely* confused. At least now . . . I know I'm in good company. Computer . . . end the program."

CHAPTER 17

"Here is the plan. Bateson is coming to the Typhon Expanse with the new *Enterprise* for war games with a single Starfleet ship called the *Nora Andrew*. On both ships, shields and weapons will be reduced to bare minimum. That means we can take both ships."

"How do you know this?"

"Because I am still a commander in the Klingon fleet and I still have my resources."

"You are a dishonored liar."

"I am dishonored, but I am no liar. And while you stand aboard my vessel, I am your commander, not your father. You will treat me with respect while you are on my ship."

Until this moment, Gaylon had been trying to avoid eye contact with either Kozara or Zaidan, but now he turned to look. Zaidan had clamped his lips, obviously surprised by the calmness with which his father had made those statements.

Kozara was acting like another man from those minutes when Zaidan had come aboard. The commander now seemed to radiate confidence and planning. This change was mystifying even to Gaylon, who knew Kozara as well as anyone ever could.

The commander folded his hands before his chest and ran one thumb along the knuckles of the other hand. "The Klingon Empire has not lain idle during the ill-advised 'peace' with those people. We know how to take that ship."

"How will you and one miserable ship destroy the new *Enterprise?*"

"I do not mean to destroy it. I mean to possess it."

"Possess?"

Trying desperately to keep sense in this escapade, Gaylon stepped toward Kozara and asked, "But what if he will not engage you?"

"He will engage. He is an impatient youth." Kozara leaned forward and narrowed his eyes at the screen. "You cannot teach a young dog an old dog's tricks. But there are obstacles . . . there is an android assigned to that ship. Captain Picard's tin doll. We must be ready to incapacitate him, or he will single-handedly pull our heads off. I have researched this—the android runs on a positronic brain and neural network. We can neutralize that if we prepare."

"How do you know," Zaidan asked, "what he has in his head?"

"Because Starfleet is a friendly child. They keep no secrets. I accessed their library net, and there he was, with full diagnostics. They are too proud of him. That is one step of many. Plan . . . plan . . . we must have a plan for each step. We must hold back our advantage as long as possible. Listen to me, Gaylon."

Kozara broke his commune with the screen and grasped Gaylon by the sleeve so hard that it pinched his skin under the fabric.

"I have been in contact with the spy," Kozara said. "He is still with us."

Baffled, Gaylon came suddenly to life and demanded, "How could you contact him?"

"With my connections in the High Council. Though they would not meet my eyes, they had to listen to me. I was right— the contact was reactivated after Bateson came from the past. And here we are today, with advantages."

Kozara's son, who teetered on the brink of not being his son anymore, scowled with dripping contempt. "We have one great disadvantage. We have you. Something will go wrong. You will blunder somehow."

"I may blunder," Kozara spat back, "but at least I have made my *own* mark upon the empire and not clung to pity as my crutch. I worked ninety years in hard servility, I and all these around you. Shame can be struck away, or it can be worked away. Which have you done, Zaidan? Many have overcome worse obstacles than a gloryless father. There are other kinds of warriors than those with weapons. What have you done to deserve anything other than pity . . . my *son?* If nothing, then stand back, and watch real warriors work."

"Captain, you don't take a brand-new ship into a demilitarized zone near hostile space with reduced shields and weapons. You just don't. I'm sure you *won't.*"

"The *Nora Nicholas* is already in position, waiting to trapdoor us. The arrangements have all been made. It's all been worked out, on recommendations by Admiral Farrow and Admiral Hayes. They think, and I agree, that war games near the Neutral Zone will demonstrate to the Klingons that the Federation is not intimidated by their recent martial prancing."

"Taking a brand-new starship out is a complicated venture," Riker forcefully insisted. "Neither Admiral Farrow nor Hayes have ever done it. Respectfully remind the captain that you, sir, also have never done this."

"Neither have you."

As quickly as that the fragile truce between Riker and Bateson dissolved, and Riker felt suddenly cold on the inside.

"Sir," he forged on, "despite the handsome reports of all your department officers that the starship is ready for warp speed, there are ten thousand bugs that haven't been worked out. War games are inefficient methods for working out those bugs. We haven't even had her up to maximum warp yet. Even the hull bolts are untried. Doing this so close to the Klingon Neutral Zone at a time when there are hostilities with the Klingons—"

"I'm used to hostilities with the Klingons, remember?"

"Captain, that was ninety years ago!"

"Ninety-*three.*"

Abruptly defiant, Bateson's voice flared. Apparently, sensing he was about to be insulted, he was all done being gentle.

"That's all we ever had, was hostility," Bateson went on, now that they had everybody's attention, and that meant everybody including the squishy life-form sitting on the deck with its big black eyes blinking and tentacles around both of La Forge's legs. "What's so different?"

Riker deliberately leaned forward, knowing he was stepping over the line of decorum.

"What's different is that they've had ninety years to think about things you've missed. They're *different,* Captain, don't you realize that?"

"Klingons are Klingons," Bateson said. "They can't have changed that much."

Standing up now, Bateson met Riker's challenge head-on. From Riker's point of view, the captain stood bracketed by the presence on the upper deck of Montgomery Scott on one side and, ironically, Data on the other.

"You people have never fought Klingons," Bateson declared. "I have."

"Maybe not," Riker said, "but we have fought alongside them."

Unaffected, Bateson blinked at him. How could he be so blasted casual?

"Will, I don't care if your mother and two of your sisters are Klingons. Your ships are a little faster than ours were and a little tougher, but you've never really *fought* Klingons. You don't know what they're like to fight. I do. That's the first, best rule of any engagement. Know your enemy. *You* don't know them. *I* know them."

The resonance of the captain's voice carried with it a confidence that was both damnable and formidable. Riker at the moment could think of nothing to say. There was an irritating sense in what the captain said, and he was the only one who had actual events to back him up. He was the one who had stood off impossible Klingon odds in the past, though far past.

Cocking a hip, Bateson let the words ring, then lowered his chin and held out a flat hand.

"You want a shuttlecraft? You want to get off? You and your friends? There's the door."

The offer took Riker so utterly by surprise that it also put the argument into perspective—an argument about which there had not yet been an incident. Bateson, who remembered that, was keeping his temper and now had parried Riker into a corner.

Getting ready to box his way out, Riker settled back on his heels, took a deep breath, held it, and glanced at Troi and Geordi. Intensity of the moment traveled a psychic channel between them, and Troi reacted as if she'd been pinched. Her gaze attempted to express what lips failed to form. She and Geordi were holding their breaths too.

So were Scott and—well, Data would've held his if he'd had any.

"That's uncalled for, sir," Riker said. "This ship is brand-new and untried. We're about to tarnish her image before she even has a reputation."

Not bothered by the fact that he'd just deeply disturbed several of the officers on his bridge, Bateson speared Riker with a glare.

"Oh, well, Hell, commander, wouldn't want *that* to happen! Maybe it's too high a standard for you, but we'd better have people out here in these ships who believe in the ships. I don't want you here if you don't want to be here. You're grown-ups. Make a decision."

197

Very clear. He wasn't a by-the-book kind of man. They either accepted him for their captain or they didn't, and he apparently thought senior officers ought to be able to pick.

Or maybe he didn't, and he was just aware of the special circumstances of their being here. Riker couldn't really tell. Bateson obviously didn't want to start his command under a cloud of resentment—and, yes, he was right, they did resent him.

"That won't be necessary, sir," Riker assured. "May I respectfully recommend that shields not be reduced in power during the war games?"

"You may," Bateson said. "Scotty, please explain it to Mr. Riker."

Blinking out of his fascination with this flak, Scott said, "Shields have to be reduced in correlation with the reduction in phaser power, or else the sensors couldn't measure hull impact and record damage potential accurately."

"Thank you. Satisfied?"

Unfortunately . . . "Yes, sir."

"Very well. Now that we're finished dancing, let me explain the scenario of the war games. Everyone pay attention. The *Nora Nicholas* is a Starfleet fighter-class ship already dispatched to the Typhon Expanse, where as we damned well know there are plenty of places to hide. The mock confrontation is for us to hunt down and engage a border raider that has been disrupting shipping, participating in smuggling operations, and brokering contraband and counterfeit credits."

"Counterfeit credits?" Riker interrupted. "We don't have that problem anymore. Media of exchange can't be counterfeited anymore."

"You're deluding yourself." Bateson flatly said. "People are more creative than that. Have you ever worked anywhere other than Starfleet?"

"No, sir, I went directly—"

"Well, I have. Outside of Starfleet, there's a universe bubbling with commerce, legal and illegal. You're living in the insulated world of knowing where your next meal is coming from, Commander."

"And you're living in the past," Riker challenged. He paused, then squared his shoulders and loftily raised his chin. "We don't concern ourselves with such things in our century. We aren't interested in personal enrichment. In this century, we strive to better ourselves."

Now Bateson was the one to pause. He leaned on the arm of his chair, surveyed Riker for a long, long time, and raised one eyebrow. All the men from the *Bozeman* now looked at Riker in the same way Bateson did. All the people from the *Enterprise*-D held very still.

"Really . . ." the captain droned. "And just who is it you think you're 'better' than?"

Under the insulted gazes of the *Bozeman*'s brave crew, men who had stood down impossible odds with a ship one-tenth this size, William Riker's shoulders sank a little and his chin came down. There was no good answer for that question. Not here, with Bateson's crew silently surveying a man who had just declared himself superior without defining that.

In Troi's eyes and Geordi's, he could see he had made a mistake. Only Data failed to indict him for some transgression, mostly because he couldn't really figure out what was going on.

Morgan Bateson gave Riker no quarter. Didn't let him off. Didn't stop glaring at him. He wanted an answer.

Riker had never had to actually answer that before. He glanced around, broiling under the gazes of the *Bozeman* crew, who had indeed paid their dues every bit as much as he ever had.

With his expression he offered a truce. "I'm sorry," he appeased. "That did sound arrogant."

"Yes, it did." Bateson still didn't let him off the hook. "You people these days, you think you're better than everybody. You look down your noses at the conflicts of the past as if we had wars because we thought they were fun. I've got news for you. It's no fun. Someday you're going to have to fight unthinkable odds too, and on that day you'll remember me. You'll find out that there comes a time when you have to stand up and hit somebody. And before you start looking at me like that again, remember that I didn't build this floating fortress by myself."

"That doesn't mean we have to bait potential enemies by staging war maneuvers in their front yards," Riker said.

Evidently Bateson had had this argument before. He was so relaxed he'd have stuck his hands in his pockets if he'd had any. Instead he just gripped the command chair and leaned on it. "But it *does* mean that we have to be prepared to fight and become familiar with the areas of space where the fighting will most likely take place."

"Sir, communication science is better than it was ninety years ago. You're fooling yourself if you think they're not watching every move this ship makes."

"I don't know if that matters much," Bateson said. "When you're expecting a desert war, you don't practice swimming. When we expect conflict in the Typhon Expanse, we don't stage war games at Rigel. Starfleet crews have to be familiar with the conditions, anomalies, and cosmic configuration where the conflict might actually happen, don't you agree?"

"In theory, yes."

"That's what we're doing. Will, I'm not being contentious as a hobby. Some time after the *Bozeman* disappeared, peace broke out between the Federation and the empire. I'm one of those people who think we're the only side really being peaceful. Just look at the Klingon Empire. It's perfectly acceptable in political situations to gain by murder. A simple disagreement can mean a fight to the death. And we have a treaty with that! The Federation actually recognizes that as a legitimate government, and thereby we say it's okay to behave like that!"

"The Federation," Riker told him sternly, "recognizes the High Council because it *is* the de facto government. We try not to make value judgments."

"Well, you'd better start making some. When I came forward in time ninety years, I was relieved that the Federation still existed. Then I paid closer attention. The Federation's foreign policy these days is nothing short of burlesque."

"We're at peace. Peace, Captain. With your attitude, do you even know what that means?"

Apparently Riker hit a chord with that one. The captain lowered his chin and his eyes smoldered. "I know one of the charms of peace is putting off thinking about things that are ugly. The willful lack of candor and foresight are precisely the ingredients to create a catastrophe. Those who avoid the lessons of the past create conditions for the next disaster. It's one of the worst mass delusions since Stanley Baldwin lied to the English people about the Luftwaffe. If you want peace, you must prepare for war."

Taking sustenance from Troi's encouraging eyes, Riker shook his head in dismay and protested, "Captain, that is the most flagrantly irresponsible crock of paranoia I have ever heard. You should be ashamed of yourself."

"Maybe. But that last part wasn't me talking."

Knowing he was being baited, Riker decided to field the blow. "All right, who was it?"

"George Washington." Cockily Bateson flared an eyebrow. "You want to tell *him* to be ashamed too?"

Tipping his head, Riker accused, "Sir, are you comparing yourself to George Washington?"

Bateson shrugged unapologetically. "We had better hold ourselves up to great people, or we will certainly fall short."

"Granted, but I honestly believe we're provoking trouble by displaying our anticipation of it!"

Furiously Riker pointed at the glittering panorama of the Typhon Expanse opening before them, hoping to make an illustration before one made itself.

Unaffected by the bolt of volume from his unhappy first officer, Bateson looked at the forward screen for a few moments as if appreciating what he saw out there. An almost nostalgic quietude came over him, and his voice was now as mellow as Riker's had been fierce.

"If we stumble into a big problem five years from now with

shrinking forces, obsolescing weapons, and a leadership that doesn't know how to design a serious campaign, we won't get much ballast out of saying, 'Hey, we tried to be nice.' The Federation *can* fall, Will. We can be overrun and we *can* be demolished. Complacency is a disgrace."

"Strong words, Captain," Riker said, matching the lowered tone. "But I'm frankly terrified that a ship of this power is commanded by a man who thinks that 'peace' and 'fooling ourselves' are the same thing."

"I've told you you're free to go," Bateson offered again. "You can call it 'peace,' but I still don't buy it. Do you, Mr. Scott?"

"Never have, sir."

Experienced, tempered, and almost amused by what was going on here, Montgomery Scott was a full captain and that had to be considered. He was also one of James Kirk's original crew and had pioneered the unknown reaches of space back when that really meant something. He was "Mister" on this voyage because there could only be one person called or referred to as "captain," but that didn't lessen the ballast of his opinion.

Damn them both, Riker thought. *This is making my teeth hurt. I've indulged in negotiations with sworn enemies that were more fun than this.*

"Mr. Scott," he asked, "do you concur with this line of thinking?"

"I do," the famous veteran said. "And so do *your* admirals, who commissioned this ship."

"If the Federation knows what's good for it," Captain Bateson took over, "it'll get ready to fight Klingons the old-fashioned way. You'd better start training your field operatives because there are things they have to know."

Irritated beyond temper now, Riker grumbled, "Sir, we *do* know how Klingons fight."

"No, you don't. You're only—what are you, thirty-five? The oldest active-duty admiral in Starfleet is only seventy-nine. You guys know how they wage a cold war, not a real war. But, believe me, the Klingons are always thinking about the real thing."

Again Riker scowled and raised his voice. "Respectfully submit, sir, the captain is obsessed with Klingons."

Bateson shrugged. "Maybe. What difference does that make? It doesn't matter how we hone our skills as long as we hone them. If it's not the Klingons, you can be sure it'll be somebody else. Maybe somebody worse."

Troi by now was standing with her arms tightly folded, no longer pretending to work as the others were. There was a certain political decorum on the bridge when officers were having a dispute—keep to your work, keep your eyes on your board, and unless you're invited into the conversation don't even look in that direction. Almost everyone was managing to do that, except Mr. Scott, who didn't care what anybody thought of him, and Deanna Troi. Her gaze reminded Riker sadly that Bateson could very well be right—the NCC 1701-D crew members had already wrangled with worse than the Klingons, and they probably would again.

"Well, Mr. Riker?" Bateson asked directly. "Either comply, or lead a mutiny, or get off the ship. Now's the time. You can think what you want about me. We don't ignore Klingons where I come from."

Wishing he had never accepted this post, Riker thought bitterly of Captain Picard and endured a keen stab of loss. Perhaps it was only nostalgia. Perhaps it was something else.

Haunted by actions he hadn't even taken yet, he wondered—did he want to gain command by becoming this ship's Fletcher Christian?

And he *had* accepted the post.

"I won't be leaving until this shakedown cruise is completed," he said, making the condition clear. "And you are the captain of the ship. I won't be the one to change that, sir."

"Does that mean you're complying with the plans as they stand?"

"It does."

"Very well. Then carry on, Mr. Riker."

"Aye, sir."

"Entering the lateral quadrant of the Typhon Expanse, sir."

"Acknowledged. Sound general quarters. Yellow alert."

At the comm station, Wizz Dayton responded to Bateson's order in that clean, crisp way that had rumbled down through history, a series of relays and repeats that greatly reduced the chances of error.

"General quarters, aye. All hands, battlestations. Go to yellow alert. Repeat, battlestations, yellow alert. Engineering, secure from warp speed. Go to full impulse."

Scott gave a satisfied nod. "Full impulse, aye, sir."

"Somebody take George Hill below."

An ensign rolled out of his seat at the secondary science console. "Take George Hill below, aye."

As acting science officer, Lieutenant Wolfe instantly transferred the controls of that console over to his primary console. Riker watched with undeniable satisfaction at the efficiency of the crew. Everything, so far, seemed to be fine. Data at ops, Andy Welch at the helm, Gabe Bush in his second officer's chair, Mike Dennis taking the position at tactical, Deanna Troi on her way into the turbolift to take her station at sickbay, Geordi LaForge at the impulse engineering console, and Mr. Scott at the main.

Engineer Perry and a couple of others hurried into the auxiliary turbolift and headed back down to the engineering decks where they were stationed, replaced almost instantly by three armed Security guards who came out of the lift as the engineers went on. The three guards took positions at the lift doors and stood back, out of the action.

"Mr. Riker," Bateson addressed, taking his command chair, "defensive measures."

"Defensive measures, aye, sir. Weapons on standby, Mr. Data. Shields up. Confirm power reduction."

"Deflector shields up, weapons on line," Data repeated studiously. "Power reduction confirmed, sir."

"Short-range scanners on full search mode."

"Full search, aye, sir," John Wolfe responded from main science.

"Threat assessment, tracking and targeting systems, confirm ready."

"Threat assessment ready, sir," Wolfe reported.

Data said, "Tracking and targeting systems read functional, sir."

Riker turned to Bateson. "All confrontational and response systems are standing by, sir."

"Thank you. Have a seat. This'll be fun."

"Captain, picking up a warp trail already," John Wolfe reported.

"They're here," Bateson said. He patted his chair's arm. "Now we'll see what this debutante can do. Everybody keep your eyes open. We'll probably have to take the first hit. After that, we'll have a fix on the bogey. The first thing I want to do is take a series of his running fixes and plot his method of tight maneuvering. That'll be you, Mike."

At tactical, Mike Dennis said, "Ready, sir."

On the main screen, several nebulas and clouds floated in a spectacular panorama, some closer than others, some intermingling slowly, very slowly on the scale of cosmic time, so slowly that they seemed engaged in an unending kiss. The colors were stunning. Over three active years, Riker had forgotten what this sector looked like. Jewel-toned wonders of nature sprayed everywhere, mounted on the velvet trophy shroud of open space. Bright marigold dust streaks glittered like brocade in the middle of the screen. To the left were two moth-winged clusters intertwined, heavy with sparkling minerals the colors of sherbet.

To the right and below were a half-dozen disruptions in various shapes, still shrouded in the impact clouds from the asteroids that came free out of the belt at the edge of this solar system.

The sun here was far off, but very bright, casting glorious light upon all these wonders. *What a lovely area of space, like a giant casino. Too bad it was so close to restricted space. Hardly anybody would be able to enjoy it.*

At once he felt privileged. Sometimes he forgot to appreciate his special position in life.

He turned to mention some part of this, but instantly dismissed it when a hard hit from starboard knocked the ship sideways in space. Half the crew fell or fumbled, but scrambled back to position almost instantly, except for Mike Dennis, who went down on a knee—and apparently it hurt. He took a few seconds longer to pull back to his post.

The lights on the bridge flickered. The ship whined with strain as her systems tried to pull her back to her heading, but she recovered faster than Riker could think about what should be done to make her recover.

"Whoa . . ." Bateson looked around at the flagging lights. "I had no idea that lowered shield power would make that much of a difference—"

"Sir, that strike was ninety-seven percent Starfleet phaser power!" Mike Dennis reported. "Why haven't they reduced their output?"

"Sir, I'm reading full shields on the other vessel," Data reported.

"Identify that ship," Bateson ordered. "Confirm registry as the *Nora Nicholas.*"

"Confirmed, sir," Wolfe said instantly. "Emissions and configuration are Starfleet standard."

That was fast, Riker thought as he pushed out of his chair. He just couldn't sit down once the ship had been struck. Why had the hit been so hard?

"Could there have been a miscommunication?" he asked.

"We had direct acknowledgment from Captain Brownell. I spoke to him myself." Watching the smoldering green cloud from which the hit must've come, Bateson seemed as if he were trying to look with X-ray eyes through that soupy mess. The cloud churned and boiled, stirred up by the movement of the ship hiding inside it.

"Increase our shield power," Bateson said.

"That'll take seven or eight minutes, Captain," Scott said, but he started working.

"Weapons?"

"Require five minutes to bring phasers up to full power, sir," Data reported. "Photon torpedoes are not on line, in accordance with Starfleet War Game Regulations."

"How long to get them on line?"

"Nineteen minutes, sir, from main engineering."

Bateson turned around. "Scotty, can you get that done?"

"Sir, I can do that," Lieutenant Wolfe volunteered. "My minor was quantum physics of motive powered projectiles."

"Scotty?"

"Let him do it, sir."

"Go, John. Scotty, keep working on the shields."

"Aye, sir."

"Geordi, take over main science."

"Aye aye, sir."

"Mike, target that ship."

"Targeting," Mike Dennis responded as Wolfe hurried past him and disappeared into the turbolift. "Sir, the cloud is obscuring sensor contact. I can't get a true fix. I get general movements within about a hundred meters."

"Another hit coming in!" La Forge shouted suddenly, and hardly were his words out when the ship was rocked again, then again almost instantly.

The ship screamed in protest as nearly full-power phasers blasted her lowered deflectors. The lights flashed again, this time with more violence than the last, and there was obviously real damage crackling through the systems.

"LBD shutdown!" Dennis called out over the noise.

"Losing liquid helium in the loops," La Forge said at the same time. "We've got heat buildup. Attempting to compensate."

"Shields, Scotty," Bateson urged.

Scott didn't look up. "Working on it, sir, but that second hit took out two polarity generators. They knew our shields would be reduced and they're trying to keep them that way."

"Time to repair?"

"At least thirty minutes, sir!" Scott didn't wait for an order or anything else. He snapped his fingers, said, "La Forge, take over here! Dennis take science! Data, take over tactical!"

"Aye aye, sir!"

"Aye, sir!"

Scott ducked into the turbolift and was consumed by the gush of the tube door.

Musical posts again. Riker's stomach tightened. What was going on? Not war games, that was for sure, unless the admirals were *really* out to test this ship in unorthodox ways. More like insane ways.

Captain Bateson didn't contradict Scott's reassignments, but watched as the men settled into their new posts and took a moment to acclimate to the readings.

"These aren't Starfleet emissions!" La Forge blurted. "Intercept sensors indicate the contact is fourteen meters too long in hull configuration, with all the wrong emissions readings. It's definitely not the *Nora Nicholas.*"

"Could sensors be obscured by the cloud?" Riker asked.

"Not this much, sir."

Bateson looked at La Forge. "But Wolfe confirmed it!"

La Forge swiveled in his chair, insisting, "He was wrong, sir!"

"Then who is it?" Riker demanded. "Who is that?"

"And what happened to the *Nora Nicholas?*" Bateson wondered, peering at the swarming cloud in which their unidentified antagonist hid.

Dayton turned, one hand on his earpiece. "Contact is hailing us, sir . . . but it's not a Starfleet—sir, it's a Klingon signal!"

"And those aren't phasers hitting us," La Forge angrily said. "They're disruptors!"

Bateson shot Riker a glance, and looked far more stunned than vindicated. "Wizz, respond!"

"Frequency open, sir."

"This is Captain Bateson in command of the *U.S.S. Enterprise.* You are in Federation space and in violation of the

Neutral Zone treaty. Identify yourselves and prepare to stand down."

"*Morgan Bateson. Welcome home. And bid welcome to the warrior whose name you ruined. Identify yourself as the plague you are, and prepare to lose everything.*"

"Kozara!" Bateson hurled. Then he suddenly laughed, a horrible, ironic laugh. "Oh, you bloodblister!"

Riker turned quickly. "You seem to have good instincts!"

"I thought it'd be five years, not five minutes!" Shaking his head, Morgan Bateson drew a long breath and blew it out through pursed lips. "Boy . . . there are times when I *really* hate to be right."

CHAPTER 18

"Are we still hidden?"

"Yes, the cloud is obscuring us for now." Gaylon answered Zaidan's question with reserve. He did not like speaking to his son.

The whole crew was nervous, knowing what a chronic failure Kozara had been. And now they were going up against the Federation's newest, most powerful ship.

Zaidan eyed the controls Gaylon was working, and clearly understood nothing on the board. "What if he sees us?"

"He already knows we are here. He probably will be unable to take aim with this cloud around us."

"When will we come out of the cloud?"

"At your father's bidding."

"What if the sabotage is a lie? What if they have compensations? Are their weapons bigger than ours? What if . . . what if our information is wrong? What if he can see through the cloud with his sensors?"

"Then we will be destroyed." Gaylon pushed off his console and looked at Zaidan. "Now you begin to see how much can go wrong. We can be as ferocious and tough as we wish and it might change nothing. If fate turns against us, we will be destroyed."

"Then why do you follow my father?"

"Because he is our commander. If there is failure, it will never come because we failed to follow or he failed to lead. His shame is ours. We are a crew with nothing to lose. Is that not why you also are here?"

Zaidan squared his shoulders defiantly. "I come here with you because I want this one chance to get out from under my father's shame. I want a chance at honor."

"Yes, I know." Gaylon leaned forward and lowered his voice. He did not want Kozara to hear. "But we know something important which you have never learned, Klingon boy. 'Honor' may be 'luck.' What if yours is bad? How do you fault a man for that? Your father is no coward. As we go in to destroy the man who turned our luck sour, remember that. It was not Bateson who took away our honor. It was the Klingon way that only sees winning as a victory."

"Scotty, we've got to have those shields!"

"Coming, sir. Got roughly fifty percent and building."

"I'll take it. Red alert."

"Red alert, aye."

With that order, everything changed. Systems that had lain idle now glowed to life. Emergency lights on the deck shone a soft pink, and would be red if the main lights were cut off.

Suddenly Andy Welch thrust to his feet at the helm and shouted, "Look!"

All eyes turned to the main screen. Out of the churning pot of nebula gasses and dust, the tip of a constructed mass appeared—a point. No Starfleet ship had a pointed bow.

Instantly the rest of the mystery solved itself. An olive-colored head burst out of the cloud, followed by a truncated neck, and battle-moded wings in a threatening arch.

There it was. A Klingon ship where a Starfleet ship was supposed to be. A Klingon ship on this side of the border.

"Andy," Bateson said evenly, "sit down, take a deep breath, and come about and engage the enemy."

"Captain!" Riker stepped into the command arena. "We have to withdraw and call for backup! He's got something on us or he wouldn't try this. Without some kind of edge, it would be crazy. He's got to have an edge."

"Kozara's crazy. Most Klingons are."

"No, he's not, sir, or the Empire would never have given him a fighter and let him come here. That ship can't catch us if we don't want it to."

"I'm not going to run. I set him up and he fell for it, and we're going to take him down."

Riker stared at him blankly for a moment. "So you *were* baiting the Klingons. This 'powered down war game' was a lure to pull them across the border."

"That's right, and they fell for it, and we're not leaving without springing the trap. Data, put our strongest shields to him. Phasers ready . . . fire!"

The ship thrummed with power, but not enough power. A ship geared for war games couldn't be brought up to full power in a matter of seconds.

On the screen, Kozara's ship angled into the phaser streak and took the shot easily on its strongest shields. Even underpowered, the starship packed a punch compared to a smaller fighting vessel like that, and the Klingon ship wobbled. But the shields held.

And the return fire plumed through space with enthusiasm—full disruptors, almost to the level of Starfleet's full-phasers. Of course, the *Enterprise* didn't have full-phasers with which to respond, or even full shields with which to deflect the disruptor fire.

The enemy shots cut through key areas of the starship's hull, and reports flashed in from all over the ship.

"Inertial baseline system's faltering, sir!" Dennis said, just as La Forge called over his snapping console, "I'm getting breach of integrity in the deuterium flow!"

"Plasma distribution manifold just collapsed," Data reported. "Prefire chambers are shutting down."

"Does that mean we can't shoot?" Bateson asked.

La Forge was apparently already on the problem. "Hamilton reports they're working on it, but they're undermanned."

Riker held onto the helm console as the ship shuddered under return fire and took hits on her reduced shields. "Sir, I *strongly* recommend against this course of action."

"What do you recommend?"

"I recommend withdrawal." Riker called up all his personal restraint to keep from adding *what else?*

Bateson shook his head. "We can't give him the idea that Starfleet will run before we're even on our knees. Don't you understand? This is a test. They're testing us. They haven't fought us in a century. They want to see if we still have a backbone. Come on, propulsion! Maneuver behind him. We're bigger, but we're more maneuverable too. Stretch yourself, Andy. Push!"

At the helm, Andy Welch was sweating like a pig. "Okay, aye . . ."

"Push! She won't break. Phasers, target the fighter's aft section. He'll have all his shields forward. Get him where he's weakest. He won't expect that. Fire at will."

"Aye, sir," Data responded, and enabled the phasers.

Streaks of controlled energy bored through space and struck the Klingon fighter on the aft underside, and the whole ship lurched.

"No breach of the hull," Mike Dennis reported. "Phasers aren't powerful enough for—Captain, I'm getting MJL overload!"

"Where?"

"Right here!"

Riker started toward Dennis. "Get away from it!"

The overload blew out of the subprocessor housing in a funnel-shaped plume, driving Mike Dennis straight backward with sheer force and Riker back the way he'd come. He skidded to the carpet on his side. At his feet, Dennis landed flat on the lower deck, his face flecked with burns.

As Riker scrambled to him, Dennis's hands and arms were scorched to shreds.

Near Riker's left ear, Bateson punched his chair arm panel. "Sickbay! Medical emergency!"

"Medics on the way," the acknowledgment came from a voice Riker didn't recognize.

"Gabe, take over tactical," Bateson ordered.

Bush blinked, stared, held his hands close to his chest and twisted them together.

Riker looked up. "You've got your orders, Mr. Bush. Get up."

"Don't order me around," Bush said, but with little force. He got up, though, and found his way past Dennis without stepping on the injured man's legs—quite an accomplishment.

"Bridge, engineering."

Tapping his combadge, Bateson responded, "Go ahead, engineering."

It was Ham Hamilton, speaking for himself. *"Cap, systems are shutting down all over the ship. We've got some catastrophic failures to handle. Can we have a few minutes of buffer?"*

"I'll try. Andy, bend off a few thousand kilometers," Bateson ordered then. "Give me some room to maneuver."

"Aye, sir . . ."

The forward screen swirled, and the starship veered away, leaving the Klingon ship behind by half a nebula or so.

"Is he following?" the captain asked.

"Negative, sir," Bush reported. "He's holding position."

"Why would he do that?"

Riker stood up. "Captain, you got trumped and you're not seeing the warning signs."

Not so caught up in having his own way that he wasn't going to pick up on that, Bateson openly asked, "Warning signs of what?"

"Systems are shutting down all over the ship. It's sabotage!"

"Don't be ridiculous."

SHIP OF THE LINE

The captain's words drove a spear of frustration through the middle of Riker's chest and left him breathless. Bateson was consumed with the bravado of what fighting Klingons used to be.

The argument took a tense sabbatical as two medics piled out of the lift. With help from La Forge, they dumped Mike Dennis onto an antigrav gurney and buzzed him back into the lift. Now the deck was clear, and both Bateson and Riker had taken the chance to think.

"This ship is brand-new," the captain went on, but to his credit there was a tinge of doubt in his voice as he continued to think about what Riker had said. "When would it have been sabotaged?"

The flicker of contemplation, a hint that Bateson was ready to admit he was wrong if he could be proven to be, made Riker grip his tone like a pair of reins and keep control of it. "I don't know, but we should back off to make repairs and notify Starfleet."

"We're going back in to engage the enemy, Will," Bateson said, calm as a rug.

"Why take the chance, sir? It's one ship out here in the middle of nowhere. All right, they've got a few shots on us. So what? Let's go alert Starfleet. Sir, we've got a ship undermanned by two-thirds, and most of those men are tech specialists, not field officers. These men and women were the designers of the systems. That doesn't mean they're the best at using them in actual battle. They can run the ship, but not necessarily fight with it."

Bateson gestured at the distant ship on the screen as it hovered in wait of their return. "You really want me to risk having Kozara go back to the empire and tell them how weak our new starship is?"

"The Klingon Empire has already heard all our messages," Riker told him. "Sir, we've been duped. Kozara knows the ship isn't weak. He obviously had advance knowledge about the war games powerdown *and* he had design information about this vessel because he hit us right where it hurts most. And on top of all that, he's betting you'll do just what you're doing. That's why he's not chasing us. You said 'know your enemy.' Sir, your enemy knows *you*. And he's had ninety years to get it right!"

"Ninety-three." Bateson smoldered.

"Sir, we're not clean slates to each other anymore," Riker plowed on, now desperate to make his point. "They know how many ships we have, we know what they've got—it's not those days anymore. There's communication between the empire and the Federation. Believe me, they *know* we're not weak. It gives you and me the option of retreating. We don't have to fight to the death just to make a point!"

"Hey!" Gabe Bush dropped to the command arena from the upper deck and drilled a finger at Riker's face. "Show some respect, you phony prig!"

"Gabe!" Bateson stood up, grasped his loyal lush by both arms and pulled him back. "Down, Rover. This is no time for pluck and spunk. It's his job to point these things out."

"Not with that cocky attitude! He doesn't get to talk to *my* captain that way. Some first officer!"

"Back, back . . . that's it. Upper deck. That's right. Man your post."

Bateson steered Bush up toward the science station and let a few seconds go by. Then he turned back and casually took his seat again.

"He's right about one thing. It's an attitude thing, Will. The Klingons were at pseudo-peace with you your whole life. This is my time again. Don't you notice a difference in tactics? Kozara took the past ninety years learning to be sneaky, just as I suspected. To get familiar with Starfleet tech and tactics—"

Defying Bush's warning and still in the grip of anger, Riker closed in on the command arena, pressed a hand to the captain's chair enough to pivot it so Bateson had to look at him, and stormed. "This time he's after the wrong man. The Morgan Bateson he knew is gone. You're not paying attention. You've forgotten how to be vigilant. You're just playing with a new toy. Withdraw the ship before you get us smashed."

A hand of smoke drifted by from the smoldering hardware trunk, but they both ignored it. Riker saw the captain's eyes redden with the acrid smoke and felt his own eyes begin to burn and itch, but still he didn't blink.

Neither did Bateson. "Is this finally your mutiny, Mr. Riker?"

Caught by the captain's sudden charisma, Riker backed off a pace and took his hand off the command chair. "I already said I wouldn't do that."

"At least you're a man of your word. Bridge to engineering."

"Engineering, Scott here."

"Scotty, how are you doing down there?"

"We've got you some phaser power back now, sir, but it won't hold for long. Shields are holding at forty-two percent. They'll take glancing blows, if your helm can handle it."

"Then I'm going back in."

"Understood."

"Andy, one-third impulse, attack maneuver. Data, fire as your phasers bear."

"Aye, sir."

The starship peeled back into the core of the Typhon glory and swirled around the Klingon ship, which was taking some suspiciously lazy maneuvers out there.

"What's he doing?" Riker demanded. "He's not even dodging."

"Fire, Data!" Bateson ordered.

"Firing, sir."

Even reduced phasers were a frightening and formidable weapon against the blackness and the puff of nebula where Kozara had been hiding. The phasers sliced across the Klingon ship's lateral shielding and miraculously broke through. Burns saturated the greenish hull and blistered the ship from stern to midships.

"Got him!" Bateson shouted, thrusting a fist into the air. "We found a weak spot! Keep hitting him right there!"

Without response, Data continued firing, surgically cutting Kozara's ship down to the bone, at least in that one quarter.

Riker didn't know the configuration of that ship's guts, but hoped there was something critical in that section.

Just as the starship rode out on her one victory, Kozara opened fire again with full disruptors.

The starship was caught on the underside of her main section, and the deck heaved up under Riker's feet. Half the crew was thrown upward, only to come crashing down again as the gravitational systems fought to compromise and the ship screamed her way back to her heading. She didn't know she'd been hit, so she was trying to keep on the same course, which actually made the hit even harder.

"Guidance is compromised, Captain," Bush called from tactical. "He's going after our impulse maneuvering capability!"

"We're shallowing into the nebula!" Welch blurted. "I can't stop it!"

"Starboard thrusters, full power," Bateson ordered. "Mr. Riker, you do it."

Aggravated beyond reason, Riker spun to the nearest propulsion access and fired up the thrusters manually.

The ship began to slow its faltering toward the nebula, and gradually angled back onto a plane with the Klingon ship. "Stabilized," he reported.

He turned, and Bateson was glaring at him as if Riker's prediction of disaster had caused it.

"Did he hit us again?"

"It's not destruction, sir!" La Forge argued, "It's not damage. It's coded shutdown, and we don't know the codes to put the systems back on line. We have to completely reboot the system, and that means total shutdown and restart simultaneously from Main Engineering, Impulse Engineering, and—"

"All stop! Hold position!"

"Captain, Mr. Riker's right!" La Forge continued. "It's got to be preplanned! He's got somebody on this ship, shutting things down!"

Bateson's head lolled as he closed his eyes tightly and moaned, "Goddamn it . . ."

"Cap," Wizz Dayton interrupted, "he's hailing."

"Put the son of a bitch on."

"Dog."

"Butterfly."

"We stand against each other again."

"In two new ships."

"And yours is falling apart."

"Is it? Have any parts hit you? Because I wouldn't want to scratch that royal coach. I'll send some men right over with a couple of shammies."

"And we will eat them."

"The men or the shammies?"

"Both."

"What have you done with the Nora Nicholas?"

"Was that little boat yours? Such a tragedy. But they got in my way."

"Are you saying you destroyed those people?"

"Why would I say? I have the upper hand. I am old now, Bateson. My years have been spent in shame because of you, but that is nothing now. None of this is for me. I am lost. The fates will sooner or later get me again, but today I will prevail. I will turn the fates around this one time, trick them once, and then I will disappear and never give fate a chance to get me again. And my son, who spat upon my name, will no longer live in my shadow. After today there will be no more of this idiotic 'peace.' Today, there is a new empire."

"And you're its herald?" Bateson taunted. "I wouldn't pick you to carry any flags. You're too easy to beat."

"Forget that, Bateson. I can no longer be shamed. I am doomed to dishonor. I accept that. My honor is nothing. I know now that not everyone gets honor. I have nothing to lose. My name is smashed. Only the name of Zaidan can be saved."

Kozara stopped talking then, leaving the starship crew to stare at the screen, at the hovering Klingon fighter, and realize the complexity of their enemy's motivations. Scary . . .

Riker looked at Bateson, but didn't speak. The channel was still open. They would hear him if he said anything.

But Bateson didn't look back at him. The captain instead was gazing at the ship out there. After several very long moments, he parted his lips.

"I'm sorry about your son, Kozara. I wouldn't wish that on anyone. Your Klingon system of honor has destroyed him, not me or Starfleet. He shouldn't be saddled with your failures. That's not why I stood you down that day. But for my part in it, I am sorry it had to last so long for you. No one should—"

"Keep your pity. The time is past for that. I have changed in many ways. And so have you, in so much less time. And I thank you for one thing—you are so predictable now. In gratitude, I give you my gift for the sake of old times."

"Morgan, he's beaming something over!" Gabe Bush quickly said, staring into the science scopes.

Jumping up out of his chair, Bateson demanded, "Will the shields hold?"

"Not at this percentage, sir," Data told him.

Bush gripped his controls. "It's coming through!"

"Is it a boarding party? Guards, your sidearms."

"Ready, sir!"

The three Security men came forward from their posts at the turbolift doors and stood with weapons at the ready in three positions on the upper deck. From here, they had clear shots at anyone on the bridge.

"Not a boarding party," Bush gasped. "Not enough mass . . . I don't know what—"

The whine of transporters cut him off. For critical seconds all they could do was stand and wait, and Riker instinctively backed up onto the upper deck and put his shoulder blades against one of the vertical pylons. If their readings were wrong and it was a boarding party, he wanted kicking room.

The squeal of the transport invaded the bridge and made the crew wince in anticipation. No one knew what to do, but everyone was poised to fight.

As Data stood up from his post and turned, a ringlike device materialized on the deck beside him, so unidentifiable that nobody did anything but stare at it for an important second.

Then it glowed white-hot and made an electrical *snap*.

Data's mouth fell open and his eyes flared. His entire body went rigid, and almost as quickly collapsed to the deck in a heap.

"Positronic neutralizer!" Riker choked. "They took him out!"

Before anyone could say anything else, the whining of transport beams piled in on them again, this time by the half-dozen. All around the deck, five or six beams glowed. In each place, each beam deposited a dull gray cylinder.

When the beams faded, Riker kicked the nearest cylinder away—a silly move, because nothing could help them now.

As the bridge flashed with sudden pounding impact, the last thing Riker heard was his own warning shout, just before the sound of his own body dropping to the deck.

"Grenades!"

Part Three

A HARBOR OF
DOUBTFUL
NEUTRALITY

Last night at wheel watch I put a star in my port foreshroud and steered by it, and for a little help put what looked like a star cluster off the fores'l leach and steered also by that. Turned out not to be a cluster at all, but a comet. So I had a comet to steer her by.

D. Carey, personal log
0130 hours, May 2, 1997,
Revenue Cutter *Californian*

Parts of this book were written
on board, during that voyage.

CHAPTER 19

"Captain Kirk?"

The briefing room was solemn as a church. Dust-blue walls and the cool efficiency of an undecorated table didn't help the mood any. Black chairs, brown table, simple triscreen computer display in the middle.

Picard moved around the table to a place across from where Captain James Kirk sat with his shoulders slumped and his hands limp upon the tabletop. His olive-green tunic was more casual than the topaz one, a little less formal perhaps.

This didn't look like the same man at all. There was no fire in these eyes. Not a muscle twitched. The charioteer was gone from inside him, all the energy sapped. He sat as if harnessed there, staring at the table before him. For a moment, it seemed almost as if the holoprogram had frozen.

Then, Kirk sighed.

"Captain?" Picard attempted again. "Are you all right?"

Kirk didn't look up. He uttered only a weak, "No."

"What's wrong?"

"Transporter accident. I've been split in two."

227

Perplexed, Picard tilted a little to one side and checked. "You look all right . . ."

With an annoyed flicker in his dull eyes, Kirk glanced at him. "You're looking at half a man."

The irritation instantly faded, and Kirk's eyes fell again. There he sat, an echo of the man Picard would have recognized, the captain who was mellow but intense, sedate until riled, an allegory to the ship he commanded. Today, something was very wrong.

"I don't understand," Picard said. "What made you this way?"

Rather than respond directly, James Kirk tapped the controls of a desktop panel.

"Captain's log," he began, "stardate 1672.1. Specimen-gathering mission on planet Alfa 177. Unknown to any of us during this time, a duplicate of me, some strange alter ego, had been created by the computer malfunction. The duplicate isn't really a duplicate as such . . . he's . . . half of me. Half of my personality. We only discovered the accident when Scott beamed a local animal on board, and a few moments later the transporter activated itself, and a second animal beamed aboard. Except it wasn't a duplicate—it was an opposite. Shortly thereafter, Yeoman Rand and Geological Technician Fisher were assaulted . . . apparently by me. Crew members report that the counterpart is temperamental, but clever. Apparently, I have a dark twin aboard. We think his base instincts are in control. He's loose on my ship. And he knows the ship as well as I do. Even worse . . . I seem to be losing the will to fight him."

He paused, apparently also losing the will to continue his log entry. After a moment, he simply clicked the mechanism off and sat still again.

"I've got men trapped on the surface below," Kirk said. "The temperature's dropping. We can't use the transporter until we find out how to make it stop splitting anyone who uses it. It's a frozen waste down there . . . I feel so distracted . . . I keep forgetting things. My strength of will is slipping . . . The crew is losing faith in me. My command . . ."

"Can't you use a shuttlecraft to bring those men up?"

"The ionosphere's crystalized. Can't get through."

"You could blast your way through with phasers."

"And risk atmospheric shock waves on my men? We have to fix the transporter . . . somehow . . ."

The briefing room door parted without a signal and Mr. Spock strode in, clearly grim with the day's events. It seemed unbelievable, but in this time of technological wonders and strange uncharted science, such things were possible.

Spock paused, gazed at his captain briefly, then, much as Picard has asked, he wondered, "Are you all right, Captain?"

"Check on the men, Spock," Kirk said immediately. "Never mind me."

Not contented by that, Spock went to the end of the table, to a computer terminal, and punched the comm. "Mr. Sulu, report your status."

"Sulu here . . . all hands accounted for. The blankets you beamed down were shredded by the transporter process."

Kirk tapped the comm nearest him. "Scotty's working on the transporter. How's it going down there, Mr. Sulu?"

"It's already twenty degrees below zero . . . can't exactly call it balmy . . ."

Kirk tapped off the comm and looked at Spock. "Isn't there any way we can help them?"

Spock bowed his head, almost in shame. He was deeply pained by the strain in Sulu's voice and the fact that there seemed to be no answers. "Thermo-heaters were transported down, they . . . duplicated. They won't operate."

The comm blessedly interrupted the terrible litany of failure. "Mr. Spock?"

"Spock here."

"Transporter technician Wilson found injured near the captain's cabin. Says the imposter called him by name, took his hand phaser."

"Acknowledged. Continue the search."

Haunted now by the fact that his distorted counterpart was armed, Kirk began, "We've got to find him before he . . . but how?"

Spock drew his brows together, but with a glimmer of hope. "Apparently this double, however different in temperament, has your knowledge of the ship. Its crew. Its devices. This being the case, perhaps we can outguess him by determining his next move. Knowing how the ship is laid out, where would you go to evade a mass search?"

"The lower levels. The engineering deck."

"I'll get hand phasers for us," Spock said. "I'll meet you in the main section in ten minutes with a search team."

"No team," Kirk said. "Just you and me."

"Captain—"

"Please, Spock . . . no arguments."

Sympathy crimped Spock's features. Troublement and emotion crackled just below the blanketing surface.

"Very well, sir," he said, almost as dejected as Kirk. He swung off the table and quickly left the briefing room.

Picard moved to the place where Spock had been and watched James Kirk. This Kirk, this belevolent, drained man, had no fire in his eyes, no pulse of multiactive thought. He was instead passive to dullness, but clearly battling with himself. He had lost a piece of himself, a critical piece—the piece that made him want to command.

Had Picard lost that too? Had he lost more than a ship? A piece of himself?

If so, he suddenly wanted to find it.

"Strange," he murmured. "We always imagine that if we could take away all the agression and base needs, the dark gut reactions of human beings, we would have a superior man. You don't look very superior right now, Captain Kirk."

"I don't feel superior," Kirk said. "Besides, benevolence is easy—just make everyone an android with the brute programmed out. Would you put your android in charge of the ship on a long-term basis?"

He looked at Picard—a startling instant, until Picard remembered that the computer had his record and logs just as it had James Kirk's.

"Data? . . . No, not long term," he admitted. "Not yet. He has the intelligence, but he doesn't have the instinct. He can follow a line of logic, like Vulcans—"

"But Vulcans haven't prevailed as the strong shield of the galaxy, as you might imagine they would. The synthesis of the two parts of us has allowed humans to be the prevailing wind of the galaxy." Kirk listened to his own words, then sighed. "And I've lost it."

"I wonder," Picard said quietly. "Is that bit of evil in us really the thing that makes us strong? The tough side—getting angry, the survival instinct . . . is that what makes us move faster, think harder . . . some call it an edge. 'Eye of the tiger.' But every brute has that."

"Then what do I have?" the mild Kirk asked. Bitterness cut through the sorrow in his face.

"You have the thoughtfulness of command," Picard told him. "You have the elements that allow the survival instinct to become creative. You have what it takes to stay calm when others are losing control. It's crucial. Especially for command. The captain has to be the last one on board to lose control."

Kirk gazed at the tabletop, his fingers interlaced there. "And it's what makes you realize there are things bigger than your own survival that are worth dying for. It's what keeps me at my post, fighting the big odds even though I know we're going to die now and it's worth that."

Picard sat on the edge of the table. "Like Bateson did," he recalled. "Why you die . . . the reason you fight. The cruder side of us would run."

"I don't want to run," Kirk uttered. "I don't want to fight. I want to hide."

Picard gazed at Kirk, empathy pulling at his chest. Kirk had men on the surface in trouble, and was facing the loss of his career because he couldn't handle command anymore. There was more, though—Kirk was also dealing with the lonely personal problem that perhaps he would never be put back together again. The men on the surface might die, but then their misery would be over. A new commander would take the ship, and the future would move on. But there might be no way out of this for Jim Kirk. Had technology broken down one too many times? Would one of him forever be a monk, and the other forever in a cage?

Kirk's uncertainty haunted Picard—reminded him too much of himself a short while ago, when he was talking to Riker. All those doubts . . .

He peered at Kirk critically. "You *do* have insecurities, don't you? The intrepid hero—that was just a persona for you, wasn't it?"

"In some ways," Kirk admitted. "I wondered sometimes whether I was the best captain . . . or just the luckiest."

"Come now," Picard chided. "You were an interesting type of leader. Your profile is a rocky road, to be sure, but you ultimately prevailed in most situations because of your strength of will. So much so, in fact, that many captains have stumbled by trying to be too much like you in the wrong situations."

"They shouldn't try to be like me," Kirk said. "If all captains are cut from the same program, then we'd be too easy to beat. No one wants ships of the line commanded by a set of clones."

Here was a man toward whom almost every cadet in the academy aspired, and he was dismissing the idea that any one man could be an ideal captain. Picard grinned through his surprise, with a touch of nostalgia. He too had tried in his youth to be like James Kirk. And Kirk was right—it hadn't worked for him.

"The power of command seems so elusive to me now," Kirk groaned. "He's vital to me . . . and I don't know how to get him back . . . back inside me, where he belongs. Where he won't be . . . wasted."

"Wasted," Picard echoed. "Interesting way to put it. You shouldn't have beamed down into unstable conditions, Captain. Now you're debilitated. Unable to help your stranded crew members. You're weakened now, yet the decisions are still yours to make and you can't make them. You shouldn't have been part of the away team."

"Away team?"

"Landing party."

Kirk thought about that, then even through his hesitations, he said, "No, I had to go. I have an unwritten contract with my crew. I ask them to do incredible things sometimes. I ask them to take risks, fight, maybe die. I have to show them that I'm willing to bear the same risks. That's the way it always was . . . in the wars of the past, 1812, the American Civil War, France and England, Napoleon—the officers raised their swords and went out in front, and asked the men to follow. And the men did. They could see that their officers thought there was something worth dying for. They lost a lot of officers, but they knew the value of morale."

Picard uttered a grunt of understanding. "Yes, the Klingons say, 'It's a good day to die.' Humans say, 'It's a good *reason* to die.' Still, Starfleet changed things after your tenure. They urged captains to stay on board, so the captain would be fully able to command if things went wrong."

"They had the same thing in my time." Kirk shook his head. "We just ignored it. When I lose crew, I always feel as if I've failed, even if I won. That's why I led the landing parties."

"But you're not a general in an old-style war, yelling 'Charge!'"

"Yes, I am," Kirk said, and this was the first thing he'd said with his old conviction. "And everybody sees me out there, and all their lives they never forget what they saw. That's the deal I have with my crew members when I say, 'Go out there and probably die.' It's a lot more powerful if you add, 'I'll go with you.' The cause we choose to fight for is more important than all of us. We agree on that. It's our contract. The captain goes in front of the army, not behind it. The captain takes the first wound."

"If you're debilitated," Picard tried again, "you can't see to your men. You're the most important person aboard—"

"No, I'm not." Kirk's eyes flashed to him with a hint of the fire that had been buried. "Where did you get that idea?"

"Well . . . I think it's obvious."

"And I think you're crazy. I'm more expendable than any of my crew. I'm the *least* important person aboard. The most junior technician on my ship is more important than I am. I'll let myself be killed before I'll hand over any of them. And they all know it. They know I'll fight for their lives. So they're willing to give them. And you are too," Kirk said, giving Picard that dangerous look, as if he could see through his skin into his heart. "That's why within a month of taking command, you started beaming down and breaking that rule. The admirals sit back in starbases and say, 'You folks go risk your lives.' They've forgotten the need for junior officers to see their captains willing to take the same risks."

The room fell silent for a few long moments as the two simply gazed at each other in a weird kind of mutual understanding, and Picard felt as if he were being dissected—but by his own hand.

"Could that be why," Picard began slowly, thinking hard, "could it be why you disliked the admiralty? You didn't want to stop going in front?"

"Yes," Kirk said instantly. "It's that part of us that makes us say, 'No more.'"

In a jolt of his old self, he slammed the table with the flat of his palm.

Picard stood up. "So the crew, the ship—they're more important to you than your own life? I never knew that about you. Only the bravado has come through history. But the crew and the ship were what you really cared about."

Kirk paused, touched the table, ran his hand along the grain of the imitation wood. "The ship . . . if you ask a designer, it's just a mass of metal and circuits. A gathering of electrons. But ask someone who sails her . . . she's much more. She's the physical manifestation of our ideals. Work, exploration, protection—all the great things intelligent beings can be and do when we get together. The ship is our home, our commonality. It's our meeting place."

Picard started to say something, then decided to listen. He wanted to hear this part.

Waving a finger toward the ceiling, Kirk glanced around. "It's important. At a time of crisis, the ship gives us all a single goal. Stand fast for the ship, and we'll survive. That's the connection between the people and the symbol. A ship is more than a symbol. She's our island of survival."

Now Picard suddenly felt the bubbling of his own sentiments, and took a breath that made Kirk look at him, and wait.

"When I lost the *Stargazer,*" Picard said, "the loss almost crushed me. That was my first command. I was one of the youngest captains ever to command a Starfleet vessel. It hurt so much that I started pushing back. I changed the way I thought about ships. I convinced myself that only the people mattered. When the *Enterprise*-D was wrecked, I was too cavalier about it. I'd conditioned myself not to care . . . after all, it's just a hunk of metal, isn't it? That's what I trained myself to believe all these years, but I'm troubled now. Now that I've actually lost her, it's different. It's months later, and she's still gone—somehow I didn't expect that. Somehow I didn't think she was *truly* gone. I'm afraid the crew took my example and didn't bother to care about the ship either. And so she really is truly gone. And not only gone for us, the crew . . . but everyone else in the Federation. I lost their flagship. I didn't remember to care about the ship until it was too late. I forgot that the ship is important."

James Kirk was watching him, in a most disturbing and real-blooded way. "That's how it is. The ship is your reason to stick together. She defends you time after time, and you defend her. You keep each other alive until the last possible moment. Then one of you makes the ultimate sacrifice. It's natural. We're not the captains of ships. We're the captains of ideals."

Feeling a warm ball of understanding rise from deep in his chest, Picard watched the young Kirk and both hurt and rejoiced with him. So much, in such a compact package.

Somehow he felt as if he really weighed less. The loss of the ship had been mortally chilling, and somehow to let himself take that loss personally actually helped. And it helped to look at Kirk, to see this young man bearing the same burdens, yet never being paralyzed by them.

"Computer," Picard said suddenly, and surprised himself with the quick change, "I want to speak to the other Kirk."

Instantly the scene blurred and changed to the lower decks, Main Engineering. Very quiet . . .

He was alone. No one else was here. These muted blue-gray walls were somehow more comforting than the briefing room, perhaps because there were so many shadows, and red-painted accents and partitions. A dozen steps away, the main engineering control panels were slick black, offset by a wide poppy-red trunk base. Ceiling-high circuit trunks created a forest of obstacles and shadows, and the faint throb of matter/antimatter power made the place eerie.

Picard stood in a shadow, and watched for a moment. Had the holoprogram made a mistake? Was he alone here?

A scrape behind him answered that question, and he spun around.

"Dear God, *there's* the fire!" he blurted.

Yes, there it was. A pair of eyes like an angry cat's—an angry tiger's. In spite of himself, Picard flinched at the power of those eyes, and the phaser in the young captain's grip.

No—it wasn't a counterpart. This was the real James Kirk, not a fake, not an imposter, not even a duplicate. It was—a portion, like a cross-section or a diagram. This was the untempered critical-mass core of James Kirk.

Here, here before him, crouched and ready to pounce, phaser forward and eyes aflame, was all the severity, all the dash and spirit, the mettle and grit that history remembered about James T. Kirk. This creature forgot the other Kirk entirely, left the studious authority behind, drowned in the raw energy. This young man's face was pasted with sweat, his teeth gritted, his eyes cups of rage. This was pure gale-force Kirk.

"My goodness," Picard murmured in bizarre admiration. "What a remarkable creature you are!"

"I'm the captain!" the counterpart said. "That other one's telling lies. He's not the captain. *I* am!"

Even beneath the animalistic fury, the voice was undoubtedly James Kirk's. It carried the same positivity, each word an uppercut. Dauntless, yet somehow threatened, this Kirk stalked the engineering deck, knowing he was being hunted.

And he was good at this too—he kept his back to cover, put one shoulder down, kept his weapon up.

"You know what happened, don't you?" Picard began, seeking for a line of common awareness.

"Transporter malfunction." Kirk leaned back against a pylon, and pecked out into the main deck area. "That other one's looking for me. He's telling the crew lies about me. I have to get him first."

Slowly, Picard stepped toward him. "But he's part of you. You can't survive this way. You'll have to be put in a—"

"Back off!" Kirk snapped.

Wrenching the phaser around to Picard, Kirk sucked the breath back in between his gritted teeth, as if he were a wolverine trapped in a hole. His turbulent eyes, like arrowheads, were ringed with wet dark lashes.

"I don't need him. I'm better now. I'm stronger. I'm more decisive. I *take* what I want. This ship is mine. No one will ever take her away from me. She's *mine.*"

"If you're stronger," Picard challenged, "what are you going to do about those men on the planet's surface?"

The angry Kirk seemed to have forgotten about those men. Reminded now, he simply said, "They knew the risks. He's coming!"

Bending his knees, Kirk ducked sideways, then moved out. Picard lagged back and watched.

In an office area, the other James Kirk, the one in the green shirt—the mild one, the worried one—slowly moved through with a phaser. Probably set to stun, Picard realized, and at once noticed that this Kirk, the one in gold, had his phaser set on full power. He fully intended to kill if he fired it.

Would he fire it? How much intellect was left in him? Did he understand that two halves of a person could not survive apart? That one would be overcome by weakness, the other by violence? He saw that now, in both their faces.

The two had seen each other. They faced off within a shadow from a divider grid. Both had phasers. Both had fears.

The fear was shining brightly in both of them, and it was rather a shock. How would each overcome it?

Or could they at all?

At first the animal Kirk had been stalking the mild Kirk, but now something changed. The animal began backing away. The mild Kirk came forward. The strange dance continued. Back, back . . .

"You can't hurt me," the mild Kirk said. "You can't kill me."

The animal's phaser wavered between them.

"You can't," the mild one said. "Don't you understand? You need me. I need you . . ."

The movement stopped. Something in those words made the animal Kirk pause in his backing off. He raised his phaser. His teeth came together and his eyes tightened in pure rage.

"I . . . don't . . . need . . . you!"

The phaser wavered. He still didn't fire.

A flash of blue behind him then—Spock!

The Vulcan grasped the side of the animal's neck and pinched the nerves.

The savage Kirk's head snapped back, a horrible grimace showing the shock of paralysis. His hand clenched on the phaser, but the convulsed muscles in his arm pulled the hand up and sideways—and it fired! The streak lanced into a circuit trunk and blasted a hole the size of Picard right in the side. Sparks flew, and this side of the pylon vaporized.

Spock let go, and the feverish, vicious form of the negative captain dropped to the deck.

The other Kirk looked nauseated with misery, perhaps even stunned at the savagery with which his other half had set his phaser on full power.

He knelt slowly, his face matted with disgust at what he saw on the deck before him, the unconscious boyish twin of himself, the shame of humanity. The bad half.

Kirk was a starving man gazing at a poisoned dinner. He wanted it—he didn't want it. He had to have it, but it was sickening.

They'd caught him . . . but it wasn't enough. Now what?

"Computer," Picard quietly said, "let me see the resolution of this."

Everything blurred again, and he was standing in the transporter room of the first *Enterprise*.

Between Kirk and Spock, sagging and dazed, was the terrorized other twin, weak now and clinging to Kirk. Something had made him afraid, and he felt his fear full-throttle.

"Have you fixed the transporter?" Picard asked.

Spock was the one to answer. "We used bypasses to tie directly into the impulse engines and get the transporter working."

"But it might kill me," Kirk added. "We tried it on the duplicated creature from the planet."

"Did it put him back together?"

"Yes. But he died. Spock thinks it was blind terror that killed him. He thinks I can overcome that with . . . intellect."

"Don't you think so?"

"It doesn't matter what I think . . . I can't live this way. Compassion is only one piece of humanity. I'm afraid . . . but I have to take him back."

"Not only fear," Picard observed. "You're embarrassed."

Kirk struck him with a leer. "Wouldn't you be?"

Spock took the sagging twin's arm and urged the other Kirk to move toward the transporter platform. Up they went, and Kirk embraced the part of him that had nearly destroyed him.

There was something different now in the mild Kirk's face—resolution. He was determined to see this through. That hadn't happened with the tiger half, Picard recalled. The savage Kirk had faltered. This one didn't.

"Hold onto him, Captain," Spock said, and stepped off the platform.

"Mr. Spock—"

The science officer turned before he was down the step. "Captain?"

Kirk gazed at him with a layered expression. "If this doesn't work . . ."

He said nothing else, and for a moment Picard waited to hear the rest, but there was no more.

Spock's dark eyes softened. "Understood, Captain," was all he said.

Picard didn't know what they were saying to each other, but he suddenly thought of Riker.

And that was all the good-bye they got.

Spock stepped behind the transporter console and enabled the mechanism, while Dr. McCoy looked on in unshielded worry.

Pring—the console began working. The faint whine made Kirk—both—stiffen in reaction. Lights began sparkling, and the panel of energy did its work. Both Kirks dematerialized.

Picard was glad. Whatever happened, this terrible personal ordeal would be over. Then, in a moment of silly realization, he remembered that Kirk hadn't died here and now.

How absurd to have forgotten!

The transporter room fell quiet, but for the soft thrum of contained power. How long would it take? Picard didn't know about these old-style devices. They were more touchy than transporting in his time, he knew that much.

Behind the console, Spock seemed almost to fidget. McCoy did, without trying to hide the fact. He glanced at Spock, but restrained himself from urging. Apparently the process needed a certain amount of time. Were they guessing?

Then one light, only one, came on near Spock's left hand. He instantly enabled the transporter process, and the sparkling lights appeared again where two Kirks had been standing before.

Softly, peacefully, as though to apologize for having been broken, the transporter beams were almost musical as Captain James Kirk materialized and stood upon the platform—alone.

No one spoke. Picard held his breath. How much damage had been done? Would the captain need therapy? Treatment? Counseling? Would Spock take command for a time?

Kirk blinked, wobbled a step, looked at Spock, at McCoy.

Finally, McCoy could stand it no longer. He leaned forward and gasped, "Jim?"

The word was almost like a slap in the quiet room, but Jim Kirk drew a tight breath and stepped down from the transporter. He jerked a thumb over his shoulder and ordered, "Get those men up here fast!"

Relieved and not hesitant to show it, Spock nodded forcefully. "Right away, Captain."

Kirk stepped out of the way, and McCoy went to the console and started ordering a medical unit to come up to the transporter room.

Stepping to Kirk's side, Picard said, "Congratulations. I'm glad it's over for you."

"Over?" Kirk clenched his fists. "I still have to live with that part of me . . . knowing what I'm like without him. He took away everything that made me strong. Everything that let me make quick decisions. Everything that made me protect myself, my ship, my principles—"

"Your intellectual half came to understand the value of the brute," Picard said. "The brute never learned the same. He thought he was better that way. The intelligent part of you was the part that learned something."

"That's what intellect does," Kirk said, watching the transporter platform as three of his crumpled, half-frozen landing party materialized. "It makes the future wider than just today."

"Yes," Picard agreed. "Captain, I owe you an apology. I was

laboring under a legend. I never saw you as having doubts to overcome."

"What kind of man doesn't?"

"I don't know." Finding himself smiling, Picard said, "But suddenly I feel rather better about myself too. And I understand now that you never lost your edge because your talents and your heart's desire were the same. You wanted to be the commander of a ship. I had the talent to command, but my heart's desire had too many other attractions. That's why I've avoided the admirality. The same as you. And why Riker avoids senior command. That rule about captains being too important to go on away missions—yes, yes, that's it. We who make the decisions want to share the risks. I *do* want command more than anything else. Until today I never really knew *why*."

"Now you do."

Picard squared his shoulders, feeling better than he had in years, and smiled. "Captain Kirk . . . thank you most sincerely. May I shake your hand? I never did that, and I believe I should."

Kirk's hand was warm, his handshake tight and confident. A good grip, and the feeling sustained Picard in his new decisions.

Then a knock came on the outer wall. "Captain! Captain Picard? How does this door open?"

"Captain Reynolds, one moment. I'm coming. Computer, end program."

He watched with satisfaction and some regret as James Kirk nodded in companionable farewell, and the program disappeared. Once again he was in the simple yellow-lined black grid of this small holodeck.

"Door open," he said.

Captain Reynolds came in just as Picard added, "End program," and now they were standing in the empty holodeck grid.

"We're entering Cardassian jurisdiction," Reynolds informed Picard. "How do you want to handle this?"

"I was intending to go in and negotiate. That's all over. I

don't feel like negotiating anymore. Change course immediately. And give your men the sidearms I provided."

Chip Reynolds paled a bit with the realization that things weren't going to go smoothly. To his credit, he made no argument and didn't waste time with questions.

"Whatever you say . . . it's your charter."

Picard stepped to the holodeck computer access and removed the cartridges of James Kirk's logs. "And give these back to Mr. Riker. I won't be needing them anymore."

In a ship detached far from superior authority, there was nothing a captain might not do . . .

Hornblower and the Atropos

CHAPTER 20

"You!"

"Yes. It's me. Picard. Jean-Luc. SP dash nine three seven dash two one five."

"Son of . . . Yvette and Maurice Picard . . . born Labarre, France . . . former captain of the *Stargazer*—"

"Former captain of the *Enterprise*-D."

"Ah . . . I hadn't heard. Do you mean to have revenge on me? Will you torture me in return for what I did to you? Picard, you're a peacock pretending to be a hawk. You're not the type for revenge. I know that much."

"You're right. Revenge would never be motivation enough for what I'm about to do."

"And what is that? Go ahead and do it."

"First, Madred, I'll tell you why."

"Tell."

Cardassia's most famous interrogator cautiously remained seated behind his desk. To stand would be to give something away. Mustn't have that.

Before him, Jean-Luc Picard strolled slowly into the large

expanse of the interrogation room without glancing around. Of course, Picard knew the lay of this place. He had spent many severe hours here.

"There are several Starfleet and Federation spacefarers missing in or near Cardassian space," Picard said tonelessly, "and we know you have some of them held hostage as you held me. You have them, and I want them back."

Madred kept his hands upon his desk, knowing that Picard would know about the signaling device under the desk. Certainly the captain had anticipated that. This ruse of being alone here was not Picard's way. He was a team man.

So where was the team?

"What makes today different from yesterday?" Madred asked, prodding for information.

"The difference is the Klingons," Picard said. "They've set their sites on Cardassia for war. You know it and so do I. If the Klingons attack Cardassia, you're going to need the Federation at your side. At the very least, our neutrality. You're holding Captain Kaycee Fernando of the escort ship *U.S.S. Durant,* his command staff, and several of his crew. You're also holding, we believe, Captain Brent Atherton and the survivors of wreckage from the satellite tender *Tuscany.* Starfleet patrols recovered wreckage of both ships, including several dead personnel and evidence of Cardassian presence aboard."

"Silly magic. You have no such evidence."

"On the contrary, you underestimate Starfleet forensic analysis capabilities."

Studying Picard's manner for vindicatory hints, Madred decided not to prod for details of forensic tricks. In Picard's pale face and smooth brow, his simple black commando clothing and cool self-control, Madred saw a reflection of how physically different their peoples really were—his own steel-gray face, its corded features and scaly exterior arteries, his typical Cardassian uniform of metallic fibers . . . many differences.

Picard was not wearing a Starfleet uniform, but commando

fatigues instead. Madred wondered whether that was for his benefit, or Picard's. Was this a covert mission? Had Picard snuck into Cardassian space? How had he gotten past the portmaster's armed guard ships? Had he stowed away somehow?

Interesting questions. Madred restrained himself from asking them outright. The answers would come, slowly, with time.

As Picard approached the other side of the desk, Madred felt a queasy commonality with this man. They were both humanoid, of course, as Starfleet tended to put it. Arms, legs, heads, a face with two eyes, a nose, a mouth—in a galaxy of uncounted bizarre life-forms, they were practically twins. They had similar ambitions, desires, and needs, which Madred regularly preyed upon and knew very well. He could distill most humanoids down to the common needs and fears—Terrans, Romulans, Klingons, even other Cardassians.

A flashing memory of those Cardassians he had tortured came unbidden into his mind. He shook it off.

Picard was looking at him with a slightly scolding expression now.

"Did you really think," the captain asked, "that drinking tea in front of me would make me talk to you?"

Madred tipped his head in a shrug. "Simple, but often effective to the thirsting. After all, I'd left you hanging from the ceiling all night. I'd blistered your innards with my subcutaneous implement—"

"Yes, your pain device is gaining legendary status. Not for its innovation, but for your tired use of it. I had no information to give you, Madred. At least, not about what you were asking. It's a torturer's biggest problem. What happens when your victim really doesn't know? How do you live with yourself?"

"I do well enough. Of course, I'm not a heat-treated dandy like you, so I must have trouble in life. We can't all be Picards, can we? I suppose it's an occupational hazard of mine that one of you would eventually come back for revenge. It's the nature of my work, you see."

"I told you," Picard clarified, "I'm not here for revenge. What you did to me simply wasn't bad enough to go to all this bother. I've had worse heckling from petty criminals I've arrested. Otherwise, what's a little physical discomfort? Some spasms and cramps?" He flexed his fingers and looked at them. "I seem to still have all my digits, all my limbs . . . you weren't even atrocious enough to maim me. You thought you were debasing me by stripping my clothing off? You forgot I'd been through Starfleet Academy hazing. Just keep your hands on the desk—"

"I will."

Madred pressed his palms to the glossy desktop. He had inadvertantly lowered one hand to his lap, but even if he could reach the signal button, he didn't want to do that yet. He was interested in what Picard was saying, and in why.

They had spent many hours together. Madred had plumbed for Picard's inner weakness and found a most uncomplex man with a great deal of grudgeful determination. The captain was also stoutly unimpetuous. His presence here had no doubt been long considered. Madred kept that in mind. He would have to think quickly and be very careful in order to match Picard's preparation.

To that end, he said nothing, but let the captain continue to speak. Such moments as this tended to make truths bubble to the surface.

"When you told me the *Enterprise* was burning in space," Picard went on, "I knew you were lying. You were just too casual about it. Too neutral. You should've pretended regret, acted sympathetic, even embarrassed. Maybe begun to unshackle me. I might've swallowed that. But you showed nothing but the satisfaction of telling me, so I knew you were lying. You also promised to kill me, but then you didn't. I had no reason to pay attention to you after that. You shouldn't say things you don't mean, even to captives."

"Good advice," Madred accepted. "I'll put it down in my book of wisdom from inelastic ninnies."

Very odd . . . he had expected to see some retaliatory deviltry in Picard's manner by now, but there still was none. Picard spoke of those hours of torture with the same impassivity Madred himself might have used. There was no rancor in the man. Or perhaps that was an act. Picard must be trying to vex Madred by pretending to be unaffected by those hours. That was it—trying to make Madred feel ineffective, something quite annoying to a skilled artisan.

Yes, that was it.

Madred shuddered down an instant of personal fear. Picard might be calm because he was planning something brutal. That happened sometimes. Madred was usually very calm when he had made up his mind about something. Picard might be the same kind of man. They had found themselves matched once before. Picard had not broken down.

Of course, Madred hadn't had a chance to finish before the game was raided.

"Remember what you said to me?" Picard went on when Madred said nothing else. "'Enemies deserve their fate.' You said Jil Orra had been raised with that. Oh, yes, even through the haze I remember your daughter. How old was she then?— about seven in Earth years? Eight? I was rather dismayed that you let her into the torture room, let her see me lying there on your floor, almost destroyed by your subcutaneous instrument, exhausted and wrecked at your order, at your whim . . . you excused yourself by telling me that Jil Orra understood that Cardassia had enemies and enemies deserved what they got. Now she would be about thirteen, isn't she? Fourteen?"

"By your reckoning, yes."

"I'm sure she understands now that things are not so simple. As she grows older, she'll distill the ugly truth that her father freely executed torment when no crime had been committed."

"She might." Madred accepted Picard's point.

"You weren't even a particularly imaginative torturer." Picard lowered his voice, narrowed his eyes, and looked penetratingly at Madred. "Did you think the tide would never turn?"

Madred felt strangely unmoved, though Picard was trying very hard to move him.

"Are you looking for my repentance, Captain?" he asked directly.

"Not at all," the Starfleet man said. "If the Cardassian ruling council expects Federation help to fend off aggression by the Klingons, and you had better, then now is the time to make a strong gesture of good faith. And *you* had better. Otherwise there will be legal action, no treaty, and you'll have not only Klingons but also Starfleet at your throat."

"Legal action?" A nervous laugh bolted through Madred's chest. "Are you threatening me with your Federation courts? Picard, really. What a joke."

The captain took a step back from the edge of the desk and seemed more insulted by that comment than he had by all the torture.

"We are a body of laws and rights," he said. "If Cardassia wants to deal with us, and you're going to very soon, you'll have to abide with our laws and rights and our judicial process, and treaties, and all kinds of things criminal governments don't fancy."

The room seemed chilly. Probably just the company. And large—Madred was used to the sprawling size of the "office"— in fact, he had designed it, but today it seemed rather too big. The size gave his customers a sense of smallness, insignificance. The slate floor offered no comfort to bloodless feet. The lighting here was harsh and directed, and cast shadows. It lay crassly upon Jean-Luc Picard's carved features as he closed up the small space between himself and Madred's desk.

"Captain Fernando," he demanded, "First Officer Court, Second Officer Garland, Chief Engineer Rollins, Third Officer Ballenger, Fourth Officer McClellan, Engineer's Mate Leith, and seventeen crewmen . . . Captain Atherton, his first and third mates, his wife, and nine deckhands. Their location or locations. Right now."

The litany of names actually caused a slight echo in the big room. Or perhaps it was only the way Picard spoke. Until now Madred had not known the extent of detail Starfleet knew about who was being held and who wasn't. The numbers were off by a few, but very few.

Another problem— some of those persons were no longer animate. Of course, Madred hadn't admitted anything yet. There was still time to admit nothing.

Admission might not be necessary. Picard knew perfectly well that there were captives held by the Cardassians. In fact he knew it firsthand. Denial would be silly.

The captain stood with a barrister's posture before Madred, one shoulder slightly toward the desk, one slightly away, and there seemed to be something important about not blinking.

The effect was not without its success.

"I understand you," Madred offered. "Times do change. I would be lying to shrug and say that Cardassia is not interested in the support of the Federation against the Klingons. That is no secret, obviously, and you already said I'm a bad liar. Perhaps we can avoid a grim scene, Jean-Luc. Perhaps I'm ready to deal. Perhaps you can tell me . . . if I had possession of these missing people, what if I appease you with a few of them?"

"I will not be appeased," Picard said sharply. "You hardened me, Madred, during those days of torture. After you, the Borg got a hold on me. Compared to them, you're what we call a burlesque show."

"Mmm, so I've heard. You're not the first, you know," Madred told him, rocking back in his chair. "Others have thought to take vengeance on me. I've felt the wrath of the 'hardened.' Do your worst."

"Oh, I will."

Not a hollow promise, Madred was certain. He had not believed Jean-Luc Picard would do petulant harm upon another living being, but then again . . . much of this man remained an unknown quantity. And people could change.

"You know, this is interesting, Picard. I watched your eyes

just now while you called out those names. You know what? I'm still torturing you. You're so drowned in your own hauteur that you don't know I'm still in control. What I say now, if I tell you I have them, or tell you I don't, you're still at my whim. Isn't that curious? Even with you in charge, the great stonelike Picard, I'm still getting information."

"You may be getting tidbits," Picard agreed, "but your method is overall flawed. You try to get to your victim's soul by going through his body. That's the crack in your plan. You have nothing but flesh to feed on. If you can't get through to your victim's soul, then even if he dies, you've failed. You're just another bully. A pathetic little badger who thinks he can inflict the death of the soul with a bunch of little bites. And *keep* your hands up on this desk!"

"Yes . . . all right . . . well, then, what do you intend to do? I wish you would do it."

"I started out on this mission to negotiate with you for the release of our nationals, but by the time I got here I was all done negotiating. I discovered the negotiation was not with you, but with myself. Negotiation implies that each side has a choice, but you're not going to get one. I intend to start from your point of failure, Madred. I'm bypassing your body and going straight to your soul. Today we're going to have a standoff that involves far more than pain and lights."

Picard strode with annoying confidence to the door—which he didn't have to do, because the door could be operated from the desktop panels.

Madred understood there was a show going on and the curtain was about to rise. He forced himself not to smile, but felt his eyes glitter. The whole process rather fascinated—

"Jil Orra!"

His young daughter came into the room, flanked on one side by a massive Klingon. Madred burst to his feet, both hands upon the desk before him as if he might leap right over.

A Klingon! Picard had brought a Klingon into the heart of Cardassia! Why would he do that?

"Sit down," Picard ordered, pointing at Madred. "Don't take a single step."

Madred took no steps, but did not sit. He stared at the scene before him, at the two people who held his daughter by either arm, and his insides crumpled.

Jil Orra's gray face had gone clay-white with determination. Her slim hands were clenched. She wore brightly colored clothing that was distinctly non-Cardassian in style, and that worried him.

"Father . . ." she began, her voice cold.

In her determined eyes Madred saw the ghastly reflection of himself. His daughter knew firsthand what he did to others. Picard was correct—Madred had never shielded Jil Orra from the horrors of his job. He had let her see, and tried to make her understand that there were enemies, and enemies had to be treated firmly, even viciously.

Today, though, Madred saw in his daughter's eyes the full measure of knowledge about what her father did and the complete contempt in which she held him.

All that was in her eyes.

And for the first time Madred began to realize he may indeed have finally pushed someone too far.

"You couldn't break me," Picard said, as if reading Madred's thoughts. "You have no idea of my limits, but I know yours. Jil Orra is your limit. She's your breaking point, Madred."

"Oh—" Madred shook his head suddenly. "Now you've given yourself away. I know you better. This is a masterful bluff, but still a bluff. Your Lordship Jean-Luc Picard, I know you. You will not torture a child."

The captain's dark eyes hardened. "I won't have to."

"You'll have to show me what you mean."

The standoff reached a new peak. Not the summit, but a very important notch.

His own words drumming in his ears, Madred stood as still as he could manage on his shivering legs and demanded of himself that he give away nothing, at least physically.

Picard studied him for many seconds, searching for weakness or pretense, seemed frustrated not to find any, and turned to the Klingon. "Show him."

The Klingon reached into a small utility bag and took out a gleaming metal device with a glowing red panel.

"All right, Picard," Madred said. "What is that? I know you're hungering to tell me."

"Yes, I am." Picard took the device from the Klingon and held it up. The glowing red panel was counting down the numbers from 100. 99. 98.

"This is a K'luth device. Klingon warriors use it as a test of bravery. When the number counts down to zero, it sends a wave of neural disruption in a fifty-foot radius. It is a most unpleasant way to die."

"And your point, Picard?" The device in Picard's hand continued to count down. 90. 89. 88.

"A simple one. Only I can stop the countdown before detonation, and that I will not do unless you reveal the location of the captured Federation citizens, and the others as well."

"And you've brought my daughter to your little party because . . . ?"

"Because your own death would mean too little to you as long as Jil Orra lived to continue your line. Her life is something you care about. Your weakness."

"Father," Jil Orra began, her voice cold. Madred interrupted her.

"Do not fear, Jil Orra," he said confidently. "This noble Starfleet officer would never kill an innocent child, even to save dozens of other innocent lives. That is how humans are weak. It is why they will, in the end, be overrun."

"Father," Jil Orra insisted, "he is not killing me. I am here of my own free will, because of what you have done. If you will not release your prisoners and stop your butchery, I do not wish to be your daughter any longer. There is only one way I can escape that shame."

"Picard," Madred began, "you have . . . "

"I've done nothing," Picard said. "What she says is true. She is here at her own request." The device in his hands had reached 55, and were the numbers falling faster now? Madred couldn't tell. He had to think, but there was no time! Would Picard let his daughter die a horrible death? Madred had spent his life figuring the odds, but in his time, at his leisure.

And there was something about Picard, something harder. Had the loss of his ship changed him? "Your ship," Madred began, searching for data.

"Very perceptive," Picard said. "My ship. Sometimes you don't know what you have until you've lost it. I know now that ships are more than vehicles. They're an amalgam of everything we've taught ourselves to do over the ages. A ship is the echo of civilization itself, all in one package.

"We rose from the muck, taught ourselves carpentry, metallurgy, chemistry, navigation, architecture, art. . . . We discovered how to handle and use the elements of nature, right down to warping space itself. . . . We learned compassion and conquest and how to use each. Everything that mankind has learned over the eons can be found somewhere on a starship, and every kind of person as well—from a maverick who does what he likes to"—Picard paused and smiled—"those of us who see the value in consensus.

"The ship, Madred, the ship is why you could never break me and why if I face death today, so be it. I've faced death a hundred times. You've never faced it at all. Because I served on a ship, I will always have the advantage over such as you."

Picard's words rang in the room, then hung there, almost visible before Madred's eyes. Picard had changed, or perhaps Madred had misread him at the beginning. It was time for a strategic retreat. All strategy aside, Madred has to admit that his daughter's life, and her respect, were worth more than his prisoners. Picard had indeed found the crack in Madred's armor.

Madred forced himself to meet the supreme glare of Jean-Luc Picard. "All right, Picard," Madred said, "I'll tell you where your people are. The galaxy is full of people. I can always get more." It sounded hollow even to Madred's own ears. His days as master manipulator were over. Quickly, he fed a set of coordinates to the Klingon's tricorder.

"Verified," the Klingon said. "The ship reports multiple human life signs at that location."

"Thank you, Gul Madred," Picard said formally. "As for your acquiring more people, we'll see about that." The device in his hand went to 10, then 9, then 8.

"Picard," Madred shouted, "stop that damned thing! You have what you want."

"Do I?" Picard said. The device showed the number 7. Picard glanced at the ceiling. "Tell me, how many lights are up there? Four or five?"

Madred felt the blood in his body run cold. The tables had been turned against him. To his surprise, his daughter's life meant more to him than even his pride.

"Four or five, whichever you prefer!" Madred shouted. "Now stop that thing!"

The device moved from 4 to 3 to 2 to 1 to zero. Madred threw himself between his daughter and the device, to shield her with his body.

Jil Orra stepped back, and Madred found himself on his knees in front of Picard. The device emitted a buzzing sound, then stopped. Nothing else happened. The counter on the device reset to 100 and started counting down again.

"So," Madred said from the floor, "you didn't have the courage for it after all. The courage to die. The courage to kill."

"With all due respect to Mr. Worf here," Picard said, "neither killing nor dying takes courage. You thought you were teaching me pain and fear, Gul Madred, but instead you taught me that it is living that takes courage, finding a way to go on despite pain and loss. As I'm sure you will find a way to go on despite this little setback. But for now, I have business to attend to. Captain Atherton. Captain Fernando, and their crews."

Madred got to his feet and offered a congratulatory nod. "Yes," he said, "this way."

CHAPTER 21

"Ow . . ."

Somebody groaned.

Dark in here. Blurry. The smell of lubricant. New ship.

"Will, wake up. Wake up. Come out of it."

Captain Picard?

Same kind of voice—theatrical, resonant . . .

Suddenly the wallowing snapped off and Riker was rushing upward as he lay on a platform, as if he were being hoisted up out of his own grave, toward the rectangular light at the surface.

The groaning came again . . . his own. This time he felt the rumble in his throat. His head throbbed.

"Wake up."

"Captain . . . where are we?"

"They stuck us in an ASRV. You, me, and Scotty."

Lifepod. Not much in here for fighting back. Riker struggled to sit up, blinking as his eyes focused on the unconscious form of Mr. Scott, lying against the other bulkhead of the very small lifepod, and actually snoring as if he were taking a nap.

"Where's the crew?"

Bateson pulled Riker to a sitting position. "He got in the personnel files. He separated the crews and put all my men from the *Bozeman* on his wrecked ship and set it adrift. Evidently we got in a few good shots before he whipped the tar out of me."

"Where's everybody else?"

"Locked somewhere below, or in other pods. In the main section, I think. Probably a shuttle hangar, where they'd have trouble getting out. It's Kozara's way of insulting us by not letting us die in battle."

"How do you know all this if you were unconscious too?"

"Kozara wanted the pleasure of telling me. I guess he gave me a stimulant, because I woke up just as he and his baboons were shoving us in here. He made a point of hauling Data past me like some kind of big marionette with the strings cut. How did they do that to him?"

"It must have been a positronic neutralizer of some kind," Riker said, as if every hardware store sold one of those. "That tells me they knew the personnel roster of this ship. They knew an android would be aboard and that they'd have to take him out first.

"Kozara's really indulging himself," Bateson said. "He called me some names that even I don't know."

"That's saying something . . ." Stumbling to his feet, Riker wobbled and almost fell. Bracing against the wall on one side and Bateson on the other, he drew five or six long breaths before staggering to the airlock hatch. His shoulders and thighs pulsed with aches left over from the stun grenade. Even before reaching the hatch control panel, he could see through the dimness that the panel was shattered.

"They took a disruptor to it," Bateson said. "Guess they're not planning to visit us anytime soon."

"And there's no access conduit in or out of here. Too bad we don't have an air duct." Since the panel was toast, Riker took a second to squeeze his head between both hands.

Didn't help. Only made his hands throb.

"We'll have to notify Starfleet somehow that the ship's been taken and inform them of Kozara's intent to attack Cardassian holdings."

"Maybe they can notify Captain Picard," Bateson suggested. "He's in Cardassian space."

Riker looked up. "How do you know that?"

"Admiral Farrow assured me when he gave me command of this ship that Captain Picard had his own concerns and was going on a mission to Cardassia Prime on behalf of Federation nationals being held there."

"Begging your pardon, sir, but why would Admiral Farrow inform you of Captain Picard's mission?"

"Well, for one thing, the mission's not classified. For the other thing, I was reluctant to take command unless Captain Picard had other choices."

"You were?"

"Of course . . . what?—did you think I pulled strings to usurp you and him?" Sourly Bateson coiled his arms around his chest and sighed. "Well, the general opinion of Morgan Bateson around here certainly seems to be dragging in the muck . . . and unless you know Morse code and can knock real loud, there's no way to contact anybody from in this box. Kozara shut down the emergency evac system. Everything's cold."

Before Riker had a chance to do much more than react with his expression, another groan heaved across the deck and Captain Scott rolled over.

Riker knelt at his side. "Wake up, Scotty. We need you."

"Agh . . . stun bombs . . . I hate those . . . thought they were illegal . . ."

"The Klingons haven't read Starfleet Rules of Engagement," Bateson gnashed.

"Bet they have," Riker tossed the comment out as he helped Scott to his feet.

The senior engineer glanced around and fought for focus. "Where the devil are we?"

"ASRV. The hatch controls are blown. Airlock's jammed."

"Are we in the main section?"

"We don't know."

"Well, let's get out."

"Get out?" Riker repeated. "I just told you. They blew the hatch control panel."

"Panel, *pfft.*" Scott pressed past him and crossed the small space, completely ignoring the hatch controls and stepping instead past the lockers where the foldout seats were stored. There, a small door was imprinted with the words AUTONO-MOUS SURVIVAL AND RECOVERY VEHICLE EXTRAVE-HICULAR GARMENTS (LOW PRESSURE) THREE (3).

Scott tapped in a code, and beside him an environmental locker popped open. He pulled out a survival suit. The thing fell out on him like laundry falling off a line. He instantly shuffled for the breastplate gas exchange and humidity/thermal controls. He did something to the panel which Riker couldn't see in the dimness, then turned back to the hatch, slammed the breastplate up against the airlock hatch, and punched in a few more bleeps and a buzz.

The airlock rolled open. Just like that. It almost sat up and begged.

"Out," Scott invited.

"How'd you do that?" Riker gasped as he followed Scott out into the dim corridor.

"Oh, you'd have to take my course in alternative signals at the academy. New term starts in September."

"Scotty, you're a miracle worker."

"No, lad, I'm an engineer."

"Then you can tell me this—is there a way to communicate with Starfleet?"

"Sure," Scott said. "If Kozara and his playmates haven't figured out the auxiliary broadcast cutoff, I can send a limited coded subspace message from one of the Jefferies tubes. Right down around this bend is one."

They shuffled down the dim corridor, red emergency floor

lights casting weird shapes on their legs and faces. Riker got to the tube access first, and opened it for Scott. Scott's snowy hair was pink in the emergency lights as he fingered the bulkhead control panel for the tube's hatch release. The elderly man would have some trouble climbing up into that constricted space, but he was the only one who knew how to send a message from in there, and the process would slow down if they tried to relay.

As he assisted Scott in climbing into the tube's maw, Riker was already thinking ahead. He glanced over his shoulder at Bateson. "Sir, I suggest we run a guerrilla operation from down here. Make the ship unworkable for them. Capture or isolate as many of Kozara's crew as possible. He's got us trapped down here, but we've got the ship's major engineering at our fingertips. We can do this."

"Whatever battens your hatch," Bateson grumbled, lagging back.

Still supporting one of Scott's boots in his palm, Riker turned. "Captain? What's wrong?"

"What's *wrong?* Oh, permission to gloat, Mr. Riker. Will you get it over with?"

"Gloat, sir? I don't know what you mean."

"I mean this. The galaxy is a more complicated place than when . . . when I was a *real* captain."

"Now, captain . . ."

"Look, Will, I blew it. At least rub it in a little, so I don't feel so pathetic."

"You had a one-dimensional distrust of Klingons because that's what you needed to survive in your time," Riker replied. "I never said I didn't understand. You just found out that Kozara's not one-dimensional anymore. In your time, there weren't many older Klingons fighting. Since then, they've learned the value of their older warriors' experience. Cultures change, Captain."

"I didn't know they'd changed so much."

"They had to change. They had to get smarter, or we'd have

put a stop to them long ago. Peace can do funny things. They've learned a lot about us, we've learned about them. Our cultures aren't so mysterious anymore."

"He still wouldn't have taken the ship if I'd withdrawn when you recommended it."

"Sir, he wouldn't have taken this ship either way without a saboteur on board, and you couldn't have known there was one here."

"Yes . . . I wonder who it was. Which of our crew—"

"Let's not get into that," Riker warned. "The damage is done. We'll smoke the saboteur out."

"How?"

"It'll be whoever is up on the bridge with Kozara when we get up there."

"What if none of ours is up there?"

"I don't know," Riker said, irritated that he didn't have all the answers yet.

"Well, I know this for sure," Bateson said, "everybody on board was confirmed human before we embarked, except for Ensign Yuika and Engineer Ush. And *all* my crew from the *Bozeman* are human."

"Doesn't mean much," Riker told him. "Klingons aren't beyond hiring humans, and some humans aren't beyond working for Klingons. A human willing to work with an alien culture against the Federation is a very valuable commodity. Just like the spies the Federation has in other cultures. It's a fact of life in a hostile universe."

Watching Scott bump around inside the Jefferies tube, Bateson leaned against the tube's support strut. "Hmmm . . . imagine William Riker admitting the universe might be hostile. And, of course, once again, you're the one who's right."

"All right, Morgan," Riker sighed irritably, "snap out of it. We have to launch an underground offensive from down here. Would you please put me in charge of that maneuver, since I know more about large modern ships than you do?"

Momentarily startled at being called by his first name by

someone he thought didn't like him, Bateson contemplated that and came to an instant decision. "Yes, fine. Have at it."

"In that case, I need you to tell me what you know about Klingons."

"What? I was all wrong!"

"No, sir, you weren't," Scott said from inside the tube. "Better stop saying that before Mr. Riker has to get humble."

"Humble? What's that supposed to mean?"

Riker took over, saying, "It means your timing was wrong, but your approach was exactly right. I'm admitting that we've never fought Klingons full-blown like this. You were right about Klingon motivations. We all reacted just fine once it happened, but you were the only one who saw it coming."

"But I was completely surprised!"

"Doesn't matter. You knew the Klingons would eventually take aggressive action."

"Kozara's a rogue! He was coming after *me*. If I hadn't been here—"

"Kozara's no rogue. He has the sanction of the empire. That's a big difference. They saw an opportunity and they took it. Their advantage was that he knew you personally and he's had ninety years to think about your methods. He made an offer and the High Council took him up on it. I'm glad it was us, in this ship, instead of someone less experienced in a less powerful vessel."

"Dead right," Scott's muffled voice confirmed. "We'd be the cleanup crew for a slaughter."

Riker held out a hand of truce to Bateson. "I know about ships of the line from this era. You know about Klingons not as a culture, but as enemies. What have you faced that I never have? I need to know if I'm going to coordinate a counter-offensive from below decks. What do you know about Klingons that you think I should know?"

Bateson eyed him suspiciously from inside his despondence. "I might've been blustering . . . I'm sure you know they're basically fearless. They never hesitate when there's an opening.

Even when they should hesitate. They, uh, they want individual glory. Our problem a century ago was this—how do you fight a race of beings who are big, fierce, stronger than you are, used to prevailing physically, who think it's Viking to die in battle, and who are notorious sore losers? And who are absolutely fearless? They just come at you and they're very good at it. They never back down, they never think twice, they're single-minded and purposeful. That's why I decided not to retreat . . . we always thought it was the wrong message to send to people like that."

"Well, as you found out, they're not that unsophisticated anymore."

"No . . . I guess they're not."

"What do you think our advantages are?"

"Technically? I wouldn't know."

"Not technically. As humans."

"Oh . . . well, we're more clever than they are. I come from back in the days when men were men and Klingons were Klingons and the men lost. We had to figure out ways to handle that. And one thing I've always counted on is that Klingons tend to get angry and stay angry. That adrenaline thing they depend on, like the ancient Berserkers."

"Pardon me?"

"Berserkers."

Scott stuck his foot out from the tube and shook it to get their attention. "Lunatics," he contributed.

Bateson smiled in spite of himself. "They were hand-to-hand fighters in the Iron Age . . . ironically, they were Vikings. They'd go wild, strip off their mail shirts, and fight in bear skins. They were called 'bear sarkers.' That's where we get the term—"

" 'Go berserk'." Riker smiled. "I never knew that."

"Well, being from Alaska, you were deprived," Bateson said with a teasing wink.

"How do you know all this?"

"Word-origins are a great way to learn history. I never had many personal roots, and it's a way to get some."

"And another way," Riker recalled, "is building parts of wrecked ships into our lives, isn't it?" He offered a comforting smile. "Sir, I'm starting to like you better than I did before."

"Well, thanks," Bateson said gratefully. "I always liked you, even though you're a pain in the command seat."

"Thank you. Now, how do we use all this brilliance?"

"Well, I've always thought that humans have an advantage because, after a point, our adrenaline levels out and we tend to calm down and start being sneaky. Like the smaller of the schoolboys tend to get smarter than the bullies. And we don't have the cumbersome baggage of honor or the restraints of logic. We're a lot more individual, a lot more different from each other than they are.

"Good . . . I think we can use that. What else?"

"What else? . . . Well, their system, the way it was designed, what they value in their society, tends to put a whole lot of people on the front lines who all have the same talents and the same weaknesses as each other."

With some effort, Mr. Scott climbed down out of the tube entirely and added, "You got ten Klingons—you got ten Klingons."

"That's right," Bateson said. "But you got ten humans? You got ten really different methods of doing almost anything. Starfleet values all kinds of talents. These are science people, those are medical people, those are tacticians, that's a comm specialist, these are engineers . . . and we're *all* on the front lines. There are captains who came up from engineering, some who are historians, others out of cartography or spectroscopy—you come up against a Starfleet captain, and you don't know what the hell you're in for. At least, that's the way it was ninety years ago. That's why the Klingons were never able to beat the Federation. We've got them all figured out, and they can't make sense of us. It's a fabulous advantage."

Feeling somewhat warmer toward this warmonger, Riker grinned again. "So that's why it was such an insult when Kozara said you were predictable."

Bateson groaned out his misery. "Sure was. We always took it as given that Klingons were uncooperative and uncoordinated, grim and immovable, and so bigoted they forgot to understand their enemies. And look at me, Mr. Preparedness, trapped down here like a rat. I allowed my ship to be taken. It's unforgivable."

"You couldn't have known that Kozara had spent the past ninety years having the Klingon whipped out of him. He's spent the better part of a century eating his pride for dinner every night."

"Wait a minute . . . wait a minute. That still doesn't change his general technological background." Bateson contemplated. "He and his men have basically the same backgrounds, that of a warrior. They aren't specialists. Kozara won't have any scientists or tech guys with him. Even though he planned to take over a ship of the line, a mighty complicated ship with lots of labs and departments, he'll have brought only warriors with him. They can move the ship, fire the weapons, but there are lots of things on a ship like that that can confuse the very devil out of them. That's it! I *knew* I wasn't so dumb!"

Starting to feel as if they really did have some advantages, Riker smiled. "No, sir, you're not so dumb."

On a roll, Bateson took the approval with a sad nod. "What Klingons have trouble understanding is that muscles don't matter. Their hand-to-hand predeliction is silly. It's part of evolution that muscles aren't important unless you're going to remain a beast. The geek in the lab shows that brains are more important. One blue-haired old lady with a phaser could hold off an army with *bat'leths.*"

"You're right," Riker said. "I never really thought about that. How do we use all this knowledge to our advantage? We have to take the ship back, or at least make it unusable to Kozara. How do we use Kozara against himself, knowing what you know?"

Bateson shook his head now, baffled. "A Klingon to whom honor means nothing? I've no idea."

"Well, I do." Proudly, Riker offered, "And you just gave it to me. We can surprise them, and I know how."

"How?"

"By having a sense of humor."

Bateson clapped his hands once sharply. "Oh, yes! A sense of humor can be a formidable weapon against somebody who doesn't have one! Right?"

Riker grinned again. "I like that."

With both arms up the tube as he made a final adjustment of some mysterious kind, Scott contributed, "We can use that to reduce their numbers. I've got a hell of a sense of humor. You'll be surprised how much of one this ship has."

"Did you get the message sent?" Riker asked.

"Aye, I did. Low-power's the best I could do. It'll take a while, maybe four hours, to reach starbase. Unless there's a ship between here and there with the sense to relay."

"Then we'll have to get to work."

Scott finished what he was doing and said, "I can tap into the computer system from down here and get a sensor location on all Klingons aboard. We'll get 'em designated in groups, then go after a bunch at a time. If that's what you had in mind."

"Captain?" Riker turned. "Permission to begin assault on the hijackers?"

Bateson waved both hands. "All right, Will, you're in charge of the covert assault team. Gentlemen, let's start thinking dirty tricks."

"I've got a few," Scott said cannily, his dark eyes flickering in the dimness.

"I'll bet you do," Riker said, grinning. He stepped toward the auxiliary tool locker. A wrench could be a weapon with the right attitude behind it.

Then, unexpectedly, Bateson took his arm and held him back. "One condition, Commander."

"What's that, sir?"

"I don't want to kill any of them."

What? Had he heard right?

Riker openly gawked. "Captain . . . begging your pardon, sir, but what the hell are you talking about?"

"I'm serious. I don't want to kill anybody."

Speechless, and just to be sure he was hearing right, Riker looked at Scott.

"He's got me on that one," the senior engineer admitted, also staring as if the captain had grown elephant ears.

"I have a message to convey to Kozara and the whole Klingon Empire," Bateson said. "Call it a personal message, if you want."

"Kozara's planning to fly into Cardassian space and unleash quantum torpedoes on millions of innocent people! And it's no time for a message between Robin Hood and the Sheriff!"

"It's exactly the time," Bateson said calmly. "Klingons understand killing perfectly well. Nonlethal assault will leave them baffled about the Federation's intent. This is much bigger than you, me, and Kozara. We've got to keep the empire confused about us."

"Well, begging the captain's pardon, but you're completely confusing me, sir!"

Bateson managed a smile. "Eh, it's what we heroes of the past do best. There's something else, though. You recall that Kozara wouldn't say he destroyed the *Nora Nicholas,* even though I asked twice. I think he disabled her and left her crew adrift somewhere."

Unable to bring himself into that funnel of hope, Riker asked, "What makes you think that?"

"Because he'd have boasted about it if he killed them. Kozara has a cautious streak. He doesn't do things he doesn't have to do. What if this assault goes bad for him? He wouldn't want the empire saddled with the slaughter of a whole ship and crew if things go sour. I just know how he thinks. Or at least . . . I know how he *used* to think. Until I'm sure he killed our men, I don't want to kill his."

"Sir, I hope you're right."

"If I am, we might be able to get out of this without an act of war. There's kerosene all over the floor, and I don't want to be the one to throw the match. I headed off a war ninety-three years ago. Do I want to have come through time only to destroy a couple of civilizations now? Thank you, no."

Pausing, Riker ran through all this double-thinking, and decided, "Well, that does make some sense."

"Let's hope it keeps making sense," Bateson said, ready to doubt himself again, "because if they did kill the crew of the *Nora Nicholas,* then the war's already started. Let's get going. By the way, 'sheriff' comes from 'referee' of the 'shire,' from back in the days when the English language was still linked to . . ."

His voice trailed off as he crawled into the conduit tunnel.

"They're coming! Clear the deck! Clear the deck!"

Boom boom boom boom—the pounding feet of booted Klingons set the whole corridor shuddering, but Will Riker was shuddering well enough on his own as he ran along the curved corridor, just keeping enough of the curve between him and the six Klingons chasing him. If they caught up so much as two meters, they'd have a clear disruptor shot at him, and he had no weapon with which to shoot back.

So he ran. He wanted to shoot, but the so-called guerrilla assault team had no hand phasers so they had to be clever whether they liked it or not.

As Riker ran, he could almost feel the burning sting of disruptor fire between his shoulder blades—and he did feel it as shots slammed into the bulkheads behind him, spraying him with sparks and shorn-off bits of plate. He kept running, glad he was as tall as most Klingons and able to keep ahead of them.

"This way!"

It was Captain Bateson, waving to him from inside a doorway. Riker angled in that direction, not slacking his pace. Bateson disappeared inside the darkened room, and Riker plunged in after him, then instantly flattened himself up against the wall.

Pitch dark in here—except for the faint red floor lights from the corridor.

An instant later, three—four—six Klingons came piling

into the room, stinking of sweat and panting with blood-hunger.

Riker slipped back out the door behind them, and Bateson was immediately after. Giving Bateson one second to clear the door, Riker slammed his hand into the door control panel.

The door whooshed shut.

"Will, lock the door!"

The whole door panel boomed and rattled—Klingons had just slammed against it from inside. They were kicking it and pounding it with their weapons. Then there was the sound of a disruptor shot, but the door held somehow. Riker touched it—yes, it was warm.

Six of them, trapped!

"Hurry, Scotty!" he called down the corridor. "The door won't take many more shots! Turn on the program!"

"Understood." Down the corridor about ten feet, Scott worked at another panel, then said, "Computer on, Holodeck Two. Run Scott program 1A, continuous presentation, all vocal controls suspended, authorization Scott-E-five-two-seven-three."

Almost instantly, from behind the door, a terrible cackling and screeching noise rose, counterpointed with the howls and furious shouts of Klingons.

"Shut it down!" a Klingon demanded from inside.

Then others started yelling—

"Program off! Program off!"

"Where are the controls?"

"Computer! Program off! Off, you metal tank!"

"Find the door! Look for the door!"

There was no more pounding on the panel where Riker stood. However, the howling, shouting and screeching from inside got much worse.

Much worse.

"What did you do to them?" Riker asked as he and Bateson joined a beaming Mr. Scott down the hall. "What's going on in there?"

"I sent them to my great-uncle's poultry farm," Scott told

270

them. "Lots of feathers and birdie guano to slip around on. *Lots.*"

Riker glanced at Bateson, then Bateson asked, "And how many chickens were on your great-uncle's poultry farm, Scotty?"

"Oh . . . 'round . . . forty-five thousand, give or take the odd Christmas goose, sir. And for every one they kill, the computer makes two more."

Riker threw his head back and laughed. "Six Klingons and forty-five thousand chickens!"

"What battle methods!" Bateson complained. "George Washington'll be spinning in his crypt!"

Scott brushed his hands together triumphantly. "And they'll *never* find the door."

The dark squares of their sails were urgent with menace, and Hornblower's eye could read more than the mere drama of the silhouettes against the clear horizon.

Ship of the Line

CHAPTER **22**

CARDASSIA PRIME
Madred Village

"What is it?"

"Mark! Stand back. Everybody take cover! Take cover! Atherton! Atherton, take cover! Everybody down. Mark, get your backside *down*."

"It's landing! Steve, are you seeing this? It's preparing to land!"

"Nothing ever lands here! It's got to be something else. Take cover right now!"

"Or what? You'll tell Mom? That thing's landing! Maybe we can get out—"

Steve McClellan grabbed his brother's arm and pulled. "Then they're coming to kill us. Move."

Fighting his injured hip, Steve dragged Mark into the shadows where Brent Atherton, Dan Leith, and several other members of both crews were huddled.

This building had eight-inch walls of poured concrete . . . might provide some cover. Escape routes—to the right and directly behind. The left was cut off, but the right and behind were clear. One led to the sewers, one to the bank.

Once he decided they were leaving themselves a possible way out, Steve huddled and watched the Cardassian ship maneuver for a landing in the middle of the mall the Cardassians themselves had shattered.

It *was* a sight—a ship coming in for a landing. *Here!*

"They're coming to finish us," Brent Atherton said flatly. "They must've decided they don't need us anymore."

Steve didn't stop him. Everyone in the Madred Village had lived intimately with death for months upon months. They didn't coddle each other here. There was no good in it.

"Then we'll fight. We've been fighting the Cardies' way all these months, we can fight to save our own lives. We know how to do it. It's for real this time."

The lack of response, in fact the very coldness that blanketed everyone else right now, was a bitter testimonial. Other than straight surrender, there was no other way.

And if the Cardassians had decided it was time for their guinea pigs to die, nothing in the sector could stop that. The Federation crews were completely boxed in.

"Unless . . ."

Had he said that? Yes he did.

"Unless we can take that ship."

"Take it?" Mark McClellan shoved his brother around to face him. "Are you crazy?"

"It's a way off, isn't it? Look at it! Warp nacelles. We can take that vessel and get out of Cardassian space!"

"You're nuts. All right, let's try."

"Brent?"

"I agree. How many charged phasers do we have?"

"Seven, between both crews," Les reported from somewhere in the dark. "Ten molotovs, sixteen crowbars, nine shrapnel grenades, four radiation grenades, and two concussion salvos."

"Got it," Steve said, adding up the odds in his head.

"They're down!" Mark called, and everyone fell silent.

Out in the middle of the mall under the moonless night, a full-sized Cardassian warship settled hoggishly onto the cracked and pocked pavement, lit only by the reflection of its own harsh scene lights.

What a massive and ugly thing it was, its hull of flinty scales, its windowless body, its hungry weapons arrays.

How could they take a thing like that? They'd have to. This was the critical moment. Take the ship, or die here and hope posterity got something out of it.

Around him, the crews had gone utterly silent. No one moved. Not a pebble grated. In all these months, they'd learned how to hide.

Only Atherton moved—he shifted close to Steve and put his lips near Steve's ear. "Somebody's getting off."

Steve squinted into the darkness. He's never learned to see at distances quite as well as Atherton could. Yes, there was a portside hatch coming open, and a ramp dropping down. Foggy light from inside the craft obscured the humanoid forms that appeared at the top of the ramp.

One . . . two . . . three . . . four people.

Atherton's arm pressed against Steve's as they huddled together, watching.

"A human!" Atherton gulped. Out of habit he kept his voice down to almost nothing. "What's a human doing riding with Cardassians on a Cardassian fighter?"

"I don't know," Steve uttered.

"Do we fight them?" Mark asked.

"I don't know."

"Do you recognize him?"

"No . . ."

"What do we do?"

"I guess . . . I better go out and talk to them."

"Steve!" Mark gasped the cry out loud, unable to contain himself. "The hell you will!"

"Stand down," Steve snapped. "That's an order!"

"Order, hell!"

Atherton shoved Mark back. "Shut up right now! Steve, let me go. You've got more crew here than I do."

"And you've got more experience. If I'm neutralized, they'll still have you in command. I've got to go now, before I pee myself."

Brent Atherton let out a gallows chuckle. "Well, don't do *that.*"

As he stood up on shuddering legs, he heard his brother's pathetic whisper. "Neutralized . . ."

Steve McClellan moved laterally across the concrete building, then across the backs of two other buildings and down an alley, until he was well away from any of the crew. When he emerged onto the open mall, he was relatively sure he hadn't given away anyone else's position.

His hands were cold, clammy. He was sweating beneath what was left of his uniform. And shivering. Death walked with him as he crunched over the rubble toward the three Cardassians and the human.

Two Cardassians stopped coming forward when they saw him. Guards . . . both armed.

A shiver ran up Steve's spine as he anticipated the shock of an energy bolt from those weapons.

Then the third Cardassian hung back, and the human came forward.

"Captain Fernando?" the man called.

Clipped accent. Deep voice. Speaking English.

Steve couldn't manage an answer—his throat was twisted tight. He wondered whether they could see his dirty, torn, soot-caked Starfleet uniform. He hoped they could. Might as well go out proud.

All alone, he limped toward the landed ship, toward those who stood still now and waited for him to approach them in his own time.

The human was wearing plain black clothing, no uniform or

insignia of any kind. The suit looked like Starfleet commando issue, but anybody could buy that surplus. Lots of merchant fleeters wore surplus. Atherton did. Didn't mean anything.

Steve approached the unlikely pair, and stopped only ten feet back. If they decided to be aggressive, he couldn't run on his bad hip anyway. Might as well make a good-looking stand of it.

"Lieutenant," the human said, now that he could see Steve's uniform. "I'm Captain Jean-Luc Picard. Starfleet."

Steve's first reaction was cold doubt. The man stood there, not offering a hand, not stepping closer, letting Steve absorb the words.

A sudden surge of hope drove Steve's heart so far into his throat that he could scarcely respond. It took two tries.

"Lieu—Lieutenant . . . Stephen McClellan, sir . . ."

By now the story was telling itself. From half a dozen hiding places, a few nerve-wracked captive souls were appearing from the rubble in Steve's peripheral vision. They were coming forward, slowly, doubtfully, hopefully.

As the others appeared one by one, the human who said he was Picard requested, "Lieutenant McClellan, make your report."

Steve swallowed a ball of dust. "Yes, sir . . . I regret to report . . . Captain Fernando is dead, sir. So are all our senior officers, including our chief engineer."

Jean-Luc Picard now moved forward, and the empathy upon his strong features was undisguised. "McClellan, I'm sorry. Are you in command?"

"Ah—affirmative, sir."

"That's most commendable, young man. By rising to this challenge, you've brilliantly demonstrated what rank protocol is all about. Go on."

Steve parted his lips to say thanks, but nothing came out. He closed them quickly, pretty sure that the captain could hear his heart slamming against his breastbone. Around him, tentative after so many months, members of both crews came forward, the lights from the Cardassian ship showing off the clothing that hung on their thinned bodies.

McClellan's Starfleeters and Atherton's sailors . . . Steve waited until Atherton arrived at his side and they could stand together.

He tried to speak then, but had to wait. Throat still tight. His tongue felt twice its size.

"Captain Picard," he struggled, "this is Captain Brent Atherton, of the satelliter *Tuscany.*"

Picard smiled in a mellow way and offered his hand to Atherton. "Captain, so glad to meet you. Are you all right?"

Pale, Atherton gaped at him. "Are we . . . going home?"

"Yes, you'll be going home."

Picard raised his voice now so all who were beginning to cluster around would hear. He seemed anxious to tell them what they all wanted to hear.

"You'll all be going home! Your medical needs will be seen to immediately, and then right away you're getting a three-course dinner."

He smiled, let that sink in, then dropped the smile and turned to the nearest Cardassian, the only one not carrying a weapon.

"Come here, Madred."

Steve McClellan flinched as Atherton grabbed his arm and squeezed it. They both stared.

"Madred," Steve whispered.

Was this a trick?

The Cardassian, a man who had dominated their lives since capture, had been lingering in a shadow between the harsh streak of illumination from the ship's scene lights. Now he came forward and Steve remembered his face from hours upon hours of torture and sorrow.

He knew Brent did too. Everyone did. Mark, Dan, Les, Peggy, everyone.

The gathering on the mall turned as cold and stony as the rubble upon which they stood. Fear crackled from man to man.

"Go ahead," Picard said to the infamous Cardassian. "Apologize to these people."

Madred came forward to Picard's side, but left a good two strides between them. He faced forward, looked out at the gaggle of castaways, and took the time to meet eyes with Steve and with Brent.

"My apologies. I have stolen your lives. They will now be given back."

"What about the other Madred Villages?" Brent Atherton blurted out. "Are they shutting down too?"

Madred paused, and plainly this was the part he hated. Interesting—the apology was nothing to him.

"The other installations . . . will be purged also."

Maybe it was real. Steve glanced at Mark, then at Brent. Maybe it *really* was happening. They weren't drifting toward delusion.

"All right, Picard," Madred said, turning. "You've proven to me that you are no longer merely a benign tumor. You are a barracuda. Granted. Allow me to be in awe. You have what you wanted. Now I want my daughter."

"That will be up to her, Madred," Captain Picard said fluidly. "You'll have to win her back."

Madred balled his fists and went up on both toes. "I want her back!"

"Then act decently and honorably. She will return to you." Picard raised a communicator, and only then did Steve notice the captain wasn't wearing any kind of combadge. "Picard to *Half Moon*. Captain Reynolds, commence beamdown."

"We're ready, Captain. Energizing."

"Thank you, Captain."

279

"What's going on?" Atherton demanded.

"It's all right, Captain," Picard assured. "Just a little unfinished business between myself and our gracious host over here. Stand by."

Steve choked out, "Standing by, sir."

Twenty meters away, transport beams sizzled into form, three of them. Humanoids . . . a human woman . . . a Klingon . . . and a Cardassian teenaged girl.

Must be Madred's daughter.

New respect caused Steve to stare for a moment at Jean-Luc Picard. Kidnapping? Not exactly Starfleet method.

"Jil Orra," Madred uttered, clearly relieved at her return.

The teenager stepped forward then, leaving the doctor and the Klingon behind. "Captain Picard. I can speak for myself."

Picard stepped back. "Very well."

"Father, I wish to explain. I am the one who contacted the Federation and told them about your prisoners. I told them you were holding Federation nationals, and Klingon, and Romulans, Orions, Deltans, Lenzhai, and at least one Andorian, and where they could find you."

"Why would you do this?"

"Because you lied to me and I felt foolish growing up to believe lies. You humiliate me when you lie."

"What lie have I ever told you?"

"You said that the enemies of Cardassia deserved their fates, and you were their fate. You said we must be vigilant against all who are not Cardassian. Then I found out you were also capturing and torturing Cardassians. You even have Cardassian Madred Villages. How could you do that? Using your own people as experiments? I found out you never let any of these people have their freedom, even after they have served you in terrible places like this. I could understand that for our enemies. But I couldn't sleep at night knowing that you never let your captive Cardassians go free either."

Madred's voice went to a low grinding. "You . . . contacted . . . the Federation? You?"

"Yes. And I will continue working with them, and with anyone else who wants to believe that not all Cardassians are like you."

"You're only a little girl!" the father burst. "You can't know what you're thinking!"

Beside Steve, Brent Atherton bent over and placed his hands on his knees, breathing deeply as if he were about to retch. But is wasn't that, Steve knew. He stood beside Brent and watched the weight of the past months' horror roll off those shuddering shoulders. While the weight of responsibility had been bearable, this relief was almost overwhelming.

Silent as they witnessed the drama before them, Steve put his hand on Brent Atherton's back and just stood there with that simple tactile contact assuring them both that all this was really happening.

His daughter took another step or two toward Madred.

"When I was much littler," she told him, "you took me into your torture room and you let me see men like Captain Picard sprawled in agony on your floor and you didn't think I was too small then to see your version of the truth. So now that I'm older, I see more."

"You are a traitor!" the father burst.

"I'm a Cardassian and I'm more loyal than you are. Cardassia has to have a future, and your kind of brutality will be bad for us in the long run."

"How can you do this?" Madred demanded. "You're my daughter! I love you!"

"And I love you," the girl said. "But I want to sleep at night again."

"She's got principles, Madred," Picard interrupted them. Stepping forward, he took charge of the situation again. "Your daughter found out you're an equal opportunity monster. You'll even brutalize your own. No matter what you've gained from your actions, you have paid a large price—your daughter's respect. I don't know what it means to you, but it would mean a great deal to me. And because of Jil Orra, I shall always remember that any race, no matter how monolithic, is made up of individuals who must ultimately think for themselves."

He was about to say more, when his comm unit beeped. *"Captain Picard."*

"Go ahead, Captain Reynolds."

"We've been sent an emergency communique from Starbase Twelve. Sir, the Enterprise *has been hijacked!"*

"You're not serious!" Picard blasted.

"I'm afraid so. And it's warped into Cardassian space, not too far from here, and it's cutting up signal outposts on its way to Cardassia Prime. Making just an awful mess—"

"Who in God's name hijacked it?"

"A Klingon called Kuzar."

"Kuzar . . . you can't mean Kozara!"

"That's it!"

"My God . . . Bateson!"

For an instant Picard indulged in thinking what a buffoon Bateson was to let his ship be taken, but he couldn't think that about Riker. There must've been mitigating circumstances— something that had given Kozara an advantage.

Captain Reynolds gave all this a moment to sink in, then said, *"Starbase wants to know if you have a suggestion for heading them off. It'll take six hours for another fleet starship to arrive. By then the* Enterprise*'ll be at Cardassia Prime for over two hours. They could slice up a whole continent before anybody could shut them down."*

"What about the Cardassian defense fleet?"

"All but two of their ships are on the Dominion and Klingon defense perimeters. They'll take even longer to get here."

"What are the two ships?"

"Fighter-transports. Not very big by comparison."

"No, but a combined attack might serve."

"What do you want to do?"

"Stand by."

Feeling as if he were in a dream, watching a show in which he could not participate, Steve looked at Atherton. Due to familiarity, Steve knew the other man still suspected a trick.

Captain Picard moved closer again. "I'd been hoping to take you home for a well-earned rest, but as you just heard, the new starship, the *Enterprise*-E, has been hijacked in the Typhon Expanse by a disgruntled Klingon commander. He's been initiating a series of raids leading toward the center of the Cardassian civilization. He's threatening to unleash the power of the Federation's new flagship on the innocent civilians of Cardassia Prime and its surrounding settlements."

" 'Innocent,' " somebody mocked from behind.

Picard let the grumble run through the crews, then looked at Steve with such intensity that Steve thought one of them was about to melt.

"As the senior Starfleet officer in the sector," Picard announced officially, "I'm taking charge of the situation. Mr. McClellan, I will appropriate two more Cardassian ships of the class you see behind me. I'm conferring upon you a field promotion to the rank of lieutenant commander. You'll take charge of one ship. Captain Atherton, I believe you deserve command of the third ship. We also have with us the *M.F.P.S. Half Moon,* upon which we've mounted a swiveling dorsal-turret phaser cannon in anticipation of close-quarter battle. Any of your crews who wish to be with you shall be at your sides. I shall command the fleet. This is obviously an extremely dangerous CQB exercise. We may be liberating you only to have you killed in the line of duty. The ships named *Enterprise* have for generations been the forward symbol of Federation integrity in the galaxy. Now that is at stake. I'm offering you the opportunity to finally fight for something beyond yourselves, and to show the Cardassians what the Federation is really all about."

Picard paused a moment, gazed at Atherton, at Steve, then scanned the shivering crews clustering around them. He seemed determined to meet eyes personally with each individual.

"In consideration of your unparalleled service and bravery," he spoke resonantly, "I shall make this a voluntary mission. However, I won't delude you. No less than the noble heart of the Federation and millions of innocent Cardassian lives rest upon your shoulders. Yes . . . I'm asking you to risk your lives and your newfound freedom for the safety and security of those who have imprisoned you, who've tortured you. My friends, this is your chance," he finished, "to show them what you're really made of. Will you come with me now?"

His voice thrummed through the bombed-out square.

Cold hands shuddering, Steve McClellan stood there on his aching hip, digesting the fact that he was still alive and that there was food inside that ship for him and his brother and their shipmates, and he couldn't make so much as a squeak of response.

Should he answer for all the others? Should he—were they waiting for him to speak for them?

What was Atherton thinking?

Should they—

Steve almost jumped out of his skin when Atherton let out a suddenly whooping cheer beside him and raised both hands into the air. Instantly a bigger cheer erupted from all the former captives, a soul-raising shout of participation and hope.

Steve looked around to see who was making the noise, and it was himself. Himself, his brother, and everybody with whom they'd been stranded here, shouting and cheering, hugging and some actually dancing.

Invigorated, Steve swung back to Picard. "Sir! May I offer the services of the crews of the *U.S.S. Durant* and the satellite tender *Tuscany!*"

Another high cheer backed him up.

Picard reached for Steve's hand and pumped it. "Lieutenant, I'm proud of you. Starfleet is proud of all of you. The entire Federation owes all of you its pride and gratitude. Everyone, follow me on board! Our mission . . . stop the *Enterprise!*"

And the timbers creaked and the rudder groaned and the wind whistled and the sea hissed, everything blending into an inferno of noise as he clung shuddering to the rail.

Ship of the Line

CHAPTER 23

"Keep your voices down. There are nine Klingons right behind this bulkhead, manning the warp propulsion. We're at warp now. Lord knows where he's heading."

"He's heading into Cardassian space, sir."

"How do you know that, Scotty?"

"Directional readout charts. Right on that wee screen over there."

Bateson and Scott were in front of Riker as they all hurried through a doorway, hoping the Klingons in the next chamber wouldn't come out before they were safely behind closed doors.

They had no hand phasers. They'd raided an auxiliary arms cabinet two decks up, only to find that Kozara knew enough about computer systems to drain those phasers even as they hung on their charging mounts. Useless. Except maybe for throwing, and any hammer would serve for that.

Why was Kozara going into Cardassian space? Nothing good. Klingons thought Cardassians were slightly more than reptiles. Cardassians thought Klingons were overspined children. At the moment Riker thought they were both right.

Kozara could've gone into Cardassian space and stirred up trouble just fine with that Klingon fighter he'd set adrift. Why would he bother taking this—

Instantly the question answered itself.

"Scotty, we've got to hurry," he urged. Suddenly he was cold all over, as the larger picture showed itself across the panorama of his mind. "Do you have another idea?"

"I have one," Bateson said. "It's pretty base."

"Basic is good."

"Not basic. Base. There's a subtle difference. Scotty, can we get a view of that area without having them see us?"

"Think so," Scott answered, and plucked at a computer console in the corner of the room. "Security cameras ought to be working—there you go, sir."

An angled picture of the warp propulsion monitor cubicle cleared on the small screen. Seven . . . eight Klingons in view, having some kind of argument.

"Where's the audio?" Riker asked.

"Doesn't seem to want to come in." Scott plucked a little more. "If I tamper, the unit might light up."

"Don't do it then," Bateson ordered. "We'll just watch." He carefully, quietly crossed the deck to a janitorial closet and disappeared inside. Agonizing seconds slogged by before he came out again, with an armload of cleaning and disinfecting chemicals, and oddly, a first-aid kit. "Scotty, Will, feed these ingredients into the computer and come up with a formula."

Riker squinted. "A formula for what?"

"Now, *this* ought to turn their crank."

"Oh, my God . . . this is disgusting! Look at those numbers!"

"Especially with those first-aid chemicals included, Will. Scotty, are you ready?"

"When you are, Captain."

"Fire away."

"Operation Skunk, firing away, sir."

Riker and Scott worked together from two separate consoles, combining—very quietly—the ingredients of the medical sub-station into a computer-constructed formula, for a specific result. The chemicals themselves had been rather crudely introduced by Captain Bateson into the ventilation system from a duct access down the corridor, in heavy concentrations. Disinfectants, sterilizers, cleaning agents, solvents, medical salves . . . now the captain was back, the door was closed, the screen was showing the Klingons next door, and the computer was taking over.

Finishing his sequence, Riker hurried to Scott's console, where Bateson hovered over Scott's shoulder. Together they all looked at the small screen, which showed a ceiling view of the eight—oh, there were ten now—Klingons.

Ten. That was all of them in there, according to the thermal registry in the computer.

Ten more . . . would it work?

"Their sense of smell is stronger than ours," Bateson murmured as he peered over Scott's shoulder at the working Klingons. "When's it going to start?"

Scott hunched over the controls, delicately adjusting a dial. "Any second now . . ."

On the screen, four Klingons' faces were toward them, with the other six standing with their backs to the recorder. They continued their argument and kept working at the controls. Riker wished there were sound, but that would be too risky. Systems were scrambled all over this ship, thanks to the sabotage they'd suffered. Better not risk tampering too much. The ship would require a full sensor sweep when this was all—

"Look!" Bateson pointed at the screen.

Two of the Klingons had stopped working. They were glancing at each other, frowning, wondering. One more started glancing around. One waved at the air in front of his face. They kept eyeing each other.

Now, one by one, two by two, the rest of them noticed something less than flowery in the room.

One Klingon pointed a finger and shouted at another. The second waved his hands furiously, then pointed at another Klingon. The first Klingon clawed at his eyes and tried to plug his nose.

"They think it's each other!" Riker crowed.

Bateson actually giggled. "I wish I'd thought of this back at the fraternity house. How it must stink in there!"

"It's got to *reek* in there," Scott corrected. "And it's about to get mighty worse."

He cranked more on the dial.

On the screen, the Klingons began gagging. Two of them retched. Another scratched at his eyes and tried to block his nose and mouth with his arm.

"Masks," Bateson ordered, and handed Riker a small personal emergency gas mask. "Get ready."

"Do we have to?" Riker put his mask on, still watching the ten Klingons gag and double over at the sickening stinkpot gasses flooding the room. Six Klingons were on their knees. Two more were folded over chairs, another over a console. The assault was turning debilitating, as Scott fed a combination of methane and various other fetid odors into the chamber.

"I'm putting in enough methane to make them dizzy," Scott said. "Any more'll kill 'em. Now's the time, sir."

Bateson shoved off toward the door. "Come on, Will!"

Grabbing a box of two dozen packaging ties, Riker followed the captain out into the corridor and down to the warp control doorway. Bateson keyed the door manually, and they went in to meet the gawking eyes of dazed, nauseated, wobbling Klingons.

Even through the mask—what a stench! Riker almost threw up, but managed to hold his stomach down as he and Bateson scrambled to tie the Klingons' wrists behind their backs and then secure their ankles together.

"Aww . . ." he wheezed through the mask. "Repulsive!"

"Isn't it?" Bateson secured the last Klingon. "This is what happens when you let engineers do the cooking. Damn it, they're not armed! No sidearms! Kozara's smarter than I gave him credit for."

Riker hoisted one gagging Klingon to his knees. "We can hide them in the janitorial closet."

"Good. Let's get the hell out of this—"

"Let's inhibit the propulsion system first, sir."

"And shields. If Starfleet got our message, they'll need a way to take the ship back without destroying her.

"Let's at least do it fast."

"Oh, yes, *please.*"

"You know, my throat is still burning from that stink."

"My eyes are watering too."

"How much do you think Kozara knows about the ship?"

Riker's question was barely above a whisper as he and Bateson worked on the environmental controls. Scott, to whom fighting Klingons was old hat, was stationed in the auxiliary control room, dinking with the environmental mains. Together they were plotting mischief, but Riker was worried. Soon Kozara would discover the members of his crew missing on the holodeck and those the guerrilla squad had hidden away back in that janitorial closet. Kozara probably wouldn't find his men, but he'd know some of the prisoners were free and creating trouble. He could then track humans on the move with the bioscanners.

With his arm up to the pit in the wall access conduit, Bateson managed a shrug. "I don't know when he found out about the ship or that I was on it. Obviously some portion of this is a personal vendetta. If he found out about me three years ago, then he's had three years to track my activities, and he's known about the starship for about two of those years, right about when I joined the project. And he's had a spy informing him, but we don't know for how long. Could be hours, could be years."

"I hate unknown quanities," Riker griped. "But you know as well as I do, he could spend ten years learning about starship systems and still never know them all. I know I don't. That's why it takes a large crew to run a ship like this. Nobody can know everything."

"Give or take Scotty. I'm beginning to think he knows *everything.*"

Nodding in unqualified agreement, Riker added, "When I figure out how he got the pod's airlock open with just a survival suit, then I'll know everything too. We know more than Kozara does, and that gives us an edge."

"Until he captures us. I'm almost finished here. Adjusting localized gravitational trim . . . now. I wish we could contact Scotty."

"We don't dare," Riker said. "They could pick up on our comm signals and trace us."

"What did he say? Forty-five degrees?"

"Fifty-five degree pitch."

"Fifty-five . . . You better get out into the corridor. Let them see you, but whatever you do, stay on the outside of the centrifugal."

"Here I go. Wait for my signal."

The ship's artificial gravitational system wasn't the sort of thing Riker had ever figured for a weapon. Like walking on a planet, the gravity was just there. It felt normal. It was adjusted to feel that way, always perpendicular to the deck, so a person would be upright and feel as if he were walking on an even surface.

All that was about to change. Each deck, each stretch of corridor, had its own superconducting stator constantly spinning gravitons, so inertial potential could vary from one area to another and compensate for hard maneuvering. Waveguide conduits connected the network.

In auxiliary control, Scott had broken into the environmental systems and freed up this link of the network. Bateson now had readjusted the gravity pitch on a fifty-foot stretch of one corridor. All he had to do was push a button, and the deck would feel—well, pretty damned tilted.

Riker hurried through the ship to a door with a plate announcing BATTLE BRIDGE. Inside, he knew, were seven more of Kozara's crew, trying to figure out the master systems displays. Riker didn't know what Kozara had in mind for the battle bridge, but he meant to stop it. Possibly separate the sections, and have effectively two ships, one jam-packed with antimatter power and heavy weapons.

Heading toward Cardassia Prime . . . if not to gain back his honor, then to start a war and at least have some kind of legacy.

"Or deny this ship a legacy," Riker suddenly murmured. "That's it . . ."

Pausing briefly under the weight of that realization, he shook himself back to purposes and stepped close to the battle bridge entrance. The door sensor picked up his proximity and the door slid open.

He found himself staring at all six of the Klingons, all at once.

Then he looked down the corridor at nothing and shouted, "All hands, run for it!"

Instantly he took off in that same direction, as if chasing a whole team of Rikers on the loose. Wouldn't do any good if only two Klingons chased him.

A shout in Klingon rocketed down the corridor after him, punctuated by the pounding of hard-soled boots. He glanced over his shoulder as he rounded a corner—six . . . all seven were following!

Bateson had been right about them—instead of two or three following Riker, all seven were going after the glory, competing with each other, not thinking about how to efficiently cooperate.

Without body armor or the natural bulk of a Klingon, Riker was quicker. He managed to outpace them by about ten meters. Ahead of him was another curve. Instead of rounding that curve, he ducked into the crew's quarters straight ahead, just before the curve, and stood there in the doorway, with both feet inside. The Klingons could see him.

And he could see the fury in their eyes. A shiver raced down his spine.

"Hope this works," he gasped, and hit his combadge. "Now!"

A sickening tuck made his stomach roll. His feet were all right, inside the crew's quarters, but the upper half of his body still stuck out into the corridor and was washed with the adjusted gravity. Instantly all seven of the Klingons lost their balance and slammed hard into the starboard wall. Completely disoriented, they couldn't find the deck anymore. Some were trying to climb the wall. Their feet scratched on the short-napped carpet.

Riker hit his badge again. "Stage two, now!"

A few seconds passed, and for a moment he thought Scotty might've failed.

Then a glossy crust began forming over the carpet—frost!

The deck crackled, turned hoary white, and iced up like a skating rink. An instant later, Riker felt another wash of gravity changing, this time to pitch the whole corridor downward on one end.

As if riding a water slide, the seven Klingons howled and scratched, but couldn't stop their "fall." Scraping down the icy surface of the corridor, they swiped toward Riker, their faces plastered with astonishment and disorientation.

"Welcome aboard!" Riker called as the first one flashed past him, then the second.

Whoosh—whoosh—Squalling in rage, the third and fourth Klingons came by even faster, their legs ridiculously tangled. The fifth Klingon managed to catch the doorframe of Riker's cubbyhole and hung on, clawing at Riker's legs as if hanging from a cliff's face, and for a hideous second almost climbed inside. The Klingon's teeth were gnashing, hoping to get a bite out of Riker's ankle.

"Can't have that," Riker said simply, and assisted his friend with a kick in the nose.

Raging, the Klingon flew off down the "hill" with his crewmates, followed by the sixth and seventh Klingons, who were trying to climb each other, as if that would work.

Riker leaned as far out as he dared, his head spinning with the pull of gravity in the wrong direction, and looked down toward the end of the corridor. There stood Captain Bateson in the doorway of another quarters, throwing loading netting over each Klingon that arrived in the room. Dizzy and as turned around as undersea divers, the Klingons were disoriented enough that Bateson could quickly secure each net while the Klingons were still thrashing about and looking for the floor.

Riker hit his combadge and dared a quick message. "Cancel!"

Instantly the gravity changed again, and he had to hang onto the doorframe to keep from falling over. Seven here, ten in the janitor's closet, six chasing chickens. Twenty-three Klingons out of commission.

Happy in their victory as schoolboys, Riker and Bateson met each other in the corridor.

"Twenty-three down," Bateson said. "That leaves seventeen. Not bad for nonlethals."

"Not bad at all," Riker agreed as they ran to auxiliary control and plunged inside.

"Scotty!" Bateson called instantly. "It worked! Icing the deck was brilliant!"

But Scott was not sharing in their joy. In fact, he looked sagged and overwhelmed. "Sir . . ."

Both Riker and Bateson fell ominously silent at Scott's horrified expression.

"He's unloading the quantum torpedoes," Scott rasped. "Somehow he got 'em armed!"

"How?" Riker bolted. "The firing sequence wasn't laid in yet!"

"His spy probably told him how," Bateson huffed.

Riker rushed to Scott's side and looked at the readouts. "And he's firing them?"

Scott pointed at the firing display. "He's sure as hell shooting at something, sir."

As the blood in his body drained to his feet, Riker raised his sore eyes to Bateson's and Scott's paled faces. They gazed helplessly at each other for a few ugly seconds.

Then Captain Bateson dared to ask what they were all thinking. "Have we made it to Cardassia Prime? Could he be shooting at cities?"

"I don't know," Riker said. "But if so, our buffer's run out."

Did it matter if a grain of dust in a whirlwind retained its dignity?

Hornblower and the Atropos

CHAPTER 24

"We have destroyed sixteen outposts, primarily automated signaling centers."

"How many killed?"

"Few."

"Good. I want my options open."

"The Cardassian subspace communications crackle with terror at our presence. They know we will soon come to Cardassia Prime, and they have no fleet in this sector to stop a ship like this. Nearly all their ships are on the defense perimeter. Their own vigilance will ruin them!"

"Good, Gaylon, good. We will strike at the heart of Cardassia Prime and erase their government's seat. They will have to deal with the empire, and the empire will have to deal with me. Carry on."

Gaylon felt invigorated giving such a report to Kozara, and especially having Zaidan standing by, watching, not really understanding any of the technology of this great sweeping vessel they had stolen.

So much power! And the interior was like artwork, like brushstrokes. Like the Klingon sky before a storm.

But there was trouble also. They had now lost contact with thirty-eight members of their crew below decks. Malfunctions, perhaps, or mistakes, but Gaylon did not believe that. Nor did Kozara. There was part of a Starfleet crew trapped below, and while the firedoors and bulkheads were secured, Gaylon had no way to be certain those would stay secured. This ship was too complicated. They could be sure of exactly nothing.

If some of the Starfleeters had broken free and debilitated the Klingons below, then time was against Kozara's plan. The battle for possession of the ship was under way.

Time . . . time . . .

"Cardassia Prime in fifty-three minutes, Commander," Klagh reported from the helm.

"Hold course and speed—"

The turbolift door swished open, and just as Gaylon turned, Morgan Bateson and that Klingon-sized first officer came charging out of the lift, brandishing hand phasers.

Where had they gotten charged hand phasers?

The question dominated Gaylon's mind as he and three of his crewmates met the two angry men at the back of the bridge. The first officer fired, and took down two Klingons in what appeared to be phaser stun.

Stun! So they wanted to fight hand-to-hand. Gaylon joyfully lowered his disruptor and lashed out with a boot, tripping Bateson and sending him sprawling along the upper deck. Bateson's phaser spun out of his hand.

"Hold them back! Gaylon! Hold them!"

Disruptor fire broke across the bridge, but both Will Riker and Captain Bateson dodged it—bless those support pylons!

Riker saw the Klingon that Kozara had yelled at and noticed that this was a first officer. At least, he was wearing those markings on his body armor.

All these Klingons were middle-aged to senior types, except one—actually the biggest one. Kozara's crew . . . and his son?

Riker raised his weapon to get in another shot, and was

stunned by a hard strike to the side of his head. The pain left him dazed, and when he shook himself back, the hand phaser was gone. His arms were shackled.

Too many Klingons—too experienced to be taken this way. It had been a poor chance, trying to take the bridge before more torpedoes could be unloaded on some innocent target, but they'd taken the bet. They'd lost.

Pinioned on the upper deck by two gray-haired Klingons with good grips, Riker tried to get his wits back. His eyes gradually focused, and he saw Kozara standing over Bateson on the upper deck.

"Pick him up," Kozara ordered.

Two more of his men came forward and hoisted Bateson to his feet.

Kozara got almost nose to nose with his long-remembered enemy.

"What did you think, Bateson? I would take a ship only to let you steal it back? I have been ninety years recovering from you. You are a strange gift for the galaxy to give an old Klingon."

"You may hold the bridge, Kozara," Riker said, "but the rest of the ship is ours."

"All I need is the bridge. Our traveling is nearly over. Now all we must have is that panel." Kozara pointed, and sure enough got it right. Weapons and tactical. "I need no precision to cut apart a planet. This ship's reputation will be like flies upon dung in the street. There will never be another *Enterprise* when I finish with—"

Kozara's first officer, Gaylon, came to life suddenly from the tactical panel. "Commander, contacts! Three . . . four vessels!"

"Size and configuration."

"Fighter tonnage," Gaylon reported, squinting into the bright readouts, "three vessels bear standard Cardassian configuration, emissions, and signals. Fourth ship . . . is unfamiliar. Federation emission . . . spacelane signals . . . smaller than the others, but reads warp powered. Possibly armed."

"Of course it has arms," Kozara drawled. "Why else would they come out and challenge us?"

"Perhaps they've heard of you," Bateson needled. "And your failure of a son. Hello, Zaidan. You're a big boy now, aren't you? Too bad you don't understand what a bold warrior your father is. Even I have to give him credit. This is a gutsy way to commit suicide."

Riker smiled. Not bad.

"What is it, Kozara?" Bateson asked. "Because you were embarrassed once, you'll now slaughter millions? There's honor. And they say you don't have any. I'll have to tell them they're wrong."

"You will tell no one anything, dog. I will keep you alive long enough to watch the ruination of your great flying legend."

Bateson raised his chin. "Up thine."

Kozara blinked. "What?"

Before Riker could think of a quick answer for himself, the son of Kozara swung his long arm and clipped Bateson hard across the jawline. Bateson's head snapped back, but he stayed on his feet somehow.

"Kozara . . . do you let this boy decide the course of your actions?" he asked.

Riker held his breath. . . . He wanted to say something, felt obliged to, but some instinct stopped him. This was Bateson's show.

"Kozara," Bateson began, much quieter, "let's speak across the years to each other. You're involving everyone today—my crew, your crew, the Cardassians, the Federation, your empire—but this isn't about all these other people. It was always about you and me."

"Do you think," Kozara challenged, "I am fool enough to fight you hand to hand when I already hold the advantage?"

"No, no," Bateson said. "No . . . I don't want to fight you. You'd turn me into oatmeal. I'm trying to tell you, man—you came here and took my ship from me. Kozara . . . you already won!"

For a place crowded with people, the bridge lapsed into a stunning silence. Riker flexed his fingers and swore everyone could hear it.

Kozara stared at Bateson. Bateson spread his hands in a complacent plea.

Was it over? Was Kozara, after all these years, less programmed than Klingons of the past?

"Commander," Gaylon called, "the four ships are blocking our way."

"Warn them back."

"I did. The lead ship is hailing us."

"Put it on."

"This is Captain Jean-Luc Picard commanding this defense fleet. We are armed and ready to stop your assault on Cardassia Prime. Starfleet has been notified. Within one hour, the starships Hood *and* Defiant *will arrive. Until then, our four ships stand between you and the Cardassian homeworld. If you attack this formation or any Cardassian holdings, I will consider it an act of war against the United Federation of Planets. Think before you take action. Your entire empire will pay for your choice."*

Riker swelled up with relief and excitement, and looked at Bateson, who also was beaming. Picard! Scott's signal had gotten through to Starbase 12!

"Fire!" Zaidan shouted. "Shoot! Kill them! They cannot threaten us! We are Klingons! They are nothing! Jean-Luc Picard is nothing! He is all finished! Shoot him out of the sky and I will call you father again!"

He rounded on Kozara, who stood near the command chair now, glaring at his son with a peculiar expression of distaste.

"If you do this, you will redeem yourself," the son bellowed. "You will give me all I have been denied. Our name will not go down to shame!"

"Myself?" Kozara erupted at his son. "None of this is for myself! Do you still fail to understand? There is more in this galaxy than 'myself' and 'yourself'! There is more than the stupid, hungry self! You greedy imbecile . . . stand away from me! Take your feet up from the deck of this fine ship whose corridors you do not deserve to walk."

Stunned, Zaidan dropped back a couple of paces and gawked. His mouth hung open, as doltish as a landed fish.

"I was going to incinerate the Cardassian homeworld to undo the past for you," Kozara said. "Since we embarked together I have heard nothing but your contempt and complaints, and they begin to gnaw on me. Look around you!" He waved at Picard, at Riker, even at Bateson. "These men have fought their way back to their bridge! They deserve to keep it. Gaylon, shields down."

"Down!" Zaidan stormed.

He plunged toward Gaylon, but Gaylon was ready. He deflected Zaidan with one arm, holding him back just enough that Gaylon's left hand could freely meet the tactical control panel.

Glaring into Zaidan's challenging face, Gaylon said, "Shields are *down,* Commander."

"Weapons," Kozara ordered, also glaring at Zaidan.

Zaidan swung around to breathe fire at his father. "You are standing down? You will fight on my behalf! You will destroy them all for me! You promised!"

"A fool's promise is not binding." Kozara flamed back. "I will do nothing more for you, brat. I may be your shame, but you are mine."

Enraged, Zaidan wasted no more time on his father, but whirled around to Morgan Bateson. "Look what you have done to my father! Bulldog Bateson, I will smash you for what you stole from me!"

"Stop!" Kozara blew between them and knocked his son back a pace, away from Bateson.

Even at his age, driven by the sheer strength of his will, Kozara had little trouble blasting his powerful son back. Zaidan's fists flew wide, the fists of a construction engineer which would easily have broken Bateson's skull.

"Get away from him, boy!" Kozara flared. "He is too worthy for such as you."

Shaking out his apprehension, Bateson said, "Kozara, I really don't need your help, you know."

"And I would not help you," his old rival said, "except that you are more deserving of my effort than this sorry whelp."

The wizened commander took his own disruptor out of the holster and placed in upon the helm, all the time watching Zaidan's hatred boil.

"Now that I have this ship in my hands," Kozara said, "and I look at you, I begin to think in another way. Why should so many die for you? Why should my last action as a Klingon commander be on your behalf? What have you done to help yourself but be born alive? Must honor go only from the father to the son? What kind of civilization do we have that the child cannot honor the family until the father's shame is dissolved? Whatever turn the fates vomited upon me, I never whined like a brat. I never moaned. I never blamed anyone else for my failures. I never clung to the successes or shames of those who came before me and sought to flog myself with them and make strangers pay. I no longer care about myself, Zaidan, and as I watch you today, I begin to care less and less about you."

"Well put," Bateson offered. "Kozara, you're a man of honor no matter what anybody says."

"Yes, yes," Kozara drawled. "And you are better than I care to admit, human. Better than my son."

He turned away from Zaidan, and did not look again at his son. Instead, with rather shocking direction of purpose, he poked at the comm link on the helm. "Captain Jean-Luc Picard. This is Commander Kozara of the Klingon Advance Assault Squadron. Come and take this ship. I no longer want it." He waved at Riker and Bateson then, and said, "Tell him or he will not believe."

Riker didn't actually believe it himself. Was it a trap? No, couldn't be.

Still suspicious, he slowly moved to the comm link. "Captain, this is Riker."

"Mr. Riker, do you have control of the bridge?"

"I believe so . . ."

"What does that mean?"

Rather than respond immediately, Riker looked at Kozara. Kozara looked at Zaidan. Zaidan looked at Bateson.

Reading something in his old rival's control of the moment, Bateson turned to Riker and said, "Tell him the bridge is ours, Mr. Riker. I'd like him to beam over."

Riker felt his face crimp in a frown, but he couldn't figure out a reason to disobey that order. Captains. Weird.

"Captain, we have the bridge. Captain Bateson requests that you beam over immediately."

"Acknowledged. I'll comply. Stand by."

"Standing by."

Around the bridge, Kozara's crew members stood in surreal satisfaction. Whatever they had come here to do, they didn't want to do it on Zaidan's behalf. They didn't think he deserved it. Odd—they'd been willing to slaughter a planet, a civilization, at Kozara's bidding, and now just as easily stood down at his whim.

With new respect Riker watched Kozara. There must be something in him, for his crew to do this unexpected thing.

In fact, Kozara seemed more satisfied by this surrender than embarrassed by it.

Before Riker could reflect further, a single transporter beam sizzled onto the upper forward deck, and a moment later, Jean-Luc Picard was standing there.

Was he ever! Fully armed with a phaser rifle, this was a different Jean-Luc Picard than Riker had ever seen before. His bearing was supremely confident, and from the moment the transporter beams faded away, he was undeniably in command of this bridge.

"Stand down!" he snapped to the cluster of Klingons.

"They're stood down, Captain," Bateson said, stepping forward with two disruptors he had collected from Gaylon and another Klingon. "Of his own choice, Kozara has decided to modify his course of action. He is not our prisoner. His men are not under guard."

Picard didn't believe for a moment, but when Riker stepped

305

forward with his back to Kozara, the captain's expression changed.

"Confirmed, sir," Riker said, and gave him a little flare of a brow for good measure.

Just for a moment, Picard actually looked disappointed. Was that right? Riker looked again, but the moment was passed.

"Very good," Picard said. "Number One, take tactical and run a diagnostic on the ship's systems. Give me an overview."

"Aye, sir."

"Captain Bateson, your lip is bleeding." Picard stepped down to the command arena with Bateson and Kozara. "Are you hurt?"

"I'm all right," Bateson told him with a shrug that was becoming emblematic. "Sorry to spoil your fun."

"Yes, I was rather looking forward to it," Picard told him, still holding the phaser rifle, but pointed now at the deck. "Where's your crew?"

"Set adrift on Kozara's derelict ship, back in the Typhon Expanse."

"We'll pick them up. And the others?"

"Mostly they're locked belowdecks, in the pods and lower levels. We're breaking them out few by few."

"Well," Picard sighed, "that's certainly a better welcome than what I expected."

"What about your mission, Jean-Luc?" Bateson asked.

"Yes!" A flare of success bolted from Picard, so pleasant that Riker turned and looked, just to help enjoy it. "On those Cardassian ships out there are the crew of the *Durant* and the satellite tender *Tuscany* . . . at least those who are still alive. Their captains are commanding those ships. It's a good job, you know, when a man gets to bring—"

"Captain!" Riker suddenly had to interrupt as half his board lit up. "I'm reading a Klingon warship on approach vector— fighter class!"

He waited for orders, but didn't know which captain to look at for those.

Picard tilted his head cannily at Bateson. "Captain, it's your command."

Bateson waved a hand. "Oh . . . no, sir, you took the bridge. I was a captive here. You're in command."

Hesitating, Picard glanced at Riker, then back at Bateson. Would he take it?

Riker held his breath. It was a fine line—Bateson was the assigned captain, but he had lost the ship. Picard was the senior officer reconfiscating the vessel.

"I'm not taking the ship, Captain," Bateson warned during the pause.

"Well," Picard finally answered, "all right, very well. Would you take tactical, please, and check on phaser power?"

"Aye aye," Bateson responded, and Riker caught a bit of joy in his voice.

Incredible! Bateson was actually having a good time. In fact, both captains were.

"Number One, please take the helm," Picard requested.

"All we have is quantum torpedoes," Riker told them as he settled tightly into the helm chair. "We compromised phasers from belowdecks before we came up here."

"Picard to engineering. Mr. Scott, do you read?"

"Scott here. Welcome aboard, sir."

"Thank you. We've got a hostile encounter and we need phaser power. Quantum torpedoes won't maneuver quickly enough."

"Working on it, sir. My handiwork's hard to untangle."

"Quickly. Picard out."

"Attack position," Bateson ordered. "Full about."

"Full about, sir," Riker said. It *did* feel good to have his hands on the helm!

Beneath his touch, the big ship pivoted mightily in space, shouldering through the punishment of an asteroid cloud, toward the oncoming Klingon ship.

They could see the ship on their screen now—a strong warship rigged for battle, coming in with its fins down like a shark about to attack.

Picard gripped the arms of the command chair. "Scotty, I need that power!"

"One more minute, sir."

"Not good enough. Captain Bateson, give me communications to McClellan, Atherton, Reynolds, and Mr. Schoen on the ship I was commanding. I want them to move into formation."

Riker was looking at the forward screen, maneuvering the starship so that her weakened shields faced the approaching Klingon fighter as much as possible. If they had to take more hits, he wanted the hits to come on the starship's most narrow profile. She was sluggish—the result of espionage, sabotage, and being in the hands of too many crews with too many conflicting goals—himself, Scott, and Bateson included. They hadn't done the ship any favors down there.

"Hail the Klingon ship," Picard snapped.

There was a force in his voice that Riker hadn't heard in years, and damned infrequently at that. Riker actually turned to look.

"This is Captain Jean-Luc Picard commanding the *U.S.S. Enterprise*. Identify yourselves and stand down immediately. You are stood off by the combined fleet before you. Respond immediately or face the consequences."

The comm link crackled between the two systems. For a moment there seemed to be no answer coming. Then a voice sprinkled across the tract of open space.

"This is First Officer Gabriel Bush flying the imperial warship Klacha macha pucka yucka-yourmother'samoose *or something. Anybody know how to make this lobster pot go out of battle mode?"*

Bateson perked up instantly and called, "Gabe? Is that you? Are you all right?"

"I'm wicked, sir, and so's Wizz and Mike and everybody."

"Is that monster Kozara's ship?"

"Sure is. Sorry to be late. Took us a bit to get'er moving again. Listen—we found the crew of the Nora Nicholas. *They're alive and well, stranded on a planet in the Typhon Expanse."*

"Understood—glad to hear it. Gabe, there could be a saboteur on board working for the Klingons. We can't find him here."

"We found him already, Morgan. It was John Wolfe. Only he's not the real John Wolfe. He must've killed the real Wolfe and taken his posting just before he transferred on board the Bozeman."

"How in hell did you find that out?"

"Mike Dennis actually found him. When we figured out there'd been sabotage, he remembered that Wolfe was the one who told us nothing was wrong just before everything started going wrong. Anyway, under some creative encouragement, he fessed up."

"Are you in command, Gabe?"

"Amazing, isn't it? You know what? I kind of like it, sir. Better watch out. I'll be after your job."

"Gabe . . . I don't know what to say. You sound just wonderful."

"Feel all right too, sir. I guess there are more important things than my personal pain."

"Glad to hear it. Stand by." Smiling sentimentally, Bateson quietly said, "Captain Picard, my crew is standing by for your orders."

Picard nodded, looking a little like he had been hoping there'd be a fight. "Thank you. Actually, Captain Bateson, I'll leave it to you. What do you want done with Commander Kozara, his crew, and their ship? If you like, you can take command of that ship and pilot it back to Starbase 12. Another trophy for your exhibit, perhaps?"

Bateson considered the idea for a moment, seemed to enjoy at least the picture of it in his mind, then looked for a long few seconds, oddly, at Zaidan.

"Mmm," he uttered then. "I don't really need another trophy. After all, how much glory can a man take?"

He pushed off the tactical board and went to stand before his old rival as Kozara stood in silence on the lower deck beside the helm.

"I, Captain Morgan Bateson," he began, "stand humbled before the Klingon Kozara. I was your dishonor, and you chased me down. When the power to destroy our civilizations was in your hands, you found the strength in yourself to pause and think. You raised yourself above common revenge. You are a true commander. You deserve to be in your ship."

Purely astounded, Kozara stared blankly, disbelieving what he heard.

Riker pivoted around in his chair and stood up, as Captain Picard came to Bateson's side.

"I agree," Picard said. "On the brink of interstellar conflict, we found a way to work together to stop it for the sake of old times. We all faced our pasts, Kozara, and we put them to rest. There is good to be had today, to see that we're not all at one another's throats all the time. I will forward a record log of this to the Klingon High Council on your behalf, with my personal seal. Despite open hostilities and extenuating circumstances, you comported yourself in an honorable manner and did not kill arbitrarily. We in the Federation do not forget such things. You are honored among your enemies."

In nothing short of shock, Kozara looked as if his head were about to fall off.

Gradually, he gathered himself and came to attention before the two Starfleet captains. "I accept," he said.

It was about as close as a Klingon could get to a thank you, but that was in his tone.

"Shipwide sweep transporter beam, Mr. Riker, Klingon physiology," Picard ordered. "Send these gentlemen back to their vessel."

Despite having his orders, Riker was staring at Bateson. "Sir, I didn't think you had that in you."

Shrugging, Bateson sighed. "Acting like adults is no fun," he muttered. "You know what? You boys live in a bizarre century, that's what."

CHAPTER 25

"Captain, I was very proud of being in Starfleet when you did what you did. A few slight differences, and I'd have done the same thing."

"That's too bad," Morgan Bateson responded as he walked beside Picard toward the crew lounge. "What's command without a little variety?"

"I don't think anyone can accuse you and me of being clones, Morgan."

"No, they can't, Jean-Luc, they can't. I hope this isn't inconveniencing you, the crew insisting on a formal welcome for you as their official commander."

"Oh, well, I have to confess," Picard said as they rounded a corner toward the lounge, "the ulterior motive is to give you and your own crew a rousing send-off."

"I think we've both been cornered."

"I think we have."

"Jean-Luc, before we go in . . ." Bateson paused before their proximity triggered the lounge door. "Let me say that I admire you. You're an excellent synthesis of old and new. I hope you'll take my apology for my contributions to what happened. I had all the fire and fight of the old century, but none of the restraint of the new."

"You were right about the Klingons," Picard told him quietly. "They were massing to attack. The Cardassians were in their sights, but certainly the Federation wouldn't be far after. You circumvented that by attracting Kozara. If you hadn't, their attack would've been better planned, less spontaneous, and probably far more deadly."

"Thank you. But . . ."

"We all have our inner questions," Picard interrupted him. "The past few days have helped me put into words many things I never thought about being a captain. It's helped me a great deal, especially now that . . ."

"Now that you've been made official commander of the *E*-E. She suits you better than she does me," Bateson said. "And I don't think you'd fit on a destroyer. I want to thank you privately for sticking up for me with the admiralty and recommending reassignment. I thought they'd hang me."

"You're too valuable for that. Command of the *Roderick* is no desk assignment. You'll be the last line of defense for whatever comes. And I know you believe trouble will come."

"It's brewing on too many fronts to ignore. I still believe that. When the Klingons and Cardassians and Romulans become free societies, then I'll look again. Until then, no. But thank you again, really."

"You're quite welcome. Let's go in before we have to get a charter for this club, shall we?"

"Yes, let's."

Picard felt a spring in his step as he led the way through the double door panels into the crew lounge.

When he and Bateson entered, they were walking side by side, and that is how they stopped short, both staring at the crowd of mixed crew before them.

From wall to wall, the lounge was lined with Picard's crew and Bateson's.

At the apprearance of their captains, the happy crowd broke into applause and whistles.

Picard was speechless, but Bateson leaned to him and muttered, "They like us. They really like us."

"I think you're right," Picard noted.

The crews laughed and descended on them.

They were pulled to the buffet table, where Riker and Bush were waiting, indulging in evil grins. Even George Hill, Bateson's squishy mascot, had one coil around a wine goblet and another around Bush's ankle.

"Number One," Picard drawled. "I'll get you for this."

"Well, you're welcome, sir. We just wanted to make you feel at home."

"Oh, well, this'll do it. Mr. Bush, how are you?"

Bush smiled. "High and dry, sir. Looking forward to duty on board the *Roderick*. I think that ship fits us better."

Bateson smiled, glanced at Picard, and shrugged. "Guess we think alike," he said, hanging an arm around Bush, who indeed looked far better than he had the last time Picard had seen him.

Picard accepted a goblet of a pleasantly scented burgundy and raised it immediately. "To our ships!"

The intermingled crews cheered again, and raised the toast.

When the glasses came down again, Picard said, "It's my pleasure to offer Captain Bateson and his crew a proper send-off to their new assignment aboard Starfleet's newest destroyer. However, Captain Bateson, I do have a bit of news for you and your men. In appreciation for all you have done, for your sacrifice and your resilience, Starfleet has accepted Mr. Riker's recommendation that, at its launch next week, the *U.S.S. Roderick* will be redesignated the *U.S.S. Bozeman II,* registration number NCC-1941-A."

The crews were stunned silent for a moment, then erupted into a whoop of approval. The crew of the new *Bozeman* fielded hugs and shoves from the crew of the new starship. For about six seconds Bateson stared at Picard, turned a couple shades of pink, then accepted a handshake from Riker and returned it with speechless gratitude in his eyes.

And Picard was happy to glow from the sidelines at this excellent turn of not-very-pleasant events. Everyone had what he wanted.

Including the newly assigned master of the sixth *Starship Enterprise.*

CHAPTER 26

U.S.S. Enterprise-*E*
One year later

"What do you have?"

"We finished our sensor sweep of the Neutral Zone."

"Oh, fascinating . . . twenty particles of space dust per cubic meter . . . fifty-two ultraviolet radiation spikes . . . and a class-2 comet. Well, this is certainly worthy of our attention."

Jean-Luc Picard dumped the report on his desk and shared a glance with his disgruntled first officer. Will Riker was not happy either.

Riker was looking at him as if he wanted to walk up to Picard's inner sanctum and knock. Or maybe kick.

"Captain," Riker began, "why are we out chasing comets?"

That wasn't the whole question, of course. The other end of it was something like, *"when the Borg are on the warpath again and making a straight line for Earth?"*

They both heard it, even though Riker had been too polite to actually say the words.

"Let's just say," Picard tried to answer, carrying his cup of hot tea on a little voyage to nowhere, "that Starfleet has every confidence in the *Enterprise* and her crew. They're just not sure about her captain. They believe a man who was once captured and assimilated by the Borg should not be put in a situation where he would face them again. To do so would introduce an 'unstable element' into a critical situation."

"That's ridiculous! Your experience with the Borg makes you the perfect man to lead this fight."

"Admiral Hayes disagrees with you."

The comm whistled, a blessed interruption—Deanna Troi's voice. *"Bridge to Captain Picard."*

Picard steeled himself for another wonderful report on quasars or dark matter. "Go ahead."

"We've just received word from Starfleet." Troi was being unusually contained, as if she were working to sound impassive. *"They've engaged the Borg."*

Without bothering to thank her or engage in amenities, Picard locked eyes with Riker and instantly said, "I'll be right there. Number One, let's go."

Riker was already on his feet. "They're on a direct line for Earth."

"I know that."

They went through the ready-room doors almost side by side, even though they didn't really both fit. The bridge of the *Enterprise*-E was their second—no, their first home after a year in space. All posts were manned by familiar faces now, especially Mr. Data just now taking the seat at ops.

Before he made two steps inboard, Picard ordered, "Mr. Data, put Starfleet frequency one four eight six on audio."

"Aye, sir."

Riker found the self-restraint to sit down at his post, but Picard couldn't manage to sit.

Instantly the comm system, the whole bridge, was flooded with panicked voices, undergirded by other voices working to stay calm and dispense orders. A chill struck Picard, and he could tell Riker felt it also—they knew the sounds of desperation.

"Flagship to Endeavor—*stand by to engage at grid A-15!"*

"Defiant and Bozeman, *fall back to mobile position one!"*

"Aknowledged!"

"We have it in visual range . . . a Borg cubeship on course zero mark two one five!"

"Speed, warp nine point—"

"WE ARE THE BORG. LOWER YOUR SHIELDS AND SURRENDER YOUR SHIPS . . ."

"All units open fire! Remodulate shield protection!"

"They've broken through defense perimeter—"

"Cube is changing course—zero two one mark four—"

"—sixteen others have been—"

"WE WILL ADD YOUR BIOLOGICAL AND TECHNICAL DISTINCTIVENESS TO OUR OWN . . ."

"Repeat! We need more ships!"

"Captain, report immediately—"

"YOUR CULTURE WILL ADAPT TO SERVE US . . ."

"—ninety-six dead—"

"—auxiliary warp drive—"

"Flagship to Starfleet Command! We need reinforcements!"

"Twenty-two wounded on the flagship—"

". . . warp core . . . breach!"

"RESISTENCE IS FUTILE."

The terrible mechanical voice crackled across Picard's skin. He knew that tinny voice, from deep inside. He knew that kind of intrusion, violation.

He knew it.

And he knew other things. He knew he was no longer that man. The Borg had changed him. And other things had changed him. New things.

And he knew the battle, saw it in his mind's eye, knew all the maneuvers the Federation ships, both Starfleet and private, would try to use against the garish Borg cubeship as it vectored in to threaten Earth, the hub of the Federation. And he knew they would all fail.

Rather than sinking into hopelessness, as he saw his crew doing around him, he was suddenly charged up.

"Mr. Hawk," he said to his young conn officer, "set a course for Earth."

They all looked at him. Reactions ranged from fear to shock. He didn't care. Let them be shocked. Let them be afraid. It was good for them.

"Aye, sir . . ." Hawk glanced at Riker, then put his attention to his conn and changed course.

"Maximum warp," Picard ordered.

He waited until the order had been executed. Then he turned to face all those who were gazing at him, astonished, confused, wondering if he had snapped at the sound of that Borg challenge.

Yes, he had.

"I'm about to commit a direct violation of our orders," he told them. "Any of you who wish to object should do so now. It will be noted in my log."

Of course, he didn't say he would change his mind. They knew that.

They all stood silent, waiting to see if anyone else would speak up.

The surprising response came from Data. "Captain . . . I believe I speak for everyone here, sir, when I say 'to hell with our orders.'"

Picard felt a smile rise on his cheeks, and it took all his personal fortitude from breaking into a grin. This wasn't the time for that. But he was working up to it.

"Red alert," he said. "All hands to battlestations. Engage!"

The starship hummed with power around him. He stood in his ready room, knowing the bridge was beyond that door and that he had less than thirty minutes before they would engage the Borg. Perhaps that's what he really had meant when he said *engage . . .*

No one wants ships of the line commanded by a set of clones.

"Captain?"

"Number One . . . who invited you in?"

"Just a voice in the mist."

"Are you here to talk me out of this?"

"No, sir, I'm here to make sure you don't talk yourself out of it."

At this, Captain Picard turned. "No chance of that."

Riker came to his side, and together they looked out the wide viewport at open space, the peaceful deceiver. In the curve of the viewport, they caught a reflection of the ship's seagull-silver hull and the lights of windows on the deck below.

"Bateson was right," Riker murmured after a moment.

"Pardon?"

"Morgan Bateson. He wanted preparedness. He thought there'd be trouble with the Klingons. Or Romulans, or Cardassians. Later he thought it would be the Dominion. After all that, it turns out to be the Borg. Worse than all the others put together."

"Yes, they are," Picard quietly agreed. "Ironic you should mention Bateson after all these months. The *Bozeman II* is in the defense perimeter."

"I heard. . . . Bateson's going to face down the Borg."

"Yes. The last line of defense. He's stationed there, at Earth's solar system."

"With Gabe and the whole crew?"

"Yes, they're still together," Picard said.

"Like us. Just lucky, I guess."

"Very lucky, but by design. Bateson always knew his own mind. So did James Kirk. I admired that. When the *Enterprise-D* was destroyed, I fell into a dangerous pattern of not accepting what I wanted all along. I wouldn't accept that my life had been irrevocably changed by being one of the very few captains of a *Starship Enterprise.* I accept that now, and I take it as a solemn charge. I know that I want nothing else, and nothing more."

Riker's face beamed with warmth and satisfaction, though under the circumstances he apparently couldn't bring himself to smile.

Yet there was eminent pride in the decision they had made to ignore caution. This just wasn't the time for that.

"We're all with you, Captain," Riker told him. "Any action you take, we take with you."

"Thank you, Will. You'll never know what that means to me."

"And to us, Captain. If you'll excuse me, I'll take the conn and clear for action."

"Acknowledged. Carry on. Notify me the moment we come in sensor contact with the Borg."

"Sir, it'll be my pleasure."

In the back of the ready room, the door panel breathed open, then shut again, and the room fell quiet.

Thinking of victory, Jean-Luc Picard strode to the replicator and dumped his hot tea into the disposal. Charged to the core and ready to spark, he squared his shoulders and drew a long sustaining breath.

"Tea, Earl Grey," he ordered, then stopped and thought, and a smile broke out on his face.

"Cancel," he said. "Tea," he said again, "Japanesse Green, chilled, with ginseng and honey."

NONE BUT THE POSSESSED
Memorial to our ship,
sunk off Hatteras, Dec. 9, 1996

Port-of-callers asked the way,
looking for three sticks and a big oak body,
shrouds and spars and scuppers and tars,
listening for words that sound funny.
They'd turn in at Fort Yngve's ensign,
toward the brown deck and black overcoat,
right on past the lubbers who gasped,
"That's a damn fine castle,
and a hell of a moat."

Overwhelmed and scared of the helm,
sixty-seven years of green crews
flinched at the shouts—"Cast off! Haul away!"
and then the stronghold moved.
Up went the wall of iron-red main,
heads'ls, the fore, and then some,
and her mizzed boom groaned on the starboard reach
over the great black transom.
Trees dream of being this someday,
of making those gaff-rigger sounds,
like her sienna sails calling, "Flap, flap, snap!"
as she shuddered her big shoulder down.

A tempered Clydesdale of a ship,
draft horse of Baltic trading,
she embraced both masters and timid first-glancers
who asked, "Do all these ropes do something?"
She the witchcraft and we the possessed
shook off blows from Fell's Point to Norfolk.
We must have loved her pretty good
to go so far for such discomfort.
Potomac, Chesapeake, Downeast coast,
the Stream and the Gulf and the swollen Old Man,
the Key jetty and Thimble Shoal—
we asked and asked. She said, *I can.*

She worked away the century till arrogance
shoved her deep in Prideful water.
We beg the depths, "Treat her like a lady.
We're proud we ever had her."
Our bullhearted cradle *Alexandria,*
strong and forgiving and pliant—
Our spirits sail her still, and always will.
May she be a reef as mighty
as she was a schooner valiant.

D. Carey
Deckhand and watch leader